**Praise for the novels of
New York Times bestselling author
Jo Beverley**

Hazard

"Engaging. . . . Fans will appreciate the spicy chemistry between [Anne] and Race." —*Publishers Weekly*

The Devil's Heiress

"[A] deftly woven tale of romantic intrigue. . . . Head and shoulders above the usual Regency fare, this novel's sensitive prose, charismatic characters, and expert plotting will keep readers enthralled from first page to last."
—*Publishers Weekly*

"With her talent for writing powerful love stories and masterful plotting, Ms. Beverley cleverly brings together this dynamic duo. Her latest captivating romance . . . is easily a 'keeper'!" —*Romantic Times* (Top Pick)

"Exciting. . . . The story line is filled with action, but it is the charming lead couple that makes the plot hum."
—Harriet Klausner

"A riveting, completely captivating blend of romance, intrigue, and suspense that enthralls from the first page to the last. Beverley is a master storyteller and this book, with its superb plot, fascinating characters, and lush prose, is a stellar example of her talent . . . a strong contender for best historical romance of the year."
—Romance Fiction Forum

continued . . .

continued . . .

Something Wicked

"A fast-paced adventure with strong, vividly portrayed characters . . . wickedly, wonderfully sensual and gloriously romantic."　　　　　　　　　—Mary Balogh

"Intrigue, suspense, and passion fill the pages of this high-powered, explosive drama . . . thrilling!"
　　　　　　　　　　　　　　　—*Rendezvous*

"*Something Wicked* will delight."
　　　　　　　　　　—*Lake Worth Herald* (FL)

"Jo Beverley is a talented storyteller, creating characters who come alive."　　　　　　—Under the Covers

ALSO BY JO BEVERLEY

Hazard

Jo Beverley

A SIGNET BOOK

SIGNET
Published by New American Library, a division of
Penguin Group (USA) Inc., 375 Hudson Street,
New York, New York 10014, USA
Penguin Group (Canada), 90 Eglinton Avenue East, Suite 700, Toronto,
Ontario M4P 2Y3, Canada (a division of Pearson Penguin Canada Inc.)
Penguin Books Ltd., 80 Strand, London WC2R 0RL, England
Penguin Ireland, 25 St. Stephen's Green, Dublin 2,
Ireland (a division of Penguin Books Ltd.)
Penguin Group (Australia), 250 Camberwell Road, Camberwell, Victoria 3124,
Australia (a division of Pearson Australia Group Pty. Ltd.)
Penguin Books India Pvt. Ltd., 11 Community Centre, Panchsheel Park,
New Delhi - 110 017, India
Penguin Group (NZ), cnr Airborne and Rosedale Roads, Albany,
Auckland 1310, New Zealand (a division of Pearson New Zealand Ltd.)
Penguin Books (South Africa) (Pty.) Ltd., 24 Sturdee Avenue,
Rosebank, Johannesburg 2196, South Africa

Penguin Books Ltd., Registered Offices:
80 Strand, London WC2R 0RL, England

First published by Signet, an imprint of New American Library,
a division of Penguin Group (USA) Inc.

First Printing, May 2002
First Printing ($4.99 Edition), January 2006
10 9 8 7 6 5 4 3 2 1

This book is dedicated to the memory of historical novelist Dorothy Dunnett, who died on November 9, 2001, as I was going over the edited manuscript of *Hazard*.

Dorothy Dunnett, in addition to her other great talents, was the author of fifteen sweeping historical novels centered on her beloved Scotland, and of a number of mysteries. Her fans are devoted and worldwide. I discovered her Crawford of Lymond series at age twenty-four, and delighted in her work simply as an entranced reader.

Later, when I began to try to convey my own imaginary worlds, she was an inspiration, even though the thought that *Game of Kings* was her first novel is enough to daunt any writer. My works are different in style, in type, and in scope, but I know that some parts, perhaps some of the best parts, are there because I am a Dunnett reader.

Thank you, Dorothy, for the treasure you gave me, the reader; and for the seeds you planted in my writer's mind.

One

~

"The toad. The slimy, warty toad!"

Lady Anne Peckworth snapped around to stare at her sister. Frances was working through her day's letters, and clearly one of them had called for the Peckworth family's worst acceptable insult.

Before she had time to ask, Frances looked at her and her stomach cramped.

No.

It was like lightning.

It didn't strike the same person twice.

Frances's mouth pinched as if to hold back the words, but then she said, "According to Cynthia Throgmorton, Wyvern is married. And to a nobody! A bastard daughter of a lady of Devon, who was working—would you believe?—as his *housekeeper*. She has it from Louisa Morton, who lives near Crag Wyvern and is absolutely to be relied upon, she says. Of course, neither she nor Cynthia has any idea that this gossip is of particular importance. . . ." Her furious face softened into sympathy. "Oh, Anne . . ."

What did one say?

The same as last time, she supposed.

"I hope they'll be very happy."

"Anne! The man has as good as jilted you! And after Middlethorpe, too. Father must take him to court over it."

"Good heavens, no!" Anne shot to her feet. "I could not bear to be such object of curiosity and pity." She bit her lips and controlled herself. "The Earl of Wyvern and I were not engaged, Frances. He had not so much as mentioned marriage."

"But he has been paying you such attentions!"

Since Frances was late in pregnancy and had been down here in Herefordshire for the past five months, the family letters must have been flying. Anne wasn't surprised. Her family was in a collective fret over her.

Poor crippled Anne.

Poor jilted Anne.

Poor destined-to-be-a-spinster Anne.

Late last year, their neighbor, Viscount Middlethorpe, had courted her. It had been understood by all that he would soon ask her to marry him, and she would accept. Then he'd been summoned to his estate by some problem.

She had next seen him with his beautiful and scandalous wife on his arm. Not a housekeeper in that case, but the widow of a man known as Randy Riverton, which was almost as bad.

"I wonder if this one is in an interesting condition, too."

"What?" asked Frances.

"Have your gossips not told you? Lady Middlethorpe is expecting to be confined in the summer."

"*What?*" Frances repeated, color mounting. "That would mean that the cad got her with child while . . ."

"While he was courting me. Yes. As you see, he was no great loss."

She hadn't felt that way at the time, but she'd pretended to. How else to salvage her pride?

Frances scanned her close-written letter. "Cynthia says nothing of the lady's condition. Of course, that could be the explanation."

Anne laughed, genuinely amused at the absurd situation. "I doubt it. He's been in Devon only ten days. Ten days," she repeated. "It *is* like lightning, isn't it?"

"Oh, Anne."

Frances began to heave herself off her chaise, so Anne limped over to push her back. "Don't distress yourself. It's not good for the baby. In fact, this is no great tragedy. I'm realizing that if I feel anything, it's relief."

She'd begun her speech thinking to soothe her sister, but by the end of it, she realized that it was true.

She sat in the chair by the chaise. "Truly, Frances, I have never been sure that I wanted to marry the earl."

Frances clearly did not believe her.

She tried to explain. "He needed a wife, and I liked being needed. After so many years of war, and the death of his father and brother, he was shadowed. If I could lift those shadows, it would be a worthy task. But I was uncertain. We did not have a lot in common. In fact," she said, staring at a window dismally streaked with rain, "I was never sure why he was wooing me. I thought love would come, for both of us. . . ."

Frances took her hand. "We had no idea. We all assumed that you felt warmly toward him."

Anne pulled a face. "I'm not sure I understand these emotions. But I know one thing. I do not have even a crack in my heart over Wyvern." She decided to get one thing out in the open. "I would be celebrating, I think, if not for the family."

Frances's color bloomed again, but this time with embarrassment. "We only want you happy, dearest."

"But not if I want to be happy living on as a spinster at Lea Park."

"It doesn't seem a life worthy of you, love, and," she added, "when Uffham inherits and his future wife rules the roost, who knows how it will be?"

A chill shot through Anne. "Good heavens. I've never thought of that. And Uffham, sad to say, cannot be depended upon to choose wisely."

"Precisely. You would not want to be another Aunt Sarah."

Aunt Sarah, their father's sister, lived, mostly ignored, in a suite of rooms in the north wing in the company of a few servants and a lot of small dogs. The family generally referred to her as "dear Aunt Sarah," but it really meant "poor Aunt Sarah."

If she didn't marry, would she be "poor Anne" forever? Poor Aunt Anne. Poor Great-aunt Anne . . .

To escape her sister's keen eye, Anne returned to the sofa. "You're right. I must think about this."

As cover, she picked up her piece of craft work again.

The instructions were in the magazine open beside her—*Pastimes for Ladies: a cornucopia of elucidation, education, and recreation for the fair sex of our land.* She took that to mean "the bored fair sex of the land." Only extreme boredom could have driven her to attempting to make "a charming bonbon holder out of straw."

She looked at the weeping windows that rattled with occasional gusts of wind and showed only gray sky and pouring rain through the condensation. It was May, after all—time of blossoms, lambs, and courting birds, when the world was in good order.

In a proper May she could escape the house; she could ride, and when on horseback her turned foot didn't hinder her. With speed and fresh air she would be able to handle this better. As it was, she was trapped in the house, virtually trapped in this room, since it was the only one with a fire.

Trapped in Benning Hall in the rain.

Trapped from birth in a crippled body.

Trapped from birth by being a duke's daughter, expected to marry well, expected to behave well, even when jilted.

Trapped by her loving family's damnable concern, by their need that "poor Anne" be happy.

Her hands tightened on the woven straw, and she relaxed them.

It was the unseasonable weather that had her in the blue devils. Not Middlethorpe. Not Wyvern.

She focused on the magazine, on the instructions. She had finally finished the tedious plaiting and weaving. All she had, however, was a misshapen blob.

"Squeeze into shape," the useless instructions said. She squeezed at one end, and another part popped out. She pushed that in, and the whole thing changed again. "Do you have any idea how to make this into a heart shape?"

"No," Frances said, as if she'd been asked how to clean a kitchen grate.

"I've followed the instructions to the letter, done just as I ought. Perhaps the bottom should be flatter." She turned it over and squished, fearing to ruin it.

"Throw it on the fire, dear. Such a silly thing."

"This silly thing has taken up two days of my time. I will not give up now!"

"I wish you would put as much effort and resolution into finding a husband."

Anne stared at her. *"What?"*

Frances was red again but resolute. "You need to go into society more and meet all the eligible men, Anne, rather than sitting at Lea Park and waiting for the occasional suitor to come to you."

"We have grand parties at Lea Park."

"With the same, generally married, guests."

"I go to London for a few weeks every year."

"And attend exhibitions and the theater."

"What else am I to do? Limp around routs and sit with the dowagers at balls? I do not like to walk any distance, and I cannot dance!"

She pinched the wretched basket hard. It instantly formed the perfect heart shape of the illustration.

She began to laugh. "Oh, dear. Perhaps I am just too kind and gentle for my own good."

"What? Anne?"

She waved her sister back down to her chaise. "I'm all right. I think perhaps I do need to make some changes."

"Good."

Anne put the heart-shaped basket on the table. "The problem is that I don't know what I want. I truly am happy at Lea Park, among people I know so well. I don't like meeting strangers."

"The people of your new home will only be strangers for a little while."

"But there's that limping around London first." Anne sighed. "Did you not feel a pang at leaving home?"

"No, none. I was delighted to be coming to a home of my own and out from under Mama's eye." The Duchess of Arran was a strict mother. "And, of course, I would be happy anywhere with dearest Benning."

Anne thought Benning boring. Love was a strange affair.

"I really am a strange creature, aren't I?"

"It will be different when you do fall in love, dearest. Then you will be delighted to go to your husband's home."

"I suppose so. It is the way of the world, after all."

Anne felt a special tie to her home that she hadn't mentioned—her work with the papers of the Peckworth women. She knew that her family considered it as strange a pastime as weaving straw hearts, and something she'd leave behind when she had a full life.

Perhaps they were right. At the moment, however, it absorbed her. She wished she were home now. Rainy days were a perfect excuse to spend hours with the neglected diaries, letters, and assorted documents of her female ancestors.

Idiotic to stay a spinster just for that. Not poor Anne. Crazy Anne . . .

Then she heard a faint clanging. "Was that the doorbell?"

Frances sat up, a protective hand going to her belly. "Who could be visiting on such a day? I pray it isn't bad news!"

"I'm sure not. It's probably a neighbor as cast down by the weather as we are and seeking company."

Anne went to peer through the blurred and fogged window. "Two dripping horses being led away," she reported. "Visitors, for sure."

She limped toward the door but heard rapid steps. She only had time to step back before the door was flung open.

"Hello, Frannie and Annie!"

"Uffham!" Anne exclaimed. "You scared Frances half to death turning up in this weather—" But he had already swept her into a damp hug.

He went on to hug Frances a bit more gingerly. "How is it?" he asked vaguely.

"Active," said Frances, glowing. "You did half scare me to death, but it's wonderful to have a visitor. Sit down and tell us all the news from town. You are come from London, aren't you?"

"Yes." But Uffham cast an anxious look at Anne.

So it was public now. "I know about Wyvern, Stuff."

No one in the world could get away with calling Lord Uffham Stuff except his sisters. He was a tall, handsome young man with stylish brown hair who enjoyed pugilism, neck-or-nothing steeplechases, and the wilder sort of entertainments.

"How?" he asked, clearly rather peeved. "It only appeared in this morning's paper."

"One of Frances's correspondents. I do thank you for wanting to break the news to me."

"I've half a mind to go to Devon and call the cad out."

"No! There was nothing settled between us."

Before he could say more, Frances interrupted. "Do ring, Anne. Stuff must be chilled through and starving."

"Ain't that the truth? But I've brought a guest along, Frannie, if you don't mind."

"A guest? In this?" Frances looked at the window as if the weather might have changed to sun.

"Army man. Tough as a Highland sheep. Name's Racecombe de Vere. Derbyshire family."

"Tough as a Derbyshire ram?" Anne asked.

A vision popped into her mind of a weathered, hairy specimen of huge proportions. This was alarming because she suspected that her brother had reacted to the notice in the paper by rushing here with a replacement suitor.

"Now, now, don't go scaring him away, Annie." Having confirmed her fears, Uffham turned back to Frances. "You can put up an extra guest for a day or two, can't you?"

"Of course! I'm bored to tears, and Anne is reduced to making small items out of straw. Anne, ring for refreshments. Stuff, go and bring up your friend! I plead my belly as excuse for not venturing from this cozy room."

He swept out. Anne first closed the door he had carelessly left open, then pulled the bell rope. "He's brought this Derbyshire ram for me. How absurd."

"It's a kind thought."

"At least it gives him time to cool. He mustn't call Wyvern out. There's no cause. Probably no one in society even realizes that I had hopes. . . ."

She prayed that was true. Pity—more pity—was the one thing she could not tolerate. She'd been born with a twisted foot and lived with pity all her life.

She regarded a china ornament on the mantelpiece—a shepherd and shepherdess obviously well matched and happy. It was presented as so natural and easy, this falling in love and marrying. Why was it so very tangled in her case?

She turned to her sister. "I think Stuff dragged Wyvern to me to try to heal my pride over Middlethorpe, and you can see how disastrous that was. What am I to do about this one?"

"Enjoy his company."

"Someone calling himself de Vere? The de Veres died out a century ago. He's an impostor of some kind."

Frances's eyes brightened. "Really? How intriguing. I've always wanted to meet an adventurer. Don't take everything so seriously, dear. Flirt a little. You need the practice."

"With a hairy Derbyshire ram?"

Frances laughed, and Uffham returned at exactly that moment.

Anne blushed with embarrassment. Had his companion heard her last words?

And the Derbyshire ram . . . wasn't.

"Mr. de Vere, ladies. De Vere, my sisters, Lady Benning and Lady Anne."

The slender blond man with the fine-boned features and laughing blue eyes bowed with perfect—if rather excessive—grace. "Your servant, ladies! Especially as you provide shelter, this luscious warmth, and, I am given to understand, nourishment."

Frances was blushing and looking as if she didn't know whether to be ecstatic or to laugh. Anne was wondering what had possessed Uffham. When it came to marriage, to entrusting her life to some man, she demanded someone of more substance than this.

The maid arrived and left with instructions for tea and hearty fare. Uffham threw himself into the chair by the fire, sticking his boots so close that they began to steam.

"Uffham, your boots," Anne said. "You've tracked mud across the carpet."

She turned to stop de Vere doing the same. He, however, had not advanced beyond the wooden floor at the edge of the room.

"Don't fuss, Anne," said Frances. "It is easily cleaned. Come in, Mr. de Vere."

"Perhaps I might ask to be able to change my damp clothes before eating, Lady Benning."

"Of course! Anne, take Mr. de Vere to the east bedroom. It's not far."

Not far for your poor foot. That made it hard to refuse. "Of course, but Uffham could take him."

"I just got comfortable," Uffham protested, "and the harm's done now. Only make it worse to walk back out, and I can't get these boots off without a jack. Call for someone to help me with them, that's a good girl."

Anne rolled her eyes but gave in. She rang the bell again. Then she picked up the knitted shawl she kept to hand, wrapped it around herself, and headed for the door. De Vere opened it for her and closed it behind them.

At least he had good manners. That was something. She had grave doubts about Uffham's new crony. He was too . . . slight. Slight in build and slight in manner. Slight in substance, too.

Frances had been right. He was an adventurer. Uffham had fallen into bad company again, and now he thought she might marry a man such as this?

Two

$\sim$

"I'm sorry for putting you to such trouble, Lady Anne," the man said. "If you give me directions, I am sure I can find my way. And now I'm tracking more mud along the corridors. . . ."

He sat on a chair and pulled off first one boot and then the other without difficulty. "Army ways," he said, standing with them in his hand. "Folly not to be able to get in and out of them by oneself."

Anne felt a stir of interest. She admired practicality.

"You were at Waterloo, Mr. de Vere?" she asked as they turned the corner in the corridor.

"Alas, no, Lady Anne."

So much for that. He was a desk officer. He'd doubtless never disturbed his blond waves.

She opened the door to the east room and stood back to let him enter. "I will send washing water for you, Mr. de Vere. And of course, please ask for anything you need."

She closed the door and retraced her steps, wondering why she felt so twitchy about this new invader. He'd done nothing wrong, but there was something bold about him, something that suggested that he respected no rules. With his name and manner he had to be an adventurer, a man to be avoided.

And yet, Frances's suggestion tantalized. A lady could enjoy flirtation without sliding from there into marriage, especially with a man so completely ineligible.

She didn't flirt. It had always seemed unkind and unwise to encourage gentlemen whom she had no intention of marrying. She had begun to flirt a little with Middlethorpe, perhaps. She'd never felt inclined to flirt with saturnine Wyvern.

She did need practice. She'd never been opposed to marriage, but she hadn't been in pursuit of it, either. Now, with the threat of life at Lea Park under some other young woman's rule, it was a whole other matter.

Needing time to consider this, she went down the east stairs all the way to the kitchens to order the water. Of course, the servants fussed about her going to the trouble—but then she had an inspiration.

"Please," she said to the agitated housekeeper. "My doctor tells me I must walk frequently or my limp could get worse. You must not deny me the opportunity."

"Oh, well then, my lady. Of course, then . . ." But plump Mrs. Orwell didn't seem comfortable about it.

"This wretched weather has stuck me in a chair for two days. It really isn't good for me."

"Yes, quite, I see, my lady."

Anne went back upstairs very pleased with herself. She'd spread the same word at Lea Park, and if necessary get Dr. Normanton to support her. She knew he would. He had always encouraged her to be active, and had helped persuade her parents to let her ride and drive. That had finally given her equal mobility and a form of exercise she loved.

She paused in the chilly hall as she realized that she'd never shown such skills in society. Perhaps Frances was right. She had hidden away at Lea Park as much as possible, and when mixing with society she'd done her best to fade into the wallpaper.

As she limped up the stairs, she resolved to actively pursue marriage, which meant spending more time in society. She pulled a face. It would be tedious and at times embarrassing, but she would do it. For that she did need more practice with men.

She hovered for a moment outside the boudoir and then detoured to her room. Her maid, Hetty, was there, putting away some freshly laundered clothing.

"Oh, milady. Is there something you need?"

"Just to tidy myself," Anne said, feeling suddenly as if the words "husband hunter" had appeared on her forehead.

"Sit you down, milady, and I'll redo your hair."

Forty-year-old Hetty had been Anne's maid from her nursery days, and Anne automatically obeyed. By the time the pins were out of her hair, she had come to her wits. "I don't have many minutes, Hetty, and I don't . . . Just tidy it the way it was."

"Right, milady." But Anne saw the twinkle in the maid's eye. As if to confirm it, Hetty said, "I hear Lord Uffham's brought a handsome young gentleman with him, milady."

"Handsome is as handsome does."

"Sukie Rowman caught a glimpse of him and said he looked like the angel in the window in the church."

Anne realized that Sukie Rowman was right. The angel in St. Michael's church wore a flowing robe, but she—he?—bore a flaming sword. It was a militant angel with a square chin and waving blond hair. Perhaps that was why she felt she might have met de Vere.

"Who would marry an angel?"

Hetty grinned. "That's the spirit, milady."

Anne looked at the older woman in the mirror. Surely the news about Wyvern's marriage couldn't have made it to the servants' quarters yet. "Lord Wyvern is not the angelic type."

Hetty pulled a face. "That he isn't, milady, unless you count Lucifer."

"He's a good man, Hetty."

"But carrying troubles. There's troubles enough come in life, milady. No need to marry them. You take your time in choosing."

That was startlingly frank. "Wyvern is married. To a lady in Devon."

Hetty's busy hands stilled. "Well, I never. The warty toad!"

Anne burst out laughing. Had the phrase passed from servants to children, or children to servants?

"No, truly, Hetty. There was no commitment, and I'm happy for him. Now do hurry. I must get back to help my sister."

Hetty twisted Anne's hair into a high knot and stuck in the pins. It was a little neater, but Anne noticed that it was also a little softer around her face. She thought of protesting, but there wasn't time, and she didn't want to reveal any special interest in her appearance.

Hetty put down the comb. "You could change your dress, milady."

Anne's blue dress was her plainest, and she hadn't put on any jewelry this morning other than seed pearl earrings and a gold cross and chain. . . .

Enough. She rose and turned with the blankest expression she could find. "Why would I do that?"

Hetty's mouth pinched, but she didn't argue. She did, however, open a drawer and take out the Norwich silk shawl with the deep cream fringe.

Anne picked up her plain brown knitted one.

"You can't wear that, milady!"

"You didn't complain when I put it on this morning, and nothing has changed, especially the temperature."

She flung it around her shoulders and marched out of the room, afraid that she looked her worst, but even more afraid of being a figure of fun by changing simply because a strange man had come to the house.

A man who looked like a militant angel . . .

She found both gentlemen with Frances. Uffham, now bootless, was still in the chair near the fire, but de Vere had taken the chair close to Frances. He was making her laugh.

Not an angel. A court jester.

A straw man.

A man of no substance or use.

But straw could be useful. It could be made into mats and mattresses, fans and baskets. And bonbon holders.

Her foolish, whirling mind was sign of extreme nervousness, and she feared she'd start chattering as crazily as she was thinking. She was nearly twenty-one, not sixteen!

As she went to her seat on the sofa, however, she heard de Vere murmur something to Frances, and when she glanced that way, her sister's cheeks were pink, and her eyes shining.

Flirtation. In fact, it looked more like seduction!

Good heavens, surely Uffham wouldn't bring such a man here. . . .

She forced her mind back to reason. No man would

try to seduce a woman within weeks of giving birth. But perhaps a woman within weeks of giving birth still likes to be flirted with . . .

Was de Vere simply being kind?

Tantalized by that, she took her seat on the sofa. When she realized that *Pastimes for Ladies* was still open to her project, she closed it and put it facedown. "Have I missed any delightful new scandal?"

"Would we sully your ears with scandal, Annie?" Uffham asked with a grin. "I was telling Frannie about Hester Stanhope, but now you're here. . . ."

She gave him the glare that promised sisterly retribution, and he laughed.

"The account will be in your papers any day. Tale is, she's not only adventuring all over Asia Minor, she's now the leader of some tribes of Bedouin, as well. And possibly," he added with a wink, "having a special relationship with an Arab prince."

"Lady Hester?" Anne exclaimed. "She visited Lea Park with her uncle, Lord Pitt, when we were children. She did not seem that sort of woman."

"Who knows what secret passions hide behind conventional appearances?" asked de Vere.

Anne caught a speculative glance at herself.

"What a shame," he continued, "if they remain hidden."

Good heavens! Why would he think like that about her?

"That could apply to the last Tregallows girl!" Frances interjected.

"Why?" Anne asked, thankful for a change of subject.

"Uffham says she's eloped. With a nobody! Even so, it must be a relief to all concerned. I doubt any of them would have married except for being duke's daughters with enormous dowries."

Like me? Anne thought, but she knew ˙Frances wouldn't have meant that. "Which Tregallows lady is this? They all have such strange names, and all starting with *C*. Cornissa, Candella . . ."

"This one is Claretta."

"And," declared Uffham with glee, "she's run off with

a Major Crump! Claretta Crump. It's a positive tongue
twister. And whoever has heard of a Crump?"

Frances shook her head. "She must be *extremely* plain,
poor thing. You'd think the name alone would have
given poor Claretta pause."

"Apparently her pause should have come sooner," Uffham said. "Rumor has it that she's already increasing."

Frances smirked. "We'll know the truth in seven
months or so."

Anne couldn't stand it. "How sad!"

"Claretta Crump's lowly marriage?"

"Society counting off the months."

"Piffle," Frances said. "She's forced a marriage to
someone undesirable. She deserves everything she gets."

"Or given in to passion, Lady Benning," de Vere said,
as if talking about the weather. "Passion can drive anyone off the straight path."

Anne saw Frances blush, and knew she was blushing,
too. The man was outrageous, but the Peckworth family
was not showing well before a guest. The tea tray, thank
heavens, arrived then, along with another piled high with
sustenance suitable for young men. Anne made the tea
to save Frances from the effort.

De Vere rose to pass around the cups, and a moment
later Benning joined them, perhaps drawn by a young
man's instinct for food. He was only thirty, though an
increase of the waist and a decrease of the hair made
him look older. Anne wondered what had drawn Frances to him. Passion?

Love certainly was a mystery.

"Any trouble on the road?" he asked Uffham.

"None. Why?"

"Damn colliers dragging coal wagons around, begging.
People encouraging them by raising money. Luddites attacking manufactories. Laborers burning ricks and smashing agricultural machines. Country's going to wrack and
ruin."

Uffham took a slice of pie. "The authorities need to
catch that Captain Ned Ludd and hang him."

"He's a symbol, not a person," de Vere said, "and
therefore, immortal."

"Then the authorities can hang some of his mortal followers," Benning snapped. "Those hangings at Ely should give 'em reason to think."

"Right," Uffham said. "They'll think twice before killing someone else who tries to stop their wickedness."

Anne wished they were back to social scandal. She didn't approve of the rioters, but times were hard. Peace had proved to be a mixed blessing.

Frances put her hand over her belly. "Don't talk of these things! I cannot sleep for thinking of those wicked people wandering the countryside at night burning, smashing, and murdering. It's like France all over again!"

"Madmen," Benning agreed, which Anne didn't think helpful, but then he went to pat Frances's shoulder and assure her of safety.

Uffham peered at the tray from a distance. "Pass me more of that cake, de Vere, there's a good man."

Like a good servant, de Vere passed the cake to Uffham. Then he came to Anne to have his cup refilled. Instead of returning to his seat by the chaise, however, he sat beside her.

"You frown, Lady Anne. I cannot bring sunshine, but perhaps I can bring smiles."

"Smiles, sir? We were talking of somber matters, I think. You are from Derbyshire, where these problems are serious. Can you explain the true causes of the Luddite problem to me?"

"I left Derbyshire to join the army eight years ago, Lady Anne."

"But you must have spent your childhood there."

"I suppose I must. But matters were better then, and I was carelessly young."

She suspected that he, like Uffham, would be carelessly young till he was ninety if he could manage it.

"And now?" she demanded. "You do not read the newspapers?"

"They tend to be so depressing—riots, destruction, and hangings."

So much for flirting with him. He was as frivolous as her straw heart. "People are behaving badly because their *trades* are depressed, Mr. de Vere, driving them to try to destroy the machines that have replaced them."

"A lady interested in industrial economics? How novel."

"Not at all. Perhaps ladies do not express their views to gentlemen for fear of being mocked."

His face settled into something close to seriousness. "Did I mock? I did not mean to. Are you saying that ladies together talk of industrial matters? That perhaps you and Lady Benning were doing so when we interrupted?"

Anne found her own teacup was empty and put it on the table. Even if he hadn't heard her words before entering the room, he must have heard laughter.

She longed to lie, but said, "No."

He put his cup beside hers. "Perhaps ladies hide their true selves even from one another. As, perhaps, Lady Hester did. Sad, would you not say? Imagine if her uncle had not died and left her enough money to go adventuring."

His eyes were keen, heavy-lidded, and a smoky blue gray that should have been dull but wasn't. She felt a tug of attraction but then remembered his suspicious name.

"Have you never felt the need to hide your true self, Mr. *de Vere?*"

"All the time, Lady Anne. All the time."

"A man of mystery! There is something tantalizing about that, is there not? Is that your intent, sir?"

"To tantalize you? Are you hinting that you are thirsty, Lady Anne? Please, allow me." He picked up the teapot and went neatly through the business of pouring a fresh cup of tea for her.

She watched, amused and slightly shocked. Gentlemen did not pour tea. What was more, that play on *tantalize* showed a mind as agile as his body. The sinner Tantalus had been trapped in a pool of water up to his chin, but was never able to drink.

Did de Vere plan to tantalize her? Would she be tempted but never allowed to . . . to what?

She knew what—and she most certainly wouldn't!

He passed her the cup, and she saw that his hands were a little too brown for a man of fashion, but beautiful. Long fingered but not bony, his square nails neatly trimmed. Something about those hands made her almost fumble the cup.

He put his hand over hers to steady her. It didn't help. A ripple of something went through her, and she saw it reflected in the surface of the tea. She gathered her wits, smiled at him, and put the cup down.

The room seemed suddenly too warm, but then she realized that she still had her shawl on. Such a simple explanation! She began to shrug it off, but de Vere rose to help her with it. He folded it and draped it over the back of the sofa.

A simple courtesy to make her feel as if she had been somehow stroked. Had the news and events of the day turned her wits?

She picked up her cup and took a deep drink of tea. "So, Mr. de Vere, you think all people hide their true selves?"

"Not at all, Lady Anne," he said as he sat down again. "Uffham, for example, hides little."

"But you do?"

"Of course."

She sipped, watching him. "What parts do you keep concealed, sir?"

His eyes twinkled. "All the naughty bits, of course."

A *hic* of laughter escaped her, and she almost spilled her tea. The room heated up again, and this time she didn't have a shawl as excuse.

"You are quite a wit, Mr. de Vere."

"A wit and a madman, Annie," called Uffham from across the room. "Never take him seriously."

When conversation among the others settled—on the dull topic of the weather now—Anne looked at de Vere. "That seems a sad obituary, sir."

He looked down at himself and back at her. "I hadn't noticed that I was dead yet. Wasn't there a saint who prayed to God that he become holy, but not just yet?"

Before she could form a riposte, he went on, "Doesn't that strike a chord in you, Lady Anne? That you die a worthy lady, but not be one just yet?"

"Saints are esteemed for having sinned and repented, Mr. de Vere. Ladies of English society are not."

"Dashed unfair, wouldn't you say?"

She was rescued by the nursemaid entering with little Lucy, making the modest room quite a fashionable crush. Anne welcomed the distraction. She couldn't believe she was having this conversation in the midst of her family.

She glanced back at de Vere.

Angel?

Imp from hell, more likely. He had a way of seeming angelically innocent while being completely outrageous.

"Well, Lady Anne?" he prompted.

"I have never found sin particularly appealing," she said in a tone designed to depress pretension.

His brows rose. "No desire to steal a delightful possession from one of your sisters? No urge to stick pins into them for being cruel? Not a single sour wish directed at a person unfairly blessed by fortune? No envy, no sloth, no gluttony? . . ."

"Of course. I'm no saint."

"Ah! Then we were talking about the sin of lust."

Shocked rigid, Anne glanced at Uffham to see if he might have overheard. He hadn't, thank heavens. "Mr. de Vere," she hissed, "you go too far."

"Lady Anne," he murmured back, "you are enjoying it."

And astonishingly, it was true!

"That is because I am safe within the bosom of my family, sir."

"Unwise to bring bosoms into this discussion."

Even though her bosom was slight and entirely covered by sturdy blue cloth, Anne instinctively put a hand there.

"So," the incorrigible man continued at an alarmingly normal pitch, "you think discussing lust would lead to it? It does make one wonder what orgies result when our worthy churchmen meet to discuss what passions we should not be permitted."

She lost the fight with her lips. "Mr. de Vere!"

He took her tilted cup from her and put it on the table. She saw Uffham looking at her with a hint of concern. For some reason she smiled to show everything was all right.

"Why be tantalized," the impossible man asked, "when you can drink your fill? You can talk about any of the seven deadly sins with me, Lady Anne, and I assure you I will not act on any of them."

"And I assure you, sir, that I have no desire to do so."

Lying, she told herself, was not one of the seven deadly sins, but it offended against a Commandment. She wasn't sure which was worse.

This had hurtled beyond flirtation. She mustn't permit this outrageous man to go on saying these things. He might get entirely the wrong idea. She called for little Lucy's attention, encouraging her to toddle over and show off her doll.

But the wanton hussy headed for de Vere, beaming at him as if he were an old friend and demanding to be lifted into his lap. He obliged and admired her toy, but then looked at Anne from those wicked eyes. "Perhaps we should start with envy, Lady Anne. . . ."

An arrow straight to the heart. She had felt a spurt of envy that the child prefer him to her, which was ridiculously petty.

She couldn't have met Mr. Racecombe de Vere before. She would remember the violent irritation of it.

Three

When the group broke up to change for dinner, Anne pursued her brother to his room.

"Did you bring de Vere here as a potential husband?"

He turned from the mirror, trying to pull out his cravat pin. "Good Lord, what gave you that idea?"

Well, of course he hadn't. She went to help him. "You brought me Middlethorpe and Wyvern, didn't you? Stuff, you've managed to twist this."

Concentrating on the silver pin and the overly starched cloth, she could still see his neck redden.

"Not Middlethorpe. We've known him forever. Mother might have had a word with his mother. But when he let you down, I met Wyvern, and he was clearly looking for a bride. I thought, why not? I still thought a Rogue in the family would be splendid."

She yanked out the mangled pin and stepped back. "A rogue? Lord Wyvern is a rogue? I thought him a very proper sort of man."

And why on earth would you want me to marry a rogue?

He pulled his crackling cravat loose, scattering flakes of starch.

"Your laundress is overstarching those," she pointed out. "No wonder you bent the pin."

"Don't nag. A man needs a crisp cravat to achieve the latest styles." He rolled his neck, and she heard his collar crackle, too.

"And men say female fashion is folly. Rogue?"

"Oh, yes. Company of Rogues." He shrugged out of his riding jacket. "Started out at Harrow. Makes me wish

I'd gone to school. I've a fresh coat in my bag. Get it for me, will you?"

"No. What is the Company of Rogues?"

She didn't usually pursue Uffham's conversations so keenly, but she sensed that this affected her.

He went to open his bag and dig in it. "Rogues, Company of. Twelve boys at Harrow gathered together by Nicholas Delaney. He's Stainbridge's brother. They're a legend among old Harrovians—the Rogues, I mean. Stainbridge went—"

"Stuff!" Anne exclaimed. "Stick to the point."

He glowered at her. "All right, all right. The Company of Rogues was set up as defense against bullies and cruel masters, that sort of thing. Dashed good idea, if you ask me. There was a bunch of them in Melton this past hunting season, staying at Arden's lodge. Wish I was one of them. You should see his stables there—"

"And Lord Wyvern is a member of the Company of Rogues?" Anne ruthlessly interrupted. Once started on horses, Uffham would be impossible.

"Right." He was scattering his clothes all over the bed. "And Middlethorpe. The others are Delaney, of course. Arden—"

"Stop! I don't want a list." A strange thought was stirring. "You wanted a Rogue for a brother-in-law? You sought Lord Wyvern out?"

He frowned for a moment. "I think he approached me. Can't really remember. Fine idea, though. Pity it didn't work out. As brother-in-law to a Rogue, I'd probably get into their set."

Pity.

The word was like a jab from the bent pin.

"Would you say that these Rogues look out for one another? Fulfill one another's obligations? That sort of thing?"

"You could look at it like that. Mostly friends these days, of course."

"No wonder Wyvern seemed lukewarm . . ."

"What?" Uffham had found his jacket and was staring at her. "Something wrong, Annie? By the way, Wyvern's using the Amleigh title now. Apparently there's a contestant for the earldom."

She was almost distracted, but made herself pursue the main point. "Stuff, you are not to bring me any more Rogues as suitors, do you understand?"

"Don't be put off by the name. Schoolboy nonsense."

"I simply don't want it. In fact, I don't want you to bring me any suitors at all. I will find myself a husband."

She saw an unwise comment form in his mind.

"You think I can't? Just because of a twisted foot? Lord Byron has the same affliction, and ladies swoon in his path!"

Her brother rolled his eyes. "Right-o," he said, shrugging into his jacket.

That image of the Company of Rogues drawing lots lurked in Anne's mind. "I find I do want a list of the rest of these Rogues, Stuff, so I know whom to avoid."

He gave her a bewildered-brother look, but complied. "I think most of them are married now. Let's see. Stephen Ball was in Melton, and Major Hal Beaumont. I think those are the only two still unshackled. Ball's a political man. I don't think you'd like those circles."

"Neither do I."

"Beaumont lost an arm in the war."

"I am not one to reject a cripple, but I'm resolved not to marry a Rogue."

"Right-o. Going to go to London, then, and let Caroline take you around? Marianne'll be pleased."

"You mean Caroline will be pleased."

"No. Marianne." But then he got a fixed look, and his neck turned red again. "Pleased at you having a good time," he said heartily.

Anne's heart began to pound. "Stuff, what about Marianne?"

Marianne was her sixteen-year-old sister.

"Nothing."

She limped over to him. "Stuff!"

"Dammit, but you're a devil, Annie. All right. Marianne's hot to marry Percy Shreve."

"That was a schoolroom affair!"

"*She* was in the schoolroom two years ago, but he wasn't."

"He can't be twenty-one yet!"

"Just. And he was at Waterloo. Still suffering from it,

which is why Marianne wants to get to the altar. She don't think his mama and an army of servants can take proper care of him. Load of nonsense," he added hastily. "Just bits of shrapnel here and there, and a leg that hasn't healed quite right . . ."

Anne remembered the vibrant young man, so excited to be joining a regiment two years before, and so cast down that he might have missed the war. She remembered her young sister's starry eyes, and how they'd all teased her.

"Poor man. Poor Marianne. Let them marry! I'm not going to be cast into a despair by it."

Her brother pulled a face. "Mama won't have it. If you want the truth, I think she don't care for the match. An army career ain't worth much these days even if he heals, and there's no hope of more. Percy's older brother has three sons already."

"Does a worthy man—a hero!—count for nothing? Is Mama hoping he'll *die*?"

"Don't get in a fit." He hunted among his clothing and pulled out a crackling fresh cravat. "She'll doubtless come around, but you know she's never been happy with Benning. Caroline righted the ship a bit by catching an earl, but then you've let one slip. And here's Marianne, and she wants a younger son."

Anne was assessing all this. "If I were to marry, Mama would have no reason to refuse the match, would she?"

He was in front of the mirror now, wrapping the wide cravat around his collar. "Probably not."

"Then I had better do it, hadn't I, and soon."

His brows rose, but he said, "Right-o." Then he smiled at her. "You'll make a fine wife, Annie. You have the sweetest nature. Never any trouble. And you have a handsome dowry."

It seemed as bleak an assessment as the one he'd made of Racecombe de Vere. Which reminded her. "And you swear that de Vere is not a Rogue?"

"Lord, Annie, he's my age, and didn't even go to Harrow. Some school up in Derbyshire." He turned completely to frown at her. "You're not taken with him, are you?"

"Not at all." But she couldn't help asking, "Is he so very ineligible?"

He turned back to the mirror and began to create an intricate knot. "He's nobody."

"What is his family?"

"Dashed if I know."

"What's his real name?"

He grimaced, rocking his head to create creases. "Dashed if I know." The cravat crackled, and more starch flew.

She found his clothes brush and went to brush it off. "Uffham, if you don't know anything about him and think he's an impostor, why are you carting him around with you?"

"Pleasant company. Livens up a dull moment . . ."

She knew what he meant, if *agitation* was a synonym for *liveliness*.

He picked up a new pin and started forcing it into the cravat. "When I heard about Wyvern—Amleigh now, I suppose—dashed confusing, that. Anyway, I read the paper in White's and decided to ride down here. De Vere offered to keep me company. Made the journey go faster. Useful man to have about."

"So he's a professional toadeater."

"If you like."

"He *was* in the army?"

He stretched his neck to view his masterpiece. "Not bad." Then he answered. "Oh, yes. Quite a madman in battle, or so I heard."

She stared at him. "He wasn't a desk officer?"

He turned to her. "Lord, no. In the thick of things, but then he was one of the unlucky ones shipped off to the American war and missed Waterloo. Sold out in disgust."

Anne knew it was unreasonable to feel guilty about the assumptions she'd made, but she did.

"*Are* you interested, Annie? If so, I'll make inquiries. Dashed pleasant fellow to have around."

So, it had come to that. Even a nameless nobody was good enough if he'd only take poor Anne off their hands.

She laughed and hoped it sounded natural. "A de Vere? That's as bad as a Crump. You're right, though. He's amusing company. I intend to enjoy that."

Race de Vere finished washing his hands, thinking that Lady Anne Peckworth was not at all what he had expected. Where was the quiet, crippled, conventional lady?

The reality was surprising, but it was going to make his task here much easier and more enjoyable.

For the past few months he had been secretary to Con Somerford, new Earl of Wyvern, now Viscount Amleigh again. He'd helped sort out the tangled affairs of the earldom, but in the process he'd helped sort out Con's personal affairs, as well. He didn't regret fixing things so that Con could marry his true love, but the thought of the poor crippled lady losing her last hope had weighed on them all.

Poor crippled lady? Last hope? He laughed. Con must be blind. Lady Anne Peckworth was a prize. A duke's daughter, handsomely dowered, and lovely.

True, she wasn't in the common run of beauty, but surely not every man in Britain was enslaved by glossy dark hair and rosy cheeks? As for the limp, some men would object to that, but not all. She had a brain, and wit, and the way her lips curled at the corners when she was trying not to laugh was enchanting.

So why had she even been considering a lukewarm suitor such as Con? Was she afraid of society? Had she convinced herself, or been convinced, that her limp made her an affront to the eyes? If so, that must be changed.

Perhaps she was like a nervous subaltern missing out on life by trying to be safe. Since more men died in war from disease than from wounds, it made no sense to avoid action. He'd learned the lesson early that the only way to live through a war was to live fully.

In his opinion, fashionable England had much in common with the fields of war.

The dinner bell rang—the call to battle?—so he glanced in the mirror to check his appearance, then headed to the fray. He'd become Con's secretary in order to help the officer he had most admired, and moved on to this in order to ease everyone's consciences. Once Lady Anne was settled, he could turn to doing something with his own blank slate of a life.

He found everyone in Lady Benning's boudoir except for Lady Anne.

Uffham strolled over. "What d'you think of my sister, then?" He sounded a bit truculent.

"Lady Benning or Lady Anne?"

Uffham began to turn red. "Anne, of course. Think we can get her married off?"

"With no trouble at all."

"Has to be the right sort. No Crumps."

Ah. Unusual for Uffham to be so alert to things going on around him.

"Of course not. A title for sure. A duke, if possible." Uffham visibly relaxed. "Right, right."

Lady Anne came in then looking flustered—perhaps because she'd made changes to her appearance.

Not an overhaul, and certainly not a change into a flimsy dress that would set her up for influenza, but subtle, successful changes. She'd had her hair redressed in side curls, and added some lovely pearls and a splendid blue-and-gold Norwich shawl. The cream fringe was a foot deep, and the sky blue brought out the bloom of her skin. Her fan was a silk-and-ivory work of art.

He allowed himself only a courteous degree of smile but approved. There was a fine mind working in Lady Anne. She was making the best of herself and also reminding the Derbyshire ram that she was the daughter of a duke and way above his touch.

She even cast him a challenging look.

He went to join her. "Shawl *and* fan, Lady Anne? Playing hot and cold already?"

Her color rose. It suited her. "Prepared for all eventualities, let us say."

"All you need now is a lamp full of oil."

She looked a question, obviously wary.

"To be the complete wise virgin, I mean."

"Mr. de Vere!"

"It's straight from the Bible, and a virtuous type to be."

She laughed. "You delight in shocking people, don't you?"

"But of course. I saw an experiment once where a doctor attempted to revive a corpse by application of electricity."

"Did it work?"

"Alas, no, but who knows what the effect might be on the living?"

Her look suggested that she guessed what he was up to, but if anything, she seemed amused. She was utterly delightful.

The footman entered then. "Dinner is ready, milady."

Lady Benning struggled up from her chaise. Lord Benning carefully swathed her in two shawls and gave her his arm. Uffham insisted on going ahead in case his sister should stumble on the stairs.

Perfect.

Race offered his arm to his quarry, and they progressed along behind. "If I am not too indelicate, Lady Anne, when is Lady Benning expecting to be confined? Soon, I assume."

"In early June. Hard to believe that summer is so close." She shivered as they left the room. "It isn't so terribly cold, but Frances keeps her boudoir so warm that it seems Decemberish out here."

"The interesting effect of contrasts. What surprises us depends on our previous experience."

As they started down the stairs, she glanced at him. "Your experiences have made you hard to surprise, Mr. de Vere?"

"I would have said so, Lady Anne. But you have surprised me."

Wariness sharpened her clear blue eyes, but wariness of the right sort. Not fear, but *en garde*. "To be surprised, Mr. de Vere, a person must have expectations. You had expectations about me?"

"Do we not always have expectations? Even when heading into the unknown, we have some model, or we could never be shocked."

Their speed down the stairs was set by Lady Frances, and thus snail-like. He did wonder if she would last the week, never mind into next month, but that, at least, was not his concern.

"I had no expectation of you, Mr. de Vere," Lady Anne pointed out, "because I had no notion that you even existed."

"And yet you immediately formed a model." At her look, he added, "The Derbyshire ram?"

She colored but laughed, looking altogether charming. "Touché. And I suppose Uffham mentioned me. Very well, what model had you formed?"

Race thought for a moment, then spoke the truth. "A quiet, conventional lady. With a limp. Does your foot pain you?" When she stared, he added, "Does it upset you to speak of it? I understand you have been so since birth, so I would have thought you had come to terms with it."

He learned then that she could wield a look of ducal hauteur. "So I have, sir, but your interest smacks of vulgar curiosity. Perhaps you would like me to raise my skirts and remove my shoe so you can inspect it."

"I would, Lady Anne. Very much. But only at a more convenient moment, and when you are at ease with the idea."

Pure shock. He awaited her response with interest.

They had finally arrived at the bottom of the stairs and were turning toward the dining room. Uffham fell back to let Lord and Lady Benning enter first, and one of Lady Anne's options was to complain to her brother. Uffham, being Uffham, would react physically. Race could handle the bigger man, but it would create an unpleasantness and probably damage some furniture.

Perhaps that was why she said nothing. Instead, she proceeded into the room and took her seat at the table as if his words had never been said. Excellent. She intended to fight her own battles and, he hoped, expected to enjoy it.

Lord and Lady Benning sat at either end. With five at table, he and Uffham were placed on one side, Lady Anne on the other. Once settled, she looked across at him blandly, but he detected a declaration of resistance.

He smiled at her, and she blushed a little. Or perhaps

it was a flush of irritation. Did her lips do that little curl of suppressed amusement? Yes, they did. Lady Anne Peckworth was indeed enjoying herself, which was part of his intent.

When Uffham said, "You're looking in prime twig tonight, Annie," it was proof. He wasn't an observant man at the best of times, and if he'd noticed his poor crippled sister was looking pretty, it must be like a beacon. Lady Anne was the sort of woman who looked ordinary unless animated. She clearly needed to be animated, and he was the man for the job.

As everyone settled and soup was served, Race decided to give the lady a little time to regroup. He made a comment about a soup speciality at the Old Club in Melton Mowbray, and Uffham and Benning joined him in hunting talk.

He soon found it tedious. Lady Anne merely listened, or shared an occasional comment with her sister.

He had to keep reminding himself to pay attention to the men. With the slight changes in her appearance and the gentle glow of the candles, with the flickers of fondness and amusement on her face, Lady Anne Peckworth was distractingly lovely.

He'd noticed earlier, when assisting her with her shawl in the boudoir, that her neck was long, slender, and graceful. He'd had an insane urge to kiss the line of her spine where it disappeared into her practical dress. What would they have done then, her conventional family, who didn't seem to see her for what she was?

Her features were of such perfect evenness that they could appear boring, but not when she was smiling as she was now at something her sister had said, her eyes twinkling in the candlelight. She picked up her wineglass, and he noted her long, slender hands, her fine-boned wrist. It couldn't be so delicate as it looked. . . .

"Eh, de Vere?"

He snapped his wits together. "Definitely," he said to Uffham, relying on the fact that all Uffham ever wanted was someone to agree with him.

"Good, good. We'll have a grand time!"

He discovered he'd agreed to a trip to the Portsmouth area for yacht racing. Damnation. He hadn't intended to live in Uffham's pocket all summer, and he knew nothing about boats.

He kept his eyes off Lady Anne after that. She reminded him of another aspect of the Old Club—its deceptive punch that seemed all juice and spice but hit a man like Jackson's fist.

Four

Anne had thought that being on the opposite side of the table to de Vere would be a relief. He couldn't plague her with intrusive and inappropriate comments. She found, however, that she could hardly avoid looking at him save by fixing her eyes on her soup like a gauche girl.

She was careful, therefore, to let her eyes follow the conversation from person to person, but she still saw a great deal of the knave—all of it interesting.

Though his conversation was more normal with the group, there was still the edge of the outrageous to it. It generated high spirits and laughter, but she was surprised he'd survived to his present age without obvious evidence of violent attacks.

Then she remembered that he'd been in the thick of war. No wounds from that, either? Blessed perhaps, as is said to happen sometimes with madmen.

And yet, Racecombe de Vere wasn't mad.

He was, she decided eventually, chronically mischievous. From her experience, that was even more likely to lead to violent retribution.

How old was he? Uffham had said something. They were the same age. That made de Vere twenty-four. Past the age for mischief. And if he'd entered the army at about sixteen, as was usual, he had served for seven years up to Waterloo.

She realized that she had looked at him too long and that the footman was trying to take her soup plate. She gathered her wits. Mr. Racecombe de Vere was an excellent Pastime for a Lady, but nothing more than that. In

fact, she decided with a suppressed smile, he was a very
bonbon box of a man.

By the end of the meal, however, she had to accept
that he was a delightful one. She'd thought him slight,
and he was, but in some way his slightness and bright-
ness began to make others seem heavy. His fine-boned
features expressed ready emotion, whereas Uffham and
especially Benning were leaden. Yet at the same time,
something in his eyes, especially when they glanced at
her, suggested more beneath.

She remembered her comment about men of mystery.
It could be that he was hinting at secrets to tantalize.
Women were often drawn into that trap, and yet, she
was strangely certain that he was not wooing her. For
one thing, he hardly ever looked at her, certainly not
with the long, lingering looks of the suitor.

As the meal drew to an end, she realized that it had
been the most lively and enjoyable gathering she'd experienced here, and that de Vere had orchestrated it. He
hadn't taken the lion's share of the talk, however, which
was very interesting, indeed.

She'd often encountered a wit who could entertain a
party all evening as a solo performance, but de Vere
was not that sort. Instead, he had thrown seeds that
bloomed into conversation, and sometimes intervened to
direct talk away from strife or unpleasantness. No talk
of Luddites here, or of the riots in East Anglia and the
north, or of the abandoned veterans wandering in search
of work.

Part of her chose to disapprove, to see that as a flighty
attitude to life. Had he not dismissed the subject earlier
as "depressing"? On the other hand, it would have been
tedious to hash over these matters again at the table,
and quite possibly distressing to Frances.

The meal was over now, and it was time for the ladies
to leave. Though reluctant to end this pleasant time,
Anne glanced at her sister, looking for the cue. Frances,
however, had a very strange expression on her face. It
wasn't distressed, exactly, but she was bright red and . . .
fixed, as if she had suddenly discovered that she was
glued to her chair.

Anne leaned that way. "Is something the matter?"

Frances looked at her, and it seemed she was fighting laughter along with a great many other things. "I need the gentlemen to leave, Anne."

Anne looked at the men, who were in lively discussion of a horse race. It had to be something to do with the baby. Was Frances experiencing her pains? If so, why couldn't she say so? Or simply leave as usual.

But she must do as her sister asked.

"Gentlemen," she said loudly, so the three looked at her. "Er . . . Frances would like you all to leave the room."

They looked at her sister, who still had that fixed look on her face, though she wasn't quite so red.

"What is it, my dear?" asked Benning, hurrying around the table to her. "Is it your time?"

Uffham and de Vere were already standing, her brother looking alarmed as only a man can who thinks he's about to be involved in something he'd rather avoid. De Vere, typically, looked intrigued. And ready for action.

Anne had the strange thought that if action were needed immediately, de Vere would be the one to do it.

"Please," Frances said, biting her lip. "It would be best if you left me. But," she added to her husband, "I do think that Mrs. McLaren should be summoned, dearest. And Marjorie sent to help me."

"Good God!" • Benning got a hunted look. Mrs. McLaren was the midwife. "Right. Of course. Come, gentlemen!"

He shepherded them out, but de Vere gave Anne a look as he left. A sharing of amusement and curiosity, and, she thought, a touch of support. A belief that she could do whatever needed to be done?

That was welcome. She knew nothing of these mysteries. Once the door was shut, she said, "Frances, what is it?"

Her sister still had that strange look, but now she did laugh in an embarrassed kind of way. "My waters. My gown and the chair are totally soaked. I'm *dripping*."

Anne had no idea what her sister was talking about, but when she bent to look there was a puddle under the chair. Had Frances relieved herself involuntarily?

"Waters," her sister said. "The baby is in a bag of water. Mrs. McLaren warned that this sometimes happens. But oh, dear, I'm embarrassed to stand up!"

Anne feared she looked like Uffham. She felt completely inadequate to be involved in anything like this, but she stood and went to Frances. "You don't want to have your baby in the dining room. Come on." She put her hand under her sister's elbow and urged her up.

Where was Frances's maid? Since no one had arrived yet, she said, "Can you walk?"

"Oh, yes. Or waddle, rather." Frances suddenly smiled. "It is such a relief. These last weeks are hard, and I'm pleased to have them over."

"The baby is coming, then?"

"I believe so. I hope Mrs. McLaren arrives soon."

This hint of uncertainty, of worry, made Anne begin to shake. "Will you be all right? Will the baby be all right?" She knew immediately that it was the wrong thing to say.

"Mrs. McLaren said it posed no particular dangers. I have great faith in her." But Frances's hand went protectively to her belly.

Anne put all the bracing confidence she could into her voice. "Good. Let's get you up to bed."

Frances began to walk toward the door. "I need to change, at the least. Mrs. McLaren insists that a mother walk as much as possible before the birth."

It sounded barbaric to Anne, but she was not about to interfere. She opened the door and found the men hovering. Assuming it was what Frances wanted, she made a shooing motion. They obligingly melted toward Benning's study across the hall, though Frances's poor husband looked frantic.

Anne smiled at him, hoping he took it as reassurance, but to her sister, she whispered, "I think it would be a kindness to let Benning help you, dear."

Frances gave a little laugh. "Oh, you're right. How foolish it is to stand on dignity at a time like this." She turned. "Edward, dearest, will you help me up to my room?"

He dashed forward, and Anne gave up her place to him. She followed up the stairs, but Frances turned.

"Oh, no, Anne. You mustn't become involved in this! It's not right."

Anne was torn between wanting to help her sister and dread of the event. "I don't mind. . . ."

"Even so, dearest. Please."

Frances truly didn't seem to want her there, and at that moment her sister's middle-aged maid hurried down to help. Anne stepped back and soon was alone in the hall with her brother and Mr. de Vere.

"The midwife has been sent for?" she asked.

"Posthaste," said de Vere, who was projecting a noticeable calm. When things were dull, he enlivened? When agitated, he calmed? "You are probably thinking of tea, Lady Anne. In the drawing room? Perhaps we can share that with you."

"Tea!" scoffed Uffham. "Great Zeus, I need something stronger than tea! Benning mentioned a brisk fire in his study." He strode over to the door and flung it open. "There, see. And decanters to hand. Come on, de Vere."

Anne was suddenly abandoned—but then she found that de Vere had not moved. "I wonder if anyone thought to light a fire in the drawing room," he said. "Perhaps you could have the tray brought down here, Lady Anne, where it will be warm."

"Take tea while you drink brandy?"

"A little brandy in your tea will steady your nerves." Without waiting for her consent, he turned to the hovering footman and gave the order.

The unused drawing room would be cold. Frances had doubtless planned to take tea in her boudoir, but that was too close to whatever was happening. Cowardly, perhaps, but Anne didn't want to be where she might hear terrible things.

She particularly did not want to be alone at this time. Women sometimes died in childbirth. . . .

She let de Vere escort her into her brother-in-law's very masculine sanctuary. She'd never been here before, and the roaring fire, the array of decanters, and the lingering scent of pipe smoke made it feel as scandalous as a house of ill repute.

Then Uffham produced dice from his pocket. "Hazard, de Vere?"

"That would leave Lady Anne as mere observer, Uffham."

Her brother stared at her as if checking for some strange new growth. "Anne don't want to learn to dice."

"I would think that Lady Anne would rather take part than observe."

She was suddenly aware of how much of her life she had spent as an observer, and not only of activities that her foot made difficult.

All the same, *hazard*?

"It's illegal!"

Uffham snorted. "As if anyone cares."

"Fortunes are won and lost in a night."

"Now that's true," he admitted.

"I will not game away my portion."

"We'll play for farthing points," de Vere said, "and translate them into golden guineas in our heads."

He was already moving a fine gaming table near the fire, and arranging three chairs around it and a stand of candles nearby. Shamelessly, he opened the drawers. "No dice box that I can see. I'm sure we can be trusted to roll fairly. We have our riches, though."

He spilled a bag of ivory counters onto the embossed and gilded leather table. "Consider the relief when we realize in the sober morning that the thousands we owe are mere pounds."

"Or," Anne said, sitting gingerly in the chair he held for her, "the disappointment that the thousands we have won will not purchase much."

He sat beside her. "You would hardly find pleasure in purchases made with money that others could not afford to lose."

"I wouldn't? Then what is the point of it?"

"The pure thrill, of course."

Uffham came over, bringing the brandy decanter with him, and threw himself into the third chair. "I'm with Annie. Where's the thrill in winning farthings?"

De Vere didn't argue, but he rose to get a third glass. He poured brandy into it and put it by Anne's hand.

"Fair play, dear lady. Not good form to keep your head when all around are losing theirs."

Anne stared at the glass, feeling as if she were being swept toward hell. "I do not drink brandy, Mr. de Vere."

"You just did so in your tea, Lady Anne."

"That was different. . . ." Yet Anne couldn't quite explain how. Irritating man. She ignored the glass.

He began a brisk explanation of the rules of hazard, of main and chance, and bewildering sets of numbers.

After a while she raised a hand. "I have the gist of it— I think. Why don't you and Uffham play a . . . main?"

His eyes twinkled. "A main is a round in cock-fighting."

"Which you doubtless indulge in, too."

"There are so few amusements in an army camp, Lady Anne. Especially ones that provide dinner."

She studied him. "Are you serious?"

"As little as possible. Shall we start? Uffham, you have the dice."

Uffham, clearly thinking such low stakes silly, put a counter worth twenty in the middle. De Vere matched it.

De Vere looked at her. "Why not lay a bet, Lady Anne?"

"But if Uffham wins, I lose."

"Such is life." His smile was playful. "It is, after all, only five pennies."

She put a counter with the others. "I will hold you responsible, sir."

"Oh, I am sure of it."

She realized then that he'd sucked her into his folly— and that it was a great deal of fun.

"The Main is seven," Uffham said. He shook the dice in his hands and rolled them—six and two, making eight.

"Eight is Chance," de Vere said in a quiet commentary, "and seven is Main. If he'd thrown the seven he called he would have won outright. That is called 'nicking' it."

"But now," she said, "he wins if he throws Chance— eight—and loses if he throws his Main, which is seven. Is that it?"

"Not quite, but it'll do for now. The odds are against

him. Would you care to place another bet? That is what makes it interesting, especially with many players. The losses or gains can be huge."

"So I have heard. I do not approve. . . ."

"Less talk," grumbled Uffham. "Are you betting, Annie?"

Just to show him, she put a spendthrift twenty in.

"I could refuse your outrageous wager, you know," he said with a grin, but he put a twenty to match hers and rolled the dice again. Five.

"No result." De Vere sipped from his glass. "Another bet?"

"No," Anne said, only realizing when the fiery spirit hit her mouth that she'd imitated his action. By great willpower she did not cough or gasp, but she feared her eyes were watering.

She watched Uffham's next roll through a haze, but it cleared to show a six. The shock of the brandy cleared, too, leaving a pleasant warmth. She took another sip. Now she was prepared, she began to find it most agreeable. Reminding herself that she was only playing for farthings, she put another twenty on the table. De Vere copied her.

"That's more like it," Uffham said, covering both bets, and rolled. Another six. Four. Five.

Two.

Uffham swore, then apologized.

De Vere pushed her winnings over to her. "A throw of two or three is Crabs, and always loses."

Anne gathered in her extra sixty farthings with a hoot of delight.

"I don't think this is a good idea," her brother said. "You're showing all the signs of turning into a gamester."

"You play."

"I have a large income and extremely large expectations."

"That's no reason to risk it all at dice."

"Of course I don't." He frowned upward, as if he could see through the ceiling. "I wish I knew what was happening." But then he shrugged and, with a "dare you" look at Anne, put a fifty onto the table.

Anne risked twenty. "It has to be all right," she said, as much for herself as for him. "Bad news travels fast."

"Especially over such a short distance." De Vere put in fifty. "Births take time."

Uffham called seven again, and threw eleven.

"Main has to be between five and nine," de Vere said. He rolled again. Five.

"Five is Chance," she said, "seven is Main. Those aren't good odds either, are they?"

"You catch on quickly. Up the bet?"

She pushed forward another twenty, and so did de Vere.

Uffham threw seven, sighed, and paid up. He lost the next round as well, and passed the dice to de Vere. Anne was now nearly two hundred farthings richer. To fight the giddy excitement, she reminded herself that it was four shillings and tuppence. Even so, a greed quivered in her, and she could taste the fatal fascination of play.

De Vere put a twenty onto the table, said, "Six," and threw three. Crabs. He lost and paid.

He called six again, threw six, and scooped in their money, but it was a mere forty in winnings. Anne was still ahead.

Next time he called eight, then threw six. "Despite natural instincts, one should stick with a winner. Main is eight, Chance is six. The odds are against me. A wager?"

It was a general comment, but he was looking a challenge at Anne. She put down her largest single bet so far—a fifty. Uffham put in a hundred. She wished she had, too.

De Vere rolled a five. He looked at them again, and Anne put in another fifty. It was only just over a shilling, she told herself, but every nerve was on edge. She wanted to win, and she wanted to win a *lot*. She did not want to lose.

She sipped her brandy, watching every movement of de Vere's fine hands as he shook the dice. *Not six*, she thought at them. *Not six, not six.*

He rolled. . . .

Six!

She bit back unladylike words.

De Vere scooped in her money, smiling at her like a

devil welcoming souls to hell. He took Uffham's money, too, of course, but it was hers that mattered. She took another drink of brandy and leaned forward, keen for the opportunity to win it all back.

Then the door opened, and Benning strode in.

Five

⌒

"What news?" Uffham asked.

Anne fell back to reality with a thump. Important things were happening elsewhere, and she had been rapt in gambling. Benning looked put out to find his study invaded, but merely grabbed a glass, poured himself a large brandy, and drank a good part of it.

"The midwife is here, and Frances's confinement has definitely begun. The McLaren woman says all looks well. It will be many hours, however." He took another stiff drink, then looked at what they were doing. "Hazard. Good idea." He pulled up another chair.

Like plunging from warm to cold, Anne suddenly felt improper. She shouldn't be gaming while her sister gave birth!

The household had divided into male and female, and she was on the wrong side. She'd never been alone with men like this, not even with her brothers.

She stood. "I should go. . . ."

"Where?" asked de Vere, catching her wrist to stop her. "You will be more comfortable here, Lady Anne."

Her breath snagged at the contact, and she looked, startled, into his eyes. She'd never been so boldly touched by a stranger.

She'd never felt such a shocking effect.

He let her go. It could only have been for a second since it hadn't caused comment. She sank back into her seat largely because her legs weren't quite able to hold her.

He was right, though. She couldn't be with Frances. Everyone, not least her sister, would be horrified at an unmarried lady attending a birth. In truth, she didn't want to be there amid pain and hovering death.

Nor did she want to be alone.

She wanted to be here, in this warm room, in company. Safe, perhaps, in male company, engaged in a masculine activity, far from female terrors and mysteries.

The men were already gambling again, laying bets on de Vere's new throws. Anne took another drink from her brandy glass and determined to only watch.

De Vere held the dice for some time, winning and losing, until he threw out three times in a row and looked to Anne beside him. "Dice pass to the left. Ready to play, Lady Anne?"

To take the dice seemed a final step into hell, but she was tired of being an observer—in everything. She held out her hand and he dropped the dice into it. She rolled them in her hands, warm as they were from his.

"I'm said to be lucky, sir. Perhaps I will win your fortune, farthing by farthing."

Amusement twinkled in his eyes. "I, too, am said to be lucky, and I suspect my luck has been tested more than yours."

"Playing your military career like a trump card, Mr. de Vere?"

"You're confusing your games, Lady Anne."

"Less talk," Uffham complained.

She remembered with shock that others were present. Benning, at least, seemed too sozzled to care—or perhaps his mind was upstairs with his wife. She preferred to think that.

She put a modest twenty onto the table. "Luck is tested everyday, Mr. de Vere, in small ways and large. Some tests are simply more dramatic."

"A fine way to dismiss the field of battle, Lady Anne." He matched her bet. "*Bon chance.*"

Now she had other reasons to want to win. She called seven, which she gathered was the most likely roll, but rolled eight.

Now she had to roll eight to win. A seven would be a loss.

"Odds are against you," said the diabolical de Vere. "That's the hazard of playing safe—of picking the most common number as your Main." He put a hundred counter onto the table. "You can refuse a bet if you wish, Lady Anne."

A challenge, deliberately given.

"Of course not." When the other men put down the same bet, however, her palms began to sweat. She could lose three hundred on one roll.

A hundred farthings is only two shillings and one pence, she reminded herself. She'd pay more than that for a yard of cheap cloth. All the same, as she rolled she prayed for an eight.

Eight, eight, eight, eight . . .

Seven!

She understood why Uffham had cursed when losing. She felt almost tearful to see all her lovely "money" going into other hands. She'd win it back. She put a fifty on the table, and the men did the same.

"Eight," she said firmly, and threw—Crabs. "These dice are perverse!"

"Always are, Annie," Uffham slurred with a chuckle. "Always are. You're playing with the devil's bones."

Devil bones.

She could almost see wickedness swirl around the room. This place might as well be a gaming hell. It fit her imaginary picture of one.

The last daylight had gone, leaving only fire and candlelight, and the dark shadows beyond their circle. Uffham lolled in his chair, cravat loosened, and Benning didn't seem in much better shape. He'd summoned more brandy at one point, and she thought he and Uffham had drunk a good deal of it. De Vere drank, but she had the impression that the sips were small, and his glass was rarely refilled. She thought she was the same, but wasn't entirely sure. . . .

She threw again, wondering how affected by drink she was. She'd drunk wine with dinner as usual, but then there had been the brandied tea, followed by neat brandy. As she threw and won and gathered in some money, she tried to remember whether de Vere had topped up her glass at any time. Might she have drunk two glasses of neat brandy?

She was caster for a while and though she thought she

ended up a gainer by it, she could no longer quite keep track. Eventually she lost three in a row and passed the dice to Benning.

He held them, frowning. "Wish I knew what was happening. Damnable business." He turned to her. "Anne, go and see? Don't let men up there, you know, but they'd let you."

"Intrude on the birthing?"

She, too, wanted news, but she didn't want to go there. To see things. To hear things . . .

Yet on this strange day that had swooped from *Pastimes for Ladies* to vices for gentlemen, she decided to test herself—to do something that frightened her.

She rose, alarmed by a slight waver, then got her balance. "Very well."

She limped to the door, but someone came with her. She turned to find de Vere there, holding her shawl. "You will want this, Lady Anne."

She would have liked to simply take it, but he was moving to put it around her shoulders, and there was no decorous way to avoid that. His fingers brushed against her bare nape for a moment and then were gone.

It was no more than had happened a hundred times before with her scarcely noticing it, but she felt a disconcerting shiver. It must be the effect of the strange night and circumstances, or perhaps the brandy. Perhaps that was why ladies were not supposed to drink brandy except watered, or in tea, for medicinal purposes.

She thanked him and hurried out, hearing the door click shut behind her.

The house lay silent but for the ticking of the hall clock, but it was not dark. A hall lamp had been left burning, and candles flickered in sconces on the upper landing. She stretched her ears but could hear no sounds from above. That suddenly seemed ominous. She hurried up the stairs as best she could, for once cursing her foot that made a nimble run impossible.

At her sister's door, she paused again, almost out of breath, but from fear not exercise. She was suddenly sure that something had gone terribly wrong. While she'd been drinking and gaming downstairs!

Then she heard voices in the room. Talking voices.

Low. Then sharp. Then low again. Some cries, or growls perhaps. Growls? Not screams, at least. No one sounded grief-stricken.

Then someone laughed.

With a gasp of relief Anne sagged against the white-painted panels, every muscle weakened.

Good heavens, it must be the brandy. Anne swallowed, forced herself straight, then tapped on the door with her fingernails. It seemed feeble, but a brisk knock was unthinkable.

She was about to try again when it opened a crack and Marjorie, Frances's maid, peered out. She looked a bit flustered, but otherwise normal in her cap and plain blue dress. "What is it?" she asked, quite rudely.

Anne bit her lip on laughter. The whole world was out of order tonight, when the womanly mysteries of birth ruled.

Then the maid blinked. "I beg your pardon, Lady Anne. Is something the matter?"

The maid was blocking any sight of the room and Anne was glad of it. She could hear, however. Hear clearly now. A working woman's voice with a Scots burr in a flow of encouragement and brisk instruction. Gasps and those deep groans that must, unlikely as it seemed, be from Frances.

Was she in terrible pain?

Anne swallowed to clear her throat. "Lord Benning would like to know if all is well with his wife." It came out thinly. Of course all was not well.

Was Frances dying?

Who had dared to laugh?

"Everything's fine!" called the Scottish voice. "Not long now. If you've a mind to be of service, whoever you are, you'll sober up his lordship so he's ready to welcome his bairn in decent style this time!"

Marjorie's eyes widened at this, and she turned to say, "It's Lady Anne, Mrs. McLaren. . . ."

In doing so, she opened the door further, and Anne glimpsed her sister sprawled in a low chair near the fire. The room was as dim as the gaming hell below, devilishly lit by flame.

Frances wore only her nightgown, and it was up

around her thighs. Her legs were bare and splayed, her
head thrown back as she gasped and groaned in some
extreme—

The door shut, cutting off the vision from hell.

Or heaven.

A buxom woman had been wrapped around Frances
like a mother with a child, cushioning her head on a
round shoulder, one hand between her legs, crooning
almost. Anne almost felt she could slide into her sister's
skin, into whatever raging forces racked her, into a world
encompassed by warm, loving arms and a strong croon
of encouragement. . . .

She turned to retrace her steps, dizzier by far than
brandy could account for, or even her damnable foot,
though she was unable to cope with it just now. She
lurched down the corridor with one hand on the wall,
trying to find her normal balance but thrown off by a
raging vision she could hardly tolerate. . . .

And walked right into something.

Someone.

Racecombe de Vere.

She immediately pushed back, and he didn't try to
hold her.

"Is it bad news, Lady Anne?"

As best she could tell in faint light and with blurred
vision, he was for once completely serious.

"No. Or at least, I don't think so. That woman said"—
strong arms, soft shoulder, crooning voice—"she said everything was all right."

She only realized then that de Vere still had his hands
on her arms as if she needed holding up. Perhaps she
did. Her legs were shaking, truly shaking. She wasn't
sure she could walk another step. When he pulled her
back into his arms, or perhaps simply stopped holding
her up, she didn't resist.

Racecombe de Vere wasn't at all like Mrs. McLaren—
he was hard not soft, and he wasn't crooning—and yet
her need for this came from that glimpse of Frances.
Then she thought with astonishing clarity that she could
not remember being held like this since her own Scottish
nurse, Mrs. Loganhume, had done so when she'd been
a child.

Her head fit with comfort on his shoulder. His body felt firm and warm against hers. She was leaning, limp, and he was balanced and strong. Infinitely dependable. Her heart rate slowed, her legs steadied . . .

And she became vastly embarrassed.

She stopped herself from pushing away and screeching, but she detached herself from this intrusive stranger's arms, aware of her own fiery cheeks.

"I do beg your pardon, Mr. de Vere. What you must think of me . . ." Then she saw typical humor in his eyes. "It was you, sir, who encouraged me to drink brandy!"

His eyes twinkled even more. "With delightful results, Lady Anne."

She pressed hands to her hot cheeks. "Can I trust you not to speak of it?"

Humor disappeared. "It is hardly a tale that would buy me a dinner."

She was making a complete fool of herself and lashed out again in reaction. "What are you doing up here anyway?"

"Standing ready to serve. Is service required?"

She began to snap, *No,* but remembered the midwife's words. "Apparently Lord Benning should be sobered up to be ready to receive his child. I have no idea how to do that, but I assume you do."

"But of course." The humor was back, but she knew it was of a different sort, a cooler sort, and she regretted her rudeness. Men sank into their cups all the time, however, so of course he knew how to deal with it.

As he said, "Let's have at it," and extended an arm to her, she acknowledged that she missed the warm merriment.

The man irritated her to death. He was like a faery visitor in a nursery story, come to wreak havoc and turn an ordinary family's life upside down. In fact, there *was* something fey about him, about his light coloring and slim body, those heavy-lidded wicked eyes.

As she'd thought, however, he was strong, and as they started down the stairs, she was glad of his arm. Her legs were still not steady, and her foot fought her. "I am not drinking brandy again," she muttered.

"Or gaming?"

"Or gaming." But she was less sure of that. For far-thing points it had been an exciting pastime. Certainly more so than plaiting straw.

Now she thought about it, being in the company of this man was an exciting pastime.

Flirtation. She'd been going to practice flirtation with him in preparation for an attempt on London society and finding a husband. How far away that all seemed.

How close he was.

Her breath felt different, as if it was spiced with brandy. Her heart couldn't seem to settle to a normal pace. When they reached the bottom of the stairs, the house was still and silent all around them. They were, in effect, alone, arm in arm. She could turn a little, and they could kiss. . . .

It was the strangest thought she could ever remember having. This man was a stranger and probably an adventurer.

It would only be a kiss. . . .

She remembered Frances, and reality, and the hundred and one reasons why she should come to her senses, and unlinked their arms.

"What do we do?" she asked him.

"Do?" he asked, as if he'd been able to read her thoughts. There was something about his eyes that made her think he might have been *sharing* her thoughts!

"About Benning."

"Ah. Yes." He shook himself. "We need cold cloths, as cold as can be found, strong coffee, and a pitcher of ale."

"Ale?"

"It sometimes works better than coffee. If you will point me to the kitchens, Lady Anne, I'll see if any servants are available."

"I'll go with you. They might not take orders from a stranger."

His crisp commands were irritating her, so she'd intended her comment to put him in his place. Of course, it had no effect. Words were as likely to depress this man's pretensions as a baby's hand was likely to depress a feather bed.

Baby . . .

She limped toward the kitchen, avoiding taking his arm again. "There will be servants awake on such a night, I think."

When she entered the big, warm room she was proved right, after a fashion. Mrs. Orwell, the housekeeper, was nodding in a big chair by the fireplace, a cat in her lap, but she was fully dressed. Her husband—the butler—and a footman were playing a card game at the big table. Hetty was darning by candlelight, and she leaped to her feet.

"Is there news, milady?"

The men rose, too.

"Not yet, but soon, apparently." Anne was reluctant to state that their employer was drunk. "We would like coffee in Lord Benning's study."

"Right, milady. Jeffrey, grind the beans." To de Vere, Orwell added, "His lordship called for more brandy moments ago, sir."

"You took it?"

"Jeffrey did, sir."

"I'll go and take charge. Coffee, Lady Anne, along with ale and cold cloths. As soon as possible."

Anne said, "Aye-aye, sir!" but he didn't seem to catch it as he dashed out of the room. "Insufferable man."

"Officer, milady." Orwell went to gently shake his wife awake.

Mrs. Orwell rubbed her eyes. "Is the baby here, then?"

"Soon, love, or so they say. Lady Anne's here needing coffee and the like."

It amused Anne to see the normally impeccable Orwells in disarray, and it touched her to witness the warmth between them. Not exactly passion, but something deep and real.

Another shift in her stable world, and right now she needed some stability to hold on to. Despite logic, she couldn't help thinking that Race de Vere was responsible for this rattling of reality. He must be responsible for the wanton thoughts that had just shaken her.

He was dangerous.

"Sit you down, milady," Hetty said, virtually placing

Anne in her chair by the fire and pulling up a footstool. "You're looking worn out."

Anne knew it wasn't tiredness, but she took the chair willingly enough as the servants bustled around drawing ale, grinding coffee, and pumping water until it ran cold enough.

Race de Vere. She realized that over the evening Uffham had sometimes called him that, and now it had stuck.

Racy.

An idle dilettante with racy inclinations.

Yet race also meant speed, as in a racing river, undercutting banks, carrying all before it. That fit, too.

Did people arrive at a version of their name that suited? What then of dull, common Lady Anne?

Or the nursery Annie?

Or Mouse, the name her foster brother, Tris, had always used with her. It was fond, but now it depressed her. Mouse, indeed. Small, dull, and hiding in holes. She knew Tris hadn't meant it that way, but it felt that way now.

What name did she wish she had?

Arabella. Barbara. That was nice and fierce. Florentia?

Serena.

Serena, Lady Middlethorpe, who was ravishingly beautiful and who had lain with Lord Middlethorpe back when he had not even been trying to kiss Anne. . . .

She would *not* start feeling sorry for herself, not tonight of all nights. And yet she was wishing she was not here. That Frances's confinement had waited a week until she was gone. Or that she'd retired to her room after dinner, perhaps even taken laudanum and gone to sleep.

Slowly, however, here among ordinary people and practical tasks, calm and common sense returned. She was a very fortunate young woman, born in silk with only one small trial to carry through life. If she lacked a husband it was her own fault for living like a mouse in a hole.

It couldn't be so hard to marry if she put her mind to it. She was a duke's daughter with a handsome dowry.

She would doubtless end up a mother herself one day and appreciate this introduction to the matter.

It was de Vere who had jiggled her life about so that she didn't know who she was or what she should be doing. So that she was having wild, wanton thoughts. And he was doing it for sheer amusement. When she'd asked him if he was serious, what had he replied?

As little as possible.

But then she remembered the moment of seriousness upstairs when he must have thought her unsteadiness was because of grief. And his decisive commands before leaving the kitchen.

Officer. Yes, she could imagine him in the midst of battle.

Exactly what was Race de Vere? What was real, and what was artifice?

Anne had to abandon that misty speculation to lead a procession back to the study. Orwell carried a silver tray with coffee and cups on it. Hetty bore a large bowl full of icily wet cloths. Jeffrey the footman brought the jug of ale and three tankards. Mrs. Orwell had stayed behind to keep an eye on the kitchen.

They entered to find Uffham snoring slackly undisturbed in his chair, but Benning awake if unfocused. His cravat was gone, and his shirt unbuttoned. Anne suppressed a giggle. Her stuffy brother-in-law was always neat as a pin.

"Your child is about to be born, Benning," de Vere was saying in that crisp officer voice. "You must be ready to greet him or her properly. First impressions, and all that."

Benning squinted at him. "Child. Right. Boy?"

"We don't know yet. The cold cloths."

Hetty hurried over, though Anne saw that her eyes were wide.

De Vere took a cloth and without hesitation wiped Benning's face with it. Benning spluttered and tried to fight free. De Vere prevented it with remarkable ease and wrapped the cloth around the drunken man's neck.

Benning yelled, eyes opening wide. "What the—? Plague and hell—!"

"You are needed, Lord Benning," de Vere said in a

voice that must have led men into battle. Without turning, he said, "The ale."

Jeffrey poured a tankard and hurried forward.

Anne retreated and watched in fascination as de Vere dragged her brother-in-law out of his stupor and into a state where he could form coherent sentences—most of which seemed to be blistering complaints.

"An attempt to thrash me would probably help in sobering you up," de Vere agreed. "Would you care to step outside and try?"

His voice was still precise, but an edge of impatience was audible. And tiredness. His face, she noted, was set in harder lines than she'd seen before. If it was fey, it was now from a darker version of faeryland, but in a strange way he was more beautiful like this than teasing and laughing.

Beautiful?

Yes, he seemed beautiful to her. Like the angel in the church, she remembered. An angel of the fiery, militant sort.

She realized she was leaning back against a bookcase, watching and weary, almost drifting on these astonishing events. How long was it since she had gone upstairs to find out what was happening? From here and in poor light she couldn't make out the clock. The room was still a hell lit only by flame. Uffham had slid farther down in his chair and was snoring softly.

Benning pushed to his feet, staggered, and then righted himself. "Damnation. Give me more of that coffee. Did you say the baby's born? Is Frances all right?"

"We don't know yet, Lord Benning," de Vere said. "But the midwife said it would not be long and you would want to be ready to hear the news."

"Right, right." Benning began to stagger around the room, but then noticed the servants. "What the devil are you doing here? Get on with you!"

They left, but gave Anne rolling-eye smiles as they did so. She felt like giggling, perhaps with exhaustion, and told Hetty to take herself off to bed. She could get herself out of this dress and her light corset, and she couldn't imagine sleeping until it was all over.

Then the clock on the mantelpiece began to chime, and she counted eleven. Late by country time.

Benning was lurching around the room, drinking and spilling coffee. De Vere was doing nothing but filling the coffee cup now and then.

Benning suddenly stopped. "Why is there no news? Why haven't we heard?" He glared at Anne. "When did you say the McLaren woman said the birth was imminent?"

Anne straightened, his worry kindling hers. "I didn't. She said you needed to be sober to be ready."

"Impertinent woman. Just because last time . . . Damnable business. Worse for the husband than the wife, if you ask me."

Anne wondered if deep inside he'd like someone big and soft to hold him in his arms.

"Can you go and ask again, Anne?"

She stared at him. It was a piteous, desperate request, but every muscle tightened in rejection. "Oh, no. Mrs. Orwell—"

"Just ask how long. See that everything's still as it should be. Please."

She felt nailed in place. She'd ventured off to do something difficult earlier, brave because of ignorance. Now she knew, and she didn't want to return to the fray. For some reason she looked to de Vere. His eyes met hers, expressionless.

She knew, however, she *knew* that he was daring her. No, it wasn't that. He was expecting her to, as an officer expected his men to march.

Or was he expecting her to fail?

Stiffening her resolve, she took two steps toward the door.

She was saved by it opening to reveal Marjorie, beaming, a bundle in her arms. "My lord," she declared, with excusable drama, "you have a son!"

Anne saw the sudden light in her brother-in-law's eyes, saw his unfettered joy as he marched forward to grasp the baby. "By God, by God," he said in a voice perhaps blurred with tears. But then swiftly, he asked, "And Lady Benning?"

"Is well, my lord. She said you were not to keep the baby from her for long."

"Indeed, indeed . . ." He left in a hurry, baby in his arms.

The door closed, and Anne found herself alone in the light of a dying fire with Racecombe de Vere and unsteadying, tumultuous emotions.

Six

~

She should leave. She should go to bed now. But she couldn't yet, and the only person available to her, it would seem, was this gadfly, this hard-faced officer, this fey mystery of a man.

Then Uffham snored.

Anne started, but she knew her brother. She doubted even cold cloths and coffee could restore him to a chaperon.

De Vere put another log to crackle on the fire, then went to the tray set on a side table. "The coffee is doubtless cold, but would you like some?"

Perhaps she, too, needed cold cloths. She felt disconnected from her real world, from Lady Anne Peckworth, the quiet lady of impeccable behavior.

"Yes, please." Her foot was aching, so she sat with relief at her seat at the table.

He put the cup and saucer before her. "Are you all right?"

"Why shouldn't I be?"

"I don't suppose this is a normal night for you."

"I don't suppose it is a normal night for you, either."

The candles he had set near the table so many hours ago were all burning low, sending irregular light to distort everything. She became aware of the smell of brandy heavy in the air, and the bitterness of coffee on her tongue. He hadn't sweetened it, but she decided not to complain. Bitter coffee seemed in keeping.

"I've only been involved with a birth a time or two," he said, sitting down opposite her.

"You've been involved in a birth before?"

She noted that he was drinking brandy not coffee, but she couldn't complain. He was certainly not drunk.

"An army camp is like a rough-and-tumble town, Lady Anne. Birth, marriage—or the associated bits—and death, it all happens underfoot."

"Then I hope you watched where you walked."

He laughed, a sudden, blessed relaxation. "Always, Lady Anne. Always."

There she went again. She never made risqué remarks. She was mistress of the art of light conversation that passed the time but touched on nothing that might discomfort or raise emotions.

She'd never before understood the phrase "not quite oneself."

"I try to always watch my step," he said. "A misstep, after all, can cause a fall. And a fall can cost a man, or a woman, paradise."

She focused her eyes and studied him. "Why are you here, Mr. de Vere?"

"Because Uffham is here."

"You are stuck to him like a . . . a barnacle on a ship's bottom?" But then her words summoned a most improper vision, and she hicced back a laugh.

"Now, what was that wicked thought?"

She kept her lips sealed, but he grinned.

"Mr. de Vere!"

"It was your thought, Lady Anne."

Her laughter escaped, even through her hand over her mouth.

Uffham stirred.

Anne stared at her brother in alarm. Had he heard? Had he woken? Might he remember any of this in the morning?

"Do you often have improper thoughts, Lady Anne?"

She swiveled her eyes to him. "Only, it would seem, with you, sir!"

"Ah, now that is interesting."

She thrust to her feet. "How do you *do* this? What is it that you do? You enter people's lives like . . . like a ball among skittles, throwing everything awry. I wouldn't be surprised if you started Frances's confinement!"

He stood, too. "It would be a remarkable skill if I did."

"You are a devil, sir!"

"And you are a saint? Does it not grow cold on that virtuous, unforgiving ground, my lady?"

"I'm sure hell's flames burn hot!"

"Perhaps paradise, therefore, is in the middle ground." She stared at him. "I think that's sacrilege."

"Why? If we believe in a good God, do we not believe in a paradise that will be just reward for virtue? What, Lady Anne, would you choose for eternal happiness?"

The elementary question struck her dumb. Having no answer, she sank back weakly into her chair. "Have you known great happiness?" she asked at last.

He sat opposite her again. "One of the rewards of battle is the euphoria of victory, and especially of survival. The pleasure is so great that some men cannot live without it."

"But many die. Or are maimed."

"Contrasts, Lady Anne. Contrasts." He rolled the dice over the scattered counters. They came to rest at two. "Crabs, I die." He looked up at her. "Perhaps pleasure is always equal to the hazard involved. That is why people play for high stakes, you know. In games—and in life."

Race thought that perhaps she understood him. He was not keeping her here, after all, and for her this was a hazardous encounter.

"A duke's daughter is not allowed to play dangerous games," she pointed out.

"A well-behaved duke's daughter."

"You advocate wickedness?"

"I advocate being what you want to be."

"Beautiful." She threw it like a dart. "I want to be as beautiful as Lady Middlethorpe."

He saw her realize what she had revealed. She grasped her brandy glass, then realized that it was empty. She shoved it over to him.

He picked up the decanter. "I am honor-bound to remind you that you vowed never to drink brandy again."

"I've changed my mind. A lady is allowed to do that. A gentleman," she added, "is not." But then she grimaced. "I must make it clear that Lord Middlethorpe made me no promises. Nor did Lord Wyvern."

He filled her glass and passed it back. "You have no need to be envious of any woman's looks."

"Do you claim that I am a raging beauty, Mr. de Vere?"

He gave her the truth. "No."

She laughed and toasted him. "Well, here's to honesty!" When she'd swallowed a mouthful of brandy, she added, "Lady Middlethorpe is. A great beauty." She drank another sip. "He got her with child while he was courting me."

Ah. He hadn't realized it had been quite like that. He didn't know Middlethorpe, but he'd thrash him given the chance.

"And Lady Anne Peckworth was, I am sure, completely the lady about it. No admission of envy. No spurt of anger. But what," he asked, "did you feel?"

He thought she wouldn't answer, but then she said, "Anger."

"A deadly sin. Perhaps you should have shown it."

"Not showing anger was the only way to retain my dignity. . . ."

"Pride."

"Not at all. I needed to stop Uffham from calling him out."

He wished he'd been there to support her. "A virtue, I grant you, though I don't know which."

"Wisdom, perhaps?"

"If you can, Lady Anne, by all means be wise."

She pushed the brandy away. "If I were wise, sir, I would not be here with you. I should go."

She didn't rise, however, and he was glad of it. They were progressing, but he wasn't sure she was hatched yet. "You are better off, you know, without a dutiful husband who wants another."

"True. But then there's my sister."

"Lady Benning?"

"No. My younger sister, Marianne. She's in love. With a hero. Captain Percival Shreve."

"Are you saying you love him, too?"

She looked at him with astonishment. "Of course not. He's still suffering from his wounds. They want to marry, but my mother will not permit Marianne to marry before me. I suspect she doesn't want the marriage at all because Percy might be an invalid for life. And now Lord Wyvern has married another . . ."

She blinked—tears? "I don't know why I'm telling you these things."

He spoke softly so as not to stir her. "The strangeness of a strange night. You'd be amazed at the things men tell each other around a campfire the night before battle."

"Or around a birth? You make a very unlikely midwife, sir."

He laughed in genuine humor. She was a delight when slightly tipsy, and her comment was closer to the truth than she knew. Could he hope she was feeling newborn?

She rolled her half-empty glass between her pale, slender fingers. "So now I must find another husband, and quickly. And one who will stay the course."

He hadn't counted on this urgency. "There is no need of desperation, Lady Anne. You are a prize."

She peered at him. "Did Uffham bring you here for me, after all? I will *not* be courted out of pity again."

"So I should think. And your brother, my dear lady, would shoot me if I aspired so high."

She frowned at him. "Who *are* you?"

"Racecombe de Vère."

"I mean, who are you really? Where do you come from?"

"London."

"Where is your *home*?"

"A soldier's home is where he hangs his hat."

She tossed the contents of her glass in his face.

Anne pushed to her feet, horrified at herself. "Oh, I'm sorry! I don't know what came over me. . . ." She looked around for some sort of cloth.

He produced a handkerchief and dabbed his face, seeming amused. "Don't fuss. I was being irritating as usual." He calmly refilled her glass and put it in front of her. "I was born and raised in north Derbyshire, not far from Chesterfield."

Anne settled back into her chair, dazed. He was like no man she had ever known. Perhaps he truly was fey, here to bewitch them all.

"Is your name really de Vere?"

His mouth quirked. "I know, I know. The extinct de Veres. I assure you, Lady Anne, I was born to a father called de Vere and christened Racecombe de Vere in a Christian church."

No mystery at all. An ancestor must have been a de Vere on the wrong side of the blanket and taken the name.

"I'm sorry," she said. "I was intrusive."

"Naturally so. I have been prying into your affairs all day."

She looked at him again. "Why?"

"You interest me, Lady Anne. For example, you cannot have lived entirely in seclusion. You must have had many suitors."

"Fortune hunters, or those wishing to push their way into a ducal family."

"Are you sure?"

"A lady can tell where a man's interest truly lies."

"A pleasant belief, but a gentleman can also tell if he is viewed with suspicion. Striving for heaven on earth could be a prescription for disappointment."

She tried to apply her fuzzy mind to his comments. "You think me too particular? If you do not believe in being particular, Mr. de Vere, why are you not married?"

"Have pity, Lady Anne! I'm under a year back from war and no great prospect."

"You are a younger son?"

Something in his quick look made her think he didn't like that question. Eventually he said, "No, but I ran away to the army, so my father owes me nothing. He will likely leave what he has elsewhere."

"Why would he do that?"

"Because I irritate him as much as I irritate you. It is my role on this strange stage of life."

He rose suddenly and went to fuss with the fire.

Anne watched with some satisfaction. She'd finally hit a sensitive spot on Mr. Racecombe de Vere. His family. He'd probably been cast off.

Horrid to be so nosy, but he fascinated her and in more than his background. The way he spoke, the way he teased, the way he moved. She watched him in the firelight, the lines of his body somehow made clear to her despite his substantial clothing.

Broad shoulders, long back, lean hips, strong thighs . . .

He rose smoothly, as if to emphasize the latter, limned by firelight. "Why have you avoided society, Lady Anne? Because of the limp?"

That jerked her out of foolish wanderings. "No one, Mr. de Vere, raises my deformity without a blink as you do!"

"I was not aware that it was a secret."

"It is too obvious to be a secret, but . . ." She found herself without a rational protest to make. "I simply do not enjoy idle social gatherings."

"I see. The limp is not your handicap. It is your excuse."

If he wasn't so far away, she might have flung her drink at him again. "And what is yours, sir, for being a shooting star with no fixed point in the firmament?"

"My nature, of course. Who would tolerate me for more than a month or two?"

"The army did."

"It was touch and go at times."

And that smile was back, that rueful, self-mocking smile that made her tremble.

A spent log tumbled on the fire, and light flared over him. Transient light. The fire would die soon if no one put on more wood. This wild unsteadiness would die soon, too.

She felt he might disappear at daylight like the fey creature he seemed. She could not bear for it to end just yet.

She pushed to her feet. "Mr. de Vere."

He stilled.

"You offered to serve me. There is one way in which you could."

"Yes?" His eyes were steady and wide. His instincts were very good. A wicked imp inside delighted that she finally had *him* off balance.

"I must go into society and seek a husband—but I am handicapped by a lack of experience."

"As you pointed out earlier, Lady Anne, a lady is not supposed to be experienced."

He was definitely on the defensive! Mischief bubbled up in her.

"There is experience, sir, and experience. I am a duke's daughter and thus rarely encroached upon. Because of my crippled foot, my family are very protective. A lady who has been out in society for four years could be expected to be a little more . . . knowledgeable."

He walked toward the table, watching her. Picked up his glass and drank. Drank more at one go than she'd seen him drink all evening.

"What knowledge, precisely, do you want, Lady Anne?"

What knowledge, precisely, would you provide if asked?

Astonishing to think that tonight there was nothing and no one to prevent the most wicked excess. Her family were either asleep or engaged in other matters. The servants would not come at this hour unless summoned. She had never before in her life been so unprotected— so free—as she was now in her brother-in-law's proper house, with her brother in the same room.

She flickered a glance at Uffham, but he was completely unaware.

"Kisses," she blurted.

"You have never been kissed?"

She supposed his astonishment was flattering.

She looked down and fiddled with the scattered counters. "Only in the slightest manner. If I am to encourage men to court me I need to know how to act and react."

She studied him. Faced with his silent disapproval, she added, "You say I have been discouraging, but we ladies are warned against permitting liberties. I need to know what to permit."

"In this situation, my lady, nothing."

His distancing "my lady" made her want to giggle. Who was the skittle now, and who was the ball?

"I've seen Uffham drunk before," she said. "If the room were to catch fire we'd probably have to drag him snoring to safety."

The look he shot her was as much exasperation as amusement, but he went over, hitched her brother higher in the chair. "Uffham, it's time to go to bed."

The regular snoring might have hesitated for a second, but then Uffham sagged back down in the chair.

De Vere turned to look at her, shaking his head. "Lady Anne, you have drunk too much brandy. You are going to be very embarrassed in the morning."

"I don't feel drunk." In fact, she felt alive, uninhibited by convention, and astonishingly bold. "And if I'm to feel embarrassed, I might as well have something to be embarrassed about. Would it be so very difficult for you to kiss me?"

She said it lightly, but then something cold flowed through her, washing away the glorious confidence. He didn't want to kiss her. Of course he didn't. Why did she think he might?

"I'm sorry. I should not have—"

"Anne." His voice, his use of her name alone, stopped her.

He came toward her, seeming completely steady. "I have no objection to kissing you. It is only that I do not want to take advantage of the moment."

"You are bound to say something like that. I have embarrassed you and myself."

He took her hands. "Remember. I nearly always say exactly what I want."

"*Nearly* always."

"What pressure is there here to prevaricate? Are you going to shoot me, or court-martial me?"

She found herself laughing, her hands still warmly in his. "I think you could drive a person to shoot you."

He smiled. "But not you. Or not over this. Very well. Kissing lessons." He bowed low and kissed first one hand then the other.

"Hand kissing is not much practiced anymore," she

commented, amazed at how breathless that simple contact made her. But it was two contacts—both his lips and his hands on hers.

When meeting gentlemen, she was usually gloved. When had a stranger last touched her naked hands?

"And not with the deep bow." He straightened, her hands still in his light but firm grip. "If any man kisses your hands like that, he is a mountebank. Don't trust a word he says."

"I have made a mental note of it, sir."

He looked down. "Your hands are lovely."

"My *hands*?"

He raised them, turning them in the unsteady light, her familiar hands with only two small rings.

"Lovely." He looked up, and she saw no mischief or teasing at all. "If ever, some time in the future, you feel this kissing lesson was of value, Lady Anne, send me a sketch of your hands."

She wasn't sure whether to be flattered or offended. "My *hands* are my finest feature?"

Now the mischief was back. "I would have to inspect the whole of you to make that judgment, dear lady, but I admire them profoundly."

He raised them to his lips and kissed each, a gentle but firm kiss, then looked into her eyes. "This is the hand kiss of a man who knows how to soften a woman's heart and mind." He brushed his lips over her fingers, and then over her knuckles.

She felt it on her skin, up her arms, then down, curling, into her belly.

"I see."

She heard the breathiness of her own excitement, but beneath it flowed melancholy. Lord Middlethorpe had kissed her hand like that when departing, when promising to return in a few days, with the clear implication that he would then ask for her hand in marriage.

"Is your mind softened?" he asked with an impish look.

It snapped her back to the moment, but she feared he might have seen something, guessed something. "Not at all."

"Good. It is too easy a trick."

He kissed her knuckles again, this time with lips parted so she felt breath and perhaps even moisture.

She swallowed. "How should I regard a man who does that?"

"Very warily, but he might be honestly devoted."

"I would know him to be skilled at these things. Is that a virtue?"

"Such skill is like a sharp sword—excellent in some hands, but worrying in others. Surely some of your suitors have tried this ploy."

"It never had much effect. It never felt sincere." De Vere was not sincere, and yet his courtship of her hands was having an effect. "You, Mr. de Vere, are a prime example of skilled, are you not?"

"Me, Lady Anne?" He was innocent as an angel. "I have spent most of my adult life with the army. True, there were occasional gracious moments, but if I have talents, they must come to me naturally."

"Or unnaturally."

He laughed and let one hand go. The other, he turned and pressed a kiss into the palm with what sounded like a hum of pleasure.

Her breath caught and a shiver that was certainly not of horror rippled through her. When he raised his head and looked at her, she tried to make her face blank, but she wasn't sure she succeeded. Therefore, she reacted in the only other way she could think of. She turned his hand and brought it to her own mouth to kiss.

Oh, dear. Now she knew why a man might do something like that. The hollow of his hand seemed a personal place, a private one. One not often seen or touched. It was warm and smelled softly of . . . of flesh, she supposed. It was smooth except for a ridge of scar tissue that ran straight across.

She moved the hand away and studied it.

"I grabbed a saber. I was gloved, but it was still a damn stupid thing to do. I'm lucky to have full use of my hand."

A vision assailed her—him in battle, fighting for king, country, and for his life, all fiery purpose and springsteel strength . . .

"Seduction comes in many forms, doesn't it, Mr. de Vere?"

He removed his hand from her hold. "No one, Lady Anne, is seducing anyone tonight."

Seven

~

"Of course not," she said, but she missed his touch like a long-familiar friend.

As the fire failed, the air was growing chilly. One candle spluttered wildly and then died. She should leave. She should have left long ago.

"You're right, however, about methods of seduction," he said. "Some will try to woo by being pitiful. Resist."

"Being wooed that way, or wooing?"

"Have you ever used your foot to try to snare a man?"

"I have never tried to snare a man at all."

"How exasperated some of your suitors must have been."

"Why? What do you mean?"

"You are a duke's daughter, a princess within walls of power. A little encouragement would have been welcome." He tugged her into his arms. "What would you have done," he asked, fitting her against his firm body as if it were the most natural thing in the world, "if one of those unpromising gentleman had done this?"

"Insisted that he let me go."

But she whispered it. Perhaps it was because they were so very close, but perhaps it was to avoid any chance of waking Uffham at this most interesting moment. There was no place for her arms to go except around his neck. Her heart was fluttering, and various parts of her body were, she felt, coming fully alive for the first time.

Her fingertips against his collar.

Her legs brushing his.

Her breath almost close enough to his to blend . . .

"And if he did not?" He held her closer still so she was pressed to his body along her whole length, encircled as she encircled. It had been much the same earlier, in the corridor outside Frances's room, but it had been oh so different. Then she had been weak with shock and fear, but now she felt not weak, but soft . . .

Except her breasts, which seemed firm and sensitive where they pressed against him.

"Well," he asked, brushing a kiss against her cheek, speaking close by her ear, "what would you do?"

"Scream for help?" It was the merest breath.

"If you scream, Uffham may not wake, but someone will come." He drew back a little to look at her. His eyes still smiled, but to her they were full of deep and alien mysteries. "You really should scream, you know."

"I won't. You have my word on it."

"No matter what I do?"

A shiver of fear ran through her, and yet she could not do the sensible thing and pull out of his arms. "Yes, I will scream if necessary, but I will warn you first."

"You play fair. Perhaps it is time for you to call me Race."

Transfixed by him she said, "Oh, no, Mr. de Vere. I think that would be most unwise."

His smile was sudden and delightful, digging disarming brackets into his cheeks. "Wise lady."

And then he kissed her.

It was a gentle pressure on her lips, and something she had experienced before. A gentleman or two had stolen such a kiss before being told to desist. Never before, however, had she been wrapped so intimately in the man's arms, shaped to him, melded with him. Her senses swirled out of all balance to such a tame kiss.

And to think, she could have been doing this for years!

When their lips parted, she stared at him. "Do you truly think I have been discouraging?"

"Most men would tremble in their boots at the thought of courting a daughter of the Duke of Arran."

Another log shifted in the grate, its dying flames dancing against the fine-boned edge of his face. "Are you trembling, Mr. de Vere?"

"A little. A lesson, Lady Anne. Even a man with no serious intentions can become seriously intent with a lovely lady soft in his arms in the wicked hours of the night."

She could see the truth of it in his eyes. When she sucked in a breath, she felt as if he breathed with her, as if they could blend even more closely together. "Is it too dangerous to proceed? I will scream if you alarm me."

"Are you easily alarmed?"

"I have no idea."

"Don't scream. You have only to whisper stop." Then his eyes twinkled. "If that doesn't work, pull my hair out."

His arms tightened, and his lips covered hers with sudden force that knocked out what little breath she had, whirling her into dizziness. Ruthlessly, he ravaged her, open mouthed and wet.

Some instinct made her open, perhaps to object, and he blended their mouths, silencing her. Despite faint clamoring bells of outrage, Anne surrendered.

Surrendered to his clever mouth, as clever in this as in everything else.

To his hands, moving, exploring, making nothing of her sturdy dress.

To his whole body and hers, trying to merge through layers of clothing that she had once thought protection . . .

When he stopped, when his hold loosened and she found the strength to push free, she gasped, "I cannot possibly let just any man do that!"

It was loud and Uffham's snoring halted. As one, they turned to look at him, to watch as he sagged again into deep sleep.

Dear heaven, she had done that in her brother's presence! It had been so dazzling, so staggering, that she feared the echoes might linger in the room to tell what she had done.

"You let me do it," de Vere pointed out, "and I am as close to just any man as makes no difference."

She hit him. His head shifted under the crack of the blow. Her hand stung.

After a horrified moment, she tried to rub his cheek better. "Oh, I'm sorry. I'm sorry! I don't know—"

He grasped her hand. "Calm, calm, my dear. I was being irritating again."

But he did not pull her hand from his cheek, and she felt his firm face with the slight roughness along his jaw. Because of his blond hair she couldn't see any shadow there, but in some way the roughness made his dangerous maleness more potent in the darkened room.

"It was shock at myself," she whispered. "I don't know what came over me."

"The kiss, or the blow?"

"The kiss . . . The blow . . . Both!"

"Such a shocking night."

He was laughing at her!

She pulled free and distanced herself, smoothing her gown as if every crease stood witness to wickedness. "You will not speak of this?"

"You insult me, Lady Anne." Then his expression softened. "It was not so very bad, you know."

"It was appalling!" She caught his look and shivered. "Don't pity me, Mr. de Vere. That I will not tolerate!"

"If you marry, Lady Anne, your husband will wish to kiss you that way. If he doesn't, then I do pity you."

"In marriage it will be different."

"Perhaps, but I recommend some ardent kisses before you say your vows. What if you do not like the way your husband kisses?"

She had no brandy left, but his glass still held some. Boldly, she drained it. Then she pressed the glass to her cheek, which felt hot enough to have been slapped. "I wish you had not come here."

It was, without doubt, the most discourteous thing she had ever said to anyone in her life.

The fire was down to a sullen glow, and all the remaining candles guttered. She looked at him, wanting to take the words back, wanting a great many things she could hardly put words to, feeling the truth of the words bite her. She did wish he had not come and scraped all her sensitivities down to the raw.

He seemed, for once, completely serious. "I am sorry if you think I have done you harm, Lady Anne. It was never my intent." He bowed—a proper, sober, and respectful bow. "I will not distress you again."

He walked out of the room, and she was alone. Except for snoring Uffham.

Deliberately she poured another half inch of brandy into the glass and drank it, mouthful after mouthful. What had happened here? What had made her behave so unlike herself? What had changed her?

She did feel changed. In the morning she might be embarrassed. She might even suffer the ill effects of drink. She didn't think, however, that the effects of this night would fade like a headache or a dream.

There was no mirror here, but she doubted that she was physically changed. Inside, however, she was like a shuffled pack of cards—all there, but in a different order, ready to deal entirely different hands.

Good, or bad?

Surely that was up to her.

In a few short hours Race de Vere had taught her a great deal about men and about herself. She could see now that she had let her own insecurity make her discouraging. She had never considered that her suitors might be even more nervous than she, fearful of offending her or her powerful family. And, of course, her limp doubtless made her seem fragile, to be handled with care.

Race de Vere had paid it no heed at all.

She drained the last of the brandy.

For a moment she thought of getting to know him better, but then she shook her head. Her family would be appalled, and society would think she couldn't do any better. Poor Lady Anne de Vere. It would be as bad as poor Lady Claretta Crump.

She hovered, wondering whether she was being realistic or cowardly. Perhaps Claretta was madly happy with her Crump. Perhaps sometimes a person had to be wild, to gamble, to call a Main that wasn't seven. . . .

No. Hazard had proved exciting as a pastime, but gambling was no way to live, especially with the odds so heavily against her. She touched the ivory counters rather sadly. After sifting them through her fingers, she took one and put it in her pocket, a reminder of the pleasures of the evening and the pressures of reality.

Then she picked up her silk shawl and wrapped it around herself. The room was cold now. Her knitted one would have been more practical. That was what she had to be. Practical.

There were still some weeks left of the season. She would go to London—to the Marriage Mart—and find exactly the right husband, one who could give her exactly the right life.

She wanted a home similar to Lea Park—an elegant country house and a substantial park.

She wanted a husband with little taste for London affairs. Once she had her husband she would be happy never to go there again.

She wanted a life companion who was intelligent. No stultifying conversations by the fireplace.

And not a gambler. She would have complete security.

And, of course, he must be desperately enamored with her. She could not bear to have another man drop her on the way to the altar.

Was it possible? At the moment, brandy-fueled confidence burned high, but she feared that tomorrow poor Lady Anne would return. Terrified or not, however, poor Lady Anne was going to London.

She was at the door when she remembered her oblivious brother. It would serve him right to spend the night in the chair and wake up sore all over, not only in his head. She was a dutiful sister, however, and so she went to rouse some poor servants to carry him to his bed.

Race shut the door of his bedroom and leaned against it, breath unsteady. Matters had run out of control down there. It had never been his intention to get to kisses with Anne Peckworth. Especially kisses of that sort.

That blood-sizzling sort . . .

Thank heavens she was too sensible a woman to

screech the house down. Or to take the kisses to heart
and think they signalled commitment.

Sensible!

He reviewed that assessment and headed for the
brandy decanter his kind hosts had provided. Lady Anne
Peckworth was doubtless sensible in many ways, but as
far as men were concerned, she was as sensible as a
March hare. Twenty years old, and hardly been kissed.

He'd seen her once before, months ago in London.
What had he thought then?

Conventional.

Yes, he thought, pouring brandy into a glass, if he'd
had to put a descriptive label on her that day, it would
have been conventional. Simply another aristocratic lady
at another social gathering, dressed in something pale,
pale flowers in pale hair, pale gloved hands clasped in
front of her, pale smile in place.

Nothing like the vibrant woman he'd seen when Uffham had taken him into Lady Benning's overheated
boudoir, even if her bright eye and pink cheeks were
because of her comment about a Derbyshire ram.

Did she know the song that went by that title?

As I was going to Derby, all on a market day,
I spied the biggest ram, sir, that ever was fed in May.
This tup was fat behind, sir, this tup was fat before.
This tup was nine feet tall, sir, if not a little more . . .

She'd have blushed even more at the line about the
tup's balls.

She was pretty when she blushed, even stunning.

Of course, when he thought of it, that occasion in
London had probably been not long after Lord Middlethorpe's marriage when she was still smothering
anger beneath placid smiles. Her words about Lady Middlethorpe had revealed the depth of that wound.

He itched to punish Middlethorpe, but he was one of
the Company of Rogues. Poke one and you poked the
lot of them.

Anyway, he was, in a way, here as an agent of the
group. He might have come anyway, but the leader of
the Rogues, Nicholas Delaney, had hinted that someone

should make sure that Lady Anne didn't suffer. "Can't be a Rogue," he'd said to Race. "By now I'm sure she'd shoot any of us on sight."

Race liked Delaney, and he'd thought him right. He was here, however, mostly because it was his fault that Lady Anne had lost another chance at marriage. He'd held back the commitment letter Con had written to her. If it had been delivered, Con would never have backed away.

Race didn't regret it. Con and his Susan were perfect for each other, and Anne would not have benefited from a dutiful marriage. He'd created the wound, however, and it was for him to heal it.

How could he have known he'd be affected like this?

Worse, how could he have known she would be affected like that?

Perhaps he should have.

He was attractive to women, though he didn't know why. He didn't have rugged manly looks, but at the same time, he didn't spout poetic compliments. He had neither lineage nor fortune and no ambition for greatness, and he was more likely to act the fool than the hero.

Yet women fluttered to him. He knew men who reveled in that sort of gift, but he'd found it to be a Midas touch, especially during his army years.

War was not a place where a sane man fell in love or bound himself to a woman—or brought children into the world, poor mites. Between battles, however, it was an excellent place for games. In that hothouse of danger and boredom he'd often charmed the right sort of woman into giving favors, the sort of woman he could leave happy.

But then there had been the wrong women.

Letty Monke-Frobisher came immediately to mind. Letty had been his colonel's eighteen-year-old daughter. She'd flirted with him under her father's nose and sent appalling perfumed letters. As a final insanity, she'd slipped into his billet one night dressed only in a cloak. He knocked back the rest of the brandy and went to get more. Letty had terrified him more than a host of French battalions, and after that he'd learned to be very careful.

Until tonight.

Another inch of brandy in his glass, he contemplated the bedroom door. He went over and locked it. He didn't think Anne Peckworth was the sort for such folly, but who could tell with women? With that in mind he decided not to drink any more brandy. His head was buzzing.

As he stripped for bed he reassured himself that Anne had too much sense and good breeding to chase any man, especially into his bed. He slid between the chilly sheets, turning his mind to a problem at Con's Sussex estate. Better to think about anything other than Anne Peckworth.

The feel of her in his arms. The perfect fit . . .

Con's grandfather had leased the land for ninety-nine years. . . .

With a groan, he remembered Uffham. Hell's tits. He was here as glorified servant, and he couldn't leave his patron down there in a hard chair. He rolled out of bed and grabbed his banjan.

Judging from his earlier test, he didn't reckon much for his chances of rousing Uffham enough to get him up the stairs by himself. Was he going to have to rouse servants in a strange house at this time of night? Be damned to it. He grabbed the eiderdown and a pillow off his bed. He'd roll him on the floor and swaddle him up warmly.

He went to the door and turned the knob. Why the devil wouldn't it open? Then he remembered and unlocked it, laughing at himself. He was still smiling when he opened the door . . .

. . . and saw Anne coming along the corridor toward him.

She stopped, sudden color creating her special, delicate beauty in the wavering glow of the candle she carried. After a stunned moment, he realized why she was staring at him. He hadn't fastened the top buttons of his robe, and the eiderdown and pillow were under his arm, not clutched to his chest.

He moved them, hoping that she couldn't tell how fast and deep his heart was pounding. "I'm going to make Uffham comfortable," he explained softly.

She licked her lips. Her full, soft, pink lips. The arch of her short upper lip was painfully enchanting.

The pounding intensified, drowning sense. Two steps and she would be in his arms. A few moments and she could be in his room.

A few more and she could be in his bed . . .

He sucked in a breath. Was he mad?

Her soft voice fought through the fog in his mind.

"The servants are bringing him," she said. "Now."

He heard it then. Soft voices and clumping footsteps coming up the stairs.

"We mustn't be caught here like this," he said, fighting hot blood and laughter.

Her color deepened. "No."

She didn't, however, move, and neither could he.

His laughter became a smile, and he didn't try to stop it. Magic danced in the gloomy hall like sparkling fireworks. He didn't try to stop himself from stepping forward to kiss her hot cheek, then her lips, then her cheek again, from inhaling the subtle flower perfume that would always linger as hers . . .

"Good night, my dear," he said, meaning good-bye. Then he retreated back into his room, his last image of Anne with eyes wide, cheeks pink, and lips parted in surprise.

Or hunger?

Yes, he thought, back to the door again. That had been hunger as shocking to her as it was to him. If he'd swept her into his room she might have come, and perhaps the cataclysm that followed would have been worth the inevitable, disastrous price.

He was here to help her, dammit, not to ruin her! Tomorrow he'd get Uffham out of here at the earliest possible moment, and then he'd avoid Anne Peckworth for the rest of his life.

But no, he couldn't. He couldn't hatch her out of her protective shell and then abandon her as a mere fledgling.

Temptation tugged at him. He could win her if he tried. It would mean an elopement—the Duke of Arran would hardly approve of a husband such as he—but he had one advantage to offer. He did truly care for her.

He shook his head. One person's caring did not outweigh a loving family alienated, a life of elegance lost. He'd seen marriages like that in the army, ones where ladies of high birth had run off with dashing officers. There had always been an edge of bitterness to them, especially if the mad passion that had caused the union faded under time, hardship, and too many children.

He stayed where he was, listening as footsteps and quiet voices passed by, as a door opened and shut. Uffham's. As another door not so very far away closed. Anne's.

He let his imagination follow her as her maid helped her out of her dull blue dress—was her underclothing as plain and practical, or was there lace and embroidery there? As the maid brushed out her soft, silky hair . . .

The house settled at last into the silence of the night.

Race sucked in a breath and pushed away from the door. Then, as symbol rather than precaution, he turned the key before getting back into his chilly bed.

Eight

~

Anne woke the next morning feeling fuzzy. Feeling, in fact, like a well-used horse blanket. Hetty had just drawn back the curtains, and Anne squinted at the bright light.

After a moment she decided that she didn't have a drunkard's headache. That was something. Her head felt as if it were stuffed to bursting with that rank horse blanket, but it didn't exactly hurt.

Her mouth was sticky and foul, however. She wanted water, but didn't want to move, and so she lay there trying not to think about Race de Vere. About her last sight of him.

A blond angel in a silver robe. That vee of muscled chest. That something in his shadowed eyes that had held her still, set her heart racing, stirred wild thoughts . . .

Enough! She pushed up, hissed, and gave her head a moment to settle. Then she remembered the important things.

"Is all well with Lady Benning and the baby?"

Hetty beamed. "Yes, milady, and Lord Benning's given all the servants a guinea in celebration! Are you going down to breakfast, or do you want it here?"

Down?

Where she might meet him?

He'd been *naked* beneath his dressing gown.

And he'd kissed her—kisses on cheek and lips in some way more shattering than the heated embrace in Benning's study. He'd smelled of soap and something else. Something physical . . .

Through the open door of his room she'd seen his bed

rough from his sudden rising. She'd imagined walking into that room, getting into that bed.

She blew out a breath and pushed hair off her face. Those were the feelings a woman should have about her husband, or the man who would be her husband—

"Milady?"

Anne started. Hetty was still waiting for instructions. About what? Breakfast. "Just tea and toast, Hetty. And a drink of water, immediately."

Hetty brought the water and hurried off to get the breakfast. Thank heavens she'd sent Hetty to her bed early last night, that she'd not been here to see her in whatever state she'd been in.

She pressed hands to her cheeks at the thought of what the servants might be thinking. Did they know she'd spent time—how much time?—with Race de Vere?

Then she lowered her hands and studied them. They were elongated. Not at all plump. Her wrists were bony, her arms too thin. Like the rest of her.

He couldn't have meant what he said about them being lovely.

And now she had to take her bony self off to London to find a man who would truly think her lovely, who would fall deeply in love with her. So deeply that there was no possibility of him being snared by some other woman.

She groaned. Had she really told de Vere all about that? About her feelings about Middlethorpe. About her fears?

Pray heaven she didn't have to meet him again. She hoped Uffham wasn't too under the weather to leave. She knew he'd want to. A house of birth and babies? He'd think of it like a house of contagion.

She climbed out of bed and caught sight of herself in the mirror. Heavens above! Did she usually look so tousled and wanton in the morning? She heard footsteps and quickly splashed her face with water.

Hetty returned, chattering about the baby. "Marjorie says Lady Benning is sitting up and eating hearty, milady. A right easy birth."

Then heaven save us all, thought Anne, *from a hard one.* "Go and see if I can visit her, Hetty."

Anne began a proper wash, soaping her hands, feeling kinship with Lady Macbeth, who was somewhere on the family tree. *Out, out, damned spot!* And yet, hands and face clean, she did not wish all those kisses gone. They had been far more educational, elucidating, and yes, even entertaining, than anything in *Pastimes for Ladies.*

A pastime. That was all it had been, like the straw box that must still be in Frances's boudoir. This time yesterday that had been her biggest problem.

She cleaned her teeth, which was a great improvement.

Then something shone in her eye and she turned, realizing that there was sunlight outside. She limped to the window. This side of the house did not get the early morning sun, but it was reflecting from the stable block windows, and the sky was blue.

Glory hallelujah! She could go riding. That would sort out her befuddled wits. Monmouth would be full of himself after three days in the stables.

Hetty came back. "Lady Benning asks if you will take your breakfast with her, milady. Which dress would you like?"

Hetty was already laying out shift and corset. Anne leaped back to the mundane with relief and reviewed the simple wardrobe she'd brought with her. She'd anticipated only a quiet country visit.

"The pink sprig, Hetty." That was the prettiest gown she had with her. "Are the gentlemen up?" she added, trying to sound as casual as possible as she discarded her nightgown and put on the shift.

Hetty helped her on with the corset and started to tighten the laces. "The master and that Mr. de Vere have breakfasted, milady. Not Lord Uffham, though, as yet."

If Uffham was under the weather, he was unlikely to leave soon. If Uffham decided to stay another night, de Vere might be interested in a ride around the area. Riding out with a gentleman known to her family was acceptable behavior. . . .

Anne wriggled her shoulders to settle into the snug garment. "Lay out my riding habit for later, Hetty."

She could feel her heartbeats and knew she was being wicked, but she couldn't help it. After all, even Frances had said she needed practice at flirtation.

Hetty dropped the gown over her head. Anne glanced in the mirror and was startled by how well the pink suited her. It had been ordered during her consolation trip to London after Middlethorpe. Her mother's prescription for all ills was new clothes. Since it was a summer dress, she'd worn it only once, and then it hadn't looked quite like this.

Her lips and cheeks seemed pinker, and even her breasts seemed a little larger. Hetty hadn't dressed her hair yet, and she impulsively decided to leave it loose on her shoulders, at least for her visit to Frances.

When it came to a shawl, however, she lost her nerve and picked up the plain knitted one. She wouldn't want anyone to think she was going to extraordinary lengths. She wrapped it around herself and hurried along to Frances's room, Hetty following with the tray. She only realized when she arrived that speed and shawl weren't necessary anymore. Sunshine had begun to warm the house.

She passed the shawl to Hetty as she went to Frances's bedside. "You look so well."

It was true. Frances, in a pretty peach bedjacket and lacy white cap, was blooming. A cradle draped with golden silk sat on the floor by her bed, a nursery maid beside it, ready to serve the baby.

"As do you, dear! Pink suits you." Frances beamed at the cradle. "It all went splendidly, and little Charles is a picture of health. Mrs. McLaren said she'd rarely seen such a strong feeder."

Anne tried to match her vibrant sister with the sprawled, overwhelmed woman she'd glimpsed last night and decided it was simply a mystery. She turned to admire the tiny infant sleeping beneath white, lace-edged linen.

"He's beautiful," she whispered. It wasn't exactly true, but it felt true.

"You can pick him up. He won't mind, and I want to

hold him again." Frances turned to the nursery maid. "You may go for a while, Alice."

The maid curtsied and left. Frances chuckled. "I don't think she trusts me with her treasure. They can grow too possessive if allowed. Remember when it's your turn that you must be firm from the very beginning. Don't worry. Just support his head."

Anne had dealt with babies before in her charity work, though never one quite so young. She peeled back the covers and lifted the tiny, swaddled child. His bowed lips worked for a moment, but then he settled again, a soft, warm weight. She held him close and sat on the edge of the bed.

"I do want babies of my own."

"Of course you do."

Anne glanced at her sister. "A baby requires a father."

"You have only to snap your fingers."

Anne laughed. "Hardly that."

"As good as. A duke's daughter with a handsome dowry?"

Typical of Frances to be so direct and practical. In her own way she was as meddlesome as the rest of the family. Late pregnancy had turned her thoughts inward, but now she was present and alert again.

"I would like to be married for more than my money and my family connections."

"And so you shall be," Frances said, a shade too heartily for Anne's liking.

Perhaps this new feeling of being pretty rather than passable was an illusion. After all, she hadn't lived like a cloistered nun, and she'd never been pestered by devoted admirers. It must be done, though.

"I intend to go to London, and let Caroline do her worst."

"Her best, you mean. Splendid! If a lady wants her choice of men, she must go where the most men are." But then Frances cocked her head. "What about Mr. de Vere?"

Anne stared. Had the servants noticed something and talked? "What about him?"

"He's Uffham's friend."

A flicker of excitement stirred. If Frances thought of de Vere as a possible husband . . .

"That's no great recommendation," Anne said, watching her sister's reaction. "What's more, Mr. de Vere makes no secret of the fact that he has no particular birth or fortune."

"Oh, what a pity."

It was said without rancor, which made it all the more fatal. Well, of course. What had she been thinking?

"Benning rather admires him," Frances went on. "He confessed that he got into his cups, poor lamb, and that de Vere sobered him."

"Which shows that he's had plenty of practice."

"If he's had practice at sobering men up," Frances pointed out, "then he hasn't always been drunk himself."

"I have no interest there anyway," Anne said firmly. "He's a pleasant pastime, nothing more."

Her louder voice startled the baby, who let out a wail. Anne tried to calm him, but Frances demanded her child and unwound the cloths to reveal tiny fingers that stretched for a moment, seeking who knew what.

Anne gave thanks for the distraction and sat to tackle her uninspiring breakfast. She regretted not asking for more. "Did you find it difficult to fix on the right man?" she asked, pouring fresh tea.

Frances looked up from little Charles. "Oh, no. As soon as I met Benning I knew. You will, too. It is an awareness. The man becomes special. Stands out from the others. Did you not feel that way about Middlethorpe or Wyvern?"

Anne buttered her toast, considering it. "Perhaps a little with Middlethorpe, but not with Wyvern."

"Then you've had a lucky escape, dear."

Despite all her efforts, Anne's mind swung back to de Vere. Awareness? Did being extraordinarily irritating count? What did a lady do if an unsuitable man stood out from the others? . . .

Her thoughts were interrupted by Uffham, looking surprisingly alive for this time in the morning, though his eyes were bloodshot. Anne began to tingle—but de Vere was not with him.

"Came to have a look at the little fellow before setting

off," he said, boots thumping as he approached the bed. At least they were clean now.

Setting off? Anne's stomach clenched around the inoffensive toast.

"Tiny thing, ain't it?" he assessed.

Frances pulled a face at him. "Quite big enough, I assure you, Stuff, and the picture of health."

"Good, good! I gather Benning sent for Mother. She should be here this evening." He leaned down to kiss Frances's cheek.

"What of Mr. de Vere?" Frances asked.

"What? He's coming with me, of course."

"I mean, what of his future?" Frances's eyes flickered to Anne for a moment.

Anne wanted to gag her.

"He seems to be such a capable man," Frances went on. "Perhaps he needs employment. As your secretary, for example."

Anne stared. What was Frances up to? A secretary was almost as low as a governess—and if de Vere was Uffham's secretary she'd keep meeting him.

"I don't need a secretary!" Uffham protested.

"You would if you did anything serious," Frances pointed out.

"Don't start nagging me. I can't interfere in a man's life without him even asking." He was already retreating toward the door. He glanced at Anne. "All right, Annie?"

Unclear what he referred to, she simply smiled and agreed. He passed on thanks and suitable good wishes from de Vere to Frances, and then he was gone.

"What was all that about?" Anne demanded.

"De Vere?" Frances queried innocently. "Nothing in particular. I liked him, and as far as I can tell he does need employment."

The baby began to fret, and Frances put him to the breast. It was an interesting enough process for Anne to let her eyes and part of her mind rest there. The rest of her mind was accepting that Frances had relegated de Vere to the multitude of people who were beyond the charmed inner circle of the Peckworths and the haut ton. They were to be employed and sometimes assisted, but never to be considered equals no matter what their qualities.

It was as well that de Vere was leaving, that last night had been like a faery visit, never to be repeated.

And besides, he was obviously not interested in seeing more of her. He must have worked hard to rouse Uffham and have him ready to travel so early. Even after that encounter in the corridor, and those three sweet kisses.

What mortifyingly embarrassing message had she conveyed to him? She felt as if she had a lump of dry toast stuck in her throat. She took a deep drink of her tea and then another, trying to wash it away.

She heard something and turned to look outside. Through the window she watched two horsemen ride away from Benning Hall, one on a dock-tailed chestnut, the other on a long tailed bay.

"There they go," she said, carefully careless. "Mr. de Vere rides well."

In fact, he had a perfect seat, completely one with the bay.

"Cavalry, I understand." Frances's attention was obviously all on her child.

"Yes. Quite a hero."

Anne almost wished she could see him in battle, which was ridiculous. She'd seen too many of the wounded to want more war.

In truth, she had no idea what she wanted, but she recognized that last night she'd brushed against something dangerous—the plague that ran through history impelling people into folly, danger, and death.

She remembered the Lady Anne Peckworth of the seventeenth century who had fallen in love with a Parliamentarian during the Civil War and died for it.

Last night she had been tempted. Thank heaven that temptation was riding away. Her family would have a collective fit of the vapors, and as de Vere had said, Uffham would shoot him for his impudence.

The riders passed out of sight.

Anne turned away from the window to butter a new piece of toast. "So," she said, "how do I attack the Marriage Mart?"

Nine

～

Anne left Benning Hall the next day in the family coach
with outriders that had carried the Duchess of Arran to
Frances. It took her home to Lea Park to choose clothing and ornaments suitable for her husband hunt. As
she supervised the packing, the temptation to stay was
powerful. Lea Park was at its spring best, and every
morning she rode Monmouth for miles, astride even,
without meeting anyone who might disapprove.

Riding was her time of greatest freedom, the time
when she wasn't crippled at all.

Those of her family who were at Lea Park were
pleased to see her back—her father, her two younger
brothers, and Eliza, her youngest sister. Marianne was
visiting her beloved at the Gravender dower house. At
Benning Hall, the duchess had confirmed what Uffham
had said. She didn't think it right to let sixteen-year-old
Marianne marry before her twenty-year-old sister.

No argument had changed her mother's mind, which
didn't surprise Anne. The Duchess of Arran was a
strong-willed woman, and she had her mind set on good
marriages for all her daughters. Earlier in the year she
had bent to let Anne's nineteen-year-old sister marry
the Earl of Welsford. The fact that he was an earl had
probably been the major factor, though the fact that Caroline could twist their father around her fingers had
helped. That one capitulation, however, made another
even less likely.

Another reason for Anne to marry.

Over her week at home, she said a silent good-bye.

The people on the estate and in the village who knew

they could depend on her acted as if she'd been away for months. She worried about them, but she was not, she told herself, indispensable.

There were friends here, too, of all sorts, but there was no point weeping over that. Women of her rank were born and raised to live elsewhere. In time her new home would be as precious to her as this one, and she would have new friends.

When it rained she slipped off to the muniment room to work on the Women of Peckworth, trying to get as much done as possible.

When she was fourteen, she'd heard of that Lady Anne Peckworth who'd suffered a tragic love for a Parliamentarian. She'd gone to the family archivist to see if there were any records of the story.

She'd discovered that Dr. Plumgate was a severe historian who was interested in the Peckworth papers only as they interacted with the great matters of their times. He produced an annual annotated index of them for the use of scholars, and published occasional excerpts in the *Monthly Magazine*.

He'd lectured her on her trivial tastes and tried to interest her in the letters of the duke of the time, which would educate her about the political aspects of the war.

Anne, however, had always had a stubborn streak, and she was the duke's daughter, so he had eventually shown her a small room where such idle matter was stored. Despite dust and disorder, it had been like a treasure trove.

She'd found boxes and bundles of records that were considered unimportant, almost entirely by women. She unfolded letters and opened diaries and recipe books. There were even laundry lists and household accounts.

Dr. Plumgate was right. These were nothing compared to the papers he cared for, but they fascinated her. She loved coming to recognize the handwriting of the different women, and how each document opened a window into the ordinary lives of the women who had come before her.

At first she had attacked her treasure like a child, but she'd soon realized that she risked making things even worse. She'd begun to try to organize the papers, but been defeated by the sheer mass of them. Nervous but determined, she'd returned to Dr. Plumgate.

She remembered how surly he had been, clearly seeing her as an idle disrupter of his work. He'd given her some quick lessons simply to get rid of her. When she'd returned day after day, however, he'd come to inspect her work, and after that, he'd regularly checked on her and given additional advice.

He'd also helped her learn to decipher the ancient handwriting, which was often the hardest part. He was still taciturn, but these days they had an agreeable working relationship. If he came upon anything in his important documents that related to the distaff side, he would leave her a note and reference. To her delight, she occasionally found something in the women's papers that she could alert him to.

She'd always known that she could have mobilized the dukedom in this interest if she'd wished to. She was poor crippled Lady Anne, and if she had a harmless enthusiasm she could command anything she wanted. A suite of offices. An army of clerks. Dr. Plumgate's entire attention.

She'd never wanted that. Her interest wasn't exactly secret, but it was private, between her and her fascinating female ancestors. The only servants she used were two maids whom she summoned now and then to dust a newly emptied shelf and wash it with vinegar.

Now she read again the letters and papers to do with that Lady Anne who had first stirred her interest. She had let her heart drag her into disaster. Anne, raised on stories of gallant Cavaliers and wicked Roundheads, had at first found it hard to understand how her ancestress could ever have fallen in love with the enemy.

A more subtle understanding of history had shown her that things were never black and white and that there were usually good people on both sides. Now she felt she had a new insight into the power of attraction. Had the seventeenth-century Lady Anne been appalled by her own desires? Had she struggled against them?

Better for her if her unsuitable lover had not returned her feelings. As it was, they had run away to marry. Later, she had been torn from her husband's arms and had seen him slaughtered by her brother. She'd been carried abroad when her family fled. She'd died not long after, miscarrying a child.

Had it been a natural death, the result of a broken heart, or had it perhaps been murder? The duchess of the time had been an unforgiving woman. Anne could imagine her forcing that poor Anne to take something to get rid of the child, and everyone knew that was dangerous. She could even imagine the duchess killing her child to clean away the shame.

Thank heavens she lived in a gentler time. But then, she had no idea what her parents might do if she tried to behave so outrageously. She had always been so good.

She packed away those papers and turned to her work-in-hand—deciphering the scribble of the fifth duchess's sister. When the light began to go, she realized that this was the end. Tomorrow she left for London, and she would not return here again as a home.

She carefully folded the letter, fighting a sick feeling in her stomach. It shouldn't matter. This was another Pastime for Ladies, and she would have her own house to run, children to raise. . . .

But it did matter. She looked around at the clean, ordered shelves, which still contained so many unexplored documents. She thought of the book she'd planned—a family history viewed from the women's side. She'd never have it published in the regular manner, of course, but she could have a few copies printed for her family.

A husband might not approve such an indulgence. He certainly would not want a wife who spent hours poring over old laundry lists! And in fact, unless she took all this with her, there would be nothing to pore over.

It was like a death. She stood and limped around the room, trailing a hand over boxes. She opened the one that contained her indices and notes, the basis of the book to come.

It was like a stillborn child.

Oh, this was silly. She rarely found a reference to anything important. Her fascination was mostly the thrill of reading private documents. It was almost as base as gossip.

And it was over. She put away the letter and capped her inkwell. Life involved changes, and this was another one. Perhaps her husband would have family papers and she could continue her work there when she had time.

Suppressing all sadness, she took farewell of Dr. Plumgate, then summoned her father's steward to go over the arrangements for the short journey to London. She had already written to Caroline to tell her when to expect her.

"Off, are you?" her rotund father said that evening in the family drawing room. "Don't let Caroline run you ragged, Anne."

"I won't, Papa."

"Shame you're on your way tomorrow. Uffham wrote to say he might drop by. Been down near Portsmouth. Some sort of yacht racing. But then, you saw him at Frances's place, didn't you?"

For a moment, words failed her. Would de Vere be with him? "Yes, yes I did. . . . Perhaps he'll go on to London."

The duke chuckled. "If he does, I doubt you'll be moving in the same circles. The poor boy is hounded to death. I told him—better to arrange a marriage in an orderly way and get it over with, but he doesn't listen. Modern times, modern ways. On his own head, on his own head. But I'm sure if you need his escort, Anne, he'll do the right thing."

"Oh, no, that won't be necessary, Papa."

If Uffham squired her around, de Vere might be nearby. Her task would be hard enough without that sort of distraction.

As soon as Anne entered Lord Welsford's town house, her sister Caroline exploded upon her with squeals and exclamations and dragged her to a vastly overdecorated boudoir.

Three months of marriage clearly suited Caroline. She had always been pretty, but now she glowed. This served to fix Anne's mind even more. She wasn't sure marriage would make her glow, but she was sure it would work the miracle for Marianne.

She would clear the way. She knew that once she was

out of the way her mother would not be able to block the marriage for long. Their father was too kindhearted. He believed that daughters were the wife's business, but in the end he could be brought to interfere.

As for Caroline, it was all "Welsford says . . ." and "Welsford thinks . . ." At least Welsford, eight years Caroline's senior, was a sensible man, so what he said and thought was useful.

"You are truly going to give the lucky men a chance?" Caroline whipped Anne out of her light pelisse and bonnet and passed them to a maid along with a command for tea.

"Sit!" she said, pushing Anne onto a pink sofa. There was a great deal of pink in the room.

"Caro! Let me catch my breath."

Caroline sat on the opposite sofa. "I'm sorry. I'm so excited that you are here. How wonderful it must have been to be there when Frances took to her bed. I can't wait to give Welsford a son. He is the most perfect husband!"

Caroline sighed. She beamed. She glowed.

In fact, she glowed suspiciously bright.

Was some of it *paint*?

Anne's instinctive disapproval was replaced by curiosity. Had Caroline always used paint to help create her vivid appeal? Would it work for her? If she was going to do this, she would do it to the full.

"The whole world is talking about Wyvern, of course," Caroline rattled on. "Imagine the old earl married years ago and with a son. A son, moreover, who has been acting as estate manager with no idea of his legitimacy! It's as good as a play."

Anne came alert for special meaning, especially pity, but saw none. "It's accepted, then?"

Caroline waved a hand. "It all has to go through courts and committees and things, but Welsford says it will likely stick. A Guernsey marriage, but apparently that works as well as Gretna for the civil courts. And then the lady—the mother—took up with a smuggler who is now transported, and the lady has gone after him! It is all too delicious. In fact, Mr. Lockheart is said to be writing a play around it all. And here is Wyvern—Amleigh again now—married to his rival's sister."

Then, belatedly, she went stricken.

Anne smiled. "It's all right. I wasn't going to marry him."

"Oh, good. I did think him rather dour. We can do much better than that for you now you are willing to play your part."

Anne suppressed a grimace at the *we*. Letters had doubtless been flying as her whole family campaigned to get her to the altar. It was all out of love, however, and this time she was going to cooperate.

"Frances mentioned Race de Vere."

Anne stared at her sister in shock. She'd thought that idea dead.

"But I don't know what she was thinking," Caroline added.

"Nor do I. Her mind was probably engaged with little Charles."

But Caroline was eyeing her. "Frances seemed to think there was something between you."

"Childbed madness." Anne prayed she wasn't blushing. "Why would I even think of marrying someone like that?"

Caroline shrugged. "He is amusing, and he's good for Stuff, you know. Distracts him from his wilder friends, though they do say he's a black sheep. De Vere, I mean."

"Or a black ram . . ."

"What? You *are* interested."

"I'm *curious*. He did behave well during the crisis. If there were a way for the family to help him, I think we should."

Anne felt positively saintly for making this suggestion. She had refused to search the Lea Park library for information about any de Veres of Derbyshire. That would be fuel on the fire. It wouldn't hurt to find the man employment though, and it would get him away from Uffham so she'd have less danger of meeting him.

Caroline lounged back on her sofa in a way that would have caused a lecture in the schoolroom. "It's all very mysterious. Stuff says that de Vere is an only son but is at outs with his father who never wanted him to go into the army. Even so, it must be a very minor property. I looked him up, and there's nothing about any de Veres in Derbyshire. Or anywhere, in fact. Welsford says they died out long ago."

"A bastard line, I assume."

"I suppose so. He is a charmer, though, isn't he? Prudence Littleton is absurdly enamored of the man."

"*What*?" Anne hoped that she hadn't sounded outraged.

Though they were alone in the room, Caroline leaned forward to whisper. "Stuff says she writes de Vere the most imprudent billets-doux, and she's not the only one!"

"De Vere reads them aloud for his friends' amusement?"

Caroline drew back. "No, of course not! Or at least, I don't think so. Apparently the featherhead sent one under cover to Stuff, begging him to be sure de Vere received it, as he'd not responded. Can you imagine? Stuff told only me, and I wouldn't tell anyone but the family."

Anne doubted that and felt sorry for foolish Miss Littleton. Thank heavens that she'd resisted the temptation to write him a note care of Uffham. Nothing embarrassing, of course. Merely a thank-you. But thank heavens she hadn't.

A liveried footman—a fashionable black man, Anne noted—brought a tray of refreshments, which was a relief all around. She was hungry and thirsty, and did not want to talk about Race de Vere.

As Caroline went importantly about the tasks of preparing tea, Anne absorbed the fact that for Race de Vere she was one of hundreds of tediously admiring ladies. Intolerable!

Her twisted foot had made her interested in Lord Byron, who was similarly afflicted. As a result, she'd followed the embarrassing course of Lady Caroline Lamb's pursuit of the poet.

All London had been at his feet, but Caro Lamb had carried it to disastrous lengths. Despite being a married woman and mother, she'd acted scenes in public, invaded his rooms in man's clothing, and written him embarrassing letters which *he* had not hesitated to share with others. As a grand debacle, when he snubbed her at a ball, she'd slit her wrists.

A warning there for all women who believed themselves in love, and chose to believe, despite indifference and rebuffs, that their beloved returned their feelings.

"So," she said, before Caroline could recollect the subject of their conversation, "how do I embark on my husband hunt?"

Instantly distracted, Caroline outlined an exhausting involvement in the final weeks of the season.

Anne accepted the cup of perfectly prepared tea. "Perhaps it's flattering that you've forgotten, but I can't dance."

"Bother! But you can't avoid all the balls and assemblies. It's where so much of the season takes place."

"As I know to my infinite boredom. I will sit with the older people as usual."

"And have the same result. It paints you as a wallflower. Or even a fixed spinster." Caroline sipped her tea, then nodded. "We will make it the fashion for men to sit out with you. You are excellent company when you choose."

Anne put down her cup. "You think I sometimes choose *not* to be good company?"

Caroline colored. "Oh, no!" But then she said, "You do sometimes. It's as if . . . as if you turn down your wick."

Anne absorbed that. "Almost twenty-one seems an advanced age to be learning so much about myself."

"Whatever do you mean?"

"Someone else suggested that I use my crippled foot as an excuse to avoid people."

Caroline's eyes widened. "Do you?"

"Perhaps. I weary of company after a while. It might be different if I could dance, but sitting out, there is nothing to do but talk. And"—she pulled a face—"so many people have no conversation."

Caroline was not sympathetic. "The French have a saying that it is necessary to suffer to be beautiful. Perhaps for you it is necessary to suffer tedium to find the right husband."

Anne laughed and chose a small iced cake finished with sugared violets. "As long as I don't have to marry tedium."

But then she wondered what she might sink to as time passed. There were only a few weeks of the season left. She might have to take the best that presented. She was determined on getting this done.

Caroline had cocked her head and was studying Anne with a thoughtful frown—the sort to make any sister wary. "Because you've been out for years, people are used to you. They have preconceptions. You need to signal that you are different now."

"A label, saying 'Now open for wooing'?"

Caroline smothered a laugh with her lavishly ringed hand.

Seeing the flash of them, Anne said, "I think I could like to be a bit more flamboyant with jewels." She finished the cake and added, "Shall I tell you a terrible secret?"

When Caroline nodded—clearly astonished that her quiet sister might have a terrible secret—she revealed in a whisper, "I have never liked pearls."

Caroline's eyes widened. "Oh, me neither! I adore emeralds, though." She spread her hand to show a pretty ring of five small emeralds. "Welsford says I mustn't wear heavy ones until I'm older. He's probably correct, but I have my eye on a splendid emerald and diamond brooch. A brooch is different to a necklace, wouldn't you say? And he has brought me a delicious collar of small emeralds and pearls. Pearls are pleasant enough as contrast with the brighter jewels, wouldn't you say? What about a cane?"

Anne had been flowing on the torrent of chatter, but this jerked her out of it. "*What*? Of course not. I'm not so crippled as that!"

Caroline, however, had a faraway look in her eyes. "One must make a statement. I have my rings, and"— she stuck out a foot—"my slippers are embroidered with jewels and beads."

Anne saw that indeed, Caroline's white satin slippers were decorated with small gems and beads.

"Mostly inexpensive," Caroline added, "though I do have diamonds on the pair to go with my spider net gown. But you see, they make me different. Intriguing. Do you know Mama had jewels on the heels of her evening shoes when she was young? I wish heeled shoes were in fashion."

"And I thank heaven they're not. I have trouble enough as it is."

"I suppose so. But you do need a statement. Welsford suggested the shoes because he knew it would amuse me, and of course he likes having a wife who makes her mark on the ton. He hired Philip for me—the footman who brought tea—and had a livery specially designed. Lady Welsford's livery. Philip goes everywhere with me. Another statement, you see."

Anne wanted to protest that she'd be happier fading as usual into the flock of discreet, well-born, unmarried ladies, but she knew that Caroline had a point. She wasn't a new face. It could take forever to convince the eligible men that she had changed, and she didn't have much time.

"An outward sign might help, but what sort of statement would a cane be? *Behold, here comes a cripple?*"

Caroline shook her head so her curls jiggled. "No, no, not at all! It would say . . . It would say that you're not ashamed of your foot. Oh," she said, bouncing on her seat, eyes brilliant, "not a *boring* cane, Anne. That's not what I mean. A magnificent one! Tall, more like a staff. Beautifully made and with ribbons to match your outfit of the day."

Anne began to take the idea seriously. "I confess, I like the idea of declaring my limp. I do try not to hide it or seem ashamed of it. After all, it is nothing to be ashamed of. So why not make something of it? And in practical terms, a staff could be useful. I do sometimes feel unbalanced."

"There, see! And—"

A knock at the door interrupted, and the Earl of Welsford entered, smiling. He was in many ways a quite ordinary man, of average build, with fine brown hair. He'd always been distinguished by excellent fashion sense, however, and by a keen mind. Anne had learned that he also had a kind heart.

Caroline swiveled to greet him. "Welsford! See, Anne is here at last."

"So I heard, my dear."

Anne hadn't seen them together since the wedding when Caroline had glowed with excitement and Welsford had seemed to be a very happy man. That was to be expected at a wedding, however.

Now she saw magic.

It was as hard to pin down as a sunbeam, but something bright sparked on their shared gaze. Ten years lay between them, and Caroline had always been a little wild, so Anne thought Welsford must have worked quite hard to create such a deep bond. But then, perhaps she was underestimating her sister.

Caroline took his hand and towed him around the sofa and down beside her. "We are talking about Anne's new emergence into society, Welsford. I am determined that she will be all the thing."

"But my love," he said with a twinkle, "*you* are all the thing. And I'm sure that you don't intend to vacate your throne."

Caroline frowned for a moment—Anne noticed that she still held her husband's hand, as if that were the most natural thing in the world. "We will be the dashing Peckworth sisters."

"Dashing?" Anne couldn't help but protest.

"Dashing," Caroline said firmly, and shared their plans with her husband in a torrent of words that he seemed able to follow.

"A staff? An excellent idea, Caro. I congratulate you. Wallace in Bond Street. My ebony is from there."

Caroline turned to Anne. "A very fine piece, and with a snuff box in the head. Only think, you could have secret compartments, too. Smelling salts, for example."

"I've never needed smelling salts."

Caro dismissed that with a wave. "You could be ready to waft them in front of some other, weaker woman. Perhaps you could have a place for calling cards, or for a few coins for emergencies." Caroline's eyes brightened. "And if you don't care for smelling salts, you could have a hollow at the top for ratafia." She swung back to her husband. "You have a cane with a small flask of brandy in the top, don't you? I can think of many a dull occasion when a nip of ratafia would brighten the tedium."

"I'd rather have brandy." But then Anne detected a reaction. "I suppose Frances wrote that I spent her confinement in Benning's study drinking brandy and rolling dice?"

Caroline bit her lip. "She did, yes. I found it hard to believe."

"Such a dull puss as I am?"

"Oh, no, Anne!" But then it was clear that Caroline wasn't quite sure what to add, probably because she had thought exactly that.

"The hazard was the shock," Welsford said with a wicked look. "Not a game generally played by ladies. If you've developed a taste for it, however, a private party could be arranged."

Anne refused to fluster. "Only for farthing points, Welsford."

"Which equates to point*less*, my dear."

"Not at all. I think I won almost five shillings."

Caroline turned to her husband. "Would I enjoy hazard?"

He winced theatrically. "Only for farthing points, my love. Promise me."

"Oh, certainly. What point in risking money at the tables that might be spent on fashion? Which reminds me"—she jumped to her feet—"we had best be off purchasing a cane."

Her husband tugged her down again. "Anne will be tired from her journey, love."

Caroline looked at Anne as if he'd said she might have the smallpox. "Are you?"

It had only been three hours in the coach. "Not at all, though I do intend to finish my tea."

Welsford chuckled. "The redoubtable Peckworth sisters." Then he kissed his wife's hand.

Anne watched his technique with interest. He raised Caro's plump hand, but met it halfway in a bow that seemed a meaningful reverence. Though his kiss was light, his grasp on her fingers was firm, and Anne thought the way Caroline's fingers curled over his was just as meaningful.

She looked away, feeling intrusive—and wistful. She was planning marriage as a practicality, but a part of her longed for this—to feel that a husband was all to her, the pivot around which her life swung, and that she, miraculously, was the same to him.

"Anne?"

It was her brother-in-law's voice, and she looked back, hoping she appeared unmoved.

"A suitable escort might set the right tone from the beginning," he said. "A gentleman who is highly prized in the marriage stakes."

De Vere. Did Welsford know de Vere? Was he thinking of *hiring* him to play attendant, like a cicisbeo of years gone by? Then she came to her senses. De Vere was a complete outsider in the fashionable marriage stakes.

She was so off balance, however, that she couldn't find sensible words. "You think it important?"

"First impressions, my dear. And the right gentleman will intrigue society, and thus make you intriguing."

Despite all logic, de Vere's image sat in her mind. "Whom do you have in mind?"

"St. Raven."

Caroline squeaked.

Anne felt as if her eyes had expanded. The new Duke of St. Raven had spent some years living at Lea Park, foster brother to the Peckworths. "Tris? He's like a brother!"

"But he's not," Caroline said, eyes bright. "And his escort would certainly create a stir."

"I wouldn't want to impose. . . ."

Welsford waved that away. "We're hardly asking for blood, and I'd think he owes a debt of gratitude to your family. You took him in when the duke and duchess would not, I understand."

"And wait until you see him, now, Anne," Caroline said. "He was always good-looking, but oh, my!"

Anne cast an alarmed look at Caroline's husband, but he seemed amused. "Poor man. Romantically handsome, and a young, available duke. At his side, Anne, you will be the focus of every eye."

"And the subject on every tongue," Caroline added, "in the context of marriage, no less."

"We're like brother and sister," Anne repeated.

"But he's not your brother, which is all that matters now."

Anne wanted to protest more, but she remembered her purpose. She must wed, and every weapon must be used.

"Very well, if he agrees. At least I like him and enjoy his company."

Welsford rose. "I know St. Raven well enough to put this matter to him. I think he'll do it, for amusement if nothing else."

The door shut behind him.

Anne frowned at it. "I am beginning to dislike being a source of amusement for idle gentlemen."

"Whatever do you mean?"

Anne started. She needed to watch her tongue—and get all thought of de Vere out of her head. "Just nonsense and a spinning head. This business with Tris seems so very peculiar. I haven't seen him for nearly two years. He went abroad when he inherited."

Caroline pursed her lips. "Maybe you'll see him differently now. He's *not* your brother, and how utterly delicious if you were to snare the catch of the season. Mama would take flight!"

Anne sat up. "Snare! Did you 'snare' Welsford, then?"

"No! How horrid of you."

"Then don't imply that I would do such a thing." But she sucked in a breath. They were sinking into nursery squabbles. "I'm sorry, Caroline. This whole business has me on edge."

Caroline rushed over to hug her. "I'm sorry, dearest. And this will be fun, I promise! We will find you the perfect husband. Whatever husband you want."

Anne had a vision of her family stalking her reluctant

choice and dragging him to her in a net, but she returned the hug. Caroline had a good heart and meant the best. They all meant the best.

"We're not pushing you where you don't want to go, are we, dearest? You have always been so . . ."

"Quiet," Anne filled in. "No, I'm ready for a change, and I will find a good husband. I'm not sure about perfect, however. Perhaps waiting for perfection is what makes spinsters."

"Nonsense. First we arrange the matter of the cane—they may not have such a thing ready for purchase. Women haven't used them in a fashionable way since our grandmother's time. Then we inspect your wardrobe. Yes, I know you think it sufficient, but you are no longer in hiding."

"Yes, ma'am."

Caroline grinned so her dimples dug deep. "Indeed. I am in charge for the moment. A little trimming of the hair . . ."

"Some experiments with the paint pot?"

Caroline blushed and put her hands to her face, but then she laughed. "I confess it. And you will see what a difference it can make without being at all obvious."

She went quickly to her flower-painted desk and took out a book, flipping through the pages. "Friday. That should give us enough time. We'll make your grand entrance at Drury Lane. It's the opening of *A Daring Lady,* a new play for Mrs. Hardcastle. She did a wonderful Titania not long ago, but this is a comedy. We're promised breeches and sword fighting, so all the world will be there."

She gazed into space for a moment. "We'll hold a supper here afterward, and you will be the center of attention."

Anne's mouth turned dry. Running back to Lea Park was tempting as sugar plums. She had chosen this course, however, and would stick to it.

"And, of course, there will be St. Raven," Caroline continued.

"He may not be free on Friday."

"Then he can make himself free."

"Caro!"

Caroline grinned. "I am the famous Lady Welsford, and will be obeyed. I wasn't so close to him as you, but I'm sure he'll want to help. And once you have been seen with him, the other men will flock to you."

She sank back among the cushions of her sofa, almost purring. "We are going to create a sensation. By this point of the season the new people are old and the scandals are fading. Even Byron and Brummell's flights abroad are stale news. You, your staff, and St. Raven will be the new talk of the town."

Anne grasped the teapot and refilled her cup. She dearly wished she had some brandy to add to it.

Ten

~

On Friday night Anne did drink a little brandy to steady her nerves.

She had her cane. Wallace and Sons had been willing to sell a display item, an apprenticeship piece of tulip-wood, inset with mother-of-pearl and silver in a design of winding flowers. It was taller than she'd intended—the amber knob with a fly fixed in it came to her shoulder—but she already liked it in a practical way. With the staff she didn't fear falling and could walk faster and for longer.

In all other respects, however, she felt kinship with the poor trapped fly.

A quiet ivory satin dress from last year was now embellished with an overdress of pink net and silver beads, and cut considerably lower in the neckline. The entire upper part of her breasts was exposed. She was used to thinking of herself as modestly endowed, but when she looked down there seemed to be an enormous amount of flesh on display.

Caroline's dictatorial coiffeur had trimmed her hair to curl around her face, which she quite liked, but had also insisted on a rinse that made her hair a brighter blond. Caroline thought it wonderful. Anne thought it was too . . . Simply too much.

Especially with the additional effect of face paint as used by Caroline's French maid.

A stranger looked back from her mirror. A lovely stranger—even she could see that—but so unlike herself that she feared looking a fool. Caroline was ecstatic,

Welsford was flattering, but Anne fixed her mind on St. Raven. Tris would tell her the truth.

She heard a voice, then crisp footsteps across the hall. Moments later Tris strode in—still Tris, but now very much the duke. Had he needed to go away for a year to grow into the new skin he had inherited? It wasn't anything to do with his looks, though he was even more darkly handsome, or with his elegant evening clothes. It was, she decided, simply the way he occupied space.

As if it was all his.

As, of course, it was for a duke.

She wanted to shrink back, to become invisible again, but then his eyes met hers and he smiled, and he was Tris.

"Anne." His eyes widened and traveled over her. "My, my, I won't be able to call you Mouse any longer. London will be at your feet."

He meant it. She was sure he meant it, and it was as if a tight-wound spring inside her relaxed. She gave him her hands. "As it already is at yours, milord duke."

He laughed. "Alas. If I could change my appearance and reverse the effect, I would, but I don't think fustian coats and a bald head would deter anyone at all."

"I'm afraid not, but it's because you would still be ridiculously handsome."

"And above all, a duke." He smiled in that wry way he had that accepted fate and made the best of it. She remembered afresh why she'd always liked him.

His parents had died when he was fourteen. He had been nephew and heir to the Duke of St. Raven, but the duchess loathed the sight of him—the son she had failed to provide. So Tris had come to Lea Park, welcomed by her generous parents, to grow up in a ducal household and learn the trade.

"Thank you for smoothing my path," she said.

"I am yours to command in all things, Mouse." He considered her. "It has to be Mouse, you know. I'm sure there are resplendent mice somewhere in the world."

"Dead ones, I'd think. It is a mouse's good sense not to be noticed." She led the way to a sofa and sat. "But I, of course, wish to be caught."

"Nonsense. You are the huntress, not the prey."

"A hunting mouse?"

"You are an original."

Anne relaxed the last tiny little part. He was Tris, and he was her friend, just as he had always been. It had been a strange friendship with five years between them, but when he'd first come to Lea Park, newly orphaned, dark and withdrawn, he'd formed a link with her. Perhaps simply because she'd been the quiet, crippled one.

She was sure he alarmed and even terrified some people now, but not her. Reflected in his eyes she saw herself as lovely, confident, and in control, but also as the Anne she had always been.

They were a party of four for dinner, so it was a relaxed affair. They left for the theater in high spirits, and arrived in time for the main part of the program, the new play. Anne had almost forgotten the importance of the occasion until they stepped out of the carriage into a fashionable throng all pushing into the box entrance at the same time.

She grasped her cane for support both physical and mental, and saw a few people pause to stare. Saw them see Caroline and Welsford and thus recognize her. Saw them see St. Raven and turn to whisper.

It had started.

Tris squeezed her hand.

She put on a bright smile. "Thank you. I don't know how I'd do this without you."

"The same way you rode for the first time."

It had been Tris who'd argued that she should learn to ride because it would give her more mobility, and he who'd dared, teased, and cajoled her into it.

"Terrified," she said.

"But successful."

Her smile was natural now, and she didn't mind the stares. "Thank you."

"It's my delight. You are excellent defense against the fair huntresses. They really are enough to push a man into being a recluse."

She sighed. "A quiet life is very tempting, isn't it?"

"No. You're not enjoying this, are you, Mouse? Shall

I throw you into the carriage and carry you back to Lea Park?"

He'd do it, too. "I wish you could, Tris, but I'm determined to go through with this."

"Your family could bring suitable suitors to the country for you."

"That has been tried."

His blank look showed that he had no idea about Middlethorpe and Wyvern. That was comforting. At least it wasn't the talk of the town. Now she wished she hadn't mentioned it at all, and in the crush she couldn't explain if she wanted to.

"They weren't right for me. I have to make my own selection. In the ranks of society there must be one man I can love, and who can love me."

"Rarer, I fear, is the man who deserves you."

"I seem to be very hard to please."

"So you should be. You are a princess."

"Behind walls of power?"

He looked puzzled, as well he might. She must stop letting de Vere live like a third in her company. Someone pushed from behind while the man in front slowed. Tris moved to take the pressure off her. The perfect escort.

She smiled at him. "Someone suggested that I'd frightened all my suitors away by being a duke's daughter, and by being . . . off-putting."

"If a man is frightened away, he is not worthy of you."

"But what if the hero doesn't exist who is brave enough to attempt an assault?"

His dark eyes turned dangerous. "If anyone assaults you, Mouse, he'll not be your husband. He'll be dead."

Oh, Lord. "Tris, you are not to make trouble."

"I most certainly will if it is called for."

"Trouble?" asked Caroline from her other side. "Are you all right, Anne? What a dreadful crush, but I suppose no one wants to miss this first night."

She related an alarming story of a panic on crowded stairs like these that had resulted in injuries, and some ladies ending up in rags, exposed to the common gaze. Anne was more concerned by the danger of Tris's attitude. There had always been something dark about him. Not a bad dark, but a warrior core that could and would kill.

She remembered him attacking a brawny farmer who'd been beating a maid over something. Tris had ended up with a black eye and cracked ribs, but the farmer hadn't escaped unscathed. And, she remembered, Tris had insisted that the man not suffer for assaulting a member of the Lea Park family, only for assaulting the servant.

It had been noble in its way, but she didn't need a knight-protector attacking any suitor who became ardent.

Or impudent.

The thought of an encounter between Tris and de Vere made her hair stand on end. It was a strange notion, but in many ways, they were two of a kind and could tear each other apart. The noisy press of the crowd fermented her simmering nervousness into panic. If it had been possible to turn back and escape, she might have tried. . . .

Then suddenly a door opened before her into space. They had arrived at Welsford's box.

A new noise and vibrancy assailed her—the chattering, glittering crowd within the theater. A fog of sweat, perfume, candle smoke, and oranges turned her stomach. The others were standing back, expecting her to make her grand entrance first.

"Chin up and face the lions." Tris grasped her arm to move her forward.

With a deep breath, she took over for herself. Chin up, staff forward, she walked down to the front of the box, to the place where she—and her escort—would be visible to nearly everyone in the theater.

She'd entered a theater many times without creating the slightest disturbance. Now, faces turned and a silence fell over the crowd, followed seconds later by a buzz. Mouth too dry for any light comment, she made herself smile as she passed her staff to Tris, who passed it on to Philip. Then she slowly settled into her seat at the center front of the box.

Despite the flash of quizzing glasses raised to inspect

her, she did manage to relax. The worst was over, and as usual, it hadn't been the end of the world. She glanced at Tris, who smiled as he sat beside her, inviting her to be amused by the whole event.

And suddenly she was. It was all so silly, this attention and speculation merely because Lady Anne Peckworth, somewhat improved in looks and carrying a beribboned cane, had come to the theater on the arm of the Duke of St. Raven.

Smile deepening into wickedness, Tris raised her hand. "If we're to do this properly, we should set up a flirtation." He kissed it, lingeringly, with that exact kiss that de Vere had described as the one of a man who knows how to please women.

The buzz intensified.

Without urgency, she took back her hand. "Wretch. Half society will have us engaged to marry by morning."

"Would you like to be?"

She blinked at him. "I could take you up on that and scare you to death."

"If it came to bluff and counterbluff, Mouse, who do you think would win?"

"You, and that's one reason we could never marry."

"What are the others?"

He was holding her attention and being playful to help her over the worst, and it had worked. She did worry, however, that his whimsical question might be rooted in seriousness. Might a beleaguered duke see his old friend as a safe refuge?

"We could never love in that way, Tris, and I suspect that you need a mad passion if you're to take marriage seriously."

"So do you."

"Oh no. I want a placid life in the country."

"The mouse aspires to be a cow?"

She pulled a face at him. "This mouse aspires to a fellow mouse and a quiet nest. If you promise not to force adventures upon me, I promise not to lecture you about your intimate affairs."

"I hope you know nothing about my intimate affairs." But his expression eased. "As for adventures, I'm not sure you've tried enough to know what you want."

"I've never been shipwrecked, but I'm certain I don't want that. I do truly want a quiet country life, Tris." Struck by a sudden thought, she added, "Now there, your wicked reputation could be of use to me."

His brows rose. "As occasional amusement when the boring husband is away?"

She rapped his hand with her fan. "Don't be absurd. I said your reputation, not your skills."

"And what do you know of my skills, Mouse?"

Anne knew she was blushing. "Do stop this. What I mean is, you can warn me of any poor choices."

"In the area of skills? I don't normally observe other gentlemen in action."

She almost asked for clarification, but caught herself. He was teasing and didn't need encouragement.

"I presume you observe other gentlemen at the gaming table, and that's what I mean. I have no mind to marry a man who might risk my security and that of my children for the thrill of cards or dice. So if you see one courting me, give me warning."

"That I can do as long as you don't plunge without consulting me first."

She laughed. "When have you ever known me to plunge?"

"I sense a new and dangerous Mouse. Very well, we need a secret code. If I mention mice, Mouse, beware."

"Mice?"

"And rats if the specimen is truly verminous."

"We'll seem crazed to be talking about rats and mice."

"The advantage of being a duke and a duke's daughter is that we can be as crazy as we wish to be. In fact, I think we need to distinguish between the rakehells and the gamesters. You may incline to one but not the other."

"I incline to neither!"

"Good. For gamesters, it will be farthings."

"Farthings?" She started as if a terrible secret had been revealed. Had Caroline gossiped about her night at Benning's? What did people know?

"Farthings. I would hate to ruin a man with a careless word, and I can't remember the last time I even thought

about a farthing, never mind spoke of one. Mice and
rats for the dissolute."

Her alarm simmered down. It wouldn't have mattered
anyway. The whole world could know that she'd played
hazard for farthing points in the company of her brother
and brother-in-law. It was the third player who made
the subject like nettles to her, raising an instant rash,
and that was ridiculous.

"What about nobodies?" she asked wryly.

He gave her a puzzled look. "Those, I assume, you
can detect for yourself."

To her relief, the curtain rose to reveal the drawing
room of a wealthy house. The play had begun.

Lady Rosalinde entered, played by Mrs. Hardcastle of
the famous beauty and silvery hair, complaining to her
maid about her guardian's insistence that she marry an
older man of property when she wanted a dashing
young beau.

The uncle arrived with a stern older man to present.
Then a fashionable married cousin and Rosalinde's
grandmother turned up to encourage her to seek youth-
ful delights. The heiress rejected the stern suitor. The
uncle raged, but went off to find another contender.

The cousin summoned Sir Mirabel Preen, a fashionable man of handsome appearance, but he was more
interested in his reflection in a mirror than in Rosalinde,
so he was dismissed, too.

The uncle returned with a lord this time, but he lectured Rosalinde on her duties as the future Lady Mount-
augustine, which seemed to include immense gratitude
to him. Rosalinde sent him on his way, too.

Throughout, Rosalinde's expressions were delightful,
and her occasional asides to the audience were clever,
as were those of the grandmother.

Anne leaned close to Tris. "Doesn't the grandmother
remind you of the Dowager Duchess?"

"Lord, so she does! Even to the heavy paint and salty
turn of phrase. She had us boys blushing at times."

Then the cousin's next offering arrived—Captain Jeremy Goodman, in scarlet regimentals.

The grandmother turned to Lady Rosalinde and said
in a very loud aside, "Now this is more the thing, gel.

Note his shoulders and calves, and the fine pair of thighs on him."

Rosalinde clapped her hands to her cheeks, but then she flirted with the young man and at the end of the scene turned to the audience. "Ladies. Listen to your grandmothers. I do believe that this is the perfect husband for me, a young man both brave and honorable. And oh, the thighs on him!"

The audience was laughing and applauding as the curtain lowered, but Anne thought that the women were laughing loudest.

"Assessing a husband by his *thighs*?" she murmured.

Tris gave her a look. "Turning prudish?"

"No, but . . . do you not notice? The play is about a trinity of women evaluating suitors, and mostly on their appearance and ability to please."

He laughed. "So it is. Fair is fair. Men do that all the time."

Caroline and Welsford stood to leave the box, and Tris offered Anne his arm. "I admit, I'm more interested in the play as a guide to failure. Perhaps I should take to admiring my reflection while lecturing the ladies on their future duties."

Anne rose, but then she looked him up and down. "But oh, sir, your thighs!"

"Saucy wench—"

"There's Uffham!"

Anne whirled to look where Caroline was pointing—down into the chaotic pit. Sure enough, there was her brother, cuddling a laughing orange girl, and there was Race de Vere, flirting with another. Her heart missed a beat, but she took the sight as warning.

All the women fell in love with him, even orange sellers.

"Uffham must come up here," Caroline declared, and rushed down to the front of the box. clearly intending to get his attention.

Welsford pulled her back. "Send Philip, my love."

Caroline remembered to be a respectable married lady and dispatched her footman on the errand. "Lord Uffham is to join us in the box for the rest of the play,

Philip. Make that clear. Even if he is a mere brother, he will add to Anne's consequence."

"St. Raven is quite sufficient," Anne protested.

"There is no such thing as sufficient," Caroline declared, taking her husband's arm and sweeping out of the box.

Anne shared a smile with Tris. "She's going to be insufferable one day."

"Not at all. She'll be the sort of matriarchal tyrant who terrorizes generations. Like the dowager."

They shared memories as they mingled with the elite, but Anne couldn't really concentrate on anything except the probable approach of Race de Vere.

He'd teased her and kissed her and said improper things to her. Then he'd kissed her again half-naked in the corridor. Him being half-naked. He'd stirred all kinds of feelings in her, desires even, and then left without a word or a backward glance.

Mischief, she reminded herself. He'd admitted to irritating everyone. He'd merely amused himself with her during a rainy country visit. She'd been his straw heart!

She had that straw heart on her dressing table holding hairpins but also a certain gaming counter. Innocent things to suddenly seem so dangerous. Thank God, she thought, that she was on the arm of the most eligible man in England.

Perhaps she tightened her grip, for Tris said, "Are you all right?"

She raised her chin and smiled brightly at the passing Greshams. "Yes, of course. Just a twinge of nerves. This is my first night."

"I could say something risqué, but I will spare you."

"Good."

She saw Uffham coming. He was tall, anyway, but he parted the crowd as if it were the Red Sea. He didn't have Tris's ducal presence yet, but he was what he was, and most people instinctively gave way. De Vere, of course, was with him, and Anne realized that he had a presence of his own. She had no time to analyze it.

Eleven

~

"Carrie," Uffham protested, "a play's much more fun from the pit."

"I want you up here," Caroline said. "And don't call me Carrie!"

"Frannie, Annie, Carrie, Marrie, and Lizzie."

"Very well," Caroline whispered, *"Stuffy!"*

"Children, children," murmured Welsford. "We are supposed to be giving Anne countenance, not covering her with blushes."

Uffham, red with annoyance, turned to Anne. But then he grinned. "Quite the thing, ain't you, Annie? Get you hitched in no time."

"Uffham," Tris said, quietly but almost as angrily as Caroline.

Uffham at least heeded it. "What?"

Her brother, Anne realized, was drunk. Not seriously, but enough to make him troublesome. Why had Caroline had to bring him up here?

He wasn't too drunk to catch Tris's warning, however. "Oh, right. Good to see you again, Tris. Have to call you St. Raven now, I suppose. Can't be school-boys forever."

"Some of us don't want to be."

Uffham rolled his eyes. "Don't you start prosing on at me. Bad as de Vere. Where the devil is he? Ho, de Vere, come and admire my sister Annie in her fine new feathers."

De Vere obeyed. "Plumed fine enough to take flight, Lady Anne. But remember Icarus."

What had she expected? Some expression of warmth or hidden passions?

"Are you accusing me of being a high-flyer, Mr. de Vere?"

She heard a choking sound from Tris. That was slang for a loose woman.

She saw nothing but brilliant amusement in de Vere's eyes. "Only insofar as you live with the gods in ducal splendor, my lady."

"You worry," Tris said, "that a lady in the company of dukes and future dukes is in danger of a fall?"

Anne didn't like that tone. Uffham had wandered off without performing the introduction, so she presented de Vere to Tris.

De Vere bowed like a minion, murmuring, "Your Grace. Icarus was in no danger at all, Your Grace, until he tried to fly his way out of a prison."

Drat the man. The flowery Your Graces were at complete odds with his demeanor, and he was going to drive someone to do something unwise.

"You think Lady Anne imprisoned?" Tris was still cold.

"I think Lady Anne should be careful where she flies, Your Grace. As should we all."

"Mr. de Vere was till recently in the army, St. Raven," Anne interjected.

"At Waterloo?" Tris asked, warming slightly.

"No, Your Grace."

De Vere didn't show any reaction, but Anne winced at how he must hate that question.

"Mr. de Vere was with the forces sent to America. I think it most unfair that those regiments have no medal merely because they missed the final battle, when they'd fought so many years in Spain and Portugal."

"Galling, I'm sure. And your plans now, sir?"

"Are undecided, Your Grace."

"Marriage?"

"Only to a very wealthy lady, Your Grace."

"I see." Anne hadn't known that Tris could look down his nose like that. "You plan to marry a fortune rather than earn one?"

De Vere's brows rose. "Some might say, Your Grace, that seven years in the army entitles a man to any spoils he can find. It could seem ungracious if those who stayed at home begrudged them."

Anne wanted to kick him. He couldn't know, but he'd found Tris's sore spot. Tris had longed to buy a commission, but as the precious sole male of the Tregallows, it had been impossible.

"That depends," Tris said, "entirely on the spoils. An army is not supposed to ravage its own."

"I should think not, Your Grace. It sounds positively incestuous."

"Lady Anne and I are not related."

"Did I say otherwise?"

What was all this? Anne leaped in. "St. Raven and I are like brother and sister, Mr. de Vere, even though there is no blood tie."

"And like a brother"—Tris was talking through his teeth now—"I will protect her to the death."

Thank heavens Caroline swept over. "Uffham is to join us in the box, Mr. de Vere, to add to Anne's credit."

It was not information. It was instruction.

De Vere turned to Caroline as if war hadn't nearly broken out here. "Are you sure he will, Lady Welsford?"

It was a tantalizingly ambiguous warning. Whether Caroline caught that or not, she ignored it. "Do please see that he does, Mr. de Vere."

Anne seized the opportunity to steer Tris away to mingle with other members of the ton. "De Vere would probably like to throttle the Peckworths."

"I assume he finds it worth his while to be . . . useful."

Anne frowned at him. "Do you know something to his discredit?"

"No. Why? Is he a contender?"

"De Vere?" Did her laugh sound shrill? "Of course not. But you secmed cool."

"Uffham's friends rarely stir me to warmth, but he did say de Vere prosed at him, so perhaps there's hope."

She glanced at him. "No mice, rats, or farthings?"

"Don't know him from Adam. Of course, I might

know him better under his real name." He was being arrogant in a way that was at odds with his nature.

"It is his real name."

He glanced down at her. "De Vere? Come, Anne. Any true de Vere would be trying to claim the earldom of Oxford, which would be very interesting when it's been in other hands for over a century."

They paused to speak to the Harrovings. When they moved on, she said, "He said he was a de Vere, born to a de Vere, and I don't think he gives a direct lie. Perhaps he's from the bastard line. I wish Uffham and Caroline wouldn't treat him like a servant."

"He amuses and takes care of Uffham, and for payment he has room, board, and a share in Uffham's expensive recreations. What would you call him? You seem hot in his defense, Mouse."

Trying to react to that, she accidentally smiled brilliantly at the passing Marshboroughs, thus giving them the unlooked-for opportunity to exchange trivialities with a duke. Probably something to tell their grandchildren.

She'd lived her life within the aura of high rank, but felt as if she were seeing it anew. She didn't like the way de Vere was dismissed as a nobody while people fawned on Uffham. It was the way of her world, however. One day Uffham would be the mighty Duke of Arran, and de Vere would be who knew what?

Still a nobody.

Enough of that. She was forgetting her main purpose here—to meet eligible titled men. She glanced around and saw the Countess of Flawborough, a tower of bronze including a high turban, heading her way, son in tow.

A younger son, but Anne needed practice, so she smiled at Mr. Pitt-Meadowing. She soon wished she hadn't. He had bored her before, and bored her now. The same could be said of Lord Marlowe, gleaming smile to the fore, Lord Gillmott, and Sir Shaftesbury Drum.

While listening to Sir Shaftesbury discuss the design of carriage wheels with Tris, she realized why Tris had reacted so badly to de Vere. He thought he was a fortune hunter.

How absurd. He wasn't hunting her at all. She would have to make that clear.

She supposed she could acquit these other men of being fortune hunters, too, since she'd owned her large dowry all her life and they'd ignored her before tonight. Now they were interested, but she felt that they should have been attracted to her before, should have sought her out in her rural seclusion. This new person that they fluttered to was only surface glitter.

She reminded herself that in the past she had deliberately hidden. How had Caroline put it? Turned down her wick. Or as de Vere put it, projected lack of interest. She might be shining brightly now, but she wasn't sure she was projecting interest. How could she when she wasn't interested?

And yet, she had to marry.

Not Sir Shaftesbury, however. Beyond a few idiotic words of flattery, he'd ignored her in favor of manly talk. The question was settled when Tris said, "The thing about a carriage, Drum, is to be careful not to let in the rats."

"Rats, St. Raven? Have trouble with them, do you?"

"All the time, sir, all the time."

Anne struggled with laughter as they moved on. It set a pattern for the intermission. Sometimes Tris mentioned rats, mice, or farthings, sometimes he didn't. Even the innocent men, however, went to the bottom of her list in moments. How could she end up with a list composed entirely of a bottom rung? She was relieved when it was time to return to the box, but when she entered it she paused.

For the first act she and Tris had sat in the front with Caroline and Welsford behind. Now two chairs had been added, one at either end of the front row. Caroline clearly wanted Uffham at the front to ram home the fact that Anne was a future duke's sister. She'd never imagined that it would be in doubt.

She could take one of the end chairs. Once Tris sat beside her, she'd be safe from de Vere. It would give an inferior view of the stage, however, and might be noted. Tris was already suspicious.

She settled, therefore, into her former seat with Tris on her right, praying that Caroline would marshal Uffham into the seat on her other side.

Uffham, however, took the seat next to Tris. "Need to talk to you . . ."

Anne sighed and turned to Race de Vere, now sitting to her left hand.

He was giving her a speculative look. Heavens, did he think she'd *arranged* this? She was going to murder Caroline!

She plied her fan and tried to look bored. "What do you think of the play, Mr. de Vere?"

"A wicked piece, Lady Anne, perhaps written by a woman."

She stared at him. "A female playwright?"

"Why not? And I anticipate more skewers driven into male flesh. A number of irate gentlemen were storming out of the theater at the end of the first act."

Anne looked around and noticed a few empty boxes, but not many. The atmosphere among those who remained seemed to simmer with anticipation.

Was she simmering with anticipation? She was simmering with something. There was a power in de Vere's mere presence, something that set her nerves a-tingling.

Then she became aware of a tingle of another sort. It seemed to shoot between de Vere and Tris, with her in the middle. She had thought earlier that a confrontation between them would be alarming. Unfortunately, she had been right. She could only be relieved when the curtain rose.

Lady Rosalinde was in the midst of a confrontation with her furious uncle, loudly declaring that she'd marry her Jeremy.

"He doesn't have a penny to his name, you foolish chit!"

"He has his army pay."

"No officer can make do on army pay, never mind support a wife. Be done with this."

"But I have a fortune, Uncle, that will come to me when I marry."

"Which is why you'll marry a sober, older man, you hussy."

"Which is why I'll marry any man I choose, you old misery!"

The uncle set off after her with his stick, and they dodged around the furniture until the old man collapsed wheezing onto the chaise, complaining that she'd be the death of him.

Anne was struck by the parallels. She had a large dowry, and in theory could marry anyone she chose. If she were a daring lady . . .

She stole a glance at de Vere—

And caught him looking at her.

He raised his brows. She quickly looked back at the stage, knowing she was blushing. Plague take the man. She'd like to push him over the balcony back down into the pit where he belonged!

Oh, Lord. How did he stir these outrageous thoughts?

Rosalinde had fixed on her dashing captain and determined to have him despite all opposition. The married cousin advised caution and time, pressed her to seek a titled husband, but the grandmother urged her to seize the moment.

"Embrace your future, gel. And your Jeremy's thighs in your marriage bed!"

The audience roared with laughter.

Anne thought of thighs.

She'd eyed Tris's thighs without a quiver or a qualm. She remembered ogling de Vere's thighs by firelight. Remembered quivering.

She slid her eyes sideways at eye level. He was watching the play, grinning at the discussion among the three women.

She slid her eyes down.

In the gloom, however, and with him wearing dark pantaloons, she couldn't see anything.

And what on earth did she think she was doing?

She concentrated on fictional insanity to find Rosalinde involved in a mock consultation with the audience.

"Marry money," called one female voice. "It lasts longer than muscular thighs!"

"Nay," the heiress said, "I'll exercise them enough to keep them trim and strong!"

"You're a hussy, young lady," called an older male voice from a box. It was the Earl of Brassingham, a notorious lecher if rumor was true. "Marry as your guardian says."

"But, sir," Rosalinde said, glancing up, "elderly guardians seem to always want young ladies to marry men of their age. Perhaps they seek to deny the wattles in their mirrors."

Anne wondered if steam was rising from the wattled old roué. He got to his feet, and he and his party marched out of their box.

"Probably can't bear to look in a mirror at all," the actress remarked, causing a gale of laughter.

"Heavens, she'll end up in jail," Anne said.

"I doubt it." It was de Vere. "She has very powerful friends."

"Who?"

He looked at her. "There's a group called the Company of Rogues."

"I know of them. Lord Amleigh is one. He is her friend?" A beautiful actress as well as a lady of Devon?

"More particularly a Major Beaumont, but her safety lies in the friendship—before his marriage, of course—of the Marquess of Arden."

De Vere, she thought, was the only person who would discuss mistresses with her. Even Tris might balk.

She looked at the vibrant actress again. "I'm glad."

The give and take continued.

"Old husbands die sooner," cried a woman in the pit. "Marry a dodderer."

"But have you not noticed how time drags when we're bored? A year with a dodderer could be lifetime enough to drive me to the grave!"

"A hit, a veritable hit," murmured Tris. "Don't marry a bore, Mouse."

"Mouse?" asked de Vere, glancing at them.

"A schoolroom name," Anne said.

"Ah. I hope His Grace realizes that you are not in the schoolroom anymore, Lady Anne."

"His Grace," Tris said, "does. May we watch the play?"

Anne stared fixedly at the stage as Jeremy rushed in asking what plan Rosalinde had concocted. What was she supposed to do if the men on either side of her lunged to attack?

Push them both into the pit if she had the strength. They were like fighting cocks anyway. Who could understand men? She wished she could wash her hands of all of them.

Including Captain Jeremy Goodman.

He was declaring that they must obey Rosalinde's guardian. His plan was to venture to America to make his fortune and then return to claim his fair Rosalinde.

"Idiot," Anne said, not meaning it to be aloud.

"True," Tris said. "Poor men marry heiresses whenever they have the chance. Would you not agree, Mr. de Vere?"

"It does depend on the heiress, Your Grace. Some are not worth the price. Fair Rosalinde, however, could marry a duke even if penniless."

"Only a very foolish duke. She'd settle for less."

"St. Raven!" Anne protested.

Yes, Tris definitely thought de Vere was a fortune hunter. What on earth could have given him that impression?

Her skin suddenly prickled. Was he sensing something she had missed? She didn't understand men well.

After all, she had hardly encouraged de Vere. In fact, now she thought of it, she'd been as actively discouraging as he'd suggested. She'd thrown brandy in his face, and then—oh lord!—she'd hit him after that kiss.

And then, to cap it all, she'd told him directly that she never wanted to see him again.

Oh, my. Her heart started to pound. Had he been as stirred by their time together, by their kisses, as she? She remembered that last kiss, those three light kisses in the corridor. They had to mean something, didn't they?

Was he attracted to her?

If so, what did she want to do about it?

Every time he called Tris "Your Grace" it was like a declaration that he came from a much lower social station. He was not at all the sort of man she was supposed to marry.

Lady Claretta Crump loomed in her mind.

And yet, and yet, here was Lady Rosalinde claiming her right to marry where she loved rather than for worldly position.

And then there was Lady Hester Stanhope, not fictional at all. She wasn't simply adventuring. She had taken up with a man far more unsuitable than anyone Anne might consider—not just foreign, but possibly pagan!

Anne felt breathless with possibilities and fears as she watched Rosalinde arguing with her Jeremy. So fierce she was in her fight for what she wanted. Unfair that she had to fight Jeremy, as well. He was standing nobly adamant, chin high, preaching obedience and good order.

In the end the actress came to the front of the stage. "By the stars, why am I plagued by such a noble fool? Any number of men have tried to marry me for my fortune, and yet here is the one I want and he will not play! What am I to do?"

She appeared to listen to the cacophony of suggestions, then nodded. "Yes, indeed. I will force his hand."

She marched back to the posing hero. "Jeremy, I insist that we elope."

Jeremy recoiled. "My love, you do not want to do something so likely to tarnish your good name!"

"Yes, I do. In fact, I insist on it. Tonight."

"Tonight! No, no. Your guardian has the right of it, my love. I cannot yet provide the home and circumstances you deserve."

"My money can, and once I am married my fortune will be mine no matter what my uncle says."

"We must wait until I have improved my circumstances. It will only be a matter of years—"

"Years!" Rosalinde planted her hands on her hips. "I'll be gray by then! Harken to me, sirrah! I am climbing out of my window tonight and going north. If you accompany me, you will be my husband. If not, I will find another one on the way."

"Rosalinde! You could not possibly do that."

"You think not? Try me and see!"

The curtain came down on that ultimatum, leaving Anne breathless. To cut through all the tangle of society's expectations and rituals, and seize fate like that.

Her heart raced, but was it with excitement, or with terror that she might actually be tempted into such insanity?

Twelve

~

"Oh, my," Caroline exclaimed, "if he doesn't keep the assignation, will she truly take some chance-met man to husband?"

"He will have to show up," Welsford said. "Once trapped in the role of a hero, what hope does a man have?"

Anne turned in her seat to see Caroline poke him with a jeweled finger. "Perhaps I will run off on a mad adventure so you will have to follow and be my hero."

He captured her finger and kissed the tip. "As long as you are willing to accept the consequences. I would be somewhat angry, my love, if you endangered yourself."

That sounded threatening, but her sister's eyes were bright as she slid her finger out of her husband's hold and took the wine the footman was handing around.

Another aspect of love? Not always courteous respect, but veiled threats and challenges? She definitely didn't understand love, but she itched to learn.

Tris asked her, "So what do you think of the play now?"

She took wine herself and turned back to the front. "It still amuses, but I worry about the happy ending."

"You don't think Rosalinde and Jeremy will suit?"

"No. But I don't suppose it matters. This is all make-believe."

"Yet a good play should seem real at the time, Lady Anne," de Vere interjected. "Therefore, I suspect that there are some twists still to come. Do you care to *hazard* some guesses?"

Anne almost choked on the bubbles. "That depends

on what is at stake, Mr. de Vere. What twists can you imagine? Lady Rosalinde can hardly marry *just any man.*"

She used the phrase deliberately, but saw no reaction.

"Which leaves only Captain Goodman, who doesn't please you. Because of his lowly station?"

Was that a meaningful question? She took another sip of wine to moisten her mouth, considering the implications of her answer.

In the end she settled for honesty. "It is his lack of courage that makes me doubt."

"You have no evidence as to his bravery or lack of it. He simply wishes to behave within the law. Rosalinde's uncle has the legal right to block an unsuitable marriage."

"If you were Jeremy, Mr. de Vere, what would you do?"

His smile was sudden and delightful. "Avoid the fair Rosalinde like the plague. She'll be a torment to him all his days."

"Isn't that what men desire?" she asked, glancing to her right to include Tris if he was listening.

He was, like a hawk. If hawks listened.

"Torment and desire?" he said. "You're dabbling in dangerous waters, Mouse. Marry for comfort."

"Will you?"

"Perhaps I wish better for you than for myself."

Anne glanced back at de Vere.

"I'm sure we all wish that, Lady Anne."

He seemed sincere, and that lingered with her as the curtain rose again.

Could de Vere be acting the noble Jeremy and not pressing her because he felt unworthy? What did a woman do about that?

Get with child, as it seemed Claretta Crump had? Caroline had confirmed that rumor, and that Captain Crump was a decent man with an excellent war record. He was completely unsuitable, however, having made his way in the army entirely on his merits. His father was a fishmonger.

How could such a union work?

On the stage, at least, boldness seemed to win the day. Rosalinde and Jeremy were in a real coach pulled by galloping wooden horses. The backdrop of wild countryside rolled behind to cleverly give the appearance of movement.

Rosalinde, in a tricorn hat and mannish shirt, was hanging out of the window looking backward. "All clear! We have escaped pursuit."

"I still don't think this is wise," Jeremy bleated. "And as for your clothes . . ."

"Was I to climb out of my window in skirts?"

Cheers from the audience. Some man called out, "Let's see your thighs, love. Fair's fair!"

The rougher parts of the audience took it up. Anne began to fear a riot. It wouldn't be unheard of.

The actress, however, looked out at the audience, and slowly, silence fell. "Behave yourselves," she said. "I've a skirt here with me, and I'll have it on in a moment if you're not all perfect gentlemen."

After a resounding, laughing cheer, the audience settled to the play again.

What was it like, Anne wondered, to have such control from center stage, to play people, even rowdy men, like an instrument?

"Stand and deliver!"

Anne jumped, and from the cries and shrieks, so did a number of other women.

The scenery stopped and a masked and cloaked highwayman swept onto the stage. He looked like a stray cavalier in a long richly curled wig, a neat beard and mustache, and a wide-brimmed cavalier hat with a lavish white plume. His pistol was pointed, arm stretched, at the coach.

"It's that Corbeau!" shouted someone from the pit, and the play paused under a contest of cheers and jeers.

"Clever," de Vere said.

Tris looked at him. "Who is it?"

But Uffham answered. "Damned highwayman who's been working the roads north of London for months now. Dresses in exactly that peculiar style. How could you not know about him?"

"I'm only just back from abroad. A dashing, daring sort, is he?" Tris was clearly unimpressed. "Our true hero?"

Anne stared at him. "A thief? Surely not."

"There are many kinds of thievery, Lady Anne," de Vere said. "And apparently this fellow doesn't take all of a traveler's jewels and money, only what he calls a tithe."

Tris snorted. "Romantic folly. I'm surprised he doesn't settle for kisses."

"Oh, he does sometimes—"

"Hush," Caroline said. "The play!"

Most of the audience had been exclaiming and gossiping, but now it settled.

Still Tris said, "Only an idiot would play such a dangerous game for amusement."

"Only an idiot would drive up and down the north roads hoping for an encounter," de Vere said, "but apparently some ladies of the ton are doing exactly that."

"What?" asked Anne. "I don't believe it!"

"Oh, hush!" Caroline rapped de Vere's shoulder with her fan, which seemed unfair.

Jeremy and Rosalinde had lost the argument to the persuasion of Le Corbeau's pistol, and were climbing down from the coach. The actress was in the promised breeches without concealment of even a jacket.

The audience—the male part, at least—cheered wildly.

Anne saw Uffham with his hands cupped to his face making hunting horn noises. Tris and de Vere were quiet, but she could see that they both appreciated the actress's shapely legs. Anne couldn't help think that her own legs were in excellent condition from riding. Tris had seen her in breeches, but of course de Vere had not.

Would he be appreciative?

But then Rosalinde strode across the stage with a man's confident swagger, bringing Anne back to earth. Shapely thighs or not, the effect would be spoiled by her limp.

Jeremy was still hovering near the coach. "She must not marry him," Anne said.

De Vere turned to her. "He's handsome, gentle, loving, and honorable. Respectful, even, of a guardian's rights, and anxious to make his own way rather than live off her money. Where's the lack?"

"He's a coward. You said I had no evidence. Look at him now!"

"You want him to rush the pistol and be shot?"

"I want him to do *something*. Would you cower while that highwayman was ogling your lady's limbs?"

"A pretty chicken," Le Corbeau said, leering, "with plump, tasty thighs."

De Vere looked at the stage. "No. While he's so distracted by her legs, I'd take the pistol right out of his hand. But you're right. Jeremy has lost the hero's crown."

"I stopped your coach in hopes of a plump purse," said Le Corbeau, "but I'll happily take a plump kiss instead. What say you, wench?"

Rosalinde stepped back, but Jeremy at last came forward. "So be it, if you promise to let us go on with no more demands."

"The toad," Anne muttered.

"With warts on," Tris agreed. "My money's on the highwayman now. Any takers?"

De Vere was smiling. "My money's on the daring lady. I think I see the twist coming. . . ."

Rosalinde had turned to the audience, her expression all astonishment. "A kiss!" But then she turned to Jeremy. "My hero! To suffer a kiss from this hairy villain merely to save my purse."

"What? 'Tis you he wants to kiss!"

But Rosalinde pushed the captain into the highwayman's arms. As the audience hooted with laughter and Jeremy fought free, Rosalinde said, "A bargain is a bargain, sir. You didn't say who the kiss had to be from."

Anne realized that she was applauding and cheering, and stopped, hot-faced.

Le Corbeau laughed. "True enough, you wicked wench. And a highwayman's word is his bond." He turned toward the shrinking Jeremy. "Come here, my pretty chicken—or should I say cock?"

Jeremy scuttled backward and the audience howled with laughter.

Anne knew she'd missed some of the joke. "What?" she whispered to Tris.

"I refuse to comment."

She turned to de Vere. "What?"

"Hush," he said, lips twitching. "The play, Lady Anne."

"Wretch," Anne muttered.

"Never!" screamed Jeremy, scrambling under the coach. "Never. Help! Rosalinde, give him the money!"

"But without it, how are we to get to Scotland, my love? It's only a kiss."

"I never wanted to go to Scotland, anyway!"

"I begin to wonder if you ever wanted to marry me."

"I did. I did. But that was before the breeches, before this. I am not sure anymore that you are the woman I loved."

Hands on hips, Rosalinde declared, "I see. You fell in love with silliness and skirts—with skim milk—and choke on the cream." She turned to the audience. "What do I do now? Go back to my uncle defeated?"

The highwayman held out his hand. "The purse, my pretty."

"What of the kiss?"

"But your fair companion won't pay. Will you?"

The actress eyed him for a carefully judged moment. "I gather you sometimes fence for the money, sirrah."

"You are offering to fence me?" Le Corbeau laughed, but he whipped out a rapier. "If you have a sword, I accept, you daring wench, but if I win, I'll take my reward in a fencing match of another kind."

"Oh-ho!" cried the audience.

"From Jeremy, of course," Rosalinde retorted, causing gales of laughter, and Jeremy to scuttle deeper into hiding.

Anne knew she was blushing. She'd realized what cock had to mean and was speculating about other things. "This is an outrageous play."

"But at least she's safe from Jeremy," Tris said. "She can never marry him now."

"She'll marry the highwayman? I'm not sure I care for that either."

"Perhaps she'll declare herself free of all men," de Vere said, "and go off to enjoy her money by herself."

"Like Lady Hester?"

"Very like Lady Hester."

As Rosalinde pulled a sword out of the sword case on the back of the coach, Anne considered that option. Her family wanted her married, but she could convince them she preferred the single life.

The truth was, however, that she didn't want adventure, and she did want marriage. A tranquil marriage. A quiet nest with another mouse. She glanced wryly at de Vere, who had no touch of mouse about him at all.

Rosalinde flexed her rapier and slashed it with a very expert style.

"*But, but . . . ,*" protested Jeremy.

Rosalinde strode forward. "En garde, Mr. Crow! I fight for Jeremy's honor!"

A spirited sword fight followed, back and forth across the stage.

"By Hades, but she's good," Tris murmured.

"Do you fence?" Anne asked, eyes fixed on the stage.

"It amuses me. Do you fence, de Vere?"

"I have more practice with a saber, Your Grace, but yes."

Anne glanced from side to side, praying that she was mistaken in hearing a hint of future contest. What were these two men doing? And why?

"Ah-ha!" With a cry of victory, Rosalinde disarmed Le Corbeau and presented the rapier at his throat. "I think it is the gallows for you, sir."

Le Corbeau did not quail. "Or perhaps," he said with the kind of actor's softness that carried all through the theater, "I could pay you with a kiss?"

A murmur passed through the theater, and Anne knew it came from the women. Perhaps she had murmured herself. This was the hero after all. Yet he was still a highwayman. A thief.

Rosalinde turned to look at the audience. "A saucy rogue! But I think he is too fine a specimen to hang just yet."

With a flip of her blade she untied the cord of his

cloak so that it fell away, showing him, too, in shirt and breeches. "What do you think of his thighs, ladies?"

Many ladies applauded, and the grinning highwayman turned, showing himself off.

"Are you not embarrassed to be ogled by women, sirrah?"

"Not I. Do not all cocks strut proudly to impress the females?"

Hoots and cheers all around. Uffham almost fell off his chair with laughter. Anne had her hand over her mouth, but she was laughing, too.

The actress tossed aside her sword. "And I am mightily impressed!"

She went into his arms for a kiss. A kiss so like that one in the dying light of Benning's study that it raised the hair on Anne's neck. She was burningly aware of de Vere by her side, could almost taste his mouth on hers.

Was he making the same connection? Did his skin suddenly feel too sensitive for clothes? . . .

The audience members cheered and stamped their feet so the theater seemed to shake—or perhaps it was just her, shaken by the heavy beat of her own heart.

Something brushed her arm. She started, but realized that it wasn't de Vere touching her. It was that she'd swayed against him.

She hastily straightened, swallowing and trying to bring back sanity. Then she saw that Jeremy was crawling out from under the coach, was grabbing one of the discarded swords.

"Look out!" she cried, and she wasn't the only one.

"Release her, you rapscallion! Rosalinde, desist!"

He was still on his knees, however, and Mrs. Hardcastle cast the audience a look of disgust, then turned, put her booted foot on his chest, and thrust him back on the ground disarmed.

The audience erupted in cheers, and Anne cheered, too. She'd never behaved this way at a play before, but never before had she cared so much about the activities on stage.

"I'll marry no man so unworthy of my heart!" Rosalinde declared.

"And nor will I," Anne echoed.

She'd not meant it to be aloud, and she glanced to either side. Tris was laughing at something with Uffham, but de Vere met her eyes. "So I should hope, Lady Anne. But a highwayman could not be worthy of you."

"Should I judge a man by his occupation?"

"Why not? Does it not indicate abilities and inclinations?"

"You, sir, seem to have no occupation at all."

Oh, she hadn't meant to say that! She fixed her gaze on the stage and pretended not to hear his words.

"I am busy, as always, in mischief."

Le Corbeau was on one knee before Lady Rosalinde. "Magnificent lady, be mine!"

Rosalinde, however, looked out at the audience again, posing the question. Silence settled. The actress had created the illusion that this was real, that the decision mattered.

Rosalinde looked back at the man kneeling before her. "I'll not marry a thief, sirrah. Do you promise on your honor and your soul to give up your wicked life, and be an honest man?"

Le Corbeau turned to look at the audience, but the audience simply waited.

"So," murmured Tris, "how do you vote now, Anne?"

"Will he keep his promise? If he will, then she should have him."

He made a *tsk*ing sound. "Mice, rats, and farthings. She knows nothing about him. He could live without thievery and still be a drunken wastrel on her money, and cruel to boot."

Anne kept her eyes on the stage, entranced by the lingering moment of decision. What perfect timing the actors had. "He's not giving a glib promise. If he gives it, he'll mean it."

"Silence carries such weight?"

"And he's brave. That's a great deal."

"Not in marriage. Tell her, de Vere."

It sounded autocratic, but de Vere obeyed. "There are many heroes of the war I would not wish to see you marry, Lady Anne."

The words "including you?" almost slipped from her lips. Anne watched the actors, feeling that if Rosalinde could arrive at a happy ending, she could, too.

The highwayman leaped to his feet and threw off his hat, long wig, and mask, revealing a handsome enough man beneath. He even ripped off his mustache and beard.

"Ouch," said de Vere. "Now there's a sign of love."

"Henceforth I am an honest man, and true and loving husband to the most daring lady in the land!"

The couple leaped into the coach, and coach and horses were drawn off the stage heading north, the audience cheering them on.

Jeremy was left behind with the remnants of the costume, a pistol, and two swords. Anne felt some sympathy for him. Her almost-husbands hadn't been snatched in her presence, but they had been snatched.

Would he pretend not to care, as she had?

Would he wish the lovers well, as she had?

Would he recognize the ways in which he had failed? She never had, but now she thought that perhaps the losses had been partly her fault for being discouraging, dim, and dutifully quiet.

"She was never worthy of me," Jeremy declared, and marched off stage, just ahead of some thrown oranges.

As the players returned for more applause, Caroline declared, "That was a very clever piece, and most amusing. Everyone will be wondering who the playwright is. Which reminds me," she said, shooting to her feet, "we must be on our way to be ahead of our guests! Uffham, no slipping off to your club!"

"Just to the green room for a while, Caro."

Perhaps it was his use of her preferred nickname, or perhaps simply her urgency, but Caroline gave in. "For a little while only." With a casual, "Do please see to it, Mr. de Vere," she hurried out.

Anne hoped to hear de Vere argue with Uffham, show some pressing need to stay in her company, but instead he shook his head. "I am merely one man, not an army, Lady Anne. Warn your sister not to depend on Uffham's attendance."

"I believe you could make my brother do anything you wished, Mr. de Vere."

He was politely blank. "That would hardly augur well for the duchy, my lady."

My lady, my lady. He did it deliberately to slide to the minion level. She reached out and touched his arm. "Come to Lady Welsford's on your own, Mr. de Vere."

Uffham was at the door. "Come on, de Vere!"

De Vere looked at her for a moment, then he slipped away from her touch and obeyed Uffham.

Thirteen

～

Anne hissed in pure annoyance, both at him and at herself for weakening close to begging. Why couldn't she ignore the wretched man's existence? After all, marrying him would be nearly as bad as marrying a highwayman met on the road.

The theater was emptying, leaving orange peel and stray forgotten items, curdled smells and dead candle smoke. Workers were moving into the pit to sweep and tidy for tomorrow's production of the adventure. It hadn't been real. It should not affect her.

Tris waited with her staff in hand. She took it and left the box with him. "Caroline will be frantic with impatience," she said.

"I told her to go on, that you would need more time."

Did that refer to her limp or had he noticed her preoccupation with de Vere? She was relieved not to have to rush, however, and they worked their way out at the tail end of the chattering box audience. Everyone seemed pleased with the play, excited and a little shocked.

People enjoy being excited and shocked, she realized, and wondered if de Vere knew that and did it deliberately. Hadn't he mentioned the experiment with electricity? He did it, however, like an actor in a play. When the curtain dropped it was over, and the audience was supposed to know that.

Outside the theater, carriages were queuing to pick up ladies and gentlemen, and hackneys hovered nearby. Tris summoned one of them and helped her in.

"I've never been in a hackney before," she said.

"What a sheltered life you've led."

"I know."

He settled beside her and the plain carriage jolted off. "You'll note an absence of good springs, but the seats appear to have been washed and the straw on the floor is fresh. Pining for adventures and highwaymen, Mouse?"

She pulled a face at him. "No."

"Good. I fear Rosalinde is in for a hard life."

The thought, *But a merry one*, popped into her head. "You don't believe in gallant highwaymen?"

"Not at all."

She decided it was time to turn the tables and tease him. "Perhaps the gentleman doth protest too much. In French, Corbeau means both crow and raven, and didn't you recently buy an estate near Buntingford? That's Le Corbeau's territory.

He actually gaped. "Are you suggesting that *I'm* playing the high toby?"

"Are you saying it's mere coincidence?"

"That, or a very peculiar sense of humor. Dammit, I'll cage the rascal and find out what this is all about."

"You'll have to catch him first, and he seems to be a clever bird."

His face settled to that dangerous look. "So am I, Mouse, so am I."

A shiver slid across her shoulders, because of other matters entirely. "Tris, why were you behaving so ferociously with poor de Vere?"

"Poor de Vere? You might as well say 'poor Le Corbeau.'"

"Come now. You are worlds apart, but you were fencing with him as if he were your equal."

"I have to spar with someone. It grows so boring on this chilly elevation."

Anne sighed. "Why, Tris? You weren't snarling at any of the other men we talked to."

His lids lowered, making it hard to read his expression in the light of the dim tallow lamp. Eventually he said, "De Vere is more dangerous than any of the other men we talked to."

"Dangerous? To you?"

"To you, Mouse."

She sucked in a breath. "He wouldn't dare." After a moment she added, "He's not interested in me."

"Oh, yes he is."

Despite her will, her heart began a patter of excitement. "What makes you think that?"

"Male instinct." He took her hand. "Caroline mentioned that he was at Benning Hall when your sister was confined."

"Well, damn her."

"Tut, tut."

Anne knew she'd revealed too much. "I spent the evening gaming with him, Uffham, and Benning. But that's the extent of my wickedness," she lied.

"I wonder."

"He's avoided me ever since! Look at tonight. Is he here, pursuing me? No, he's in the green room with Uffham, the enchanting Mrs. Hardcastle, and a bevy of other theater beauties!"

She squeezed her eyes shut and tried to pretend that she hadn't let such telling comments escape. Having done so she might as well go on. This was Tris, after all, closer than any of her real brothers.

She met his thoughtful eyes. "He kissed me. No. We kissed. I haven't been able to entirely put it out of my mind."

"Was it your first kiss?"

"No. Yes. Like that, it was."

She thought she heard a hiss of breath. "I'll kill him."

"No!" She tightened her hold on his hand. "I asked him, Tris. I persuaded him. He did nothing I did not want."

"Do you want him, then? I'll get him for you if you do."

"Oh, Lord," she laughed. "Are you my hunting dog, to be sent out to bring back my chosen dinner? You know I'd never want a husband who came that way."

She considered Tris, in many ways her oldest and best friend who would do almost anything to help her. "He said I was discouraging. Do you think I am?" Reluctantly, she added, "Do you think I've discouraged him?"

"Sweetheart, I don't think a cannon ball would discourage de Vere from something he truly wants."

It was gentle, almost pitying.

Oh, God. Pity.

She swallowed and stiffened her spine. "Then I must get over it, mustn't I?" She looked at him, this fine, handsome man alone with her for a little while. "Would you kiss me, Tris? As he did? A strange thing to ask, I know, but we aren't brother and sister. And I can be sure you won't make too much of it."

After a moment, he asked, "Why?"

It would be revealing again, but there was no help for it. "I need to know if it's the kiss or the man."

He drew her into his arms, but slowly. "I'm not sure if I can do this right with you, Mouse, but come, let me try to kiss you better."

His lips were warm and soft on hers, his body hard and strong. She relaxed. It was certainly not unpleasant. She pressed a little closer and opened her mouth. . . .

Then she drew back. "It's not working, is it?"

In the dim light, she saw his rueful smile. "No."

She rested against him. "What am I going to do? What if it's only like that with him?"

"It won't be. I'm too like a brother, and you're too like a sister to me. But there will be other men."

"There have to be. I am resolved to find Mr. Mouse this season."

"Lord Mouse, at least, love."

She laughed, and he stroked her back as if she were the mouse's enemy, a cat. It was wonderfully comforting, but not the tiniest bit arousing.

How strange this all was.

Finding a quiet corner in the crowded, noisy green room, Race fought the temptation to worry about Anne Peckworth.

He should never have encouraged Uffham to come up to London for Anne's grand entrance at the theater, but he'd had to know how she was. He'd thought that seeing her in triumph, seeing her secure in her proper place in her world, attended by suitable aristocratic gentlemen, would enable him to get on with his life.

It hadn't worked.

When she'd appeared in that theater box, he'd seen only terror. But then she'd relaxed, and even flirted with her handsome escort. Uffham had identified him as the new Duke of St. Raven. An eligible *parti par excellence* and an old family friend.

That had stung, he admitted it, but he knew he had no hope there, so he'd been happy for her. He'd thought his mission over until he'd remembered that Anne had not wanted a life on the social stage.

Was she being pressured into a grand match by her family? Uffham was little use there, though he'd given a sketchy history of the duke's interaction with the Peckworth family.

Perhaps being duchess to an old friend would be to Anne's taste, but he'd had to know more. When the command came down from Lady Welsford, it hadn't been hard to get Uffham to obey. He seemed terrified of all his sisters. Race could probably have dragged him to Lady Welsford's party, but enough was enough.

For now at least.

Anne was safe. He was a good judge of men, and St. Raven would protect her as securely as he would himself. But did their temperaments suit? The duke was more of an eagle than a raven, and in some ways Anne was a mouse.

Meddling, meddling.

It went beyond tidying loose ends now, though. He cared for Anne Peckworth beyond sense, but more than that, he accepted his responsibility. She was out in the world, vulnerable, in part because of his interference in her life. He had to see her safe.

"Race! How lovely to see you again!"

He pulled himself out of his thoughts to greet Blanche Hardcastle, to pay homage to her outstretched hands, and then to shake hands with Major Hal Beaumont by her side. He'd met them both in Melton, when Con had taken him to Lord Arden's hunting lodge. He'd felt close to Blanche then, perhaps because they were both outsiders in that aristocratic enclave.

In fact there was a strangely familiar pattern in their love lives. Beaumont wanted to marry Blanche, but Blanche insisted that it was unsuitable because she was a butcher's daughter who'd worked her way up in her profession by any means available. She'd be his mistress but nothing more.

Of course, Anne Peckworth was not trying to persuade him into marriage, and there was no possibility of an unblessed union.

"Isn't it time you made an honest man of him?" he said to Blanche, teasing.

"Don't you start! I grant you did well interfering with Con, but find someone else to exercise your restlessness on now, sir." Perhaps he glanced at Uffham, because she lowered her voice. "You think you can work miracles there?"

"The greater the task, the greater the achievement . . . But no. Poor man, I'm using him."

"Ah," said Beaumont, who was no fool. "Lady Anne. She certainly set everyone talking tonight. No sign of a broken heart?"

"None. The Rogues can cease fretting."

"Then why," asked Blanche, who was no fool either, "are you so attached to Lord Uffham?"

"I'm barnacle to his bottom, dear lady," Race said, and refused their laughing demands for an explanation.

Fourteen

Anne woke the next morning feeling unaccountably depressed. And the sun was even shining!

No, not unaccountably. She had to accept that she was depressed by Race de Vere's lack of pursuit. She'd spent the hours of Caroline's successful party waiting and hoping for his arrival. She could hardly remember the various men who'd paid flattering court to her.

Tris might say that de Vere was interested, but she saw no sign of it, and as Tris had also said, mere unsuitability would not deter a man like Race de Vere.

He *was* unsuitable, though. Drifting asleep, her mind had wandered into storylines better fitted to a play. He was a lord in disguise, engaged in some secret work for the government. Or in a wager. He would challenge her to marry the poor man and then reveal himself to be worthy of her in every way. . . .

In daylight she laughed at such folly. In society everyone who was anyone knew everyone.

At Caroline's party she'd spoken to three military men who knew him, one quite well. The fact that they all thought highly of him didn't help. The fact that they all, in one way or another, described him as a madman proved that they knew what they were talking about.

She'd mentioned him to Lord Kimbleholt, who was from Derbyshire. "De Vere?" Kimbleholt had said. "There are no de Veres, certainly not in Derbyshire, Lady Anne." It was a large county, but it didn't augur well.

Major d'Arraby, the one who'd claimed to know de Vere well, had said that there was a rumor that his family came from trade and had assumed the name. Surely that couldn't be true. There was no trace of the shop about de Vere, and he had been an officer.

But then, so had Captain Crump. In wartime, many men rose from simple beginnings.

De Vere was a Mr. Nobody of Nowhere. There was no hope.

Where there's life, there's hope. She imagined him marching off like Jeremy Goodman to make his fame and fortune. Or better, doing such noble service that he received a title. After all, she *had* money, so that was not the issue. Sitting up in bed, chin on hands, she decided that Rosalinde had been wrong to reject that solution.

She shook her head. It was a play! Plays didn't have to make sense, but reality did. The reality was that marriage to Racecombe de Vere would outrage her friends and family and make her a laughingstock. And besides, the man had sense enough to not be courting her at all!

She forced her mind to the eligible men, but not even a fanciful imagination could turn any of the ones she'd met last night into her heart's choice. The pick of the aristocracy had flirted with her, and her heart hadn't missed a beat.

It was enough to turn a lady to laudanum, and now here she was still on country time, awake too early, before Hetty had even brought her washing water.

She straightened and stretched. Enough of this. Last night had been only the first step. She had weeks left and couldn't have met all the eligible men yet. And perhaps some would improve on acquaintance.

She decided that she had better be orderly about her search, however. She climbed out of bed and found her journal. She opened it to a blank page, checked the pen on her desk, and began a neat annotated list of the eligible men she had met, including their virtues and limitations.

She did not include Race de Vere.

By the time Caroline wandered in, yawning, tousled, and looking, Anne couldn't help thinking, well loved, Anne had her love life in order, on paper at least.

"What's that?" Caroline asked, peering over her shoulder. "A list? Really, Anne."

"How else am I supposed to go about this?"

"So who is your favorite at the moment?"

Anne picked a name. "Lord Alderton. His sister and I are friends."

"A consideration," Caroline agreed, lukewarm. She closed the book. "You are too impatient. Simply enjoy yourself and love will come."

Love? At the moment Anne would be content with someone she could tolerate. She put her pen back in the holder, and her book back in a drawer. "So, what are our plans for today?"

Caroline yawned again. "Visits, the park. The Fortescue ball unless you wish otherwise."

"I loathe the thought of all of it, but I will suffer in order to be married."

Caroline laughed and wandered off to dress.

The day progressed according to plan. The round of visits went better than Anne expected. Everyone was talking about the play, which was a great improvement on the usual dull conversation spiced only by malicious gossip.

In keeping with her new resolution not to hide her skills, she rode Monmouth in the park, wearing her smart gray habit with military frogging, a shako-style hat on her head. She was soon surrounded by an escort of horsemen, and was glad that Monmouth stood at fifteen and a half hands. She'd seen ladies dwarfed by their escorts, and she was determined never to be ridiculous.

She overheard Lord Michael Norton say he was hurrying home to get his horse so as to be able to accompany the "fair Lady Anne," and managed not to laugh. It confirmed her belief that the life of the ton was an absurdity.

She was enjoying it, however. In fact, she was slightly shocked at how much she was enjoying all this male attention. Did all the sorry bystanders in society secretly long to be at the center, so secretly that they did not even know it themselves?

At the same time she was aware that this enjoyment

was temporary. To live much of her time on this stage, acting in this trivial play, was not to her taste at all.

Yes, she thought, listening to Major d'Arraby on her right talk about himself at length, that was the London season—a weeks-long amateur theatrical, put on at great expense.

If she was constantly alert for Uffham—and his favorite companion—walking on stage, that was her folly to hide.

At nine o' clock, in a blue-spangled evening gown, she left with Tris, Caroline, and Welsford for the ball. When she arrived, the admirers swarmed in even greater numbers, male and female.

Caroline found a moment to whisper, "You are all the rage, as I predicted. Everyone wants to be seen with you."

Anne was tempted to swing her staff to clear some space around herself, but Tris neatly dispersed her admirers and led her into the ballroom. That was a relief, but it also presented a problem.

"You're scaring all my suitors away."

"If they're worthy of you, they'll brave my frown. But don't worry. I'll have to dance, and that will leave you open to attack."

"A very pleasant way to put it, I'm sure." She couldn't help noticing the avid female eyes fixed on him. "It's quite a sacrifice for you to come here, isn't it?"

"I can handle the bitches on the hunt."

"Tris!"

He smiled. "Technical term, my dear. And in hunting, bitch is an honorary name."

They were approached then by Lord Tewkesbury, his hopeful sister, Miss Raile, on his arm. He was a handsome man and smooth, very smooth. It didn't appeal, but she supposed that over a lifetime smooth would be better than rough. He was quite a wit and had her laughing.

Then Tris said, "Gads, a rat just ran over my foot!"

Miss Raile screeched and raised her skirts. They all looked down at the innocent polished floor. People nearby turned to look.

"Damned pests are everywhere," Tris said, raising his quizzing glass to eye Miss Raile's lower legs. Sadly, they were sticklike, which was not helped by horizontally striped stockings. "It's all right, Miss Raile. I don't *think* it ran up your skirts."

The lady's eyes went wide, and she made her brother take her in search of the ladies' room for a thorough check.

Anne made herself match Tris's straight face. "Wretch. Is he, though? A rat?"

"Definitely. Drink, women, and gambling."

"Ah, well, I don't think I would care for him anyway. He likes this fashionable life too much."

"Not a candidate for Lord Mouse of the Countryside?"

"Don't sneer. There has to be such a man somewhere."

Tris sat out the first dance with her, but after that he had to do his duty and bring stars to the eyes and magical hope to the breasts of some of the ladies. Anne was promptly swarmed.

She was tempted to cross every man present off her list simply for taking part in this folly. Scanning the mass of smiles, she caught sight of Alderton holding back. He was somewhat shy. She smiled brilliantly at him and held out her hand. He went pink, but he came to sit beside her, so she could wave the others away.

"Not surprising you created such a furor, my dear Lady Anne. You look like the stars in heaven."

A pretty sentiment, but she had no idea what it meant. She gave him the sort of smile a lady was supposed to give to a gentleman who paid her flowery compliments and then settled to well-practiced conversation.

They talked of the music, which was excellent, and the gracious ballroom, which few London houses could boast of. They admired the floral decorations and some of the more interesting fashions. It was, in other words, just like the other balls she had attended over the years.

After the set was over, another gentleman took his place. In fact two this time, one at either side. Smiling, listening—it had not struck her before how happy most men were simply to be listened to, how uninterested in anything a woman had to say—she made mental notes for her list.

She must marry a man who listened as much as he talked, and who treated her words with the attention they deserved. That ruled out d'Arraby, even though he was handsome, eldest son of a viscount, and rode well.

After three sets of dances, she knew that her husband must not be fond of this life. A week or two a year if he insisted, but beyond that it was a quiet country life for her. And the ban included Bath, Brighton, and every other fashionable spot.

She mentally crossed off Lord Vane—an aptly named dandy—and Sir Pomfret de Court. Both men had shimmered with the pleasure of seeing and being seen.

She regretfully crossed off Sir Rupert Grange. He was not a peer, but he was member of an eminent family, and had a reputation for involvement with important social issues. She might like that.

However, within minutes she knew she could not live with a man who laughed like a donkey. The strange *heehaw* sound he made after each witticism was making her laugh, which convinced him of his cleverness. In fact, his bons mots were quite witty, and he was an intelligent, responsible man, so it was all rather sad.

For a moment she thought of taking him on as a challenge and somehow training him to laugh differently, or in fact, not to laugh at his own jokes at all. She stamped on that notion. She could imagine nothing more foolish than to go into marriage as an act of charity.

Pity in reverse. Horrible.

Her husband must not have a dominating mother. She made that resolution when she was again ambushed by Lady Flawborough, Mr. Pitt-Meadowing in tow, trying to ensure that he took Anne into supper.

Pitt-Meadowing was an unlikely contender in any case. He had the bloodlines, but no fortune or likelihood of making one. He was a pure fortune hunter. There were plenty of those in the upper ranks of society, and she wanted no part of them. Her husband must have a purpose in life other than to spend her money. She gave Tris a warm smile when he rescued her.

He found them a table and went to gather some food for her—an honor that would make most ladies swoon. Sad, really, that they did not suit. She could only pray that he one day find the perfect wife. She had little hope of finding the perfect husband.

Then a stir made her glance to the door. She felt her eyes widen. There was Uffham with Miss Rolleston-Stowe on his arm. Race de Vere came behind with giggly Miss Cottesly, Diane Rolleston-Stowe's adoring bosom-bow, on his arm.

Lady Fortescue must be in alt. Two eligible ducal prospects at her ball. For her part, Anne felt as Frances must have when she soaked her chair—shocked and unable to act.

In fact Lady Fortescue looked as stunned as Anne felt. Perhaps she feared a full-scale hunt, bitches in cry. Anne bit her lip to prevent any hint of that thought escaping, but she could only watch as Uffham hailed her as if she was his savior, and hurried over.

"Come to see how you're doing," he said, seating his partner in one of the spare chairs and taking the other. He seemed to be sweating slightly. Miss Rolleston-Stowe did have a very hunting-hound look on her face.

There were only four chairs at the table. De Vere commandeered two from nearby and seated Miss Cottesly, who giggled.

He said, "Good evening, Lady Anne," but then went off to the buffet tables, presumably to collect food for all four. No wonder Uffham was so fond of him. The man was indispensable.

But not, she thought sternly, *to me.*

She saw Tris notice de Vere and exchange some comments. She wished she could hear what they were. Mere pleasantries, or some inquisition? Tris had, after all, said that de Vere was interested in her.

Despite will, despite sense, the sizzle of excitement had started. If she wasn't careful, she was going to make as much of a fool of herself over de Vere as the other two ladies were doing over Uffham.

Tris and de Vere turned from the tables together. De Vere seemed to have solved his logistical problem by finding a large platter and loading it with food and bringing along the plates. Anne had to laugh. He was outrageous, but ingenious.

It was only as he put his collection down that she realized that the two empty places at the table were to either side of her. Of course. Uffham was opposite, bracketed by his hounds.

Tris gave her a plate of carefully selected food and sat to her right. De Vere sat to her left and chose items from the platter for Miss Cottesly. Who giggled. A footman came by with the wine and filled their glasses.

Interestingly, Anne didn't feel the same challenge shooting through from the men to either side of her. Was Tris not worried, or was de Vere not interested?

De Vere ate a little pâté, then said, "It's a pleasure to see you again, Lady Anne."

She would be cool and rational. "We saw one another last night, Mr. de Vere."

"True, but it is still a pleasure to see you again."

As she tried to assess that, Uffham made a remark about Berkshire and horse racing, which was apparently where they had been after Portsmouth and yachting.

When Uffham and Tris started swapping horse stories, she said, "I hope the racing was enjoyable, Mr. de Vere."

"Tolerably so, Lady Anne. I—"

"Tolerably!" Uffham interrupted, helping himself to another lobster patty. "Won a fifty guinea purse racing against that big black stallion of Arden's!"

"I did have a horse," said de Vere mildly. Then he added, "and the stallion had to carry a rider. Fair's fair."

Anne almost choked on a crumb. She knew why Uffham liked to have him around.

"I let him ride my Trafalgar," Uffham said. "Rides lighter than I do, and it paid off."

"Cavalry, de Vere?" asked Tris.

"Yes, Your Grace."

"St. Raven, please. I didn't think Arden's Viking was beatable. Was he riding?"

"Came over from his place at Hartwell." Uffham summoned the footman for more wine. "Wife's almost in the straw. I knew Trafalgar had it in him to beat Viking, and by gad, we proved it." He raised his glass. "To Trafalgar!"

They all drank, but Tris added, "And to his rider."

Anne smiled her thanks to him, but at his fixed look she knew it wasn't wise. She didn't know what Tris would do if he thought she was seriously interested in de Vere. Have him abducted to the Antipodes, probably.

Uffham leaned to inspect the platter. "I say, de Vere, those lobster patties were dashed tasty. Go and find me a few more, that's a good fellow."

Anne longed for de Vere to tell Uffham to forage for himself, but he rose and went off, just like a good and faithful servant.

"I admire your staff, Lady Anne," said Diane Rolleston-Stowe. "I wish I had an excuse to carry one, too."

Anne looked at her. "Really?"

The blond beauty blushed. "A sprained ankle or such, I mean."

The creature was trying to make an impression that would help her in her hunt for Uffham, but this was a pathetic effort. "If you sprain your ankle, Miss Rolleston-Stowe, you'd be better advised to stay at home with a cold compress on it."

"Take that advice," Tris said, drawing all the fire of the big green eyes. What was the heir to a dukedom, when an actual duke spoke to her?

"Oh, I'm sure, Your Grace," she gasped. "So kind. Of course, I hope not to sprain my ankle at all."

"Not until after marriage, at least."

"No, Your Grace?"

Anne recognized the wicked glint in his eyes and wondered what was coming.

"It's cant for getting with child, Miss Rolleston-Stowe," Tris explained.

The poor lady went pink, and Anne pinched Tris under the table on the nearest spot. His thigh. Which

meant there was hardly anything to pinch. She was sure
it was the same with de Vere's thighs. . . .

She was going mad.

"I say, St. Raven," Uffham objected.

"I say, indeed," said Anne. "We ladies do not need
to know such things."

"Yes, you do." Tris was not at all deterred. "Then
people won't be able to play tricks on you with double
meanings."

The two hounds giggled.

Giggling hounds. She *was* going to go mad.

Uffham was quite eclipsed by Tris, and in typical con-
trary manner, was looking peevish about it. "Where the
hell's de Vere?" he demanded, disregarding good manners entirely.

Anne couldn't take any more of this. She rose, which
meant Tris had to rise and leave with her.

In the corridor he said, "Are you all right?"

"Perfectly."

"Be honest. Is it de Vere?"

She looked him in the eye. "No. If I'm upset it's because I've realized that I absolutely have to marry. One
day Uffham is going to be caught in the slavering jaws
of one of those bitches, and I have no intention of being
the quiet sister-in-law under her paw."

"Bravo! But don't make a foolish choice out of urgency, Mouse."

She suspected that he was warning her off de Vere,
and of course, he was quite right. "I won't, I promise."

That day established a pattern for her life, a pattern
that soon came to feel worse than a treadmill. Morning
visits, the park, and one or two events in the evening.
As usual, she enjoyed the theater, the lectures, and
the musical soirées. However, too many of the events
Caroline dragged her to were those designed for people to see and be seen. The same people, over and
over.

They said the same things over and over, too, and yet
they all seemed so pleased with themselves. It was indeed like a play—one that was repeated day after day,
night after night. *The Daring Lady* was a great success,

still running after three weeks. Did actors weary of their parts? Especially when the most exciting player left the theater.

Right after the Fortescue ball, Uffham had gone to a house party in Oxfordshire, taking his favorite companion with him.

Fifteen

~

Anne met de Vere again nearly two weeks later at the Swinamer ball.

She arrived in some distress, for she'd foolishly agreed to attend a rout first. She always avoided them because they involved nothing more than walking and standing, but it had presented a challenge, so she'd insisted. To make matters worse, she was too vain to wear her supportive shoe for evening events.

At the Swinamers', she went up the stairs with Caroline and Welsford, trying not to limp more than usual, greeted their hosts, and passed into the ballroom. Or rooms. The Swinamers had elected not to hire assembly rooms for this event but didn't really have a large enough house for the number of guests they had invited.

They'd cleared three linked rooms in their house to serve, but the rooms were already crowded and likely to become more so. Worse, Anne immediately noticed that there were an inadequate number of chairs.

She longed to claim one, but few were sitting yet and she didn't want to be so obvious. She stood, more grateful than usual for her staff, and let the men come to her.

Lord Alderton hurried over with flattering speed. His confidence was growing, and she really must consider him. He was pleasantly ordinary in looks, with soft brown hair and a long nose. He wasn't at all overwhelming, which she liked. He didn't excite her in any way, but she refused to be sad about that. Presumably that would come in time.

No other man eclipsed him.

She watched the chairs begin to fill. Eventually she

said, "Perhaps you could escort me to a chair, Alderton."

Pleased as a dog asked to perform a trick, he crooked his arm for her and led her tenderly to a group of empty chairs. "Which one would you like, Lady Anne?"

This seemed so silly she had to bite her lip, but she thanked him and settled in the middle one. Immediately, as if someone had rung a dinner bell, she was surrounded by men. They blocked her view of the dance floor, and in moments they had moved the chairs to either side of her and filled that space, too.

Panic struck for a moment, but then she pushed it aside. She wasn't going to be eaten by ravening dogs tonight, even if Marlowe's grinning teeth were right in front of her.

"Lord Marlowe," she said, "my foot is aching most terribly. Could you find me a footstool?"

He reared back like a horse at this unwelcome command, but went, as he must.

"Please," she said quickly to the men who were pushing in to fill the space, "don't block my view of the dance floor, gentlemen."

A small space was left, jealously guarded. Anne peered through it, looking for help. She wished Tris were here, but he disliked balls as much as Uffham, and for the same reason, so she'd not asked him. She couldn't see Caroline or Welsford.

Besides, she should be able to handle this on her own.

She hated to be such a center of attention, however. She knew everyone must be aware of the ridiculous scene, and all the young ladies must be grinding their teeth. She didn't even want most of these men!

Then Lord Osmunde, rotund heir to the Earl of Balbeckstone, threw himself prostrate on the floor and beseeched her to rest her foot on him.

Straight out, her foot would have to go on his ample bottom.

"Get up, Osmunde. Please!"

She looked around for help, and her eyes collided with the laughing ones of Race de Vere across the room. Heat surged into her face, but she had to bite her lip not to smile for simple pleasure.

He was here!

"Like Lord Raleigh, you know," Osmunde said.

She pulled her attention back. "He only laid his cloak over a puddle, Osmunde."

"There, see!" He leaped to his feet with admirable agility for someone of his size. "He should have laid his person. Doubtless have won a title for it, and then King James wouldn't have topped him, eh? Ancestor of mine on me mother's side."

Clearly he didn't feel at all ridiculous. How did people like him have such thick skins?

"Please, gentlemen, do not let me prevent you from dancing."

They didn't move. She prayed for the dance music to start. Presumably then Lady Swinamer would command some of them into duty. She glanced across the room again, but de Vere had disappeared.

Had he been a figment of her imagination?

Was she going mad?

Osmunde moved into her precious gap. "I would like to watch the dancing, sir."

He shuffled to the right. Other men shuffled around, trying not to lose place. In a moment, she was going to scream.

Race de Vere walked through the opening as if the men had parted just for him, went to one knee, and placed a cloth-wrapped object in front of her. It was exactly the right height for a footstool, but since this was de Vere, anything could be under the purple brocade.

"What is it?" she asked, heart thundering. As well as his presence, she was panicked by fear of being even more outrageous. Oh, for the days when she had faded into the wallpaper.

Still on one knee he met her eyes, a twinkle saying that he knew what she was thinking. "Quite safe, Lady Anne, and it won't get you into trouble."

Then he took her foot by the heel, thus by the shoe, thus not quite touching her skin, and placed it on the object. Tingles shot right up her leg to alarming effect.

The impromptu footstool was even padded. A cushion of some sort?

She didn't dare look to see how all the titled gentlemen around her were taking this interloper, but she tried to make light of it. "If I had a title to bestow, Mr. de Vere, you would have it."

"Fool," someone muttered as suggestion.

Anne extended her hand to de Vere. "Hero," she said.

"You honor me, my lady." He kissed her hand, but then he rose, still holding it. She tugged and could not break free. She should have known not to encourage the wretch.

"However," he said, "heroes have a high casualty rate. I would rather be your fool. As your fool I could sit at your feet and amuse you while these highborn gentlemen do their duty by young ladies who are able to dance."

As if on cue, the musicians signaled the first dance. He released her hand and suited action to words by subsiding, cross-legged, to the floor.

She bit her lip. The wretch was going to have her laughing out loud. When she was in control, she smiled around at her looming suitors. "Alas, sirs, he's correct. The music is starting, and you cannot ask me to be so selfish as to claim all your attention when other ladies wish to dance."

She was reinforced, thank heavens, by Lady Swinamer, who descended upon them, smile fixed. "My dear sirs, you must take turns sitting by Lady Anne and be kind to the other ladies." She seized two by the arms and dragged them away.

Fearing the same fate, the others followed, all jealously watching to see that no other stole a move by staying. De Vere obviously didn't count. As the lines formed for the dance Anne found herself alone for a little while, with only him, still sitting by her chair.

She fixed her gaze on the dancers. "Do please get up, Mr. de Vere. You make me feel like a figure of fun."

"You, Lady Anne?" But he rose, neatly rearranged the chairs to either side of her, then sat on her left. It was all done so smoothly and efficiently that she became breathless. And by now she was watching him.

Here was trouble again, and yet she couldn't be sorry.

It was as if someone had added a thousand candles to the chandeliers.

The other seats around were instantly taken, but she was glad to see deaf old Lady Leveson on her right side.

"What is supporting my foot?" Anne asked.

"Four of Sir John Swinamer's weightier tomes, covered by a cushion and a small curtain."

Anne's eyes widened and she shifted her foot to the floor. "Sir John's collection of ancient books is quite famous, you know."

"Is it?" But then his false shock turned to humor. "You are not abusing his Gutenberg and Caxton, dear lady, merely some volumes of decades-old sermons."

She put her foot back with relief, but still wondered what might happen if Lord Swinamer realized what was going on. He was famously proud and protective of his library.

"He has a first folio of Shakespeare, I believe," she said.

"You tempt me to go exploring again. . . ."

When the first dance of the set ended Anne emerged from an entrancing discussion of books. She blinked at de Vere, almost dazed. "I assume Uffham is here."

"Am I not a barnacle? Besides, they wouldn't admit me otherwise."

"Come, come, you are hardly such an outsider as that."

"Am I not?"

In fact, he was. "You are certainly a miracle worker to persuade Uffham to step into this lions' den."

His smile was quick and delightful. "Lady Swinamer's ball as a recreation of the Coliseum! The evening will be perfect if Miss Swinamer and Miss Rolleston-Stowe come to blows over Uffham. I think I will design a new sort of fan—with spikes at the end of the spokes."

She rapped him with her own unarmed fan, then wished she hadn't. It seemed shockingly intimate.

He clearly didn't think so. He was as relaxed as a happy cat. "In fact Uffham is here to give you moral support . . ."

She raised her brows and looked around.

". . . but at the moment is gathering his courage in the gaming room. Playing hazard, perhaps. We could join him there."

A connection shot between them. "I doubt they'd accept farthing points."

"I could bank you. I'm good for about fifty guineas at the moment."

"Your winnings at racing?"

He smiled. "Precisely."

Was that truly all he had in the world? The clothes she wore had cost more than that. It reminded her that he did not belong on her list of suitors, amusing and interesting though he was.

What did she know about him? He had admitted to being the oldest son, and he presumably had the de Vere blood somewhere on the family tree. Not the sort of man she was expected to marry, but not completely impossible.

As she indulged in these outrageous thoughts, she watched the dancing, enjoying the swirl and sway of it. Sometimes at home, at private parties, she danced the simpler measures. She knew she was inelegant, but she enjoyed it. Inelegant steps, inelegant marriage . . .

She glanced to her side. "Are you fixed in London long, Mr. de Vere?"

"Perhaps you should ask your brother."

"Nonsense. You will leave when it suits you. When will that be?"

"I am a creature of whim, remember. And a fool."

"I doubt that, too." Desperately, she added, "Will you not tell me something real about yourself?"

"I am no mystery."

"Yet you are here in poverty, almost a servant, while an oldest son. Is your rift with your father so unhealable?"

Then she wished it all unsaid. Something in his eyes suggested that her question stung.

He replied calmly, however. "Not at all. We have met and blood did not run. It is simply that my father has grand ambitions for his line which I do not share. I was not, and am not, a good and dutiful son."

"You surprise me," she said dryly. "What are his plans?"

But he shook his head. "I escaped into the army, and he's never forgiven me."

There were many questions she'd like answered, but it was clear he would tell her only what he chose. "How did you escape, then? He must have tried to stop you."

He relaxed, which was when she realized that he had been tense. Since the mention of being the oldest son. Why? What question had he feared? Her curiosity about Race de Vere was as dangerous as opium, but like an opium-eater, she could not resist.

"He tried, but too late. My ally was my uncle, Colonel Edward Racecombe." He shifted to turn to her, now seeming lightly amused. "I was army mad, and Uncle Edward persuaded my father that a visit to a barracks would cure me. He was recruiting at the time, and when he sailed for Portugal, he took me with him."

She stared at him. "Wasn't that illegal?"

"Highly, but the Horse Guards weren't eager to release a new recruit, and my father did not have the influence to force the matter."

She saw him weigh whether to tell her something or not, and prayed hard that no one interrupt. If he was hesitating, it must be of importance.

"My father, you see, won a lottery."

She gaped. "Truly? I've bought tickets sometimes for fun, but I've never known anyone who won."

His lips twitched. "Now, indirectly, you do. He decided to take his fortune and become a gentleman. He bought an estate, and a wife. But first," he added, and she sensed the important thing coming, "he changed his name."

"Not de Vere," she breathed.

"I told you the truth when I said I was a de Vere born of a de Vere, but he wasn't born a de Vere. Thus he had nothing to throw into the battle. No powerful relatives, no influential friends, and not even much money. By then it had been sunk into house, land, and the trappings of a gentleman. By the time he'd bludgeoned the officials to write to my uncle about it, I'd been serving for six months."

"What happened then?"

"I was summoned into the presence of Sir Arthur Wellesley and asked whether I wished to serve king and country or go home. The implication was clear that if I answered the latter, I deserved to be shot, but I didn't want it anyway. I'd flown the coop and on the whole was having a marvelous time. The last thing I wanted was to return to the cage."

Her heart warmed at the intimacy of the moment, the trust implied in what he was telling her, but then a chill trickled after.

Now she knew. There was no de Vere blood. He was not a gentleman in any way her circle would understand the term. He did not even have right to the name he carried. He was beyond the pale—and, she suspected, that was why he had told her all these things. Had her reaction to his reappearance, her fledgling hopes, been so obvious that he felt he must warn her off?

She swallowed and grasped their conversation as refuge. "All this at sixteen," she said, wafting her fan. "Without influence or money, it must have been hard."

"You will insist on trying to make a romance out of this, won't you? I had my uncle, don't forget, until he fell at Burgos. And my father began sending me a quarterly draft for a hundred guineas. If I was to be an officer, I was to do the *nouvelle* de Veres proud. I'm afraid he still doesn't fully realize what an unfortunate choice of name that was."

"Have you not considered reverting to the real one?"

He laughed. She wasn't quite sure why. "What is real?"

Not this. The current set of dances was ending. Their time was almost at an end.

"Is the Duke of St. Raven not here?" he asked.

"No. Why?"

"I would trust him to protect you from the ravening mass of asses."

Strictly in the manner of light flirtation, she asked, "Are you not going to, sir?"

"I don't have the firepower. Here comes Lord Marlowe, teeth and footstool to the fore."

She looked through the dancing couples, and there indeed was the heavy-muscled man, bearing a footstool. In moments he would have to see that she already had one of sorts.

De Vere slipped to one knee again and reversed his procedure, gently lifting her foot off the books and putting it on the floor. It occurred to her for the first time that he must finally have had a good look at her ugly, twisted foot.

She looked down and met his eyes, his serious eyes.

"If it wouldn't embarrass you, Anne, I would kiss it." Instead, he took her hand. "Pretend, if you will, that this is your poor foot."

His lips pressed, gentle and in some strange way healing. Ridiculous though it was, she felt that if Race de Vere could stroke and kiss her foot it would instantly straighten.

And he had called her Anne. . . .

Then he rose and walked away, his bundle borne before him like a holy relic. The cream of society parted before him, staring. Then they turned to stare at her.

Anne hated it, but she didn't hate what had just happened.

Now, however, she had Marlowe placing a proper footstool before her. She praised his resourcefulness, but that didn't prevent complaints about de Vere.

"Damned impudence. Who is he, anyway? De Vere? Pretentious upstart."

"He served excellently in the war, Lord Marlowe."

"By his own account, I suppose."

"Not at all. Many men have spoken well of him."

Marlowe frowned, but then said, "Come to think of it, saw him hunting this year. Good rider."

"Cavalry, I gather."

"Suppose so." He took possession of the chair to her right. "Saw him out on one of Cavanagh's horses one day. Almost bought the beast." He settled into hunting stories, and she could smile and nod and think her own thoughts.

She knew that in the Shires at hunting time a great

deal of horse trading went on. Men who wanted to sell their horses would sometimes hire excellent riders to ride them in a hunt to show them off to best advantage. Roughriders, they were called.

She supposed that was another way de Vere had been making money. It wasn't to his discredit, but it was worlds apart. Perhaps he gambled, as well. Tris hadn't known, but he might be discovering such things now. Perhaps he was even a libertine. He'd been free enough with his kisses.

Rats, mice, and farthings.

The dance ended, and Marlowe surrendered his place to young Lord Laverly who required rather more conversational assistance. Or at least, he expected clear agreement every few moments.

She agreed that the music was loud, the rooms crowded and far too hot. She sympathized on his headache. Then he asked for her favorite headache remedy.

When she confessed that she never had any, he sighed. "You are blessed with a sturdier constitution than I, Lady Anne."

He didn't look particularly frail, but now she noticed how pale and puffy he was.

"Perhaps you need more fresh air, Laverly. I find a brisk ride clears most complaints."

He shuddered. "But this weather. It has been so inclement. Sciatica, dear lady. Been a martyr to it all my life."

Since he couldn't be much older than she was, she didn't believe him. She could trump his complaint with her foot, which also ached in the damp and which truly had plagued her all her life, but he wasn't worth the bother. He'd probably claim a fatal disease just to win the hand.

Mentally, however, she was scribbling black lines through his name on her husband list. She couldn't bear a hypochondriac.

She knew he collected glass, so she ruthlessly switched the subject to that. Soon she was back into nodding and smiling as he lectured her on the mysteries of colored stemware.

That was when she saw that Race de Vere was dancing. Wonderfully. His army life must have included such things. Officers were expected to play their part at social events. It wasn't that he performed and posed as some dancers did, but simply that he was athletic, graceful, and clearly did not have to think about the steps. It was an eight, and as he wove his way through the ladies she watched each lose a bit of her heart to his flirtatious smile.

Then she noticed that one of the ladies in his eight was Phoebe Swinamer. In fact Miss Swinamer was his partner.

Now that was strange.

Phoebe Swinamer was a raving beauty with a high opinion of herself. It was well known that she intended to marry as high as possible, which was why she was still unwed. Not for lack of offers, but because none yet had been quite to her standard. She had also doubtless driven some away. She was so cold and self-centered that even the most dazzled earl, marquess, or duke had to notice eventually.

Anne smiled and murmured some response to Laverly, but mostly she watched Phoebe wind her way through the dance, completely aware of every graceful pose she struck. The beauty wore the blank smile of a china doll until she interacted with someone she thought important, whereupon her brilliant smile flashed out.

Every time she danced with de Vere, that smile shone.

At de Vere? Anne was sure that in Phoebe Swinamer's judgment he was less than a flea. Was his charm powerful enough to dazzle that ruthless mind?

Oh, Lord, she suddenly thought, Uffham!

De Vere was Pheobe's key to Uffham.

And Uffham was just possibly stupid enough to be caught in the trap.

". . . dropped dead right under me. Shattered my nerves."

"What?" Anne turned and stared at Lord Laverly.

"Barbary Wench."

"What?"

"Heart. No sign, of course. And now Dancing Girl has the scours."

She realized he had switched to talking about horses.

A more interesting subject to her, but she did not want to listen to a recitation of poor Dancing Girl's revolting symptoms. What was more, she needed to check on Uffham and talk to de Vere.

"Speaking of bowels . . . ," she most indelicately said, then rose to walk away. She couldn't help but delight in the shocked look on his face. This London season was going to drive her into lunacy.

Sixteen

Anne found the gaming room where mostly older people were seated at card tables. She realized then that, of course, no one was playing hazard. Dice games were technically illegal, and certainly improper. Gambling was illegal, but no one paid attention to that. Most people were playing whist for penny points. One table was playing brag, a much simpler game, and Uffham was there.

She went to stand by him. He looked up and smiled. "What ho the sister. Enjoying yourself?"

"It's a ball, Uffham, and I can't dance. I've just escaped a bore."

"Good for you. Want to play?"

The other men looked a little taken aback, and she was tempted to accept just to shock them. "No, thank you. You won't be dancing, then?"

The whites of his eyes showed. "I should think not. Only came to show the flag for you."

She didn't see how sitting in the card room was doing her any good, but she thanked him and went on her way sure that he was safe for a while. She'd confer with Caroline later and find a long-term strategy to avoid the Swinamer trap.

De Vere was the one who could do the most good, however, and she needed to alert him. She was surprised that he'd been drawn in so far as to dance with Miss Swinamer, but it was possible he'd been fooled. She was startlingly beautiful, with her glossy dark curls, perfect complexion, and large blue eyes. Last year she'd almost hooked Lord Arden, heir to the Duke of Belcraven, but he'd escaped.

A string twanged in the back of her head. Arden was one of the Rogues. She remembered, too, that Mrs. Hard-castle had been his mistress before his marriage.

All useless information since he was safely married. She did a quick mental review of the names Uffham had given her to be sure there were no lurking Rogues among her suitors. She would not be married out of pity.

Sir Stephen Ball. She knew him slightly, so he couldn't take her unawares. Major Beaumont, apparently current protector of Mrs. Hardcastle. Who else? A Simon St. Bride. For a moment she toyed with the idea of de Vere being St. Bride in disguise, but then she shook her head. People knew him, people who had known him for years, and besides, despite the occasional mystery, she was sure that he spoke the truth.

She was safe from Rogues, but for respite from the pests she went to the ladies' room. She tidied herself, chatting to a couple of women who were resting there, feet up. It didn't require a deformed foot for them to ache. When a flurry of ladies came in, she knew the set had ended. Now to find de Vere.

She went out to hunt, but didn't have to hunt at all. She almost ran into him in the corridor.

"I wanted to talk to you." It spilled out brashly, so she added, "About Uffham."

He crooked his arm for her. "Of course, Lady Anne. There is a problem?"

She put her hand on his arm, aware of how much even this restrained touch affected her. It was a strictly physical thing, but quite extraordinary. Shouldn't it mean something to him, too?

She had to find out.

"Not here." She smiled as if they spoke of the weather. "You mentioned a library. Is it nearby?"

He looked at her, and she saw wariness. She gave a light laugh. "My dear sir, I have no designs on your virtue!"

It was true. She wasn't planning to tear off his clothes.

She had to fight wild giggles at the thought as he led her along the corridor and around a bend to a set of quiet stairs to the ground floor. There, he opened a door, peeped in, and then widened it for her. She entered a book-filled room lit only by one well-shielded lamp.

Anne came to her senses. What on earth did she think she was doing? She knew young ladies who made an art of going apart with men at these events, but she'd never, ever done it before.

"We should leave the door open," she said.

"Most certainly." He was still by the door, in fact, distancing himself.

She fluttered her fan. "Come now, sir, you can't possibly think I will try to compromise you. What would be the point?"

His lips twitched. "None at all." He came a few steps closer. "So, Uffham?"

Pity take her, she'd been arch to protect her pride, and rude, as well. There was no point in apologizing, however. It was all true. He was a nobody, and they had no connection except Uffham.

"Phoebe Swinamer," she said.

"You're worried that Miss Swinamer is on Uffham's trail. Correct, of course, but I think I've distracted her for the moment."

She rolled her eyes. "Mr. de Vere, no matter how fascinating you are, you will not draw Phoebe Swinamer off the track of one of the only ducal prospects around."

He was unoffended. "True, but I argued St. Raven's case. I pointed out that he was already a duke, and that he had confided to me that he wanted to marry as soon as possible."

Anne stared at him. "Did he?"

"Of course not."

"He'll throttle you!"

His lips twitched. "Like all the rest, he'll have to catch me first. And I'm sure he can cope with the Swinamers of the world." He sobered. "Does it bother you?"

"Me? No, why?"

"I think you would suit."

"St. Raven and I? We certainly would not."

"Perhaps you need to open your mind to the idea, Lady Anne. He is not your brother. He's no blood relation at all."

He was advising her to marry another man!

But she thought she heard ambivalence, and she could not forget the way he had handled her foot, kissed her hand, and called her Anne.

Stealing time, she turned to look at the shelves. "Did you say there was a Gutenberg?"

"Yes, but it's locked in that case along with the other treasures."

She went to peer through metal-barred glass. "I'm not used to being locked out of such things."

"And I'm not used to being let in. We should return to the company."

She turned to study him. "Why do you keep hammering home the differences between us?"

His brows rose. "Isn't it more that they simply exist?"

Unable to resist, she limped toward him. "I don't know if they matter."

His face became a mask, a smiling handsome mask concealing everything. "You have only to ask anyone of your acquaintance."

"Perhaps I don't care."

"That my father was a carriage maker?"

She stopped dead. A *carriage maker?* She licked her lips. "Perhaps no one need know."

It was, of course, the wrong thing to say.

Pity. That was the emotion behind his slight smile. "It's the sort of thing to come out, particularly if society's curiosity is stirred."

That should settle it—she couldn't marry the son of a carriage maker—but being close to him, private and close, seemed to make such harsh realities evaporate. Her skin tingled, and the need to touch was almost overwhelming. She put her gloved left hand on his jacket, slid it up to his shoulder.

He captured it with his own, pulled it away. But he didn't let it go. Instead he kissed it.

If only she wasn't wearing gloves.

"What is this?" she whispered.

"Folly." But he let her hand drop, pushed shut the door, and pulled her into his arms.

The kiss was everything she remembered and more, swirling down and around her like heat and honey, satisfying places that had longed for this for weeks. The taste—his taste—was a feast for the starving. She lost her grip on her staff, but he caught it and propped it up against the wall.

When he drew her close again, she raised her hands to cradle his head the better to explore him with lips, with tongue, with every inch of her sizzling body.

His mouth, hotly, hungrily on hers.

His hands, pulling her harder and harder against his hard body.

She wanted more. She crushed against him urgently, achingly, longing to fuse with him in some impossible way. . . .

She only realized when he broke the kiss to suck in air that she'd driven him up against the door. Their eyes met. Were hers as dark and desperate as his?

Suddenly he reversed their positions, driving her hard against wood panels. He grasped her chin and held her for a brutal kiss.

Brutal?

Race?

But there was something different here. Her back hurt where an edge dug into her spine and his hot mouth attacked her, his tongue thrusting deep and hard.

Then she felt his hand on her thigh, on her skin there. He had her skirt up!

No! She tried to shake her head free, to escape, to scream for help.

His lips freed hers, but his hand replaced them, blocking sound. His other hand slid between her thighs.

"Not what you want?" asked this demonic stranger.

She shook her head desperately.

"Are you sure? You did entice me here, after all. . . ."

She could only shake her head and swallow tears.

He moved one hand but kept the other over her mouth. "Far be it from me to force a lady fair. A warning, though. If you scream you could cause me a great deal of trouble, but it's just possible that you'd end up married to me, and you don't want that, do you?"

Emphatically, she shook her head.

He took away his hand and stepped back, smiling.

Anne slapped him with all the strength she had. Then

she grabbed for her staff in order to hit him harder. He was there before her and moved it out of reach.

"You'd regret it later," he said, still smiling. "I'll leave it outside."

Then he left and she sagged back against the shelves, scrubbing at her wet face. *Oh, Lord, the paint.* There was no mirror here, but she had a handkerchief tucked away. She blotted her face as best she could, trying to swamp the turmoil of feelings that burned like lye.

Her hand still stung, but she was glad, so glad, that she'd hit him like that. It was tempting to tell Uffham or Tris, who'd thrash him properly, but guilt stayed her.

She had inveigled him in here, and it hadn't really been to talk about Uffham. Unacknowledged, she'd hoped for something, for kisses, and perhaps a little more than kisses. He had held back, and she had pushed.

Pushed him over the edge.

She knew the truth now, however. At bottom he was no gentleman. He'd said she should try out a husband's kisses before committing herself, and he was clearly right.

She sucked in some deep breaths and checked her hair and headdress by feel. All seemed fine. She opened the door and peeped out into the corridor. No one was about, but her staff, as promised, leaned against the wall. She grasped it, feeling complete again, glad all in all that he'd stopped her from murdering him with it.

A bubble of wild laughter threatened. That would be a ridiculous end to her ridiculous season.

She made her cumbersome way up the quiet stairs again, then realized that they brought her out on a bedroom corridor. Taking a risk, she opened a door and was rewarded by a deserted bedroom, and a mirror. When she saw herself she gave thanks that she had checked. Her eye color had smudged, and strands of hair were sticking out. As well scream to the world about what had happened.

There was half a jug of cold washing water, enough to repair her face, though it meant removing most of her false bloom. She did away with it entirely. What good had it done her so far?

She pinned up her hair and surveyed Lady Anne

Peckworth, more like her old self, but in fine feathers. Race de Vere had said something about flying high, and warned of the possibility of disaster.

Now she knew what he'd meant. Inside her growled a place that had enjoyed his fierce assault, that had slapped him because she'd enjoyed it more than was decent. A place that wanted to fling herself out of her lofty tower and try to fly.

But Icarus's fine feathers, she remembered, had melted in the heat, and Icarus had died.

Seventeen

~

Two days later Uffham came round to Caroline's in the pouring rain to complain that "damned de Vere" had left with hardly a by-your-leave to go heaven knows where, and what the devil was he to do without him? Life was so flat.

Looking at rain-drenched windows, Anne could only agree, but her life had been flat since de Vere's outrageous behavior. Now, apparently, he had truly walked off the stage.

"Perhaps he's gone home to Derbyshire," she suggested.

Uffham frowned. "Do you think so? Never mentioned it. I wouldn't have minded a trip to Derbyshire."

Who was the barnacle on whom? It would seem de Vere pulled men to him as well as women.

"If he's gone there, it will be on personal business," Caroline said. "He might not want a stranger present."

"You think he'll be back?"

"Why not? And I do hope so. He's excellent company."

Anne looked out at the rain knowing that he wouldn't return. She had to be glad of it. She was now free to apply herself wholeheartedly to choosing among more appropriate gentlemen. There had to be at least one who was tolerable.

Five men had already asked her if they could approach her father. She'd told them all that she wasn't ready to make a decision yet, but in truth they'd all been impossible.

Alderton had not yet asked, but she suspected that

she could have him any time she chose to encourage him. Not yet. Not yet. There had to be some man in her world who could stir a trace of the same excitement as de Vere, but her time was almost up. The season was almost over.

Perhaps her practice of riding in the park was hindering some prospects. Not everyone kept a riding horse in town and besides, riding in a group did not give an amorous gentleman many opportunities.

Moreover, her equestrian abilities had caused some other ladies to copy her. Poor Miss Cottesly had been thrown and received not the sprained ankle she'd wished for, but a nasty bang on the head.

Anne decided that as soon as the weather cleared she would drive instead. She'd be able to take gentlemen up with her and give them a fairer chance.

So she sent to Lea Park for her phaeton and matched grays, and when they arrived she tooled them into Hyde Park. She had to admit to enjoying the stares and even exclamations, and thanked Tris for pressing her to learn to drive so many years ago.

As if summoned by her thought, she saw Tris with a group of men. De Vere was not among them. Of course not. She groaned that the thought had even crossed her mind.

Tris smiled and summoned her to stop. When she obeyed, he climbed in.

"You're not driving," she said, setting off again.

"Why would I want to, though I do admire your team. Are they for sale?"

"Of course not."

"Pity. Glad to see you still have all your skills, though."

"Thank you. Not that there's much chance to show them here."

"Devil a bit. Managing not to lock wheels with the other carriages requires finesse. So, how's the assault? I hear that you nearly created a riot at the Swinamers' the other night."

"Nonsense, though the men behaved badly. It's pure competition with most of them, I swear it. I don't think more than half are seriously interested in marriage."

"Probably not. We're a terrible lot for wanting the other dog's bone. So, who leads the pack?"

Wearily, she said, "Alderton."

"There's a bit of the season left yet."

She supposed that summed it up.

She tried to resist but couldn't. "That de Vere has left Uffham, casting my poor brother into despair."

"He wasn't in despair last night, but then, he was in female company."

She glanced at him. "Do I want to know?"

"Probably, but I'm not about to tell you."

"Of course not. You were there, too."

"Precisely."

She growled at him. "I don't understand men."

"Good."

"How am I to make a rational choice if I don't understand what's going on?"

"Watch the road." When she obeyed he added, "Listen to your male relatives."

He ran through her most obvious suitors, tagging some as rats, mice, or farthings, but leaving over half acceptable, including Alderton. She longed to ask if he'd checked on de Vere, and if so what he'd found, but she had enough control to resist.

"Time for me to get down," he said. "A queue is forming."

Anne slowed her horses and saw that he was correct. A number of men were standing around obviously waiting to replace him.

"They look like children queuing for pony rides at a country fair," she murmured. "I'm tempted to charge them a penny each."

He laughed. "Charge Sir Pomfret de Court a farthing."

She surveyed the group. "I see. And Marlowe probably eats rats for breakfast."

"I can believe that."

"Good."

He swung down from the vehicle. "Step right up, gentlemen. Step right up! One ride a guinea, all to go to charity."

Anne was tempted to flick him with her long whip,

but she laughed and took the guinea offered by Sir Pomfret, and set off on another circuit of the park.

Race had cut free of Anne Peckworth and London and ridden south into Sussex, heading for sanctuary at Somerford Court. He was, after all, still technically employed as secretary to Con Somerford, Viscount Amleigh. He'd parted from Con over a month ago, forced to miss Con's wedding because of the need to make contact with Lady Anne before the news broke.

He wondered what Con would think of his recent work. He hoped he never heard the whole of it.

As it happened, he met his employer three miles from the Court, not far off the London Road. Con—dark-haired, handsome, and steady—was riding out of the lane to Mitchell's farm. Race ran a quick assessment and was pleased. The steadiness that had made Con an excellent officer was still there, but now it blended with an ease that spoke of a contented country gentleman and husband.

"The wanderer returns," Con said amiably.

Race drew Joker to a halt. "I left work undone."

"I tell you, young man, the work is never done."

Con turned his horse ambling toward home, and Race fell in beside him. "The burden of the married state aging you? If not, I'm only two years your junior."

Con smiled. "You don't act it, gadding about wherever you please. So, what have you been up to? 'Matters to attend to' isn't very informative."

"I've been tidying up Lady Anne Peckworth."

Con looked at him. "I don't recall her being particularly disordered. What have you done?"

That was the officer speaking. Race knew he was on tricky ground. "Nothing to her detriment. I left the lady well and in fine spirits." Best ignore the unfortunate parting.

"You'd be bound to say that. Both for your own sake and mine."

"Con, this is me, remember? If she'd slit her wrists, I'd tell you. She was taken aback by the news of your wedding, but not heartbroken. I'm sorry if that wounds your pride."

"No, of course not. I'm delighted." Con, however, still looked as if he didn't believe it.

"In fact, she has taken her place in society and is going about finding a husband more to her taste."

Con drew his horse to a stop. "Anne? Lady Anne Peckworth? The one with the limp?"

"Yes, the one with the damned limp. Lord, you sound as if she should be kept in a locked room!"

"Anything she wants to do, of course. It just doesn't sound like . . ." He frowned. "It's not her family, is it? Pressuring her?"

"Her younger sister is eager to marry, but that's the only pressure."

"Marianne? She's still in the schoolroom." But then he frowned. "How the devil did you find all this out? Even for you, it's a trick."

"Not at all. I simply ate toads for Uffham."

Con shook his head as if it were buzzing. "You've been fetching and carrying for Uffham? Is he still alive?"

Race laughed. "Very much so, but angry with me. I've come to hide."

"Angry? Why?"

"For leaving."

Con shook his head again, but in a wondering way, and put his horse to the walk again. "Does it not grow tedious?"

"What?"

"The way people become attached to you."

"You didn't throw a fit when I left you. I thank you for it."

"I've missed you."

The statement didn't burden because Race knew Con had many friends, both near to hand and scattered, and now had a beloved friend-for-life. It was perhaps why he and Con rubbed along so well.

"To be honest," Con said, "I didn't expect you back. Your work was done, wasn't it, when I married Susan?"

"I left some papers unordered."

"That was never your true work."

Race shrugged. He'd as good as admitted in Devon that he'd attached himself to Con to straighten out his life. Con had left the army in 1814 to take up his title, then returned for Waterloo. The battle had hit him hard, but it had been the death of fellow Rogue, Lord Darius Debenham, that had been the last straw. Since Con was a career soldier and Lord Darius a hasty volunteer, Con had felt that he should have kept his friend safe—though heaven knows, there was no way he could have done so.

Race had met Con again on a hunting field in the winter and worried about him, especially when Con had inherited the added burden of the Earldom of Wyvern. He'd attached himself—like a barnacle—in order to sort things out. Becoming the new earl's secretary had been a useful device. The irony was that he'd found his vocation.

"I need something useful to do and a place to think," he said. "One that puts few demands on me."

"Somerford Court should fit the bill. Now, tell me exactly what's happening with Anne. . . ."

Race gave thanks for Con and passed the rest of the ramble home with an edited account of Benning Hall and Anne's emergence in London.

Unpretentious and undemanding, Somerford Court did fit the bill, and so did Con and his family. Susan Amleigh, the remarkable woman blessed—or cursed—with angelic looks similar to his own, seemed delighted to see him again. Con's mother and sister were warm. He paid for dinner with amusing stories about London, none of them unkind, and felt as if he were relaxing for the first time in weeks.

Con observed Race over dinner. Normally he didn't bother lingering over brandy and tobacco, especially as he neither smoked a pipe nor took snuff. Tonight he decided to create more time with Race. He wanted to know what was going on. He sent a silent message to Susan. She caught it, of course, and led the ladies away.

The table covers were drawn, and port, brandy, snuff, and nuts left between them. When the door closed on the servants, he said, "Amusing as always, but there's no need to work so hard. Consider us family."

Race took a hazelnut and broke it neatly with the silver crackers. "I don't know how to behave with family."

"Then you need to go home and find out."

"I have been home."

Con stared at him. "I didn't know that. It went badly?"

Race ate the nut. He had not yet touched the ruby port in his glass. He rarely drank much. Con had learned that about him. He seemed a wild spirit, but Con had learned that he seldom stepped beyond his own control.

"My father has married again. I have a half brother and sister."

"Good God. And you didn't know?"

Race took a sip of wine. "I knew. Perhaps it is our plebian blood, but we are not the sort for high drama. My uncle insisted that I send him duty letters, and he wrote to tell me of important matters, such as my mother's death, and later his marriage and the children."

With Race it had always been hard to detect mood. "How do things stand now?"

The shrug was so slight Con felt it might even have been a flicker of candlelight. "Unsettled." He took another sip of port then seemed to contemplate the play of candlelight on crystal and ruby wine. "He loved me deeply. Too much. It hurt him when I ran away. It's natural to avoid hurt. Love's the devil, isn't it? But is it love if it's eight-tenths possession? He planned my life to suit his ambitions. I was to be the first true gentleman of his line."

"Then you should please him greatly."

Race shook his head. "I was to make all the right friends at school and at Oxford, then go to London. If possible, I was to marry a blue-blooded lady." He looked up, amused. "He's on his way to buying a title."

"Lord!"

Con meant it as a mild expletive, but Race said, "Precisely."

Con laughed. "There's nothing wrong with that, you know. My ancestor was a younger son who got a barony for clerking for the monarch, then my great-great grandfather upped it to a viscountcy by groveling to the first George."

"At least they were working for it rather than giving interest-free loans to important people. The main problem is, of course, that any title must come to me in time."

"You don't want it?"

"Not particularly." Interestingly, however, Race's lids lowered at that question, hiding something. "The problem arises because my half brother, little Tommy, is now the apple of my father's eye."

"How old is the child?" It was a pointless question, but it covered a moment where Con couldn't think what to say.

"Five. A most promising youngster. I don't think I mentioned that this time my father had the sense to marry a sturdy, practical lady—daughter of a prosperous farming family. She seems to be thriving on giving birth and creating a genuine home at Shapcott House."

"If your father gets a title, it has to come to you not to his second son. There's no way around it."

Race looked at him, and the hair stirred on Con's neck. "Not if I were to become illegitimate."

"What? That's not possible."

"It is, as it happens. I told you that my father changed his name, choosing the damnable de Vere. And then he wanted to puff off my mother's fine connections by giving me her family name as my Christian one. Positively pagan, if you ask me. The thing is, he had gone through no legal processes to change his name but he married as Thomas de Vere. And that, technically, makes his first marriage null and void."

"Good God. He's going to bastardize you?"

"He was well on the way to it until I went home." Race rose suddenly and walked away from the table. Deeply revealing for him. "I knew that it would be a bad idea to go there, but I felt I owed him that. I had no idea . . ."

He turned to face Con, but now from beyond the candlelight. "I think he'd persuaded himself that I was nothing to him any longer, but he's my father, and in his way was a good one. He always loved me more than I deserved. And now I have placed him on the horns of a painful dilemma."

Con rose, too, with outrage. "He still wants to bastardize you in favor of this other child?"

Race made an impatient movement of his hand. "In general principle, I don't mind. There's no one in my mother's family left to care, and I've long suspected that I can never live the life my father wants. Going back confirmed it. I'm not sure what I want to do, but it's not to be squire, or even lord, of a small estate in Derbyshire. Add to that, with my mother's death, my father's mercantile blood has resurged, and he's dabbling in mining, iron-foundry, even banking."

"You'd be good at banking."

"Not really. I don't have a scrap of interest in profit." He laughed. "I could spin that off into a really bad pun, but I'll spare you." He strolled back to the table, seeming relaxed again. "I can't imagine wanting any profession where being a bastard on a technicality would affect me, and I would be delighted to have my relationship with my father uncontaminated by our clashing interests and ambitions, but . . ."

"But?"

Race, however, shook his head. He picked up his glass and raised it. "To my brilliant but sinister future!"

A play on the bar sinister of heraldry, signifying bastardy.

Con drank, but asked, "Future doing what?"

"I rather liked being a secretary."

"Your father won't approve of that," Con said without thinking.

Race's eyes sparkled. "That's the beauty, isn't it? This way, he won't care."

Con put down his glass, thinking there was more to this than he'd immediately grasped. "You are certainly welcome to consider yourself my secretary for as long as it's convenient. But it's too lowly a position."

"That does rather depend on the rank of the employer, and how he treats the secretary. You treated me as a companion."

"True. Thinking of becoming Uffham's secretary, then?"

"Tallying his gaming debts? He has a while to go before he needs one of my caliber, and he's too tempting. I'm resolved to stop trying to fix people's lives."

Con was almost distracted by that, but resisted. He tried to think of a question that would be useful. "What is it you really want to do?" he asked. "Strange sort of question, isn't it? I was a second son, so I needed a profession, but I went into the army more on a whim than a plan. Once Fred died, my fate was settled. Like it or not, it's my role to manage my estates, take part in Parliament, be a magistrate, and generally meddle in the world around me. If I wanted to be a scientist or blacksmith, I'd have to fight centuries of tradition to do it. But what sort of work, day-to-day work, would you like to do?"

Race stared at the uninspired portrait of the second viscount. "I truly do enjoy paperwork, but I'm not sure I would once it became routine. How many employers are going to conveniently inherit chaotic estates as you did?"

"Few, please God."

"I found the discovery aspect of the Wyvern estate entrancing. So much to learn in those papers—about history, legend, local gossip, and national movements. About smuggling—and strange fertility beliefs."

Con laughed. His distant relative the mad earl of Wyvern had been obsessed with his own lack of fertility and had gathered bizarre objects from around the globe in a hunt for a cure.

"I might," Race said, "like to write books about the things learned when digging into forgotten papers. I'm not sure how that is done, but there must be a way."

"I doubt it makes much money."

"I seem able to live on very little." Race strolled to the door and opened it, thus signaling that the confidences were at an end.

Even so, Con said, "You'll need a decent income when you want to marry."

"I doubt I'll marry," Race said.

Later that night when Susan joined Con in bed, she asked, "So, what's wrong with him?"

He pulled her comfortably against him and gave a brief account of Race's situation.

"Do you think he truly doesn't mind being bastardized?" she asked, stroking his shoulder, his neck, his chest. She was a bastard herself, so knew something of it.

"It would be a nine day's wonder, but everyone would know it was a technicality. The de Vere name gives him more trouble, and he's learned to cope with that. Certainly a slightly irregular birth will be no problem if he finds a way to play with dusty records and write books."

"But?" she asked.

"But?" he repeated, mind drifting almost entirely to the magic her hands were creating, to the soft silk of her skin and the delicious, familiar smell of her.

"I'm sure there's something else on your mind," she whispered against his lips.

"I have a mind?" He slipped down to taste her breasts.

She chuckled softly. "About Race."

"You're pursuing this to torment me."

"Of course."

He stroked her nipple with his tongue, tormenting her in turn. "What was your question?"

He felt desire shudder through her and smiled, but she'd always been a strong-willed woman. "About Race. Something else is bothering you."

He kissed and gently sucked, considering the question only to stretch this moment out, to linger before plunging deep. "Ah, yes. There's something about the illegitimacy that does bother him. Something he fears to lose, perhaps. He's keeping it private and that is his right, but I think it might be a woman. . . ."

Any interest in that was evaporating, however, even as he spoke the words. He surrendered to mindless passion.

Eighteen

~

The day after Anne drove in the park, she opened the newspapers to find the story there, written so as to make her sound heartless and mercenary in a time of hardship. Anne had Welsford send a notice to the papers that the money was going to the fund for crippled veterans, but despite a clamor for it, she refused to drive out again. The attention was too unbearable. Instead, determined to be her unashamed self, she walked.

She drove to the park with Caroline in Welsford's carriage, but then they both descended and walked. No one could be driven to copy her, and she couldn't create some new stir. Moreover, surely some of her suitors would be turned away by how clumsy she looked, even with her staff. She was, after all, wearing her leather boots, the right one heavily built to support her foot.

Alas, her lack of grace didn't discourage many, and she was hindered by too many men around her. But then she remembered *The Daring Lady*. If Mrs. Hardcastle could control a whole audience of men, surely she could control a few. She assessed her selection and decided that it was time. She chose Alderton and sternly waved the others away. Reluctantly, they obeyed.

Her mother always said that if a woman turned her mind to it, she could fall in love with anyone. It was time to apply her mind to falling in love with the most appealing of her court. As Alderton talked and she nodded, she reminded herself of all his virtues.

He was titled, had a pleasant estate, and as a bonus, she was already friends with his sister. She knew through Harriet that he was a good and generous brother. Tris had not found any mice, rats, or farthings. Alderton had confessed to only wanting to spend a few weeks in London each year for essential Parliamentary matters, though he did like to spend a month or two in the Shires in hunting season.

The sad fact about that was that she saw it as a bonus. There was nothing wrong with the man, but he might as well be a plaster statue for all the impact he had on her. She could link arms with him without the tiniest frisson, and didn't even want to try a kiss. Would that change in time? Surely it would.

"I say, Alderton. Fair's fair. Time to give you a chance with the lovely Lady Welsford."

Anne hadn't paid any attention to Caroline's escort, but she turned to find that it was indeed burly Lord Marlowe, showing his teeth and phrasing his request in a way that made it impossible for Alderton to refuse.

What's more, Anne saw no sign that Alderton tried. She knew that Tris would not give up a desired lady in this situation. Nor would de Vere. She remembered Tris saying that even a cannonball wouldn't stop de Vere going after something he wanted.

She took Marlowe's arm and strolled on, smiling as he talked about hunting. She was unable, however, to prevent her mind leaping on the subject of de Vere like a starving dog on a lump of meat.

A strange idea had suddenly popped into her head. She and de Vere had been growing close that night at the Swinamer ball. Becoming friends, perhaps. They'd talked about books and libraries, and she'd made the surprising discovery that he was as interested and perhaps as knowledgeable as she. Then he'd talked so freely about himself.

That kiss in the library had started like the one in Benning's study—a blissful merging.

But all that night, he'd been telling her how unsuitable he was. Had that switch to violence, that crude invasion, been yet another calculated act, designed to disgust her forever? That might mean that the earlier part of the evening had been as wonderful for him as for her, but that he'd tried to protect her from it.

Such a conclusion was probably a sign of insanity,

but she couldn't quite dismiss it. Before she settled her mind on some other man, she must meet de Vere again. He'd disappeared, but she had no doubt that with her family's powers, and Tris's if need be, she could find him.

How did she do that without alerting anyone to her interest? Perhaps she could pretend an unpaid debt. . . .

For now, though, she had Marlowe looming beside her, all big shoulders, big bones, and big teeth, and obviously a serious suitor. She wished she could ask him why.

"I suppose you spend the winter in the Shires, Marlowe."

"Of course, Lady Anne. Though when married, I might break the habit a bit."

If married to him, she would make sure he went there from November to Easter!

"Such a shame that ladies cannot hunt there," she said, simply to upset him.

"They'd get in the way, though I admit that you ride well enough, Lady Anne, to perhaps be tolerable."

A meager compliment, but one she quite liked. She didn't want him to start being pleasant. A damp spot on her face was a relief. "Oh, dear. It's going to rain."

They instantly turned back toward the waiting carriage, but it was some distance, and the rain began to come down more heavily. Her frivolous parasol shielded her for a while, but then became soaked. Caroline and Alderton broke into a laughing run, clearly forgetting that Anne couldn't.

Marlowe tried to sweep her into his arms.

"Stop that!" Panicked, Anne swung at him with her staff. She got in more of a swing than she planned, and the amber knob clunked heavily against his head. His eyes crossed and he sat on the damp earth.

Despite the rain, everyone stopped to stare. Caroline had her hand over her mouth.

Anne dropped the staff and went to her knees, rubbing the lump in his hair. "Oh, Lord Marlowe, I'm so sorry! I don't know what came over me. Please say you're all right!"

The third time she'd hit a man!

He blinked at her and then suddenly grinned, showing

more teeth than ever. "Right as rain, dear lady, to have you playing the ministering angel. Don't worry about that little tap. I must have frightened you."

Others were there by then, including Caroline and Alderton, and they were helped to their feet. Marlowe was still grinning, and Anne realized that he was grinning at her. At her body.

She glanced down and saw that her flimsy muslin dress was sticking to her. So were most of the other ladies' dresses, but because she was small in the bosom she wore only the lightest corset. The shape of her breasts was clear, and her nipples were standing out. She dreaded to think what her legs looked like.

Marlowe licked his lips. Any moment he'd be drooling. . . .

Thank heavens that the carriage drew up beside them, the hood already raised, and she and Caroline could climb in and escape.

Anne collapsed back against the seat. "I hate London!"

"You do seem to have a way of stirring trouble," Caroline said, but Anne could see that she wanted to laugh.

"This is all your fault!"

"I have arranged it so that you have all the admirers you could want. Probably more after looking like that."

Anne covered her breasts with her hands.

"To end it, all you have to do is pick one."

"But I don't love any of them!"

"You know what mother says about that."

"I'm sure you had to work to fall in love with Welsford."

Caroline's wry face was acknowledgment of that hit. "Not Marlowe, I assume. He is a fine figure of a man."

Anne saw that she was serious. The taste for men was so very different. "Definitely not Marlowe. He's a libertine."

"Is he? I wonder how you know that. I suppose it's Alderton, then."

After a moment, Anne said, "Not yet."

"Not ever," Caroline stated. "Anne, you can't marry someone you feel so lukewarm about. The right man is out there somewhere."

"Where? I feel as if I've met every peer and his brother."

"You haven't, though. And there's no great hurry, after all."

Anne blew out a breath. There certainly wasn't, not if she wanted time to think more about de Vere, perhaps to find him again.

"I suppose not. I set a target of the end of the season, though, and I do so long to get back to Lea Park."

"That," Caroline said, "would be a totty-headed reason to marry anyone! There are still house parties, and Brighton, and any number of other occasions."

Treadmill, thought Anne, but she agreed.

They entered the house, still damp, to the news that Lord Welsford was entertaining the Duchess of Arran in the drawing room.

"Mama!" gasped Anne, covering her breasts again.

Caroline looked similarly schoolgirlish. "Let's tidy ourselves. Quickly!"

Caroline ran upstairs, and Anne followed as fast as she could. Both of them were ready to go down in record order, and Anne noticed that Caroline had little if any paint on. The Duchess of Arran was a warm and loving mother, but she'd always been a strict one, too.

They entered the drawing room to find not just their mother, but also Marianne sitting beside her beloved, injured hero, Captain Lord Percy Shreve. Marianne was almost as slender as Anne, but with a robust bloom and a reddish glint to her hair.

Anne could practically smell the orange blossom around them, but she was also shocked at Lord Percy's appearance. She'd last seen him as a vigorous, strapping young man. He must have lost at least a stone and his drawn face made him look years older.

He attempted to rise, and was urged back to his seat by everyone. Anne saw that he hunched slightly, favoring his left side and leg, and was clearly in pain. Marianne rose to adjust a cushion to support his arm, looking as if she felt every stab of agony herself.

Anne had only to marry to clear the way for Marianne to take care of him all the time.

Welsford escaped as the tea tray he'd ordered arrived.

"Your father wished to attend the last weeks of Parliament," said the duchess as Caroline sat to serve tea, looking as if she were taking a test. "We took the opportunity to bring dear Percy to see a new doctor recommended by Dr. Normanton. And Marianne needs new clothes."

Consolation, Anne thought, *for not being able to marry immediately.*

She was not happy about this development. She did not need her mother interfering in her affairs.

"We're not receiving, though," the duchess continued. "So tiresome, and not good for Percy."

Marianne patted Lord Percy's shoulder and hurried over to Caroline. "I'll help serve tea. Don't try to get up, Anne!"

Anne hadn't thought of it—a maid stood ready to help—but now she felt set apart as one of the cripples.

At least Caroline passed her test. The duchess took her cup, sipped, and then smiled. "Thank you, my dear. Just as I like it.

"So difficult," the duchess went on. "Marianne's clothes, I mean. She should have her season next year, but matters might fall out differently." She sent a long look at the sofa where Marianne was back to hovering over her love. Anne couldn't decide whether that look predicted a wedding or a funeral.

The duchess sighed. "She may as well have some of the wardrobe now. Caroline, you can advise me on the latest fashions."

"Of course, Mama."

"Is Uffham in town? I haven't seen him in an age."

"No, Mama. He's in Oxfordshire, I believe."

"And St. Raven?"

"I believe he left for his Hertfordshire house."

"Naughty of him not to have visited Lea Park since he returned from abroad," the duchess said, "but I'm sure London has its charms. Hertfordshire. A new estate?"

Anne remembered that her tongue was not crippled. "Apparently he bought it nearly a year ago, Mama, wanting something close to London as well as his Cornish properties."

"Very sensible. What is it called?"

Anne shared a look with Caroline. "Nun's Chase. I think he bought it for the name alone."

Her mother tutted, but with a twinkle in her eye. "I assume he is up to no good there. Not, I hope, an attempt to revive the Hell-Fire Club."

Anne had an alarmed vision of her mother's reaction if it was. She'd probably sweep down and put all the men on bread and water for a week.

"Is that de Vere still with Uffham?" the duchess asked, holding her cup in the air. The maid moved instantly to take it to Caroline to be refilled.

Anne drained hers and held it out, too, giving herself a few minutes breathing space. "You have met Mr. de Vere, Mama?"

"He has visited Lea Park with Uffham. He seemed a good influence on the dear boy, and I understand he was very helpful to Frances in her little emergency. Frances always could be impetuous."

Anne shared a look with Caroline. Apparently the duchess's daughters were expected to manage even childbirth in good order.

"He was," she said. "Useful. Especially in sobering up Benning."

"Pas devant la bonne, Anne," said the duchess. Such matters should not be spoken of before the maid. Anne was sure the servants knew all the shadier goings-on of their employers.

"We really should do something for that young man," the duchess went on. "I'm sure your father could find him a position—in a government department perhaps. He seems just the sort to move up brilliantly."

Anne didn't disagree about the brilliance, but her mother's plans stung all the same. He was viewed as a servant again.

But then, he was a carriage maker's son.

The duchess put down her cup. "I do hope dear St. Raven hasn't drawn away all the eligible gentlemen to his Nun's Chase. They are so easily distracted."

"I gather it's a small house, so it must be a small party."

"When they have a mind to it, dear, the gentlemen

can be happy sleeping ten to a room. So"—the duchess turned all barrels on Anne—"how are you enjoying yourself?"

Anne knew what that meant. "I'm sorry, Mama. I have not yet settled on a husband."

"Five offers, I understand."

"Not formal ones."

"None to your taste, dear?"

Anne thought of giving a complex answer, but she didn't want to raise anyone's hopes. "No."

"I don't mind, Mama," Marianne said, clutching Lord Percy's hand.

"This is nothing to do with you, dear. Anne, you know we would be delighted for you to live on with us at Lea Park. I'm sure in time you could bring your father and me gruel, and tuck blankets around our legs. However, I am not convinced that you want that life, despite your fondness for lurking in libraries. If you wish to be married, you must put your mind to it. It is not something to be approached halfheartedly. And sometimes," she added, "it is not wise to be too particular."

Anne was mortified by this public lecture, before a servant, even. Since her mother seemed to have forgotten the maid, Anne gestured for the stone-faced woman to go. She thought the woman sent her a flicker of sympathy as she left.

Lord Percy looked pained by more than his wounds, and her mother suddenly sported splashes of color in her cheeks. She had forgotten the maid. Anne couldn't remember ever taking command of a family situation like this, and it encouraged her to speak her mind.

"Caroline married for love, Mama. So did Frances. Marianne has stars in her eyes. Why must I settle for less?"

"As I understand it, you could *settle* for an earl, two viscounts, and a baronet of considerable wealth and lineage."

"Not all at once."

"Don't resort to flippancy, dear."

Startled at herself, Anne made herself calm down. "Then, in all seriousness, Mama, title is not the main point."

"Not the *main* point, dear, but you could hardly marry lower. Look at poor Claretta Tregallows." The duchess actually shuddered. "The man's family are fishmongers! Prosperous ones, I understand, but even so. It is extraordinary what sorts of people ended up as officers because of the trials of war."

"Captain Crump is generally admired, Duchess," Lord Percy said. "He is an excellent officer."

Anne liked him even more for that. She wished she could ask if he had an opinion of de Vere.

"The simple fact," said the duchess relentlessly, "is that by now you must have spent time with most of the eligible titled gentlemen, Anne. If your heart has not been touched, you may as well pick the most suitable." She shook her head. "Such a mistake to let you hide away for so long. These matters always become more difficult when a girl gets older. I'm sure if Claretta had married before she was twenty she would have made a more suitable choice."

Anne felt like a sulky schoolroom miss, and just as tongue-tied.

"What about St. Raven?" her mother demanded.

Anne jumped. "Heavens, no!"

"And why not?"

"He's like a brother, Mama."

"Nonsense. And didn't those Egyptians marry brother and sister? You should think about it."

"Him being the only eligible duke."

Her mother didn't so much as blink. "Precisely. Such a shame to let some other woman have him, especially as you always rubbed along so well." She rose. "Don't try to get up, Percy. In fact, why don't you and Marianne stay here while I attend to some errands." She swept out leaving the couple, Anne knew, as a living reproach to her.

In the Duchess of Arran's mind, all ladies should marry, marry young, and marry well. To do less was a sign of a weak will. Anne had no doubt that her mother had been eyeing Tris as a juicy target for years—not for Anne, but for Marianne. Now Marianne's heart had fixed elsewhere, her target had obviously changed.

Temptation flickered along her raw nerves. Marriage

would offer Tris escape from the hunt, and her escape from this predicament. It would indeed be comfortable. Was that so bad?

But then she thought of that attempted kiss and knew it wouldn't work. Even if they could bring the necessary passion into the business, their hearts would not be touched. She might have to marry for mere comfort, but she would not condemn Tris to that, too.

"Are you cold, Anne?" Caroline asked.

She must have shivered.

"Only in a daughterish manner."

Caroline grimaced in sympathy. "I thank heaven daily that I fell in love with an earl." Then she grinned at Lord Percy. "I'm sure you can't *help* being a younger son."

The man smiled, then winced, and Marianne cried, "Don't make him laugh!" She looked at Anne with great seriousness. "You are not to let our affairs hurry you, dearest. I know now how very important the deepest feelings are. You must not settle for less. And," she added with a bright smile, "Mama will be sure to let us marry soon, even if you haven't . . . chosen yet."

Anne knew, however, how every day must seem a day too long, and then, as they all chattered and gossiped a picture of Lord Percy's current situation emerged, innocently she was sure.

He was living with his mother at the Shreve dower house. The dowager Marchioness of Gravender was frantic over the state of her younger son and insisting on doing a great deal of the nursing herself.

Her fretting and weeping was hard on the invalid, but it was the treatments she insisted on that were worst. Poor Percy was being bled and even blistered on a regular basis, but didn't have the heart, or perhaps the strength, to refuse.

Bleeding and blistering did have their uses, but Anne couldn't imagine how they would help muscles and sinews that refused to heal. The problem seemed to be the large quantity of shrapnel driven into his body and the numerous operations to try to dig it out. Poor man. Having suffered a number of attempts to straighten her foot, she shuddered in sympathy.

The only way to free him was marriage and a move to a new home. Marianne's plan, though not spoken directly, seemed to involve a small house on the Lea Park estate, peace, rest, and the gentle attentions of Dr. Normanton.

When healed, Lord Percy wanted diplomatic work, and Marianne sparkled at the thought of traveling and living in many of the world's capitals. But would he survive to take up that future if things went on as they did now?

When Anne heard the duchess's carriage draw up, she went to intercept her mother in the hall. "Mama, do you not think that Marianne and Percy should be allowed to marry? They are young, but it seems very much a fixed thing, and truly, I would not mind."

"You're very kind, dear, but it will do them no harm to wait."

"It seems to be doing Percy a great deal of harm!"

"He needs resolution. A young man who cannot stand up to his mother might not make the best husband, you know."

Anne hadn't thought of that. "He's a loving son. Is that so bad?"

"No, dear, of course not."

"If I were to marry, there really would be no barrier to their union, would there?"

The duchess smiled. "No dear, unless dear Percy's health did not permit it."

There, it was clear. Quite likely her mother had accepted the inevitability of Marianne and Percy's marriage—assuming he survived. She was using it to force Anne, in particular to force Anne to marry Tris.

She met her mother's eyes in a way she could not remember doing before. "You have no fear that I will plunge into an unsuitable match in order to clear the way?"

"Of course not, dear. You have always done just as you ought."

The duchess returned to the others, but Anne took refuge in her bedroom, burning with anger. It was unfair. It was *wrong*!

It was, however, inescapable. Her mother had a will

of iron when it came to what she saw as her children's welfare. Her father, powerful as he was, left family matters to her mother. An appeal to him would not help.

It was some consolation, Anne decided, that her mother's dearest wish would never come true. She would not end up as the Duchess of St. Raven.

It would have to be Alderton.

He would make an acceptable husband, and at least she need not fear that he would try to bully her. He had been timid even when suggesting a visit to his estate. If nothing changed before Parliament ended and the fashionable throng dispersed, then she would take up his invitation and doubtless end up his wife.

Parliament completed its business and closed on July second. A few days later Anne traveled to Alderton's Wiltshire estate, with her mother as chaperon. The duchess was somewhat disgruntled.

Anne loved her mother and knew that she truly thought she was doing the right thing in pushing for the marriage with Tris. During the journey she tried to explain their feelings. She even mentioned, without the reason, their failed kiss.

"Nonsense," said the duchess. "I'm sure my feelings for your father have always been more comfortable than passionate, and it has worked out very well."

Anne wished she dared ask whether her mother thought passion ill-bred, but the answer was probably yes.

If passion was ill-bred, then the visit to Alderton Hall did not threaten good breeding. Anne tried very hard to picture herself there as happy wife and mother, but it was a formal house not helped by relentlessly overcast days.

Alderton Hall was new, the previous house having burned down thirty years before. It was elegant. It had been recently enhanced with all the latest conveniences, including a patent stove in the kitchen and two indoor water closets.

It was ruled, however, by Alderton's doting mother and grandmother, who were both permanently in residence. Both ladies were gratified to think that their son might marry a daughter of the Duke of Arran. Both were unhappy that said daughter was a cripple. Both clearly intended to continue to rule the roost.

Anne felt that she could perhaps fight one incumbent, but two?

The final straw in Anne's mind was that there were no family records older than thirty years. They had all gone up in flames.

Certainly Alderton's sister, Harriet, was as sweet and pleasant as ever, and she lived only four miles away. She was into her second pregnancy, however, and busy with her home and community. Anne suspected that they would only meet occasionally.

Alderton being Alderton, she managed to put off an outright declaration, and here her mother's plans came in useful. Once Anne gave her the hint, the duchess smoothly extricated them from Alderton Hall without unpleasantness, but with no commitment made.

Anne traveled back to London, relieved, but with her situation unimproved. She still wanted to marry, but now she didn't know where to turn.

"Why," Caroline declared when asked, "to Brighton, of course! Welsford and I are off there in a few days, and you must come. There will be different faces there and as well the whole atmosphere is different in Brighton. You will see!"

Nineteen

~

Anne had never been to Brighton. Summers had always been at Lea Park. After a few days in the Regent's summer playground, she was coming to the opinion that this had been a wise choice. She liked the country in the summer, and Brighton was a continuation of London society with an extra layer of frothy silliness on top.

Gambling, for pennies or guineas, was everywhere, and people seemed to feel obliged to stroll endlessly "taking the sea air," but in effect, meeting and being met. When not strolling, they were having picnics on just about any open space, or riding donkeys, or staging silly contests such as who could hop farthest.

She'd remarked to Caroline that she thought everyone in Brighton was bored. Her sister had been appalled, and Anne had accepted that Caroline did enjoy it, so perhaps most other people did, too. That only confirmed her suspicion that she was out of step with society in more ways than having a limp. The thought of all the enjoyably useful things she could be doing at home, such as charitable works, summer pleasures with old friends, and exploring the family documents, was almost a physical pain.

At times she became short-tempered, but it didn't seem to deter her admirers, old and new.

As Caroline had predicted, there were new faces in Brighton. Many of the officers of the local regiment had joined her court, a few seriously, and there were half-pay officers aplenty here. None of them seemed to have anything better to do than bother her every hour of the day.

She had to admit that there were some appealing men among them, at least on a superficial level. Dashing Captain Ralstone, for example, with the dark curls and laughing eyes, was very pleasant company. She wasn't sure she could or should take him seriously, however.

She began to suspect that her affairs had gone beyond courtship and become a kind of sport. Perhaps wagers were being laid. She asked Welsford, and he confirmed it, but refused to give details. "Anne, Anne, how very unsporting. It might affect your choice."

"I don't suppose the fox is interested in being sporting either, only in a safe covert. If there's anything about those wagers that might affect my choice, Welsford, then I want to know about it."

But he shook his head. "If there was anything dishonorable, you know I'd put a stop to it."

Thwarted, Anne wrote to both Uffham and Tris, insisting that they find out all the details and report to her. She dropped sealing wax on the letters and stamped her seal into it, acknowledging a coil of anxiety deep inside.

Her instinct to privacy was offended by wagers, but she wished she was more sure about the outcome than those placing bets. She might as well just roll the dice, which made her think of de Vere, which was not uncommon.

Damn the man. How dare he disappear off the face of the fashionable world?

No one had heard a word from him. His absence was made worse by how often it was remarked on. He might have been a nobody, but he had stamped an impression on the soft wax of the ton. He was remembered by ladies as a charmer, and by gentlemen as amusing. The term *madman* often came up, but always fondly.

There were other stories, too. He had helped Mrs. Hatley's son out of a disastrous entanglement, and extricated shamefaced Lieutenant Gore from a gaming hell before he'd lost all.

It would seem that he couldn't walk by anyone in trouble.

Including her?

Was that the explanation? That he'd arrived at Benning Hall with Uffham, assumed her to be broken-hearted, and set out to heal her? And then his attentions had interested her too much so that in the end he'd had to be cruel to be kind.

When she remembered driving him back against a door in frustrated passion she wanted to take laudanum and go to sleep forever.

It fit, it all fit, but then there was the memory of the way he'd handled her foot, the way he'd kissed her hand. *"Pretend, if you will, that this is your poor foot."*

Had he driven her away because she was a tiresome barnacle, sealed to him with pity, or simply because he believed himself too low for her happiness?

If the latter, wasn't it true?

She put her elbows on the desk and rested her chin in the cup of her hands. She was letting de Vere get in the way of a rational decision about her future, she knew she was. She must deal with the important question. If Race de Vere loved her, if he would like to marry her, was she willing to marry him, to be Lady Anne de Vere, horribly misaligned wife of a nobody?

In the end, she hadn't been able to resist investigating him. The Brighton libraries contained little detail about Derbyshire, but she had eventually found Shapcott Manor in a guide to Derbyshire. "A pleasant manor house in parkland, long home of the Racecombe family, but now owned by Thomas de Vere, Esquire."

That confirmed his story, but then she had never doubted that he told the truth. Fool that she was, she'd traced the few words in the book with her finger as if they were a living connection to the man who was never far from her thoughts.

When Caroline had hired an artist to do sketches of them both, Anne had asked the woman to execute a drawing of her hands. She still had it, but with no idea where to send it.

Perhaps, as she'd said to Uffham, he was in Derbyshire mending the breach with his father. If so, what did she do? Send him the picture? Write a letter like pathetic Miss Littleton? Hire a post chaise and dash up to Derbyshire?

She laughed. Everyone would think she was eloping.

She stopped laughing. If she wanted to marry de Vere, she'd probably have to elope. Her mother would lock her up rather than permit her to make a marriage like that.

Tris could probably find him. But then, if she asked Tris to do that, he'd know why, and he'd probably seek out de Vere in order to shoot him.

She could find him and flee abroad.

She sighed and stood. She was thinking like the heroine in a play instead of like a real and sensible woman. De Vere was impossible, and he was not here. She had no practical way of finding him, and if she could she didn't want to marry in a way that might cut her off from her home and family forever.

Would a truly passionate woman not care about such things? Then she clearly was not passionate.

She pulled out her list again and read the names through twice. There were additions, such as Ralstone.

Perhaps she should consider Ralstone. He had more in common with de Vere than any other of her suitors.

He was one of the half-pay officers—a cliché fortune hunter—but in fact he was heir to Lord Irlingham. A barony only, so even lower than Benning, but he would have a title one day. That should pacify her mother a little.

His family, however, was hard-put to keep up their dignity due to long extravagance and the folly of Lord Irlingham marrying twice and having twelve children, all healthy. There was little to start any of them in life, and nothing extra to support the heir in a suitable manner. She gathered that his father was also very healthy, so Ralstone's situation would not change in the near future.

But, as she'd often thought, money was not a significant factor in her choice.

Ralstone was a great favorite with all the ladies. Petty as it was, the idea of snatching up a man that other women wanted did have its appeal. He flirted beautifully, but could also talk sensibly if required. He seemed to think as he ought on all important subjects, and he had a way of looking at her across a room that implied he was lost in wonder.

Once that would have struck her as ridiculous. Now

she was at least willing to consider that he might be falling in love with her. Alderton clearly had, and Cedric Rolleston-Stowe had written tragic poetry after she'd cut his hopes short. She'd been as kind as she could to Ceddy, but she'd known she could never live with a man inclined to fly from alt to nadir in moments.

Ralstone?

She drew idle circles around his name.

There was something there. In worldly terms it would be a low match, but not impossible. She did enjoy his company. He was entertaining, considerate, and he even listened. He seemed to approve of many of her ideas, and could discuss politics and fashion with equal ease.

He was thinking of leaving the army, which was important to her. She had no taste for life as an army wife. He would need occupation, but her family could find that for him. A seat in Parliament, perhaps, or stewardship of one of her father's estates. Yes, that would be better. She did not want to spend much time in London.

In fact, on her money they could afford to lease a small country estate. One close to Lea Park, even, so she could have that and marriage, too.

There was a thought.

She decorated her circles with flowers.

Marrying a man without an estate of his own had distinct advantages. Quoyne House. It belonged to her father but was not part of the entailment. It sat just outside the walls of Lea Park. Near, but not too near . . .

Her mind was moving so quickly that she decided she needed a brisk ride to clear it. Not an amble in Brighton, but a gallop out on the downs. It was half past nine—too early for most of her suitors to be out of bed. She rang the bell and summoned her habit and Monmouth.

She kept to a sedate pace as she rode out of Brighton, one of Welsford's grooms behind, but when she reached the country road she speeded up. It was a cloudy day, but dry and fresh.

Monmouth stretched, showing how much he had longed for a good run. Anne felt as if she stretched, too, seeing Ralstone as a way to break free and get back to the country.

She could wish he wasn't quite so physical a man. It

was probably his strength and vigor that excited her, as riding a top quality horse excited her. Yet there were times when she wanted peace and a book or a box of papers. Would he allow her times like that?

She was spoiled. She hated the thought of a man allowing or not allowing anything.

Alderton would be easily managed. But he was so dull.

As she reined in on the downs to look down on the town and the sea beyond she couldn't help thinking that if she could mash Alderton and Ralstone into one person she would be close to her ideal.

What a strange state she had come to, to be trying to design her perfect husband. Laughing, she set Monmouth to the gallop and flew across the smooth downs, loving the thundering power beneath her and the fresh air against her skin—

"Halloo!"

She reined in a bit and glanced back to see a bunch of horsemen galloping toward her, Ralstone's scarlet coat to the fore. Her pestilential admirers had discovered her! Instinctively, she urged Monmouth to speed and raced to get away.

Hunting shouts echoed, and she looked for some escape. Her groom pounded alongside. "Lady Anne. Slow down, milady!"

He was Welsford's man, and didn't know her.

"They won't hurt you, milady!"

The infernal groom reached for her reins. She knocked his hand away with her crop, but began to rein in again. Fleeing like this would do no good, but she would not be *hunted*!

She drew Monmouth to a halt and turned him. Then as the group of grinning men slowed a mad urge took her.

She set her horse to speed again, right at them.

With startled exclamations, they broke apart and she flew through them and was off back toward Brighton, laughing with triumph.

It was a stupid thing to do. They chased her as if she truly were a fox, and when she had to slow to enter the town, they clustered around, exclaiming in admiration of her riding. By this evening she would be the gossip of all Brighton, and by tomorrow she would be in the papers. Again.

She glared at Captain Ralstone, riding grinning by her side, confident in his dashing good looks and charm.

His grin faded. "Did we alarm you, Lady Anne? Then I do sincerely apologize."

"You didn't *alarm* me, Captain Ralstone. It was only that I was enjoying the peace of the morning."

"It is the most precious time of the day, isn't it? And we invaded it."

His rueful expression, his understanding, melted her anger.

He reached to touch her hand. "It will not happen again, I promise you." Then, with a mischievous look he added, "If you were to summon my escort, I could make sure of it."

She found herself laughing and back in humor with him.

Why not? He would be a daring choice rather than a safe one, but why not be a daring lady?

She began to pay attention to Captain Ralstone, to truly let him woo her, but then Alderton arrived in Brighton, looking resolute.

Oh, dear. He was going to propose, and when he did she would have to say yes or burn that boat.

And then she learned that de Vere had been in Brighton just days before she had arrived.

She was with Caroline, Welsford, and a Major Trimball, strolling through a small charity fairground set up on the Steyne. They'd stopped to pay their pennies and try their hands at throwing balls into baskets when Miss Charnock, standing close by, said to her companion, "Do you remember that Mr. de Vere? He had the trick of this. Won three gifts for his fair companion before the stall holder refused him another go."

Caroline turned to them. "Racecombe de Vere? Has he been here recently?"

Anne was trying so hard not to show any reaction that she doubtless looked like a stuffed dummy.

Miss Charnock, a plain but pleasant lady, said, "Oh, yes, Lady Welsford. A week or so ago. My brother and

I met him at a large fair up on the downs." She introduced her brother, a man as plain and pleasant as herself. "Richard knows him quite well, don't you, Richard?"

"Has a mad streak, but a fine soldier," Major Charnock said.

"He was with the lovely Miss Trist," Miss Charnock said, "but I gather she has returned home to marry a neighbor, leaving many a broken heart."

Was de Vere's heart broken? Anne wanted to ask, alarmed by the sharp pain in her own. Instead, she said, "An heiress, I suppose."

"Oh no, Lady Anne, not at all. That was what made her so fascinating. A penniless beauty who looked set to steal a great catch. She was companion to the Deveril heiress, however. Now there was a fortune, and a scandal to go with it!"

"And she is snatched up, too," Major Charnock said, pretending suffering. "By a hawk, no less."

"What?" Anne was beginning to think that her wits had turned.

He smiled. "Major Hawkinville. A fine fellow who deserves good fortune and a pretty bride. Lives in these parts, too.

"Is Mr. de Vere still in Brighton?" Caroline asked, saving Anne from trying to find a way to ask without revealing anything. It would be hard when she was feeling slightly faint.

"I don't think so, Lady Welsford. I believe he was staying with the Vandeimens, though, if you wished to inquire. I assume you heard about Lord Darius Debenham?"

Anne listened as from a distance to discussion about the miraculous reappearance of the Duke of Yeovil's younger son who'd been assumed dead at Waterloo but had turned up alive though still suffering from his wounds. It had been the talk of England a week or more ago.

"Made his way from France," Major Charnock said, "and somehow turned up at the Vandeimen's house on Marine Parade. Remarkable!"

So remarkable that Anne wondered if de Vere had waved a magic wand. He had been here, right here, just days before she had arrived! And now, typically, he had melted into air again.

The Vandeimens. She didn't know them. She could find an excuse to call, however.

Oh, good heavens, she couldn't do a thing like that! It would be as bad as Lady Caroline Lamb invading Byron's rooms in hot pursuit. And anyway, de Vere couldn't be in Brighton anymore. Daily lists were produced of everyone present, of comings and goings. She could not have missed his name.

The Vandeimens would know where he'd gone. . . .

No. She would not be a bitch on the hunt.

Or a bitch in heat, she thought, remembering her appalling behavior. If the man was interested in her, he would have no difficulty in finding her.

And if he was nobly preventing her from taking a disastrous step?

What could she do about that? Kidnap and seduce him?

That evening at a musical soirée, Ralstone adroitly captured the seat beside her and amused her with a story about a donkey race on the downs that day. She made herself think about what a pleasant companion he could be.

Not as fascinating as de Vere, but not tedium.

Later, she agreed to a stroll in the lantern-lit gardens, to a pause in a discreet corner, and to a kiss. If she was considering him, she should follow de Vere's advice and try out his kisses.

Don't think about de Vere.

Ralstone was gentle at first, but when she didn't protest, he became more ardent. There was even, she thought, a little tingle from it. No sign that he might turn wild and grope her in unthinkable places, thank heavens.

Afterward he smiled at her with obvious optimism. "You encourage me to ask a special favor, Lady Anne."

"Yes?" she asked warily.

"The Regent has sent out invitations to all the military men in Brighton for a special assembly at the Pavilion on Friday. We are commanded to bring a lady, however, to represent 'the Britannia that we saved.' I quote."

She laughed with relief. "Are we to wear helmets and carry shields?"

"I don't think so. But you are to present your escort with a favor to wear."

"As in a medieval tournament? I hope he doesn't plan a joust."

"If he did," Ralstone said, capturing her free hand and pressing it to his chest, "I would be honored to fight under your colors."

It was overly dramatic, but she could grant this request at least. "Of course I will be your lady, Captain Ralstone. I am honored."

He carried her hand to his lips with such fervor that for a moment Anne worried that she had unwittingly agreed to marry him. But when he glanced at her, alerted by something, she smiled brilliantly and made herself relax.

When they returned to the soirée, she saw that Alderton was pouting. Her mental pen hovered over his name ready to strike him out, but then she made herself be sensible. In all ways that mattered, he would still be the wise choice, and if he was upset that she'd gone apart with Ralstone that was because he was in love with her.

She had made herself think about Alderton Hall. It had to be possible to move his mother and grandmother. There wasn't a dower house there at the moment, but one could be built. In a matter of months. They would still be in and out, she was sure, but they wouldn't be under the same roof.

She knew that if she was firm enough she could get Alderton to do anything she wanted, so he would adapt his house to her taste. He had an excellent stable, and it was good riding country.

Lastly, she had realized that she probably could take her papers with her to a new home. No one at Lea Park was interested in them. She could continue with her work.

Yes, life at Alderton Hall could in time be made much like life at Lea Park, and Alderton would be a much more comfortable husband than Ralstone.

She was not at all sure she could make Ralstone do as she wished.

She dismissed him and let Alderton take her for refreshments.

"A fellow like me don't have much chance when a man like Ralstone's in the field, does he?"

"Don't be foolish, Alderton. You have every advantage over him."

"Not with the ladies."

She gave him a playful look. "Are you suggesting that we ladies lack judgment?"

He opened his mouth once or twice, looking distressingly fishy. Then he laughed. "Oh, I see. I apologize. But a certain dash does catch the eye. Works the other way, too. Didn't really notice you until you spread your feathers this year, Anne."

It was, perhaps, tactless, but she rather liked his perception and his honesty. She'd much rather have that than perfect tact. Ralstone never said a wrong word.

They were in an anteroom that was deserted at the moment. She turned and put a hand on Alderton's shoulder. "Such honesty deserves a reward," she said, turning her face up to him.

The whites showed around his eyes, and she wondered if he would bolt. It was good, she told herself, that he was alarmed by an offered kiss. He was no libertine.

Did that make Ralstone a mouse or rat? She should get Tris's advice on that.

Thought was drowned by Alderton's mouth pressing hotly to hers, but only for the briefest second.

She blinked at him, but he had already moved back, out of reach. She supposed he was the wise one. Someone might come upon them here. That kiss hadn't been much to judge a man on, however, and had certainly not had any tingling effect.

Later in bed, like a person probing a sore tooth, she reviewed kissing de Vere, comparing and contrasting.

She hadn't shrunk from him. She grimaced at the dark ceiling. What point? He hadn't needed a kiss to shorten her breath, to make her toes curl, to make her smile for the simple pleasure of seeing him.

As Alderton had smiled at her? Did Alderton search

rooms for a glimpse of her, long for her, dream of her? . . .

Did Ralstone?

Her heart pattered as if a trap had closed.

Did she *love* Race de Vere?

Oh, no—she couldn't! This affliction was insanity, not love!

For some reason, however, she hardly slept that night, tossing between the sensible choice, the daring choice, and the impossible one.

When Alderton called two days later and asked her to drive out with him, she accepted without much thought. It was only as she sat beside him in his sensible gig that she noticed his set chin and pallor.

Oh, no! That kiss had been the encouragement he'd needed. He was going to pose the question, and she wasn't ready yet.

And yet, and yet, Alderton was the obvious choice. Ralstone was all flash and dash, and despite his charm, at heart he was selfish. She knew it. Alderton was not. He would give her all she desired.

De Vere was impossible. If he suddenly appeared before her and asked her to marry him, she would have to say no. There was no other rational response. She had to accept that.

As they drove along the Marine Parade, Anne looked out at the gray sea and turned her mind to falling in love with the Earl of Alderton. He was an excellent driver. That was a major point in his favor. He was well enough looking, titled, wealthy, kind, honorable, and he loved her.

What possible objection could she have?

She realized that her list of qualities seemed familiar. . . . Oh, no! They echoed what de Vere had said in Drury Lane about Captain Jeremy Goodman. Would Alderton hide under a coach and leave her to face a highwayman?

Idiotic question. It would never occur, and if it did, she was sure he would not. He would make her just the sort of husband she was supposed to have.

As they left Brighton in the direction of Hove, a pleasant tranquility settled on her agitated mind. She would marry him,. and everything would all be as it should be. Her family would be delighted. No one could pity her choice. Marianne and Percy could wed. Perhaps in a double wedding.

As if to settle the matter, a bundle of rags and seaweed tumbled across the road, startling the horses. Alderton brought them under control without difficulty.

She complimented him on his driving, and he blushed with pleasure. She remarked encouragingly on his excellent stables at Alderton Hall, and he glowed. They chatted of yesterday's weather, and today's weather, and the forecast for tomorrow. They were in perfect harmony.

They kept on driving. When and where would he ask her? After all this, if he didn't, *she* might ask *him*!

Then he stopped the curricle at a quiet spot, and his tiger ran to the horse's heads. Anne waited to be assisted down, wishing her heart hadn't begun a mad pounding. She wasn't nervous. This was no great affair.

It would be the absolute limit to swoon, though.

If he behaved as she expected, then this would lead to kisses. To make matters easier, therefore, she left her staff behind, trusting entirely to his arm. He led her along a rough path to a place with an excellent view of the sea, but which was shielded slightly from the carriage by some bushes.

Had he scouted out this spot ahead of time?

Something about that struck her as ridiculous, and she fought nervous laughter. He hadn't planned for wind. Close to the sea, the breeze became brisk, whipping her skirt against her legs, making her clutch her bonnet.

He took his arm from hers and went to one knee on the earthen path. She couldn't help thinking that he would have a muddy stain on his knee. "Alderton, please . . ."

"I must speak." He swept off his hat and held it over his heart. "Dearest Anne, you must know how I feel. . . ."

He spun off into a speech he had clearly memorized and practiced. Anne hadn't the heart to cut him short, but now she truly felt as if she were on a stage, as if she might look aside and see a vast audience rather than the indifferent sea.

None of this seemed real.

None of what he was saying seemed real.

Was it really the dearest wish of his heart that they two be joined in connubial bliss? She supposed it must be, or he wouldn't be here on one knee spouting all this stuff.

Could he really promise her perfect happiness? . . .

He'd stopped speaking. He was waiting for her answer, beseechingly.

"Yes, of course I will."

Those were her lines. What else could she say?

He rose, tears of joy in his eyes. Tears stung her eyes, too. She wasn't sure they were joy, but she did feel relief. It was done. It was finally done, and her feet were set on the most solid, sensible, safe path.

"As soon as I have returned you to your sister's home, my dear, I will go to Lea Park to talk to your father. He can have no objection."

"No, I'm sure not." But he was holding out his arm to lead her back to the carriage.

"Shouldn't we kiss, Alderton? Properly."

He blushed. It was definitely a blush. "No need for that yet, my dear."

"Need? I would like you to kiss me."

He looked around as if seeking escape, but then he took her hand, leaned closer and pressed his lips to hers as tentatively as last night. Anne remembered de Vere recommending passionate kisses before commitment.

She moved forward, put her arms around him, and kissed him back. She felt him tense. When she opened her eyes, his were open, staring at her.

She moved back. "Alderton, do you not want to kiss me?"

He was red from his neck to his hair. "Of course, of course. But this is neither the time nor the place, Anne."

Anne supposed that there was some slight chance of someone passing on the road catching a glimpse of them. Months ago she would have been as excruciatingly aware of that as her husband-to-be. What had become of her?

She felt the heat in her own cheeks. "You are right. I'm sorry."

He tucked her hand into his arm. "Not at all, my

dear. A little warmth only increases my anticipation for our future."

That, she supposed, sounded promising. But as he helped her into the carriage and they turned back toward Brighton, Anne's feeling of accomplishment began to sink beneath a tide of unfulfillment. This didn't seem quite as it should be.

Middlethorpe had felt more passionate than this, and he hadn't proposed. She was sure that if he had, when she'd said yes, there would have been more . . . connection.

Alderton glanced at her, catching her eye and smiling. "I understand, Anne. At a time like this a lady can't be expected to chatter."

He turned his eyes forward again and began to whistle.

Anne wanted to press her fingers to her head. Though it didn't ache, it felt as if it ought to. Captain Ralstone had summoned more passion. And as for de Vere—!

"Don't go to Lea Park today," she said.

He looked at her. "Why ever not?"

She didn't know except that she needed more time to grow accustomed. Could she say that? Then she remembered. "Tonight is the military assembly. I've promised to attend with Captain Ralstone."

"You must decline, my dear. It is not suitable now you are engaged to marry me."

"It isn't that sort of event, Alderton. The officers are supposed to take a lady to symbolize Britannia. And I have given my word."

He frowned. It was close to a sulk. She remembered how she'd felt about his sulking.

"If you think it best," he said at last. "But that does not prevent me from traveling to Lea Park."

A flutter of panic began to build again. What had she done? She'd thought Alderton would be easy to manage, but no sooner had she said yes than he was sulking over not getting his own way.

She thought quickly. "If you wait a day, I can go with you, Alderton. We can receive my father's blessing together."

His stiffness melted into a smile. "A very suitable sentiment, my dear. By all means." He reached out and patted her hand. "I should not begrudge another man one evening with you, when soon you will be mine alone forever."

She smiled back, but something was wrong with this. On a stage, spoken by the right actor, those words would thrill. Here in this real world, they sounded like cell doors slamming shut.

Was she making a terrible mistake? Or was she simply letting the impossible get in the way of the sensible again?

Twenty

In mid-July, Race returned to Somerford Court from Crag Wyvern in Devon, where he'd been tying up a few more administrative loose ends. He knew it was weak to return. Lady Anne Peckworth was in Brighton, and he should avoid the vicinity entirely.

He was back because of a small item in a scandal sheet read by the Crag Wyvern housekeeper.

The *London Enquirer* had been lying open in the kitchen, and Anne's name had leaped out at him.

In fact it had said Lady Anne Pxxxxxxxx, but that had been enough to snare him. According to the paper, she had played fox to a bunch of military hounds on the downs near Brighton, creating great admiration by her brilliant equestrian talents. It went on to say that a large number of gentlemen were pursuing the beautiful young lady, both in and away from the field.

It sounded as if Anne was in trouble.

He'd visited Brighton with Con and Susan, staying with their friends the Vandeimens. It had been pleasant enough, but he had been impatient with the pointlessness of it. When the daily sheets had announced the imminent arrival of the Earl and Countess of Welsford and Lady Anne Peckworth, Con and Susan had decided to avoid embarrassment by leaving. Race had been happy to go with them.

He'd soon decided that six miles wasn't far enough for his weak willpower. He'd come up with reasons to return to Con's old estate in Devon and removed himself entirely.

He'd enjoyed another dip into the affairs of the late
mad Earl of Wyvern, and it had given him the chance
to take notes of some of the more interesting matters
for a possible book, but all the same, it had been slightly
flat, like ale that had stood too long in the jar.

Life felt slightly flat these days, and he knew why. It
was the same reason a small item in a paper had drawn
him back here. When he reached the place where the
road to Somerford branched off the Brighton Road, he
felt the tug. She was there. So close. Possibly in distress.

Was she in danger? Was she being harassed? Where
was her family who should be taking care of her? Where
was the Duke of St. Raven? Why hadn't he heard of
her engagement to marry St. Raven, or some other suitable man?

He made himself continue on to Somerford. He'd find
out what was going on from six miles away, and deal
with it from six miles away, too.

He rode around to the Court stables, then entered the
house from the back. The first person he encountered
was Susan Amleigh in an apron, supervising the washing
of the corridor walls.

"Race! My goodness, you startled me, turning up like
that. All finished in Devon, then?"

"Yes, and it's pleasant to return to sanity."

For some reason that made her laugh. "Oh, Lord. If
only you knew. Con!" she called. "Here's Race back
admiring our sane world."

Con came out of his study, grinning, too, and Race
knew instantly that something had changed. For the
better.

"What's happened?"

Con insisted on Race going into his study with him,
and on ordering ale for them both. Susan came along,
still in her apron, clearly looking forward to the telling.
Race was amused, but he was also delighted. Whatever
it was, was good news.

When they both had tankards of ale, Con raised his.
"To Lord Darius Debenham. We found him, Race.
Alive! But that's the end of the tale."

"What?" But Race drank the toast, then went to shake

his friend's hand. He knew how much Lord Darius's assumed death at Waterloo had wounded Con. "But how on earth did this happen? Where has he been?"

What followed was a complex story of a French spy, a kidnapping, a death, and the elopement of Con's friend and neighbor Hawk Hawkinville with the Devil's Heiress. Race listened, shaking his head.

"A simpler story's been put out for public consumption," Con said, "but that's what really happened."

"And they call me wild! I'm put out to have missed all this."

"You're in time for the wedding, at least," Con said.

"What wedding?"

"Hawk and Clarissa. They never made it to Gretna, so they're doing it properly in Hawk in the Vale tomorrow."

Race encouraged Con to fill in the details of that adventure. Susan waved and went back to work.

Eventually Race said, "A grand affair. I wish I'd been part of it."

"More appealing than the Crag Wyvern paperwork? It must be growing dreary for you to be back so soon. You've been gone what? Ten days?"

"I've done all I need to there."

Con topped up Race's tankard. "I'm glad you're here for the wedding, since you missed ours."

"Speaking of which," Race said, hoping he sounded only curious, "what news of Lady Anne?"

"She's in Brighton still, but that's all. Why?"

"I read an item that suggested that she'd been chased on horseback on the downs."

"What?" Con looked at him as if he were mad. "I think the papers make up most of these things when it comes to the aristocracy."

"And I think they rarely need to. It was a scandal sheet, but it had the ring of truth."

"Dammit, what's her family thinking of?"

"Precisely my question."

Con looked at Race. "I know that look. You think I should get the meeting over with and make sure she's all right."

"You have to meet sooner or later, and as I said, I don't think she'll bite."

"Who knows what she'll do if she's charging all over the place on horseback? Armed with a fanciful staff, too, I gather."

"Not on horseback, I assume."

Con laughed. "All right, all right. I'll consider it. Van and Maria are coming in from Brighton for the wedding. They'll have the latest news."

Race didn't feel in the mood for a wedding, but he played his part. At least he didn't have to amuse the company. The couple did that themselves by dashing off to their home with unseemly haste.

Con laughed and toasted them, then he and Lord Vandeimen hosted the village party until nightfall. The Vandeimens hadn't mentioned Anne yet, and he was reluctant to raise the subject.

Race couldn't help noting that this event was even further proof that he had no hope with Anne. These men all had deep roots here, unlike his father at Shapcott. But then a scrap of gossip reminded him Hawkinville's father had been a man very like Race's—an outsider who had bought his way into a manor.

No, it wasn't the same. Hawkinville's father was blueblooded. In fact he had now inherited a title of his own which would come to Hawkinville one day. It hardly mattered. The Hawkinvilles, like the true de Veres, could trace their line back to the Conquest, a far greater matter than a mere title.

Race thought his father a more thorough gentleman than Squire Hawkinville.

Hawk's father had charmed his way into both manor and fortune, then treated his wife shamefully. Race's father had bargained fortune for manor, and kept his part of the arrangement. He'd restored Shapcott Hall, and provided a life of elegance for his wife.

The world would not care about that. It was bloodlines not virtue that mattered.

There'd been times, many times, when he'd imagined persuading Anne into marriage and making her happy.

He suspected that he could do the first, but he doubted that he could do the second for a lifetime. He would be asking her to climb down from her gilded heaven to wade through the mud here below.

Nor would their marriage be attended by universal joy like this one. Her family would at best be disappointed, society would snigger, and her friends would drift away. What did he have to offer in return? No family, no home until he made one, no real name. He'd suffered the constant reaction to the name de Vere. Was he to ask her to become Lady Anne de Vere?

"Cheer up," Con said, slapping him on the back. "It's a wedding. Ah, I know your problem. You want to get married, too."

"Definitely not. I've my life to sort out."

"You haven't done it yet? Think of it as papers to be shuffled."

"Organized. Shuffling is the opposite."

"Ah, that must be why I never quite got the hang of it." Con was a bit tipsy. "So, have you decided what to do about your father?"

Race accepted more ale from a rosy-cheeked girl who blushed at his smile. "Oh, yes. I wrote to him from Devon to tell him to go ahead with the annulment."

Con shook his head but asked, "What now? Delighted as I am to have you around, I feel it's time for you to leave the nest."

Race laughed at that. "Yes, mama bird. I thought perhaps I would go to London and inquire about things like archives and libraries. There has to be an occupation there somewhere that would suit me."

Con pulled a face, but then he dug a card out of a pocket and scribbled something on the back. "If you need anything, look up Sir Stephen Ball. He's a friend of mine, and he probably knows a fair bit about that sort of thing."

Race looked at the address scribbled on the back and the words "All assistance."

"Thank you. A Rogue, I assume."

"I think you'll like him. In fact, if you wanted to continue in the secretary trade . . ."

"Doesn't he have one?"

"Probably. He's the sort to always have use for more. Always digging into something."

Race tucked the card away. "Susan was unwell this morning. Am I to wish you happy?"

Con blushed. Or perhaps it was just a glow. "Yes." He turned to look around at the happy village, and at his wife dancing and laughing. "It's a perfect world, isn't it?"

"Definitely," Race said. What else was there to say on the sun-kissed evening of a happy wedding day?

But then Con turned back to him. "You're right about Brighton and Lady Anne. But if I have to go to go there, you should come, too."

Race tensed. "You don't need me. I told you. She bears no grudge."

"If not to protect me, come for pleasure. The renovations on Vandeimen Hall are finished, so Van and Maria are giving up the Brighton house next week. They suggest we visit them for the last few days."

"I don't care for Brighton."

"I'd like you to come," Con said in the direct, honest way that he had. "It's been a crazy summer with very happy endings, and you've been part of much of it. This will be the end of many things, and the beginning of the rest of our lives." He put a hand on Race's shoulder. "I'd like you to come with us simply as a friend, Race, to tie up the last knot."

Race looked out at the merry, tipsy village and surrendered. Con was right. A stage of life was coming to an end.

"Put like that," he said, "how can I refuse?"

Three days later Race rode into Brighton with Con, alongside Susan in the carriage, amused as always by the elite in frivolous mood. One group on the promenade seemed to be playing blindman's buff, and others were bobbing along on small donkeys. A large sign promised a race between a Captain Philips and "Backward Barry," apparently over a mile, to be walked backward.

He couldn't stay here long, though. Normally he was the one using mischief to lighten the sober. Here he was tempted to either go too far or take to Methodism. He would spend a few days with his friends, check on Lady

Anne Peckworth from a safe distance, and then be on his way.

He caught himself scanning the Marine Parade for a glimpse of her, but a sudden flurry drew his attention to an approaching open carriage.

"The Regent," Con said, bowing when the genial fat man waved vaguely in their direction. "He declares that he doesn't want any formal fuss here, but would be very put out if ignored."

Race hadn't seen the poor man before. He was extremely fat, looked very uncomfortable in his fashionable garments, and despite the smile, rather sad. Vague ideas of improvement drifted into Race's head, and he hastily blocked them. He had no desire to take up Brummell's abandoned crown.

They drew up in front of the Vandeimens' bow-fronted house and were soon entering. Maria Vandeimen emerged from the front room declaring, "Welcome! We have such a treat for you!"

She was in her thirties and possessed of natural elegance, but at the moment her eyes sparkled with mischief.

"Race," Con said, stopping dead, "tell them not to take away the horses. We may need to leave."

Vandeimen, young, blond, and dashing, with a saber slash across his cheek, joined his wife. "Not at all. You won't want to miss this."

"What?"

"The Regent is holding a grand reception tonight for all the military officers in Brighton."

"Lord save us." Con pretended to head toward the door again, but was towed back by Susan and Race.

"The Regent will probably be in uniform," Con complained, as they dragged him into the drawing room, "and claiming again to have fought at Waterloo. Men only?"

Maria ordered tea. "Oh, no. You are all to have adoring ladies on your arms to symbolize Britannia, and you are to wear favors."

They all sat. "You have my sympathy, Van," Con said. "It has to be too late for us to get invitations."

"But would we leave you out of such a treat? We sent

immediately to say that two other gallant officers would be here."

"Traitor."

"Not at all. The implication is that any veteran officer present in Brighton who fails to show up will be viewed as malingering."

Con was still humorously complaining, but Susan poked him. "I've wanted a chance to see inside the Pavilion." Her attention turned to Maria. "What should I wear, and what favors should we make them wear? . . ."

In minutes, she and Maria had drifted off discussing fashion. Van instantly changed the refreshments from tea to ale, and the atmosphere made the subtle shift to masculine.

Race smiled sympathy at the other two. "I'm saved from this affair by not having a convenient lady."

A footman came in with the jug of ale and tankards. Van sent him away and poured himself. "Think again," he said, giving one to Race. "Maria's niece Natalie has just arrived to dabble her toes in social waters before a proper plunge next year. She's an excitable sixteen, and she, too, is desperate to get inside the Pavilion."

Race winced, then saw Van take it amiss, thinking he didn't want to bother with a mere girl.

"I have an unfortunate appeal to the young," he said quickly, trying, by limiting it to "the young," not to sound like an cockscomb. "I've been plunged into some embarrassing situations."

Van assessed it, then nodded. "We'll warn her, but she's very sensible about these things. Continental blood. She's the orphaned daughter of a relative of Maria's first husband."

Talk moved on to friends, horses, and sports, and Race could only hope that this Natalie was as sensible as her uncle thought.

He was thinking over another problem. He'd intended to lie low in Brighton. Last time he'd come here with Con, he hadn't attended society affairs. This reception might throw him into the same company as Anne, but it was impossible now to back out without giving offense.

It sounded as if the assembly would be a crush where

it would be easy to avoid her. In that case it could be useful—it would be an opportunity to gain a true impression of how she fared.

When Susan and Maria returned, they brought the young lady with them. Lord save him. She was plump, huge-eyed, almost bouncing with excitement, and rushed over to sit beside him on the sofa.

"I do thank you for escorting me, Captain de Vere! I can't wait to see the Pavilion. Do you think the Regent will pinch my cheek? They say he does that to all the young ladies."

"Not unless you learn to behave like a young lady," said Vandeimen. "Race, I make known to you Miss Natalie Florence. Natalie, Mr. de Vere. As he's sold out, the captain is inappropriate."

Unrepressed, Natalie dimpled and held out a hand. "Thank you again, Mr. de Vere."

Perhaps this would be all right. Her eyes were bright but met his directly, and only natural color flushed her cheeks. As a test, he took the pretty hand and kissed it.

Her eyes widened, and her full lips parted. He thought he'd made a mistake, but then she said, "Mr. de Vere, could you teach me all about flirtation?"

"No." It was a sharp response that sprang directly from Benning Hall. He immediately softened it. "Not *all*. But a little, perhaps, if Lord Vandeimen promises not to shoot me."

"I make no such promise."

Race let the girl's hand go. "Alas, my dear, you are too well guarded."

She gave a teasing pout, but the smile she sent Vandeimen showed she didn't take his threat seriously. Race did. He had no doubt that Vandeimen would eviscerate any man who harmed this charming girl. He himself would be next in line.

He was reassured about her, however, and even began to look forward to the evening. He gathered it would be her first true social event, so being her escort would certainly blow away any tedium. Tedium? With the possibility of meeting Anne Peckworth again?

If Anne was there, who would she be with? Not St. Raven, who was not a veteran. Would her escort be the man she had chosen? Race wondered what he would do if she was throwing herself away on a cad.

A tingle in his body was a warning. He'd felt this way sometimes before battle—when he'd expected something exciting, or dangerous. Or even disastrous.

Twenty-one

~

When the ladies came down in the evening, Race had no complaints about his partner. Natalie was no beauty—her hair was mousy, she was short, and he suspected that she'd always be plump. An enormous zest for life fizzed in her, however, and someone—presumably Maria Vandeimen—had excellent taste.

Natalie's stiff ivory silk gown was exactly right in its simplicity and severe cut, with only the most subtle trimming of deep blue to match her eyes. The bodice was low enough on her full breasts to be interesting while still being modest, and her jewels were delicately made of pearls and sapphire chips. Suitable yet unusual, and a reminder to the world that Natalie could be assumed to share some of her uncle's wealth—the uncle being Maria's first husband, Maurice Celestin.

People in society wore jewelry as a statement of their wealth, and people like Maria—born into one of the best families in England—knew the language in every subtle nuance.

From the deep recesses of his mind came the memory that his mother had only ever worn simple ornaments, even though his father had given her some lovely pieces. What had that meant?

Natalie came straight to him, dimples deep, with a knot of sapphire blue and white ribbons in her gloved hand. "For my hero!" she declared.

Laughing, he went on one knee before her so that she could pin it to his sleeve. He fought back a memory of kneeling like this before Anne when he provided that footstool. What would it be like if this were Anne and they were going to this event together?

Instantly the other ladies demanded the same from their gentlemen, and amid complaints, they complied.

They all set out in high spirits.

"With any luck," Vandeimen said, "the prince will be in some uniform of his own design, dripping with gold cord and glittering orders."

The Regent, however, was dressed in severe civilian evening dress, though his shirt collar was insanely high and stiff, making any movement of his head perilous. Race suspected that he was tight-corseted, as well. He looked red-faced and breathless.

This was the man who had once been called Prince Florizel because of his beauty, and who seemed never to have become at ease with himself. At fifty-six, he still was not true monarch, and his blind, demented father looked set to live forever.

Race took that as warning not to drift through his own life. For now, he settled to his duty for the night—to give Natalie a perfect evening.

It looked to be easy. She was enchanted by the Pavilion's Asian decorations and by the effect of massed, glittering uniforms and medals. Race was sure she'd rather be partnered by a serving officer than by a past one, but she was too well raised to show it.

Spirits were generally high despite inevitable thoughts of the missing. All these men had come to terms with loss—one had to or else go mad. There were the wounded, of course, as reminder. Scars, eye patches, empty sleeves, and the awkward gait of the wooden leg.

If Anne was here, perhaps she'd feel less peculiar. He kept constantly alert to avoid an accidental encounter. He hadn't seen her yet. Perhaps she wouldn't be here at all.

He forced relief over acute disappointment.

There were men who carried worse marks of the war than any here, Race knew. Those hideously scarred by burns or by a saber through the face. Those confined to their beds or a wheeled chair. Those destroyed in the mind.

They were the forgotten, the reminders of the truly dark side of war that civilians preferred to ignore. . . .

He shook off the mood and squired Natalie around. She behaved perfectly, but her excitement and delight were infectious, and she was soon everyone's darling. Heaven help the beau monde next year.

Many of the men flirted with her, men of all ages, but she took it in the playful spirit it was offered. As Vandeimen had said, she already had a touch of Continental sophistication. Race did notice a few subalterns who looked dazzled. No harm in that, but he'd keep a close eye on her.

Then, as he and Natalie rejoined Con and Susan, he saw Anne.

He noticed her by a flurry of excitement. Couples were moving toward a point like moths to a candle, and the candle was a lady carrying a tall staff decorated with a line of golden love knots. Her gown was pale silk, but shot through with gold. Straight and slender, Lady Anne Peckworth truly shone like a flame.

He fought through breathless bedazzlement to notice detail. This gown was not an older one smartened up. The lines were subtly dashing in the way only the very best mantua-maker could achieve, and the bodice was extremely brief, making her breasts seem fuller than they actually were. For a moment, he could imagine walking over and claiming some right to possess those breasts. . . .

He sucked in a breath and turned away, pretending that he knew what the hell Con and Susan were chatting about.

Insanity, need, and deep gnawing loss probably had him pale. Was he shaking? Natalie was chattering to Susan and no one seemed to notice anything wrong. Weeks ago, he had consciously surrendered any slight chance he'd had of claiming Anne Peckworth as his own. Since then it had seemed a minor ache.

Now it was like a lost limb, lost sight, lost life.

What had he done?

What had he done?

Sanity swooped back with beak and claw, and the buzz around became voices. He had done what he had done for her, not for himself, and now it was even more cor-

rect. She was queen of her world, able to take her pick
of the best. It was all exactly as he'd wished.

He could look back at her now.

She wore a pearl collar on her elegant neck, but sparkles there spoke of diamonds, increasing the flame effect. More glittered in her headdress that he realized
was vaguely reminiscent of Britannia's traditional hel-
met. And the staff, braced on the floor beside her, held
at an angle, was actually Britannia's spear.

She'd come as Britain's warrior goddess, and her demeanor fit the part.

Bravo, Anne. Bravo.

"Who is that?" asked Natalie, wide-eyed.

"Lady Anne Peckworth, daughter of the Duke of
Arran."

"She's beautiful."

And she was. Not just beautiful as he found her, but
in everyone's eyes. Unlike the Regent, she had grown
into herself, and that confidence along with all the skills
available to her had created genuine, remarkable beauty.

Strangely he felt a pang of loss for the uneasy, uncertain lady he'd teased into brandy and hazard once, a
long, long time ago, as distant as the battlefields of
Spain.

She was smiling and chatting with the ladies and gentlemen around her, laughing at what was clearly a risqué
touch of flirtation. She rapped one gentleman on the
hand with her closed fan. No trace of shyness or nerves.

Then, another moth was drawn—the Regent. Among
bows and curtsies he quickly raised Anne, and Race
heard him say, "No, no, Lady Anne, do not strain
your foot!"

"Good God."

Race glanced sideways at Con. "You see."

"I do. But, good God . . ."

"You don't approve?"

"I . . ." Con shook his head. "Of course, I'm delighted
if she's happy, but . . . what has become of her?"

"You'd rather she was still the mouse?"

Con gave him a funny look, and Race knew his tone
had been razor-sharp.

"Lady Anne," Race said calmly, "seems to have developed poise and confidence and to be very happy. Do not begrudge her that."

"You're right. I suppose we put people into roles and then expect them to stay there." As the Regent moved on, Con twitched at his cravat. "I had better go and speak to her."

"She won't bite."

"She might skewer me with that spear." But Con held his arm out to Susan. He glanced back at Race. "Are you coming?"

"You'll survive without an escort."

Con and Susan began to navigate their way across the crowded room. Casual observers would see nothing wrong, but Race knew they were both wound tight with nervousness, fearing that Anne would create a scene.

She wouldn't, Race knew, but he was fighting an urge to go with them, or to hurry ahead and warn her. Anne was skilled at hiding her reactions, but in a moment of surprise—?

It was all right. He saw no hint of discomfort or awkwardness when she first spotted Con. When they met, her smile seemed genuine, and she gave her hand to Susan without hesitation.

Some tension inside him relaxed.

Perhaps she would have followed this path anyway, but he'd like to think that his meddling at Benning Hall had played a small part in her blossoming. He'd like to think that his cruel treatment of her at the Swinamer ball had brought her here, too, blasting away any tendency to be distracted by him.

Who was she with tonight?

A man stood beside her, dashing and darkly handsome in his uniform, the knot of gold ribbons on his arm almost drowned by gold braid and frogging.

Who?

Good God, it was Dashing Jack.

Dashing Jack Ralstone, nicknamed for his reckless bravery in battle, but also for his reckless indulgence with women. A hero, he thought wryly, remembering Benning Hall, a worm of worry stirring. Was Dashing Jack simply her escort for tonight, or was there something more serious going on?

He checked on Natalie at his side, but she was happily chatting to three young couples not much older than she—subalterns and their ladies.

He pretended to be observing the crowded room, but in fact kept most of his attention on Anne and Ralstone. Con and Susan had moved on, and the crowd around Anne shifted as couples came and went. Race watched every nuance of her interactions with Ralstone. Not good. Her smile was too warm, and his was too confident.

Ralstone had been a good man to have around in battle, though he'd been inclined to dash off in reckless heroics. He'd been good company in an after-victory carouse, too, but Race had never felt inclined to call him friend.

He wasn't a drunkard, but he was much like Uffham about it—likely to slide into drink when he didn't have anything better to do. He wasn't a rake, but he was a womanizer. They came so easily to his charm and good looks, and he wasn't the sort to refuse a gift if pressed upon him.

Once or twice, he hadn't been so careful of the lady's reputation as he should have been. There'd been a couple of duels, but no one had been seriously injured. Wellington's opinion of duels was too well known.

He gambled, but not to excess. . . .

Good God, all that said was that Ralstone was a typical officer. Nearly everyone drank to excess sometimes, and enjoyed the thrill of dice and cards. What man rejected the offers of lovely ladies? Ralstone did at least have the kind of birth and family connections that wouldn't shame Anne. He had a title coming to him one day.

Enough. It was time he gave her credit for knowing her own mind. Which meant he'd better apply his mind to avoiding her.

He claimed Natalie and took her off to explore the lavish oriental decorations and meet new people. He watched with amusement as she finally became flustered by the obvious admiration of a redheaded ensign not much older than she. Young Armscote had been at Waterloo, however, and perhaps something of that lingered in his eyes. His partner was his sister, who clearly did not mind his wandering attention.

Race flirted mildly with the sister for a while, trying hard not to make an impression, and was relieved when another young couple joined the group, leaving him the outsider.

It left his mind vulnerable to Anne, however.

Would Ralstone be faithful? He was more rake than not. Some rakes changed when they married for love, but most? And was this love? That felt like a mean-spirited question, but some instinct was saying that Ralstone's happy glow was not love but triumph.

Of course, winning a bride like Anne would be a triumph. If he were in that position, he'd probably be crowing like a cock. But his crow would be love, not victory. . . .

Love?

He felt like bashing his head against one of the crimson walls. He couldn't be so stupid as to be in love with Lady Anne Peckworth!

Love. He noticed Natalie's bright eyes and Armscote's flushed cheeks and separated them before they fell into the same fate. Because of his distraction, he was probably too late. The best thing would be to find her another young officer and dilute the effect.

He should apply that advice to himself, but he couldn't imagine any other woman stirring his interest at the moment. He remembered saying to Con that he was unlikely to marry. He had to assume that all this would fade, that he'd change his mind one day, but at the moment . . .

At the moment he had the absurd temptation to seek Anne out and follow her like a puppy simply for the reward of being close.

He took Natalie for a turn in the lantern-lit gardens, hoping fresh air would blow away insanity. It was a pleasant relief from the heat and smells of the crowded Pavilion, but it did nothing for his brain.

He couldn't stand by and let Anne throw herself away on Ralstone. But what else could he do?

Alert Uffham?

He wasn't sure he had any influence with Uffham anymore. His rough break with the Peckworth family had seemed a good strategy at the time—remove temptation entirely—but now it was turning round to bite him.

And anyway, what could he say? That Ralstone was not entirely a sober, upright member of society? Neither was Uffham.

Neither, come to that, was he.

Quickly bored with gardens, Natalie asked that they return to the house to explore more chinoiserie. Anything to distract his mind. They went back inside, then, as they approached the end of the gallery, they came face-to-face with Anne on Ralstone's arm.

Twenty feet or more separated them, but now that people were all over the Pavilion, the crowd here was thin.

Her eyes widened, her lips parted, she paled, then flushed. With anger? No. He didn't want to think it, but he thought the anger had come a heartbeat after something else, something he'd thought he'd killed.

He did the only thing he could for her—he sent a message that he had no interest. He inclined his head and turned his attention to Natalie and a Chinese lantern over their heads. If he'd been with an older, more worldly-wise woman, he might have set up a blatant flirtation, perhaps even gone so far as a kiss, but he couldn't do that to Natalie.

He could only pray that Anne and Ralstone would go by without speaking. Anne wouldn't approach him, he was sure, but he'd served with Ralstone for a year at one time and a few months at another, and encountered him here and there all over the Peninsula. He might come over to talk.

In a mirror, he watched Anne and Ralstone move into the long room and past. Saw her glance toward him, caught her eyes in the reflection. Wide, blue, steady, and completely unreadable. Then she moved out of reflection like an actor moving off stage.

He led Natalie onward, toward the arch and the picture of the Chinaman there, painted on glass. Real and unreal. Solid and fragile. His head was buzzing again, but he would recover once they were safe.

But then the Regent swept in with his entourage and

chose them to speak to. Race's name gave the prince some problem.

"De Vere? De Vere? Thought there weren't any de Veres any more. Going to claim the Earldom of Oxford, then?" The prince was clearly worried that he'd been left in ignorance of something important.

Race gave the answer he used when he wanted to avoid complications. "Not at all, sir. A very minor branch, and—if you will forgive me—on the wrong side of the blanket."

"Oh, I see! And your home, sir?"

"Derbyshire, sir."

"Good, good. Grand place, Derbyshire. All those peaks . . ."

The prince went on to make some remarkably sensible comments about the war, and seemed to share all Race's disappointment at missing Waterloo.

He pinched Natalie's full cheeks, and Race feared she'd burst into giggles, but she managed to only beam at the prince, which pleased. Her honest delight at the Pavilion style pleased, too, so that the royal personage delayed to talk to her about his treasures.

By the time the prince bustled off to another couple, there was no sign of Anne. Race took Natalie off to explore the Pavilion in the opposite direction. This was going to be a strange hide-and-seek evening, but he thought he could manage it. After all, Anne must be as keen to avoid him as he was to avoid her.

Twenty-two

$\sim$

Anne laughed at some joke of Captain Ralstone's that she hadn't heard, trying desperately not to show that she was shaken.

Race de Vere was *here*, with no warning. She'd not seen his name in the daily list of arrivals, but then she realized she'd been so distracted all day that she hadn't even looked.

Even so, she felt betrayed.

And he'd had a pretty, glowing child on his arm. Who was she? How did he acquire this string of adoring ladies? And she was so young. Too young.

She was immediately shamed by her anger. Despite everything, she was jealous. Sharply jealous.

Have some pride, Anne!

She suggested to Ralstone that they join a group—safety in numbers—and concentrated on the conversation there. She fixed her entire consciousness on Ralstone as he told a lighthearted story about military life.

Why on earth did de Vere have to turn up now of all times, when she'd finally committed herself to Alderton? He must be fey! She felt almost fevered, unable to concentrate. She'd been that way all day, however.

Had she known without knowing that de Vere was here?

All day a conviction had been growing that she could not marry Alderton. She'd accepted him, which meant she was bound. To the best of her knowledge, no Peckworth lady had ever broken an announced engagement. On the other hand, nothing was announced yet, which meant she had a brief opportunity to retreat.

It was always possible that some fire, some passion would ignite between them after marriage, but doubt was filling her like cold water in a well. There'd been nothing, absolutely nothing in his kiss except discomfort and embarrassment. Imagine a life, an intimate life, like that.

And so, this evening, she had begun to turn to Ralstone. She had to marry. Apart from all the practical pressures, she was going to go mad if she had to play this game much longer. And here was a handsome, dashing hero whose tender kiss had made her toes curl. His family was acceptable, and if his fortune was small, that could be corrected.

As she'd moved through this evening on his arm, her assurance about it had calmed her soul. He had a wicked edge to him, yes, but she was willing to admit that she found it exciting. She didn't have Tris's assessment of him, but she would before she committed herself.

It was clear that the officers who'd served with him in the war thought him an excellent fellow, and there had even been a few anecdotes to his credit. He flirted and charmed with suspicious ease, but she couldn't really complain about that. His devotion to her seemed genuine.

She must have been encouraging Ralstone because he was becoming more attentive, more possessive by the moment. If she encouraged him a little bit more, he would propose.

She made a vague reply to a comment she hadn't heard, suppressing a desire to giggle. Was she really going to allow one gentleman to ask for her hand in marriage when she was already promised to another? What had become of perfectly behaved Lady Anne Peckworth?

And now de Vere was here, like a prickle down her neck and a quiver in her stomach.

He'd turned away, however, as soon as he'd seen her. Could anything be more clear than that? She'd wanted his place in her life cleared up, and now it was. She made herself focus entirely on the story Ralstone was telling to the group, to considerable laughter.

Perhaps it was her intense concentration, but she began to see that the anecdote was a little mean-spirited. The butt of his joke didn't deserve such treatment, and his laughter at his own story sounded brash.

As did everyone else's.

She remembered one aspect of marriage that she'd tried to keep in mind. She would end up friend to her husband's friends, part of his circle.

Who exactly were Ralstone's friends?

Oh, did it matter? He would have to accommodate to her friends and family, too.

They moved on toward another group. "Wasn't that Racecombe de Vere who bowed to you a while back, Lady Anne?" he asked.

Anne felt as if he must notice her start, but he seemed oblivious. "Yes," she managed to say. "He's a friend of my brother's. I hardly know him at all." *Stop babbling, Anne!* She calmed herself and asked, "You know him, Captain Ralstone?"

"We served together a time or two. Amusing company, but a dashed madman at times."

Anne knew she should leave it at that, change the subject, but her will crumpled. "In what way?" she asked, pausing as if to study an exquisite porcelain vase.

"Don't want to tell stories . . . ," Ralstone said, but then proved willing enough. "After all, it's nothing to his discredit. He was put in charge of a flogging one day and switched the whip for one made of ribbons."

Anne stared at him. "What? Why?"

Was de Vere truly mad? That might explain his strange behavior.

"We were under a Major Underwood at the time. A tyrant and getting worse. He'd have the men flogged for a missing button. Course, nothing anyone could do. Chain of command and all that."

"Yet Captain de Vere refused to carry out the punishment?"

Madness because of the risks, but a glorious sort of insanity, noble and just.

"Oh, he carried it out, but with the ribbons. Claimed there'd been nothing in the order about what the man should be flogged with. Old Underwood practically had an apoplexy and ordered de Vere flogged in the man's place. With the cat."

Anne felt as if her heart missed a number of beats. "He was *flogged*?"

"No, no, my dear lady. Of course not. The men set up a racket, and the commotion brought our colonel by. Ended up with Wellington involved. Equal blame laid on de Vere and Underwood, but Underwood was transferred to Irish duties. Poor bloody Irish." Then he colored charmingly. "Your pardon."

"No matter," Anne said, still fixed on the horrible idea. "Was Captain de Vere in danger of being flogged?"

In spirit, at least, he was a martyr.

But Captain Ralstone laughed. "Of course not, Lady Anne. Officers aren't punished in that way. Would erode the respect of the men, you see. That was why Wellington rid himself of Underwood."

The glowing light around de Vere's image faded. Mischief. That's what it had been. Typical mischief. No wonder, however, that he'd said it was touch and go in the army at times.

Another couple joined them, and Ralstone mentioned the incident with de Vere. It seemed to have made the rounds of the army. Colonel Emerson thought it amusing; Major Crispin, a mad piece of nonsense that could undermine authority.

Anne, however, settled on the result. De Vere had saved a man from an unjust flogging. She wanted to ask if these officers would have carried out the punishment as ordered, but she knew the answer. They all would. Including Ralstone.

"Captain de Vere suffered no consequences at all?" asked Mrs. Crispin.

"Only a terse public comment from Wellington that if de Vere ever disobeyed the letter and the spirit of an order of his he'd have him shot."

"So I should think," said Crispin.

Anne found that she had to speak. "Surely it shows Mr. de Vere in an admirable light."

The sudden silence showed how outrageous her objection was, but she no longer cared.

"Strange fellow, though," Ralstone said quickly. "Always had his men laughing, even as they waited for battle. Drove some of the other officers distracted. He called his men the Laughing Corpses, but they didn't seem to mind."

"Thank God I never had him under my command," said Crispin. "Sounds cracked in the nob to me."

Anne couldn't stop her response, though she tried to soften it with a smile. "If I were waiting to face the enemy, Major, I would rather do it laughing than quivering."

"Doubtless why we don't send petticoats to war, Lady Anne." With a stiff bow, he and his wife moved on.

Colonel Emerson said, "Never did have much sense of humor, old Crispin." Then he and his lady moved on, too.

"You are ardent in de Vere's defense, Lady Anne," Ralstone remarked. "He is important to you?"

Heat flooded her. She'd not thought of that in her instinctive support. She laughed. "Not at all! He is merely a friend of my brother's, and seems harmless enough."

It seemed so wrong to dismiss him like that, but what else could she say?

We drank brandy together, then kissed in a most improper way, and later I wished I had the wild folly to join him naked in a bed, or the even wilder folly to let him fondle and ruin me in a library during a ball. And, yes, I like his mischievousness and wit, and now I admire his courage and honor.

"Harmless?" Ralstone seemed to find that amusing, and she read beneath it the fact that de Vere had killed, as a soldier must. It shivered down her spine and through her nerves. She glanced around at smiling gentlemen realizing that all of them must have had days that ended with blood on their hands.

Her attention was caught by someone—a rather solid young woman in a bold blue gown and turban on the arm of a rugged officer.

"My goodness, it's Claretta!"

Ralstone followed her gaze. "Oh, Crump. Yes, he did very well for himself there, especially for a trade officer."

She wanted to poke him with her spear. "I must go and wish them well." As they crossed the room, she added, "She's cousin to my foster brother, the Duke of St. Raven."

"I'm sorry, Lady Anne. I didn't realize she was a connection of yours."

She wanted to tell him that wasn't the point, but they were already across the room. "Claretta. You're looking splendid, and it must be because of your fine husband."

"Anne!" Claretta hadn't magically become a beauty, but her bright smile and shining eyes made Anne suddenly feel that parts of the world were just as they should be.

Anne was introduced to Captain Crump, and she found him to be a no-nonsense man with a kind heart. His face was square, his brown hair cropped short, and his build could best be described as robust. She couldn't help feeling that he and Claretta would have very solid, robust children.

That reminded her to sneak a glance at Claretta's shape, but with her normally heavy build and a fussy gown it was impossible to tell. What did it matter anyway? They were happy.

She chatted to the couple, liking Captain Crump more all the time. His voice had a touch of Cockney to it, she thought, but it didn't matter. His words and manner were gentlemanly.

As Crump and Ralstone exchanged polite remarks, Anne said to Claretta, "Congratulations. He's wonderful."

Claretta smiled. "He is, isn't he? I hope you do as well, Anne. You should. You've become quite a beauty."

Anne felt like saying, *And what good has that done me?* but she simply smiled. "I hope you're not having any difficulties?"

"With people?" Claretta shrugged. "There are a few who turn up their noses. We don't care for them. We

like a quiet life anyway. Of course, it might have been
sticky if the parents were still alive, especially mother."

She pulled a face that made Anne smile.

"And I must say," Claretta added, "that Cornelia is
being difficult. We never got along, though, and of
course she married Tremaine. He might be an earl, but
he's a pill. I think she's jealous."

Anne smothered outright laughter. It was all too true.
In fact, it wasn't funny. It was a lesson about what could
happen when a lady married for rank without considering the nature of her partner.

Was Claretta a lesson about the opposite? That the
daring seizure of an unsuitable husband was worth it in
the end?

"Spoiled for choice?" Claretta asked, and eyed Ralstone. "I like the look of that one."

"So do I," Anne said, and it was true. Ralstone was
wonderful to look at.

"The betting seems to be on Alderton."

"He's a good man."

Claretta gave Anne a surprisingly shrewd look, as if
she sensed Anne's ambivalence, but a burst of laughter
distracted them both. Anne looked across the room and
saw Race de Vere enter the room in the midst of a high-
spirited group.

Enter fool, stage left. Yet he wasn't a fool except in
the classic sense of the one who was allowed to prick
the pride of a king.

The Laughing Corpses. If she were a soldier facing
battle, she truly would prefer to be under his command.
What's more, she'd rather face life laughing, too.

Their eyes met across the room for the briefest moment, and then he turned to his partner, the glowing
young girl.

The cut again, and yet it wasn't. She knew it wasn't.

It was more like being accidentally kissed.

Had she given de Vere the impression earlier that *she*
did not want to acknowledge *him*? After their last encounter, it wouldn't be surprising.

As conversation flowed around her, she thought back,
tried to recreate that second of decision and reaction.
She'd been so startled, she'd simply stared. Not even a

smile. Oh, heavens, had it seemed she had been cutting him? It was, after all, for her to acknowledge him.

Then their eyes had met in the mirror. Such a strange moment, that, as if they were on two stages separated by glass. She knew now that she'd been searching for encouragement, for any hint that she could approach without embarrassing herself.

And all the time it had been her move to make. She was the lady, he the gentleman. She was the duke's daughter, he virtually her brother's servant.

It seemed that they had spoken through glass all along except for that one brief time in Benning's study when she had dared to reach, and the barrier had dissolved.

But no, it had disappeared again at the Swinamer ball. For a while. She must do something to dissolve that barrier again. She must, before she could consider marrying anyone else, be it Alderton, Ralstone, or any other man.

She must do it for herself, and for him, but also for the other men. How terrible to be married as second best.

And she must do it tonight before Race de Vere slipped out of her world again like a member of faery.

And if he wasn't being deliberately distant? If he wanted her?

He was still nobody.

Her family would still be appalled.

The ton would still snigger as they had over Claretta. . . .

It was as if glass shattered. She no longer cared.

She would be like Claretta. She would claim the man who could make the world glow for her.

When she looked again, however, Race had gone.

As soon as there was a break in the conversation, she said to Ralstone, "I do long to explore a little more." She took leave of their group and headed in the direction Race and his party must have taken.

How to find him in this place? And how to get time alone with him?

Ralstone put his hand over hers on his arm and squeezed her fingers. "Our minds are in accord, Lady Anne. I, too, would like some time alone together."

Oh, Lord. Not now. Not yet.

Twenty-three

~

"You are looking glorious tonight," Ralstone said softly, leaning so his lips brushed her ear. "So like a queen, I fear the Regent will try to steal you."

Idiocy. She twitched away. "He is already married. Or were you thinking I might become a royal mistress, Captain?"

He colored. "Of course not." But he moved closer again. "You know what I want you to become, Lady Anne."

He paused then, holding her left hand since her staff was in her right. She realized that they were in a short corridor that was deserted for the moment.

"Anne, you know I long to call you wife. Do I have reason to hope?"

His dark eyes were long-lashed and so very serious. She had encouraged him this far, she knew she had, and he deserved some kind of answer, but her heart was a thundering panic in her chest. First Alderton. Now this. What a mess she was making of things.

"I wouldn't be here with you, Captain Ralstone, if you didn't have hope."

His smile was beautifully rueful. "Jack. Can you not bring yourself to call me Jack?"

De Vere had asked her to call him Race.

She'd refused.

"In private, perhaps . . ."

His smile instantly radiated optimism. Confidence, even. "Then when may I speak to you in private, Anne?"

"It would be improper . . ."

He squeezed her hand. "I understand. You are so strong, so brave, that sometimes I forget that you are a delicately raised maiden. . . ."

Then he bowed reverently to kiss her hand.

Anne bit her lip on shocking laughter. What had Race said? That she shouldn't trust a man who bowed before her as if she were a saint. . . .

He lingered there, and she glanced around praying no one come upon them like this. Her prayer wasn't answered.

Race and his partner came around the corner. They stopped. Her eyes collided with his, no glass between them now.

His partner smiled in delight. Anne saw romantic visions dancing behind the big eyes and wanted to scream a warning. Then Race turned her, and they disappeared back the way they'd come.

Ralstone straightened, and in her dazed pity, she smiled brilliantly at him. He smiled brilliantly back, clearly thinking the delicately raised maiden was in the bag.

She, however, could only think of how to follow Race. No, how to get him alone.

Ralstone was saying something about a meeting. She made some reply, but hurried them in the direction Race had gone. She knew Ralstone was taking her behavior as maidenly embarrassment and felt cruel; but she could focus on only one thing.

Race.

She had to talk to him. She had to explain that the kiss had meant nothing. She had to find out what he felt.

She cruised the rooms with Ralstone until her foot began to ache, but caught no sight of her quarry. Had he already waved a magic wand and disappeared? She didn't think so. Absurd as it seemed, she felt his presence.

Impossible to have the meeting, though, with Ralstone by her side. Why hadn't she thought of that?

She had to get rid of him.

"I need the ladies' retiring room," she said with the hesitancy suitable for such a delicate subject.

Every inch the perfect escort, he discovered the location from a footman and escorted her down a corridor to an out-of-the-way spot. Of course, it was impossible for him to wait. Imagine the ladies having to pass a line of escorts on their way to the chamber pots!

"Perhaps you could wait for me in the central saloon, Captain Ralstone." Far enough away that he could not watch her emerge.

He bowed and left, and Anne went into the room blowing out a relieved breath. This wouldn't get rid of Race's companion, but it was halfway.

She didn't need to use the screened close-stools, so she sat to rest her foot. The spacious room contained perhaps a dozen ladies, some simply sitting as she was, some being tidied by the waiting maids. Of course, she knew everyone, and everyone knew her. Without reason, she felt sure that they all knew what she was up to.

All that was said, however, was praise of her costume and of her handsome escort.

Then she heard de Vere's name.

"Natalie's safe. Mr. de Vere's something of a devil with the ladies' hearts, but she's not ready for that sort of folly yet."

Anne saw that the speaker was Lady Vandeimen, who had been Maria Celestin, and before that had been Maria Dunpott-Ffyfe. She was talking to Lady Harlesdon, an older woman with a sour tongue.

"Girls are ready for folly from the day they get their front teeth, Maria. Be careful."

"I am, Clara, but I think it's good for them to cut those teeth on the dashing handsome ones. They're not so susceptible later."

Susceptible. The word pierced Anne like a pin piercing a bubble, and her mad confidence began to leak.

"De Vere does seem to have a fatal appeal for women," Maria Vandeimen was saying. "I don't know what it is. Perhaps that he appears to genuinely care. He has a very kind heart. Ah, Natalie, my dear. How are you enjoying yourself?"

Anne openly watched as the girl joined the older women, chattering of the wonders of the Pavilion as

Lady Vandeimen tidied her frothing curls. There was not one word about Race, so the fatal appeal had not struck there.

Anne found herself paralyzed by doubts, however. Was she simply another foolish woman to whom he'd been kind, who imagined herself special to him? Every instinct cried to retreat and protect her pride. To find Ralstone, to *engage* herself to Ralstone and show Race de Vere that he meant nothing to her.

To avoid that cruelest affliction—embarrassment.

But she had never been a coward, and she knew that if she didn't attempt to find out the truth, it would linger in her forever like a poison. And, she suddenly realized, if the girl was here, Race was free of her for a short while.

She grasped her spear and left the room, going down the corridor to reenter the more populated areas of the Pavilion. Where was Race likely to be?

Anywhere.

Ralstone was waiting in the saloon, so she could not go there, but she could wander everywhere else.

If only she could go quickly and unobtrusively around the place, but her foot made her slow, and her fame made her noticeable. And of course, everyone, from footmen to prince, wanted to be of assistance to the poor crippled lady.

She only prevented the Regent from sending for Ralstone by hinting for a personal tour of the room they were in. By the time that was finished she was sure Ralstone must appear in search of her, and that Race would be tied to his Natalie again.

Then, by miracle, he walked into the room—alone.

Before he could retreat, the Regent said, "Ah, sir! De Vere. It is de Vere, isn't it?" As Race bowed, the Regent continued, "I give you a rare treasure, sir, the hand of Lady Anne Peckworth."

Anne looked at Race and could see her own startlement in his face. Did he feel the same sharp longing?

The Regent tittered. "Just my little joke." But he placed Anne's hand on Race's arm, patting it. "Find her escort for her, there's a good man."

Then the prince was off to speak to someone else, and

Anne was, at last, alone with Racecombe de Vere. Alone in the wandering presence of dozens of other people.

Perhaps it was the desperation that had built in her over the past little while, but she was almost shaking. It certainly felt as if sparkles were dancing into her from the contact of her hand on his arm, and as if the air were suddenly thin.

Say something, Anne. Say something!

"I was surprised to see you here, Mr. de Vere."

Did it sound normal?

Heavens, did it sound as if she thought he shouldn't be here? As if he didn't deserve to be here?

She was staring ahead.

She couldn't look directly at him.

"Do we know where to look for Captain Ralstone, Lady Anne?"

Was he so anxious to be rid of her?

"I'm afraid not," she lied. "Do you not have a lady to care for, Mr. de Vere?"

"She has been recruited to play the harp."

"Shouldn't you be with her?"

"A devoted lieutenant is with her at the moment. I was definitely de trop."

She had to look at him and found him smiling.

"She's very good," he said.

I play the harp well, too. Thank heavens she didn't let the words out, but was he truly fond of the child? If Natalie was a relative of Lady Vandeimen's, it would be a brilliant match for him.

Not as brilliant a one as marrying *her*.

She had him by her side, and to herself, which she had wanted. What should she do? She could hardly say, *Is there a chance that you might marry me?*

"Perhaps if we stroll around, Mr. de Vere, I might encounter Captain Ralstone."

"By all means, Lady Anne, if it does not bother your foot."

"Not at all, especially with the staff."

"A charming new one. Do you have many?"

Was this all there was, this banal conversation? Surely not. He could hardly be expected to behave here as he had in the privacy of Benning's study, and he still might think her displeased with his company. They'd been forced together by royal command, she realized, and she still hadn't managed to smile at him.

Grasping her courage, she did just that. "I think I am able to enjoy my staffs as a result of our time together at Benning Hall, Mr. de Vere."

He seemed to study her, but she could not decipher it. Why did he have to be so hard to understand?

"I'm delighted if I was of service to you, my lady."

My lady. He was retreating behind subservience again. She would not let him go without settling matters.

"These rooms are very hot," she said. It was true, but merely being with him was making her hotter. "I cannot wield my fan, hold your arm, and use my staff at the same time."

She meant him to ply her fan for her, but he disconnected them and moved slightly apart. She opened her silk fan with a snap. "Perhaps we could step outside for a moment."

He stayed perfectly still, looking at her. "Why?"

She realized then that they were in that same short corridor that gave an illusion of privacy but could be invaded at any moment.

"For fresh air, sir." But she knew she had to address what he'd seen earlier. She waved her fan, long training preventing her from flapping it like a demented bird. "You came across me here earlier, Mr. de Vere. Did you, like me, think of a lesson in hand kissing at Benning Hall?"

"I thought mainly that Ralstone wasn't the man for you."

"Ah." She stilled her fan and looked over it. "And pray, who is the right man for me?"

Oh, dear heaven, she sounded intolerably arch, but might he be leading up to a proposal? She had her answer ready.

Yes. Against reason, against sanity, it would be yes, yes, yes!

His brows rose. "Provide me with a list of your suitors, my lady, and I will tick the suitable."

Her hand clenched on her spear so that the metal

bands bit through silk gloves. Retreating into coolness, she snapped her fan shut. "It is none of your business, sir."

"You seem to be making it my business, Lady Anne."

"Because you interfered in my life!"

He stepped closer and gripped her hand over the spear shaft. "Don't make a scene."

She almost said she would if she wanted to, which was madness. She wanted to jab him with the spear, which was perfectly reasonable, but impossible. Then a group strolled into the corridor, casting them a casual but interested glance. Had he heard their approach?

With a forced smile, she flexed her hand to shake off his, but he was already removing it.

"What a nest of misunderstandings we have, Mr. de Vere," she said lightly as the other party moved by and on. "It would not bother me if I never saw you again."

"I'm delighted to hear that, Lady Anne. I would not want to be a bother to a lady. But don't marry Ralstone."

She itched to murder him. "If I wish to, sir, I shall. And there is nothing you can do to stop me."

"I could tell Uffham certain things about him."

"What things?" If Ralstone was a scoundrel, where did that leave her? Stuck with Alderton. She realized then how very much she didn't want to marry Alderton.

"Duels, for a start. And women. I told you that a hero would not necessarily make a good husband. The Duke of St. Raven said the same thing, as I remember. Is he not one of your suitors, too?"

Tris? Her mind felt as tangled as neglected yarn. Simply to save face she said, "Of course."

Ralstone had killed men in duels? Over women?

Pride made her go on, "In fact, I am considering St. Raven's proposal now. So you don't have to concern yourself about Captain Ralstone. Speaking of which, I should find him."

She turned away, but he caught her arm. "Considering? Now you've found your feet in society, isn't marriage to St. Raven the ideal? He truly cares for you."

She summoned generations of pride to her tone. "You are impertinent, sir."

"Of course I am. It's my stock in trade. What are you going to do?"

She pulled sharply away from him. "It is none of your business. Approach me again, and I will hit you again, this time with intent to do serious injury!"

She turned and limped away, cursing the fact that she could not stalk, but giving thanks for the spear that lent her some dignity. Oh, God. Oh, God. If only she'd not sought out that horrible interview. He truly felt nothing for her except a strange meddlesome pity.

He wanted her to marry Tris, did he? If she'd been on the point of it, she might have backed away simply to thwart him. Now, however, she had to marry someone just to prove something to Race de Vere.

Ralstone.

Duels?

Alderton.

Cold kisses.

It had to be Ralstone, in part because Race de Vere had told her not to. At least there could be honest passion there. He'd doubtless fought duels to defend the honor of fair ladies, which was not such a bad thing. And she had responded to his kiss.

She passed by a pair of complacent china lovers that did not know the danger they were in. She could easily have swung her spear and smashed them into smithereens.

Twenty-four

~

Ralstone was dutifully waiting in the central saloon and came forward with flattering pleasure and relief. "I was worried about you, Anne."

"I encountered the Regent."

"Royalty must take precedence," he said with a smile. "Do you wish to sit and listen to the music?"

She saw the plump girl performing brilliantly on the harp. There was no reason to be jealous of the child, and yet at that moment Anne couldn't stand the sight of her.

"No. I need some fresh air."

He looked startled at her tone, but took her arm. "Come then, I know where we can go outside."

Soon they were in the lamplit garden. The night air was chilly after the heat inside, and Anne wished for a shawl. The cool seemed to go to her feet, too, and she hesitated about encouraging Ralstone here and now.

Tomorrow would be soon enough. It was time to start to behave properly. She could not possibly engage herself to one man while engaged to another. Tomorrow she would free herself from poor Alderton before picking up matters with Ralstone. She needed to get Tris's evaluation first, as well.

To deflect Ralstone now, she looked for a group to join. Lord and Lady Amleigh were with the Vandeimens and another couple. That would be safe and would prove to the Amleighs that she suffered not a trace of hurt.

Just as she was about to suggest joining them, Race de Vere came out of the Pavilion with his partner, and walked that way—to be greeted as a good friend.

Race and Amleigh?

The other gentleman was one-armed. She'd talked to him earlier. The name had seemed familiar. . . .

Major Beaumont. One of the Company of Rogues!

Her throat became so tight, she felt she should be wheezing.

Lord Amleigh—a Rogue.

Major Beaumont—a Rogue.

Race de Vere. Not a Rogue, but clearly a close friend of the group who seemed to regard her as their personal charity case. She hastily turned away and let Ralstone take her to another part of the gardens.

She'd always wondered what could have caused de Vere to spend so much time with Uffham, and now it was clear. It had been a way to get into circles he could not normally join. He'd been on a mission, sent by the Company of Rogues, to tidy up the unfortunate mess that was Lady Anne Peckworth.

Not by offering marriage. Heavens, no. Simply by shocking her out of her quiet ways and into society where she would marry and be off their collective conscience.

And tonight she had pursued him like a pathetic puppy begging for treats!

"Anne," Ralstone said, taking her hand.

She realized that he had led her into a quiet corner of the garden. Conversation and laughter was only a murmur—laughter at her?

"Are you ready to answer me, Anne? Don't keep me in suspense. Will you make me the happiest man in Christendom?"

Anne felt apart, apart from any semblance of reality. She wasn't even on a stage anymore, performing for a faceless crowd. It was as if she'd floated away to another dimension, one where she was alone.

She realized that she had been playing a part for weeks, secretly sure that at some point Race de Vere would return and reality would recommence.

"Anne?"

She looked at Captain Ralstone, positively delicious in his scarlet uniform, his dark eyes searching hers for hope. She could at least make someone happy.

"Yes," she said. "I will marry you." Deliberately she added, "Jack."

He took her hands and kissed them, raising them up to his mouth this time, and gazing into her eyes. "You have made me the happiest man in Christendom."

She almost pointed out that he was repeating himself, but it was time to begin a new role in the play of life—loving, tactful wife.

"When?" he asked.

Immediately, she wanted to say, but it would take a little time to manage, even with a license.

But then she remembered de Vere's threat to tell Uffham about women and duels. Was he going to snatch even this from her?

"I want to elope," she said.

Ralstone's delight turned to blank shock. "What? There's no need of that, love."

Unsuitable laughter tickled at her. This was all too like poor Jeremy in *The Daring Lady*! But now she'd thought of elopement she was as set on it as Rosalinde.

If they eloped, de Vere would have no chance to make mischief, and she would have no time to lose her nerve. What's more, there would be no question of this suitor being snared by a passing beauty.

She thought of Susan Amleigh. She was a fine looking woman, to be sure, especially enhanced by love and happiness, but her face was rather strong with a long nose and a square chin. She'd still swept Amleigh away. It would *not* happen again.

She looked Ralstone in the eye and lied. "My family doesn't approve of you. It will take forever to change their minds."

"Why? What stories have they heard? I can answer any accusation!"

"They have heard that you duel."

Guilt flashed over his face. "I confess it. But they were cases of the honor of ladies, Anne. I swear it."

She smiled. She'd known it must be so. "Would you fight for my honor, then?"

He pulled her into his arms. "Of course. I'd kill any man who offended you."

In a play, on a stage, it would be pure romance, and Anne indulged for a moment in the vicious pleasure of Ralstone killing de Vere. Reality was never far away, however, and reality threw up an alarming picture.

She pushed away from him. "If we elope, Uffham will pursue, and there'll be a duel, won't there?"

"I fear so, love. I'm no coward, but that would be scandal and disaster."

Reality locked around her again, and she sighed. "It was a foolish idea. I'm sure there will only be a little delay. A few questions of your commanding officers will doubtless appease my father."

He took her hands. "But delay will distress you, won't it? It is my task in life to save you from all distress. I would marry you here, now, tonight, if it were possible, Anne." He turned her left hand and pressed a kiss hotly into her palm.

This time it didn't stir the right response. She could hardly expect it after a night like tonight. To compensate, she pressed her hand against his lips.

He looked at her quickly. "You are passionate. I knew you must be under that cool exterior." He nipped at the base of her thumb, almost to the point of pain. "Let us elope then. Why wait when we know we are perfect for one another?"

"But Uffham—?"

That bite had sparked something in her. Something wicked, physical, hot. It reminded her of de Vere's attack, which had appalled her, but afterward had seemed so exciting. She was doing the right thing here, and she wouldn't let de Vere spoil it.

Ralstone pulled her to him and kissed her, kissed her as de Vere had kissed. His mouth commanded hers so that her senses swam. He was big, bigger than de Vere. Her head was stretched back and she felt powerless.

Was it thrilling or frightening?

One of her hands was at his nape, and she tightened her fingers in his hair, wondering if he would stop if she yanked on it.

He growled. It was a growl that resonated down in her own throat. This was certainly not like Alderton.

Alderton! Her eyes flew open and she saw stars above.

She was still engaged to marry Alderton, and was here sealing a pact with another man. At this rate she'd soon be kissing in the streets!

She pulled back and he freed her lips, smiling. "I've frightened you. I apologize, but I'm a passionate man, and you've been driving me wild for weeks. The thought that in days you could be mine forever . . ."

The look in his eyes turned her breathless. Yes. Once they were married, he would sear any other man from her mind.

"But what of Uffham? I cannot disappear and not be pursued, and I couldn't bear a duel."

"Well, in fact," he said, "I think we can do it."

In her mind it came out like a purr, a purr from a beast that had its dinner in its paws. But it was the way of men to hunt, and she had allowed herself to become the prize of the Marriage Mart. If he felt triumphant, it was not surprising.

"How?"

"You will visit my sister, Ellen, at Greenwich, love. She's married to a naval officer who is at sea, and would enjoy the company. Of course she won't have the chance. I will immediately take you on north."

Anne considered it, impressed by his keen mind. Better and better. She appreciated a fine mind.

"So I will arrive there in all propriety, in Welsford's coach, with Welsford's servants, and no one will know I have left. Will your sister not object?"

"Not when it means our happiness."

"It's very clever. But I will have to take my maid, and she will likely object."

"Is there no way to leave her behind?"

Anne assessed the problem, feeling more and more that this was a play she was planning, not her life. The plan could work, but she would still have to return to reality one day and break the shocking news.

She summoned up the picture of happy Claretta Crump and took the next step.

"How big is your sister's house?"

"Not very," he confessed. "I'm sure you know that there's little money in my family, and many to divide it amongst, and her husband, Yelland, has had little luck with prize money and such. But you will not actually be staying there, love."

Anne shook her head. "That doesn't matter, but it will be excuse to leave Hetty behind. I'm sure she won't mind a week to visit her family."

He brought her hands to his lips again, kissing the knuckles. "Then all is set, my love, my heart, my life, if you still wish it so."

"*Volo*," she said, remembering the old Latin marriage vows.

"*Volo, utque*," he replied. I wish it, too.

It should not surprise her that he knew Latin, for he would have a normal gentleman's education, but it sealed their pact and soothed her nerves. He was large and physical and dashing, but he was a well-educated gentleman with a clever mind and a sensitive soul.

Despite flutters of panic, she went on tiptoe to kiss him. "We are going to be blissfully happy!"

He kissed her back. "My dearest, darling, Anne, we will. Your trust means more than I can say. And you *can* trust yourself to me. As of this moment, you are my treasured wife." He twisted off his signet ring. "I cannot give you a proper ring as yet, but keep this as testament to my devotion."

He pressed it warm into her hand, and lacking pockets in her slim evening gown, she popped it down her bodice. His eyes followed it and a sudden stillness in him dried her mouth.

Passion. It was what she wanted. The absolute commitment that passion implied.

Wiser to return to company now, however. "We really must go back inside. It would not do to raise suspicions. In fact, I think I should go home." She grasped an excuse she was coming to rely on far too much. "My foot, you know . . ."

He was concerned and careful as they returned to the Pavilion, and during the short carriage ride home. He made no attempt to use the privacy to kiss her again.

How wonderful it would be to be cherished and protected by a man like this.

Then she was chilled by a new problem. "Ralstone—Jack. What if we encounter people we know on the road? Even if I wear a veil, there's my limp. I'm not sure there is another young lady in England who walks as I do."

"Damnation. I don't suppose you can not limp for a step or two?"

"If I could, don't you think I would?"

He squeezed her hand again. "Yes, of course. Foolish of me. But you're right. That plays merry hell with our plan."

Anne would not give up now.

"What if I were to travel as an elderly widow? I could use a short cane and stoop a bit. With a mourning veil and dull clothes, no one would suspect. You could be my attentive son—no, grandson—escorting me to a funeral."

He pulled a face. "That takes the shine off it a bit, love." But then he smiled again. "Anything that gets us to our happy destination. And speaking of destinations, here we are at your sister's house."

He handed her down and escorted her into the house, taking farewell with a kiss on her hand. Looking into her eyes, he said, "Until tomorrow." Too quietly for the footman to hear, he added, "Granny."

She laughed as he left—and no one could feel hollow when laughing, could they?—then went to her room. The first thing she saw was a straw bonbon holder on her dressing table, and the pearl counter inside it.

There was no fire at this time of year so she crushed the straw in her hand, then opened a window and tossed both items out. Tomorrow she would be on her way north and soon Racecombe de Vere, upstart tradesman's son, would know that he and his advice meant nothing to her.

She tossed and turned that night, but it was entirely because tomorrow she would have to face Alderton and break his heart.

At the first acceptable moment she sent a note to him, then fiddled around the reception room awaiting his arrival. He arrived bearing flowers and a blissful smile. It was not a pleasant interview.

Eventually, fighting tears, she managed to convince him that there was no hope, that she thought of him as a brother. His tears escaped, and she found she wanted to cuddle and comfort him, indeed like a sister. Why hadn't she realized that earlier?

And why must that swoop back memories of the corridor outside Frances's bedroom. Of the midwife enveloping Frances inside, and de Vere's supportive embrace of her?

Soon, soon, Jack Ralstone would be her lifelong support. He would be as good as de Vere.

Better.

When Alderton finally left, Anne did let her tears fall, and she knew she was weeping for more than his pain. Unfortunately Caroline came in then.

"You're receiving early, Anne— Why, what is the matter?"

Anne let her sister draw her to the sofa. "Only Alderton," she lied. "I refused him. He cried, so I am crying in sympathy." She found her handkerchief and blew her nose. "It seemed the least I could do."

"Oh, poor Alderton. But indeed, he is a little dull for you."

Anne eyed her sister. "Would you have thought so a few weeks ago?"

"No. But you've changed."

"It's only costumes and paint."

"I don't think so. So, who is next in line? You have your pick."

Anne took the plunge. "I have promised to visit Captain Ralstone's sister in Greenwich. Today."

Caroline's eyes widened, but if she had objections she didn't speak them. "So it's to be Dashing Jack, is it? He'll certainly be more fun than most."

"Dashing Jack? Is that what they call him?" Was she making a terrible mistake?

"It's what some of the army men call him. Because he dashed into battle, I gather."

Anne's panic settled. "He intends to leave the army, of course." Had they actually discussed that? She couldn't remember. "It will be many years, God willing, before Jack inherits, so I was thinking that we could find an estate of our own, perhaps close to home."

Quoyne House.

Had she and Jack discussed that, either?

Caroline nodded. "You always were fond of Lea Park, weren't you? Do you think Ralstone will like to become a country squire, though?"

The hint of doubt was reasonable. Anne was sure they hadn't talked of all this. When had they had time?

"We could still have it as a country home. Perhaps he will take a seat in Parliament."

"Perhaps." Caroline cocked her head. "It seems very much a settled thing."

Anne swallowed. "I think it is."

Caroline leaned forward and kissed her. "Then I wish you very happy. And, of course, we will all tear the skin off him strip by strip if he causes you a moment of distress." She rose. "If you wish to leave today, I had better tell Welsford so he can arrange the carriage."

Anne sat for a moment after Caroline had left, absorbing the fact that Caroline thought her choice good but daring. *A Daring Lady,* she thought, biting her lip. If she encountered Le Corbeau on the way north she'd think she'd slipped out of reality entirely, even though they'd be passing through his territory. She wondered if Tris had found out if there was a connection between the name and his title.

Tris. She'd intended to check with him about rats, mice, and farthings. Too late now. She'd burned all her boats.

Ralstone would not be a placid husband, she knew that, but that was part of his appeal. He loved her and was an honorable, intelligent man. If she wasn't exactly in love with him yet, she would be once she set her mind to it.

She rose and went off to instruct Hetty as to what to pack for—ostensibly—a week in Greenwich. A significant advantage of Ralstone's quick-witted plan was that she could take a trunk rather than have to sneak away a few clothes. She thought carefully and added the pink sprig dress to wear for her wedding.

Two hours later, Anne left Brighton in Welsford's private chaise, Ralstone riding beside. She worked hard to take casual leave of Caroline, as if she really was returning unchanged in a week, but she was astonished that the truth wasn't written on her face.

Despite Welsford's excellent horses, and the prime changes his name commanded on the road, Anne had five hours of travel to think and rethink. She did her best to concentrate on a book she had purchased weeks ago and not had time to read—a history of Jeanne d'Arc in French. She was trying to gather a body of knowledge about women who had made their mark on their times. It was certainly a story to make her own fears seem insignificant. Even at the worst, no one was going to burn her at the stake.

They arrived at Ellen Yelland's small terraced house at three-thirty in the afternoon just as Jeanne had been handed over to the English for trial. Anne watched the Welsford carriage set off back to Brighton as if it were the Burgundian army leaving her in the hands of her enemies.

She shook her head. She had always been inclined to identify too much with the characters in books. She turned to greet Ellen Yelland, soon to be her sister.

Twenty-five

⌒

Race tried to put Lady Anne Peckworth out of his mind. He'd hurt her again, however, and he burned to try to slap some sort of apology or explanation over her wounds. It couldn't work. Perhaps if he gave her reason to hit him again, she'd feel better.

The morning after the military assembly, however, he couldn't resist trying to find out a few facts.

Maria Vandeimen was part of that world so it was easy to discover that the Duke of St. Raven had been disappointingly absent from the last weeks of the London season. He had hosted a gentlemen's house party at his Hertfordshire house and then traveled to his various estates, most of which were in the West Country.

Yet Anne had said he'd proposed.

Race risked a direct question. "I thought at one point that there would be a match between him and Lady Anne Peckworth. When I saw them in London they seemed very fond."

Lady Vandeimen was working effortlessly on a lovely piece of embroidery. "There was certainly talk, but it has come to nothing. She is here, and he is not."

"They might have an understanding."

Her brows rose. "Why make a mystery of it? And why encourage other suitors?" She took some tiny stitches then snipped off her thread. "The Earl of Alderton is making a complete cake of himself over her, and Captain Ralstone obviously has high hopes."

"She was with Ralstone last night. Not much of a match for the daughter of a duke."

She picked up another thread and squinted as she

threaded her needle. "His family is good enough, though strained by too many children, and he is the heir." She smiled at him, work paused for a moment. "I certainly cannot disapprove if she has chosen love rather than grandeur."

Race knew Maria had eloped with a foreign merchant for love when younger, then married a penniless young lord recently.

"How low could a woman like Lady Anne marry without inviting ridicule?" He knew Maria Vandeimen might see the meaning behind the question, but he also knew she would make no mention of it.

After a quick look she began her steady stitching again. "It is always a delicate question. For her to marry outside of the aristocracy would be startling, but if there was wealth or high renown . . ."

He watched her complete a charming violet as she continued.

"Generally speaking, a lady takes the rank and situation of her husband. A grand marriage raises her high, an inferior one sinks her low. It is assumed that she will be intimate with her husband's family and friends, and adjust her behavior to fit in with them. Of course, someone like Lady Anne, born to the highest station short of princess, nearly always marries beneath herself, and she will usually draw her husband into ducal circles to some extent, which is part of her value."

"So," he said, "marriage to St. Raven would be excellent, to Alderton comfortable, but to Ralstone a little déclassé."

She stilled her needle and looked at him. "And to you," she said gently, "very peculiar."

He laughed. "You don't know the half of it." After a moment's thought he told her. "My father was a carriage maker before he won the lottery and decided to be a gentleman."

Her brows rose, but she took it well. "An honorable profession, and a reasonable ambition, though hard to achieve."

"In fact, he's pretty well done it. I gather he'd always liked to think of bettering himself—education, good clothing, and such—and in the course of his trade he met many of the upper class. Once he had money, he moved far from his previous environment and bought a manor and a lady. I assume my mother completed the polish. He's more bluff country squire than elegant gentleman, but he doesn't embarrass himself. And he is a gentleman in every way that matters."

"I had the impression from Con that you were at odds."

"Only because he had ambitions for me that did not include the army. And, of course, that I would drive a saint to drink."

She laughed. "Then avoid saints. The world doesn't need to know this story."

"The world always knows these stories, especially when its curiosity is aroused. And, of course, there is his unfortunate choice of gentlemanly name."

"De Vere? Yes. It does raise instant curiosity."

"And suspicion. My father doesn't seem to notice, or perhaps he doesn't care, especially now he's married a farmer's daughter. Like should wed with like, don't you agree?"

She was embroidering again. "In general I do, but there are other like things than rank." She glanced up. "Despite your lineage, you fit in perfectly among aristocrats, Race, and I have to feel that you would be sadly out of place among the trades."

He laughed. "Absolutely. I haven't the steadiness for it, for a start." He rose, deciding not to burden her with the last twist in his reality. It was doubtless academic as far as Anne Peckworth was concerned.

She stopped her work and looked up. "Love and general suitability are more important than bloodlines, Race. I truly believe that. And if a match stirs talk, the world loses interest in time, especially if the union seems happy."

Race knew, however, that her first marriage, the marriage into trade, had not been happy.

He raised her hand and kissed it. "At least I can claim most worthy friends."

He left, accepting that any whimsical dreams of groveling to Anne and winning her were idiocy. Even if he could persuade her into marriage, he wouldn't wish it on her. He was objecting to Ralstone at least partly on grounds of rank, and Ralstone had him beat to flinders on that score.

On the other hand, Ralstone didn't feel like the right man for Anne. At the moment she appeared to be Queen of the World, but he knew that underneath still lay the quiet lady who did not believe in her attractions, who'd been hurt by two disappearing suitors, and then by himself.

She was perhaps driven by hurt pride, and also by a need to do the right thing—to please her family, to soothe everyone's anxieties. If she married unwisely, she would behave as Maria Vandeimen had. She would present a well-bred contentment to the world when she should really wrap her staff around her wretched husband's head.

Did Ralstone know and love the real Anne? Race had to answer that one question before he put this all behind him. His past acquaintance with Ralstone made a visit possible, and he hadn't ever known a man in love who didn't want to talk about the object of his affection.

He walked briskly to the post office, where it was easy to discover where Jack Ralstone had his lodging. Five minutes later, he knocked at the door of number ten, Charles Street, a narrow three-story house on a narrow street. It was opened by a narrow man with an apron over shirt and breeches. Race had the ridiculous image of the man being squeezed and stretched to fit the house.

"May I help you, sir?"

"I believe Captain Ralstone has rooms here?"

"Had, sir, had. He left this morning."

That struck Race as strange. "To take other rooms in town?"

"No, sir. He was leaving Brighton."

"Suddenly?"

"Indeed, sir." The man eased back. In moments he would try to shut the door.

"Back to Shropshire, I assume, on family business."

The suggestion of familiarity with Ralstone's affairs relaxed the landlord. "He did not say, sir."

"Not bad news, I hope."

Did this mean he'd proposed and been rejected? Or

had he gone to Lea Park to speak to Anne's father? Surely in that case he'd plan to return.

"Captain Ralstone was in excellent spirits, sir. Whistling, in fact." At that, the man seemed to decide that he had gone too far, and firmly shut the door.

Race didn't try to stop him. That well was drained, but he needed to find another. There were any number of explanations for Ralstone's behavior, including the simple one of running out of money. Brighton was expensive in the summer.

He stopped on the seafront, sucking in salty air, trying to let the brisk wind blow the dross from his mind so he could think. It was instinct, this panic beating in him, but his instinct was often right. There was nothing for it. He had to visit Anne to be sure.

He laughed, hoping she'd switched spear for staff. He'd take being beaten over being impaled.

When he inquired at the Welsfords' however, he was told that Lady Anne was unavailable. She might have instructed the servants to bar him at the door. As a last throw of the dice he asked for Lady Welsford. He was immediately admitted as far as a small, flower-filled reception room.

Anne truly wasn't here?

Had she left town with Ralstone? In that case, the only destination could be Lea Park to get her father's blessing on their union.

Too late, too late.

Not for himself, but for her.

Caro Welsford walked in, eyes brilliant with curiosity. She was what—nineteen?—but with lineage, training, and an understanding, loving husband, her poise grew day by day. Soon she would be one of the rulers of the polite world.

Different spheres.

"Mr. de Vere, I gather you wished to speak to Anne. I'm afraid she has left Brighton for a while."

"To return to Lea Park, no doubt, Lady Welsford."

She cocked her head, lips pursed. "No," she said at last. "She has gone to visit Captain Ralstone's sister in Greenwich."

"Greenwich?" he echoed, as if she'd said the moon.

It was an idiotic response, but he felt as he had once when a nearby cannonball had blown him off his feet.

"It is a perfectly respectable location, Mr. de Vere. Captain Ralstone's sister is apparently married to a naval officer."

Not quite so bad as Lea Park, but the same to all meaningful purposes.

"I assume this is a prelude to an announcement, Lady Welsford."

"I assume so too, Mr. de Vere." After a moment she added, "Do you think it wise?"

Did she have doubts, too? He respected her shrewdness and chose his words with care. "I'm sure Lady Anne has considered matters carefully, and that her family will advise her."

"Oh, indeed. But if she is set on it, she will doubtless have her way."

Was there really a double conversation going on here? Was she asking him to interfere?

"I know nothing particularly to Captain Ralstone's discredit, Lady Welsford. Just the sort of behavior forgivable to men at war."

"We are no longer at war, Mr. de Vere."

She *was* expecting something from him, but he had nothing to give. Anne had made her choice, and he had given as much warning as was reasonable.

He bowed. "When you see your sister again, Lady Welsford, please convey to her my best wishes for her future happiness."

"She will be back in a week. You will be able to speak to her then."

He smiled. "I don't think we're on speaking terms, and besides, I am leaving Brighton today."

"To go where?" she asked, with all the blunt arrogance of her blood—and even as if annoyed.

"Into the future, Lady Welsford." He bowed again and took his leave, but she stopped him near the door with a hand on his arm.

"You and Anne are at odds, it would seem."

"We have hardly been at evens, Lady Welsford."

Her brows snapped together, and if she'd lived in earlier times he could imagine her ordering him off to the dungeons. But then she smiled. "You have done well by my family, Mr. de Vere. If you ever require help that I or Welsford might be able to give, do not hesitate to approach us."

She was young and arrogant, but she had a strong core of wisdom and decency, and in that she reminded him of Anne. He took her hand and kissed it. Then he left the Peckworths forever.

Twenty-six

~

Anne paused in Greenwich only long enough for a light meal and for Ralstone to settle the details of the carriage he was hiring from the local inn to take them to London.

Anne was dismayed to find that she didn't immediately take to her future sister-in-law. Ellen Yelland had similar looks to her brother, but on her the dark eyes and hair seemed somewhat harsh. She was inclined to grovel to a duke's daughter, but also to make broad comments about marital bliss. She also whined about her straightened circumstances so much that Anne wondered if she was supposed to slip her a few guineas before she left.

Anne spent part of the time writing a letter to Caroline lightly describing her enjoyable stay in Greenwich. It felt truly deceitful, but she had to do it. Caro would expect some news. Ellen agreed to send it in two days.

Then she transformed herself into the elderly widow. She'd chosen to wear a dark gray traveling dress and Jack had found a black cloak, veiled bonnet, and a crook-necked cane. She hated to give up her staff, but she did it. She insisted on taking it with her, however, for later. It unscrewed in the middle, so could fit in her trunk.

Then, the elderly widow, she was ready to leave, to finally end all chance of going back. She did not let herself hesitate. Before leaving, however, she gave Jack two guineas and asked him to give them to his sister as if from himself, so it wouldn't seem like charity. She didn't begrudge the money, but it seemed a strange beginning to this adventure.

Then they were on their way. She leaned back in the well-worn carriage and made herself relax. It was done. She smiled at the handsome man beside her, the man who would soon be her husband. "Everything has gone so smoothly! You are a genius."

He smiled back. "But of course. I have managed to win you."

She blushed, as much from being alone with him as from the compliment. "But truly, your plan is so clever. No need to hurtle up the Great North Road afraid of pursuit, and instead of a few boxes or even a bundle, I have a trunkful of clothes with me, including an elegant dress for our wedding."

He took her black-gloved hand and kissed it. "Don't tell me what it will be. It's bad luck."

She tugged her hand free, teasing, "I don't think you should be doing that. Not to your ancient grandmother. Am I Mrs. Ralstone?"

"Not yet. But soon. Very soon. Mrs. Ralstone, mine to treasure. For now, however, I think perhaps you should be a great aunt. It is just possible we might meet someone who knows me, and who knows my grandmothers. Better to invent someone. You can be . . . Mrs. Crabworthy!"

She laughed, but then he dug in his pocket and produced a narrow gold band. He peeled off her left glove and slid it onto her finger.

"Should we?" she asked.

"My ancient great-aunt should have a wedding ring under her glove, my sweet."

"She could be a spinster."

"I admit, I like to see it there. It was my mother's."

Touched, perhaps to discomfort, Anne pulled on her glove again. "Are you sure this isn't unlucky?"

"We make our own luck, love, and now I am the luckiest man alive."

It was exactly the right thing to say. When would the little knot of anxiety inside her release and let her be completely happy? Perhaps not until Gretna.

He touched her chin. "Why the worry, love? Is it me? I won't embarrass you on the journey, ring or no. My word on it. It will be exactly as if you were my great-aunt."

"Should I slump into the corner and fall asleep snoring?"

He laughed. "If you wish."

"I'd rather talk." Anne realized that her hands were locked together and relaxed them. "We don't know a great deal about each other, do we?"

"Only that we love and will make each other happy."

His soothing comments were beginning to frustrate her.

"Tell me something. How did you end up in the army?"

He leaned back, long legs stretched as far as the coach allowed. "It was church, law, or the military, darling one, and I never fancied the navy. Better way to money, of course, during wartime, but I shouldn't like to drown."

"No thought of the church, I see."

His grin was answer enough.

"Did you enjoy army life?"

He shrugged. "At times. At others it is not something suitable for a lady's ears."

She took his hand. "But perhaps for a wife's ears? I would share your shadows, Jack."

He kissed her glove. "No need of that, my pet. There are no shadows anymore. I am home, and the most blessed of men."

There he went again, but really, she was the most difficult woman to please. The future was settled. The dice cast.

Crabs. A losing throw at dice.

Worthy of crabs . . .

"You do intend to sell out, don't you?" she asked.

"Of course, but it won't bring me much money. My promotion to captain was dead man's shoes. I didn't pay, so I don't get anything for it." He put on a leer. "I'm marrying you for your money, wench."

She laughed, delighted that he could joke about it. "So what will you want to do?"

"Rest, relax, enjoy myself." His lids lowered seductively. "Enjoy you, my bride. I think that will take all my time and energy."

She swallowed. "Did I mention Quoyne House?" Her voice seemed to squeak. She quickly described her plan. "It's a charming house, and not too large. Just four good bedrooms, and of course," she added, feeling absurdly awkward, "the nurseries. The farmland is excellent, but it has been leased out to a variety of tenants. I'm sure there will be improvements you can make."

"Perhaps after this your father won't give us the estate."

"I'm sure he will not be so angry as that."

But was she? She had never done anything so outrageous, nor had any of her brothers and sisters.

He squeezed her hand again. "If he kicks up about it, we can find some other home. You'll still have your portion."

"Yes, of course, but it will be all right."

"I hope so. I hope for your family's favor."

"They only need to see me happy." She didn't want to speak of it, but she must. "Because of my foot, you see, they have always fussed over me. They don't expect me to do anything grand, only be happy. I think they will like to have me living close to Lea Park, to see me nearly every day. They'll be checking up on you," she teased. "Caroline threatens to skin you alive if you upset me."

He seemed taken aback, so she hurried on, "Just teasing, love. Uffham is bound to marry one day, so our children will have cousins to play with."

He said nothing, still looking . . . dismayed?

"Don't you agree?" she prompted.

Instantly, he smiled. "Completely, my love. I am simply enjoying your enthusiasm."

"Do you not like the idea, Jack? If so, I'm not set on it." Despite a pang, she tried to make that true. "We could purchase some other estate. Perhaps," she added nobly, "one close to your family."

But he laughed at that. "Lord, no! An occasional visit will suffice there. I hope we'll jaunt to town now and then, though."

Compromise, compromise. "Of course. We will generally be able to use Arran House. It is kept ready for family year-round."

"How grand. But if you prefer the country, I won't drag you off to London to keep me company. In fact, if I'm going to be there by myself, it would probably be better to keep a small set of rooms."

Compromise. Compromise. "Perhaps you would like a seat in Parliament. My father has any number of them in his pocket."

"I'm sure he has, but politics, my angel? Good to serve one's country and all that, but I've been abroad at war so long I'm not sure I understand what's what."

Jack certainly wasn't marrying her for chance of preferment. Of course he wasn't. He loved her.

"It will all be as you wish, Jack."

"That's my girl. And I don't suppose you'd want to be a political hostess, living in London throughout every sitting of Parliament."

She smiled. "You know me well, don't you?"

A strange thought crept into her mind, however. She felt much the same about Jack as she had about Alderton. She'd rather like him to be away for long stretches of time.

That didn't seem the right thought to have on the way to her wedding, but married couples did not have to live in one another's pockets. Her mother rarely accompanied her father when he went to London for debates in the Lords or other matters of State. . . .

So many uncertainties and concerns. It would be the same if they were planning a wedding in a church. The problem here was that they were compressing it into days, even hours.

He smiled and tugged at her black bonnet ribbon, loosening it. "We can't have you worrying, sweetheart. I'm sure this is giving you a headache, and it's dashed ugly. You don't need a disguise in the coach."

In moments the mourning bonnet was off and tossed casually aside. She knew what he was up to now, and that flutter of panic started again, but it was time to get over it.

Yet hadn't he promised to treat her like an elderly relative? To free him of his promise, she smiled and touched his cheek. "A kiss would not embarrass or dishonor me, Jack. In fact, I would like it very much. And I do trust you not to go further than we ought."

"We are as good as married," he said, drawing her into his arms, pressing his lips to hers. Then, for the first time, his hand settled on her thigh, and through her dress, began to explore.

She thrust aside all thought of Race de Vere and surrendered to the inevitable.

Twenty-seven

~

Race took a coach to London. He'd find cheap lodging there and perhaps use his introduction to Sir Stephen Ball. What he needed was enthralling work to drive Anne out of his mind.

As London drew close, however, he found that he was not free yet. Somewhere along the way a memory had popped up in his mind.

Lisbon. An aristocratic colonel's daughter and a British diplomat. The young lady had accompanied the diplomat's mother to Cintra in the hills to escape the summer heat, but from there she'd run off with her lover. Her parents had not learned of it until she did not return a fortnight later. Too late by far to interfere. Ralstone had been in Lisbon then, too. Had he remembered it?

Impossible. Why would Anne do such a thing?

But then he remembered his threat to blacken Ralstone's name. Had that pushed her into disaster? He had to check to make sure that she was safe in Greenwich with the respectable sister.

He got off the coach at Brixton, leaving his bags to wait for him at the coaching inn in London. He managed to hire a horse, though it wasn't much of one, and arrived in Greenwich at just gone five. He stopped at the Ship, which seemed to be the only inn there. He didn't know the name or address of Jack Ralstone's sister, but assumed it would be easily found.

It was easier, and more disastrous, than he'd thought.

A mention of Ralstone's name to the innkeeper, a Mr. Birt, produced the information that Race had missed him. "Received bad news from his home, sir, and set off an hour or more ago with a grieving relative."

"His sister?"

"No, sir. An elderly lady."

"Who walks with difficulty?"

But the man shrugged. "I couldn't say, sir. My men took the coach to Mrs. Yelland's house to pick the lady up. They said she seemed old and frail, poor thing. Deaths hit them hard when their time is near, you know."

He rambled off into stories of people he'd known who succumbed soon after attending a funeral.

Race pretended to listen, weighing options.

It was possible that an elderly relative lived with Mrs. Yelland, and that Jack Ralstone had offered to escort her somewhere for a funeral. Possible, but damned unlikely. What better disguise for Anne than widow's weeds and age?

"Heading north, I assume," he said when he had the chance. "Captain Ralstone's home is in Shropshire. I'm heading north of London myself and might meet them on the road. Any idea what route they planned to take?"

The innkeeper eyed him, clearly wondering if there was trouble involved. Race did his best to look harmless, and it seemed to work.

"My coach took them as far as the Swan in London, sir. That's as far as I go, you see. You'll doubtless learn more of them there."

Race found that the fastest way from Greenwich to London was up the river when the tide was right. It was, and there was a boat leaving soon. Ralstone had left at half past four—Birt kept a log—and would have arrived in London in about an hour. Assuming he did not have to delay there for a suitable carriage and team, he might be assumed to stop for the night at Ware or Huntingdon when the sun began to set.

Mr. Birt poured them both ale as they waited for the boat, and happily speculated on all the possible routes north, along with the benefits and disadvantages of the various inns, and the effect of an elderly relative on speed and rest.

Race let part of his brain gather these details while

trying to come up with a plan. They had to be heading for Scotland, probably Gretna Green. North of London the main road split for a while. With luck, he'd get a clear direction at the Swan, but if the postilions had not returned there, or were on another run, he'd have to go blind, feeling his way.

Birt was probably right about them stopping at sunset. They would think themselves safe from pursuit so wouldn't need to push beyond reason.

What would they do when they stopped? Would Anne insist on propriety, on waiting for the wedding? Or would Ralstone want to secure his prize?

He looked at the ticking wall clock. Five-thirty. How was he going to catch them before nightfall? He didn't have the funds to hire a fast chaise, or even a decent horse. If he'd had his wits about him, or if he'd accepted that he'd have to check up on Anne, he could have borrowed from Con before leaving Brighton.

If they planned to anticipate the wedding, would they wait for nightfall? He knew how possible it was to make love in a carriage but it wasn't the way it should be for a woman's first time. It would be Anne's first time.

He saw the boat coming in and rose, interrupting Birt in midsentence. Something about Le Corbeau.

"That highwayman still plaguing people?" he asked, as he paid for the ale. He was down to a few guineas.

"No, sir, like I said. Caught him two days ago, they did!"

"Good news."

"That's to say," added Birt, walking with Race to the door, "they caught someone the magistrates swear is him. Pawning a ring taken from a lady not a week ago. But the man in question—a Frenchie, sir, so that fits— claims he won it at dice." Birt gave a face-twisting wink. "Have to see whether the crow still flies, won't we?"

Race spared a moment's pity for the Frenchman who could be just as he said. Feelings still ran high in England against the French, and the man could hang without real proof against him. That, at least, was no concern of his.

He arrived at the Swan With Two Necks in Lad Lane by hackney, just over an hour later, but in such a busy place it took time to find someone who remembered the officer escorting the elderly lady.

Race knew now that he should have checked Ralstone's sister's in case the grieving ancient was real and Anne was still there. Too late now. He was committed to this throw, and in his heart he knew he was right.

He talked the dispatch clerk into checking his log and found that the first set of horses had taken them to Enfield. He had the road, but no means of travel.

Then he remembered the card that Con had given him. Perhaps the gods would smile and Sir Stephen Ball would be in his Brooks Street rooms. As he went there he tried to plan for the worst, for catching up with Anne too late, after she was ruined.

She wouldn't be ruined unless the world knew about it. The disguise she was wearing helped there. If he returned her to Greenwich and then to her family, perhaps no one except him, her, Ralstone, and his sister need ever know. He'd make damn sure that Ralstone and his sister never spoke of it.

And what if she didn't want to be saved?

He'd do it anyway. If she insisted on marrying Dashing Jack, she could do it properly, from Lea Park, in virtue and orange blossom.

The porter at the door to the elegant gentleman's rooms was obviously not impressed by the dusty traveler. Race gave him the card to take up to Sir Stephen, trying to make new plans if the man was away. Most sane people spent summer away from the city.

In moments, however, Sir Stephen came down himself to take Race up to his rooms.

It was interesting how different the Rogues were. Solid, stable Con; mercurial Nicholas Delaney; and now this tall, vibrant man with the clever eyes and the quick brain. Race liked him immediately.

Ball's rooms were furnished with exquisite and expensive taste, but they had the feeling of not mattering. He probably lived so much in his mind that his surroundings were irrelevant, and yet some instinct saved him from the fusty disorder of the eccentric.

There was no time for further acquaintance, however. Race explained his situation, and within fifteen minutes, all was in hand. Ball sent a message to Con in case any assistance should be needed near Brighton—discretion was apparently taken for granted—and promised to make sure that Ralstone's sister was kept in line.

He'd sent a servant to the livery stable that had his patronage, and Race emerged from the house to find a superb bay gelding waiting for him, ready to fly.

Ball insisted on lending Race twenty guineas, some of it in small coins. "In case you need ready cash. You can repay me at your leisure."

Efficient and tactful.

At the last minute, with Race already mounted, Ball said, "A marriage between you and Lady Anne Peckworth will not be easy to arrange."

Efficient, perceptive, and frank.

"I don't think to marry her."

"The Rogues have an interest in her happiness."

"I know. Delaney asked me to look out for Lady Anne."

After a moment, Ball said, "I see. Good luck," and waved Race on his way.

Even though the new horse was ready to eat up the miles, it wasn't possible at first. London was too crowded. Once out of the city, however, he could let the horse stretch, and it proved to be as gallant and fast as he'd hoped. He made short work of the stage to Enfield, surely cutting a half hour off their lead. There he learned that they'd planned a change at Ware.

He pushed the horse on, being sure not to press him too hard, and made Ware by nine. With any luck they would have stopped here for the night.

The sun was down, however, when he reached the Saracen's Head, and the place was hectic with travelers who were stopping for the night. It took fifteen minutes and bribery before he found out that Ralstone had gone on nearly two hours earlier with no specified stopping place. Was he going to have to check every inn on the Great North Road?

"What of their postilions?" he asked. "Are they back yet?"

"Nay, sir. And likely they'll stay the night where they stopped, unless they get a late run."

Race suppressed curses. "What's the farthest they'd go?"

"Buntingford, likely, sir, though they might push on to Royston."

The man looked suspicious, so Race tossed him an explanation. "They're hurrying north to my grandfather's deathbed, but we received news that he's rallied and there's no need for haste. Hate to rattle my poor granny's bones, you know."

The man warmed. "I hope you find them, sir. I'm sure they must have stopped for the night by now."

Race was, too, and it gnawed at his gut. He swung back onto his horse, who was suitably named Horatio and seemed to be thoroughly enjoying the adventure. Race wished he could say the same.

Then the gods smiled.

As he was leaving the yard he had to pause to let a coach roll in, and the head ostler called out, "Here's Jim and Matt back, sir! They took your couple on from here."

Race turned to the two postilions. Their horses had been taken from the shafts, and new ones were being put in, with new postilions to ride and guide them.

The postilions were sitting on a bench to pull off the heavy boots that protected their right legs from crushing.

He went over. "I gather you took a couple north earlier, sirs."

They both looked up, and he saw the experienced glint of greed in their eyes. He produced two crowns this time. "An elderly lady who walks with a cane and a dark-haired military gentleman."

The crowns disappeared into pockets. "Buntingford, sir. Stopped for the night at the Black Bull. Now the Crown's the better place, sir, but the gentleman asked for the quieter house. On account of the grieving lady, you see. Though I 'as to say as the gentleman looked happy," the man added with a wink. "Likely money coming."

Race nodded. "Thank you. Can I expect any problems on the road?"

"Smooth as a lady's hand, sir, though the light'll be gone soon. We delivered 'em two hours ago. Stopped there for a meal, we did, then picked up the business coming back south."

Race mounted again, end in sight, knowing that this time he had to ride as fast as horse and road would allow.

He set off knowing all speed might not be enough. The light was going, and soon all good people would seek their beds.

Including Anne and Jack Ralstone.

Beds, or bed?

Twenty-eight

~

The clock struck ten as Race entered Buntingford. The main street was deserted, the inns lining it were quiet. He gave thanks that he didn't have to hunt through them. Lights glimmered in some windows, but there seemed no sign of lively activities apart from flambeaux burning by each inn's door. To Race, the flames gave night a hellish touch.

Too late, too late chimed ten drawn-out times, and he slowed the tired horse down to a walk. A few minutes now would not help, and the horse needed to start to cool down.

The Black Bull turned out to be one of the oldest inns, with crooked black timbers and small-paned windows. No lights showed except the flambeaux by the door and a glimmer from the stableyard arch to the right.

He dismounted and led his mount through the arch into a stableyard as old fashioned as the inn. Stables and coach-houses ran around it, but on his left wooden steps went up to a gallery in front of the inn's rooms. By the light of the lantern hanging up there he thought there were eight. All were dark and silent.

He burned to charge up the stairs, to burst through doors in search of Anne and Ralstone, but that would create the scandal he was trying to avert.

To Race's right, lines of light gleamed through a closed pair of shutters. He was about to knock on the door next to the shutters when it opened, and a wizened groom came out. "Stopping here, sir?"

"Yes."

The groom took the horse and unsaddled it. Race

took off the bridle, partly to get the necessary over so
he could question the man, but also to give the sweating
horse its due. He told Horatio how pleased he was with
his service and praised his effort.

The groom carried the tack away and came back with
a blanket and bridle, then began walking the horse
around the yard.

Masking his urgency, Race kept pace. "I was delayed
on the road. I was supposed to meet a friend here—a
Captain Ralstone. Strapping, dashing sort of man with
dark hair." Since he didn't know what story the couple
were telling, he kept it vague. "Heading to a funeral . . ."

"He and his relative be here, sir, but in their beds
no doubt."

Beds. Thank God.

"What rooms?" he asked, making it sound casual.

"Seven and eight, sir, and the private parlor in between." The groom sent him a suspicious look. He
seemed a watchful sort. He'd certainly sound the alarm
if Race tried to break in.

Perhaps there was no need. They'd taken separate
rooms.

But then Race realized that they'd have to if Anne
was pretending to be an ancient.

"Can someone take Captain Ralstone a message for
me?"

"No one up but me, sir, and I's the stables to take
care of. Anyway, they're in bed." He nodded toward the
rooms above and indeed, all the windows were dark.

"I'll take a room beside them, then, to be sure to
catch them in the morning before they leave. I assume
you have the keys?"

The man still looked suspicious, but he said, "Aye,
sir. Just wait while the horse cools."

Race approved of the priority but ground his teeth.
He took the horse. "I'll walk him while you find the
key."

For a moment it looked as if the man would refuse,
but muttering, he went back into his room and returned
with a key on a big ring.

Race took it. Number six. "I'll find my own way." He

slipped the man a sixpence, hoping it would mollify him without raising suspicion.

He didn't run up the stairs, but urgency pounded in him. Even up close, there was no sound from numbers seven or eight. He hadn't asked if there were other guests, but there were no sounds from any of the rooms.

In his haste, he couldn't seem to find the hole for the key. He steadied himself, inserted it, and turned it, opening the way to a dark room. Glancing back he saw the groom still walking the horse but watching him, as well.

Race went into the room, groped for the candle that stood waiting by the bed, and carried it out to light it from the tin lamp. Then he gave the groom a cheery wave before going into his room and shutting the door.

Leaning back against it, he sucked in a deep breath. He'd never felt this sick dread before, not even before the most harrowing battle.

He quickly assessed his room. A simple enough place, not that he cared. He was more interested in the fact that—God be praised—the rooms had adjoining doors. Common enough so that larger suites of rooms could be put together for families.

He went to press his ear to the door to room number seven.

Silence.

Did the room house Ralstone or Anne in righteous slumber, or the two of them together? If they were together, what did he do? Break in and drag them out of one another's arms? Perhaps Anne truly loved Ralstone. Perhaps Ralstone truly loved Anne. Perhaps they were entwined naked in the bed, supremely happy.

He sucked in a breath. Even so, this was not the way to go about it, and the elopement was his fault.

He sat on a bench and tugged off one muddy boot. Like an enemy in ambush, thoughts of Benning Hall attacked. . . .

Anne in that plain blue dress, the dull woolen shawl huddled around her, but looking more beautiful than she had at the Pavilion dressed in flame. If he'd been able to predict the future then, and been wise enough, he would have fled.

Her hair had been pulled back carelessly and pinned into a knot high on her head, leaving her untouched face to speak for itself. An ordinary face, but one that became extraordinary with every emotion. Lovely arched brows over lively eyes. Soft lips, as soft to kiss as they'd looked. A wicked sense of humor.

Despite everything, he grinned.

Barnacles and Derbyshire rams.

Poor Lady Anne, indeed. He yanked off the other boot. She was no such thing, and he wouldn't let her become it.

Slowly, Race drew the bolt on his side of the door, relieved to find that it was well-greased and silent. He lifted the latch, but it was too much to hope that Ralstone had conveniently unbolted it on his side.

Most old inn doors did not fit neatly, however, and this was no exception. A half-inch gap gave space to insert his knife.

This bolt, too, was well greased and made little noise as he eased it back, fraction by fraction. All the same, it wasn't a silent progress, and if anyone was awake in the room, he or she would have to notice.

Race's unruly sense of humor imagined Ralstone lying there watching the bolt draw back, waiting to see who the intruder was. Not even remotely funny. The man would surely have a pistol pointed.

The bolt was finally free.

Time to get shot.

He opened the door cautiously, praying it wouldn't squeak, preparing pacifying words. He felt inclined to murder, but above all he wanted to avoid scandal.

No fisticuffs. No shooting.

At least, not here.

The room was dark and silent. The only light was his own candle left beside his bed. He was suddenly sure that this room was empty, and it was like a sword in the gut.

They were together in the other bedroom.

Swallowing bile, he went back for his candle and then moved on to the next door. It was unbolted, of course, and led into the parlor. He walked around the plain dining table to the last door of this journey. No lock to hinder him. Nothing but his own reluctance to face the truth.

He pressed down the latch and went in. He heard the rhythmic breath of sleep. Holding still for a moment, he waited to see if either of them would be wakened by the light of his candle. When there was no sign of it, he went farther into the room.

The curtains around the heavy old bed were drawn to. A quick glance showed a valise on the floor and men's clothing thrown over a chair. Then he noticed two bottles and two glasses on a small table. Had Ralstone made Anne drunk in order to have his way with her?

To hell with this. He strode forward and dragged back the musty curtains with a rattle of rings.

Ralstone grunted something and turned away from the light.

Race just stood there.

Ralstone was alone in the bed.

For a moment he thought he must be mistaken. He peered for Anne on the far side, her slight form hidden in some way. But she wasn't there. He gently closed the curtains again, though clearly Ralstone was too drunk to care.

Relief almost staggered him. He should have known that Anne had too much sense and goodness to give herself to Ralstone before she was married.

But then, where the devil was she?

He went back to the other bedroom, though he was sure he couldn't have missed her. A small trunk with the initials AP in brass was full of a lady's clothing. He lifted an expensive Kashmir shawl that he remembered all too well. That distinctive perfume rose from it—a complex blend of flowers and spice, subtle, ladylike, discreet, but promising.

Anne.

He rose and looked around again. So where the devil was subtle, ladylike, discreet Lady Anne Peckworth?

On the white cloth on top of the chest of drawers lay a piece of white paper. Suddenly frightened, he went and picked it up. His candlelight glinted on something beneath. A plain gold ring.

Married already?

That crazy panic fled. The ring must have been part of their pretense—but why had she left it?

Why had she left?

What had Ralstone done?

Dreading the worst, he put down the candle and unfolded the note. He'd never seen Anne's writing before, but he would have known it was hers. Neat, small, but with interestingly generous loops.

Dear Captain Ralstone,
 I am deeply sorry to have raised your expectations . . .

That's one way of putting it, Race thought grimly.

 . . . but I find we would not suit. I ask you not to pursue me. I am quite safe.

Relief made him want to smash something. *Anne, Anne, you idiot! How can you be safe? Where have you run to?*

She'd eloped, devil take it, done heaven knew what with Ralstone here tonight, and then she primly decides they won't suit, and takes off into the night?

He'd wring her bloody elegant neck!

When he found her.

Before, pray heaven, she fell into even worse disaster.

He longed to drag Ralstone out of the bed and beat him to a pulp, but it would raise the house, and anyway, there wasn't time. Anne, pampered and protected Anne, crippled Anne, was out somewhere in the dark night, alone.

Thank heavens Le Corbeau was in jail. This was the heart of his country. Except perhaps the authorities had the wrong man. Race was sure the dashing thief was not as amiable and noble as portrayed on stage.

He went back to his room and pulled on his boots. Then he paused at the door.

What was he going to tell the overwatchful groom?

Where was he going to look?

What was Ralstone going to do in the morning?

Cursing every second wasted, Race went back into the

other room, careless of the noise. his boots made. He picked up the note Anne had left, noticing now that it was engraved with a coat of arms. He shook his head and tore that part off.

Then he took out his pencil and added at the bottom,

Say what you must to explain your missing relative but protect the lady's name and bother her no longer. Any scandal will require satisfaction.

He wrote it in Greek characters, which any gentleman should be able to read, but no servant would. He didn't sign his name. Ralstone might even think it from Uffham, though not if he knew Uffham's hotheaded temperament.

Then he went back to his room and made himself think. Profit and loss, lists of numbers, indexes. Think of it like that.

Which way would she go? Was she on foot? How far could she walk, even with her staff?

Maps. He had his book of maps. He dug it out of his pocket and opened it to the page that covered this area. Despite his infuriation with her, Anne Peckworth wasn't a lunatic. If she'd set off from here, she had a place to go, and it would be closer than London.

With his finger he traced circles out from Buntingford. The map included side panels with details of local houses of significance. Aspenden Mount, Broadfield Manor, Widdiall Hall . . .

Hell's tits, for all he knew, any of these places could be owned by a friend or relative.

Then his finger stopped.

Nun's Chase.

The estate of the Duke of St. Raven, which had rapidly become famous as a desirable invitation for gentlemen who wanted liberal amusements. Anne was going *there*?

Even as he questioned it, he knew it was right. There was a bond between her and the duke that ensured her safety, even if she arrived in the middle of an orgy.

He hoped.

He stared at the dot on the map, wondering if in the

end all was going to work out. Was Anne already there, in St. Raven's arms, realizing that he was the ideal match after all? He had to wish for it, but he also had to make sure she'd made it there through countryside made disorderly by highwaymen, and by homeless vagrants and troublemaking Luddites.

Damn fool. He checked the mileage.

Three miles from Buntingford to Nun's Chase. Not far at all, but he didn't think Anne could walk that far, especially at night. She was probably sitting beside the road in tears.

He shoved the map book away and went out, locking the door behind him. He ran down the stairs to the coachyard and into the stall where the groom still worked, brushing down the slit-eyed, happy horse. The man looked at him, still brushing, not seeming surprised.

"I find I have to leave," Race said, holding out some coins. "This should pay for my room."

The man stopped brushing and took the coins. "I'm afraid I'll have to check your pockets, sir."

"O, thou good and faithful servant." Despite his urgency, Race waited as the man felt his pockets for stolen items.

The man stepped back. "No offense, sir."

"None taken." Race looked at his horse and asked, "Do you have another horse I can take?" For this mission, a cart horse would do. He was only riding at all to be able to carry Anne.

The man nodded and walked down the stable to stir a sleepy black. "He's been here a couple of days and could do with some work, sir. He's a bit of a temperament, so I haven't given him to the regular sort of rider, if you see what I mean."

He already had a saddle blanket on the horse and now added a saddle. The horse shook itself and looked around, ears pricking.

Wonderful. Race knew what 'a bit of temperament' meant. "Is he going to fight me?"

"Oh, no, sir—nothing like that. Not if you're firm with him."

Race gave the horse a look that he hoped conveyed that he could be very firm if required. He bridled the horse himself to make that clear, led the horse into the yard, and then mounted. If Anne was walking along the road to Nun's Chase, the rest should be easy.

Judging from matters thus far, however, he had little faith in any of this being easy. Least of all, now he came to think of it, not getting her staff wrapped around his head when he found her.

Twenty-nine

Anne paused, leaning on her staff and flexing her foot. She was close to tears, but they were as much of anger as of misery. Anger at Ralstone, but mostly at herself.

What a fool she was! She deserved everything that was going to happen to her. She probably deserved to end up married to Jack Ralstone, but she wouldn't. She would not pay for her stupidity with her life.

How far had she come?

How far to go?

She looked up at the moon and the stars, but if they could tell people where they were, she couldn't decode it.

The real question was, how far could she walk?

The signpost outside Buntingford had said three miles to Tris's place. That hadn't seemed so terrible a distance with the whole night to make it, but she'd overestimated her strength. Her cane had made walking easier, but it could help only so far, especially when the cloudy moonlight concealed ruts and dips.

Her ankle was feeling the strain, but her legs were positively aching. They were unused to continuous walking. Perhaps she should have come up with a way to hire a horse at the Black Bull, but she still couldn't imagine how to do it without creating a stir. Her one principal thought had been to make sure that no one ever knew that the old lady who'd arrived there with Captain Ralstone was in fact Lady Anne Peckworth.

Her legs hurt and even felt weak, and her spirits weren't helped by the eeriness of being out at night.

At first she'd found it liberating. She'd been alone—completely alone and unfettered—for the first time in her life. As she'd moved farther away from the civilization of Buntingford, however, every scurry of an animal, every hoot of an owl, had made her start.

She hadn't encountered anything dangerous except a startled badger that had snarled at her. She'd jabbed her staff at it, and it had slunk away. An owl had swooped overhead on whirring wings, but it hadn't been hunting her. She'd heard a fox bark and the squeal of an animal caught in some predatory jaws.

Not her. She had no reason to be afraid out here, but it was starkly clear in the depth of night that for some creatures death was just a jaw-snap away. And this was the territory of Le Corbeau. She'd not heard of him hurting anyone, but away from the theater she did not believe in gallant criminals. She didn't want to encounter him. But then she remembered that he, thank heavens, was in jail.

She looked at the winding road ahead—simply a gap between dark hedgerows. It lay empty and silent, as if she were the only person left in the world. That suggested safety, not danger.

On the other hand, it almost felt as if she had been transported out of human ken. Wasn't that what faery stories said? That people out at night could be bewitched by the faery folk, trapped for their amusement or forced to dance to death?

She shivered, and it was partly because of the chill breeze. She hadn't known how cold a summer night could grow, and though she was wearing her black cloak and bonnet, they didn't give much protection over the light summer dress she'd changed into for dinner with Ralstone.

At least she was wearing her boots.

She didn't like being out here. She didn't like it at all. If only she'd been able to stay at the inn, to demand a new room for herself and a chaise in the morning to carry her back to London, to her father's town mansion, where the servants were always ready. Back into the security of ducal power and privilege.

Might as well print the story in the papers. The inn

servants would know who she was, then, and what she had done. The story would be up and down the Great North Road with tomorrow's traffic.

In that situation, her family might want her to marry Ralstone, or Ralstone might find some way to persuade or compel her. She'd fled in terror that she might somehow end up married to him. For all the days of her life.

Tris would prevent that. Tris would do whatever was needed to get Ralstone out of her life, to prevent scandal, and return her to her family with no one else knowing. She had only to reach Nun's Chase before morning, before Jack emerged from his disgusting drunken stupor and took action.

Grimly, she set off again. Putting one foot in front of the other again and again, eventually she would arrive. She surely must have walked half the distance.

She should have *stolen* a horse. She'd thought of it, but a squint into the stables had shown a night groom there, very much awake and alert.

She stopped again, close to tears. She was going to have to sit down and rest, even though she feared that she might not be able to get started again. And she ached to sleep. She'd hardly slept last night for nerves, and not at all tonight. Tiredness weighed in her joints and scratched at her eyes.

She looked around, hoping to see some shelter, even a cow byre. Failing that, something to sit on other than the damp ground—a stile, a rock, a tree stump.

She could see only the dark hedge running along either side of the lane, with the occasional tree looming high out of it. Then she made out a gate ahead. That must go somewhere. Even if it only led into a field, she would be off the lane.

If Jack woke and came in search of her, he wouldn't find her. She'd thought him too drunk to stir, but what did she know of how he reacted to wine? She didn't know him at all.

That was the trouble.

She hadn't known him at all, and when he'd dropped his guard and begun to reveal his true self, she'd seen that she'd made a terrible mistake.

She forced herself into motion again, limping toward

the gate, leaning heavily on her staff. But when she got there, it was held shut by a rusty iron pin. She tried to force it out, but her hands were too tired, too chilled, perhaps too weak to move it.

Weak. That was what she was. Any notion of strength had been an illusion, like the belief of a fawned-upon lord that he was clever or handsome. She was a paltry, weak, stupid woman.

She leaned on the rough gate, looking into a field that was a complete mystery in the dark. After a moment, she rested her staff against it and draped her arms over it, letting the top bar take her weight. She might even be able to sleep this way, the hard bar digging into her chest. She let her head sink forward, closed her eyes . . .

She started, shuddered, and forced her eyes open. She couldn't go to sleep here! She made herself stand straight and take up her staff again.

Then she glimpsed a light.

Through another hedge to her left. A little, flickering light.

A farm. A cottage. Some sort of shelter. A place to rest in safety. She tried to judge route and distance, but the dark made orienting herself peculiarly difficult, as if the land around followed no pattern that she knew. If she continued along the road, however, there had to be a lane soon. A lane leading to that sanctuary.

She set the tip of her staff to the ground and pressed on. The hedge hid the light, but she held to the faith that she'd seen it, that a place was there, not far away.

She thought she saw a gap in the hedge but closer to, she saw only a stile. Would there be a stile on a lanc leading to a house? Surely they'd want to drive a cart or gig down there sometimes. . . .

Then she heard a voice.

A man's quiet voice, then a laugh.

She froze. Was she that close to the house? But what were people doing up, laughing, at this time of night?

A figure nipped nimbly over the stile, swaying lantern in hand. She saw others behind him, carrying things.

Sticks. Axes. And their faces were darkened.

Her light, her precious light had been these men, and they were up to no good!

She froze, praying that in her black cloak and bonnet she might be invisible, but then the man with the lantern turned and stared right at her. "Someone's here," he hissed.

Her face. His face was visible even through the soot or dirt he'd smeared on it. Hers must be white as the full moon.

She couldn't run, so she had no choice but to wait, shivering with cold, weariness, and fear. She tightened her grasp on her staff, willing to use it if she had to.

The man with the lantern came over, boots crunching heavily on the road. His lantern was tin pierced with many holes, and though not very bright it blinded her to him so his voice came out of a void. "Who're you, then?"

Her tongue stuck in her mouth.

"Come on! What you doing out here, and who be with you?"

A solid country voice, and a solid sweaty smell with him, and fear. Frightened animals were the most dangerous.

"No one." She'd found her voice, though it was breathy. "I'm walking to a friend's house!"

"At midnight?"

Anne tried to imitate Hetty's country accent. "I have no money to pay for a room, so I must walk."

She sensed other men coming closer, dark shapes beyond the holes of the lantern. Then they began to spread out, to encircle her. Panic tightened her throat, and her heart was going to burst.

She couldn't step back, for she'd bump into those behind. She turned one way and then the other, trying to keep them in sight.

"Where's this friend live, then?"

Attack was the best form of defense. She stood as tall as she could, gripping her staff. "What business is it of yours? And what are *you* doing out at midnight?"

She could guess, but she hoped they didn't know that. She'd seen sticks and the glint of metal. Axes, perhaps.

Not poachers. They didn't go out in large groups.

These men were machine-breakers. They thought their living would be taken away by a new machine—a threshing machine perhaps—and were set on smashing it. They were risking their freedom and perhaps their lives to do it, and might murder a witness.

The men were silent except for the odd shuffle or rustle of clothes. She could smell them, though: unwashed wool on their bodies, onions and beer on their heavy breath, and something else. Something primitive, violent, and dangerous.

By day they were probably decent enough farm laborers, like the ones she greeted cheerfully at Lea Park— hardworking sons and fathers. But here, at night, they were menace, and her heart beat like a frightened bird.

She could say that she hadn't seen any of them clearly, that she wouldn't be able to point them out tomorrow, but would they believe her?

A hand grasped her staff just below hers. The lantern shifted so she saw his face. Long, suspicious, big crooked teeth. "This is a fancy stick for a wandering pauper."

Someone grabbed her cloak from behind. "Fancy cloak, too."

She fought to keep hold of her only weapon, trying to twitch out of the hold on her cloak. "I've fallen on hard times. The cloak was charity. Let me be!"

"Can't do that, luv. Who knows who you might run off to?"

She pulled fiercely at the staff. He let go suddenly so that she fell back onto her bottom, at their feet. They laughed.

She screamed, *"No!"* at the vague but potent threat that hovered over her.

Then she heard it, felt it through the earth. Hooves at the gallop.

"Soldiers!" a man cried, and they began to scatter, but the horses were already on them. On her. She fell to the ground, arms over her head.

Thunder of hooves in her ears and through her body. Confused yells and shouted orders.

"Hide!"

"Run!"

Then: "It's only one man. Get him!"

She peeped, and then sat up.

A huge dark horse was wheeling and kicking. Too

close! She rolled toward the hedge, hearing her straw bonnet crunch, then peered out again.

Men were fleeing, calling to others to run, but some had stopped to fight, long sticks and heavy blades catching the moonlight. The horse reared up over them, and they fell back. The magnificent rider brought the horse down and turned it. The horse kicked out behind with a force that could have shattered heads if the men weren't already backing away.

Horse and rider turned and charged, the rider hitting out with a weapon of some sort. Cavalry! Had the military come to her rescue?

It broke the rabble. The men scattered, rolling under hedges, fighting one another to get over the stile. . . .

She sat up and almost cheered, but then she realized this was disaster. She couldn't be found like this! Hastily she began to squeeze back farther into the shadow of the hedge, trying to find a way through it into the field.

Crack!

A pistol? `

She stopped to see the horse riderless and rampaging.

One horse.

One rider.

Not the military.

And now her rescuer had been shot. She must help. . . .

To her shame she stayed frozen in her lair, afraid of being identified, afraid of being hurt.

She stayed there as the villains fled, their crashes and cries fading. The horse stamped and jerked. Wounded, too? She should help the poor horse. . . .

And then she heard a murmuring voice.

She shuddered, resting her head on her hands. The gallant man wasn't dead at least.

He might be wounded, though, and she must help him. Perhaps he need not know who she was. She crawled away from the hedge, amazed by how deeply she'd pushed herself. She had to tug her cloak free of one hawthorn spike after another, scratching her skin at times.

Surely no one would recognize Lady Anne Peckworth in this bedraggled creature.

By the time she could stand the horse was calmer, and she thought she saw six legs not four. The man was standing on the far side of the horse. Thank God. He didn't seem hurt at all.

She froze under a new thought.

Perhaps it was Le Corbeau.

If so she was grateful for his help, but all in all, she'd rather not meet him. Would he hear if she moved again? If she turned her back, would her black clothing make her invisible?

As her heart calmed, she made out the soothing murmur. "There, there, my fine brave fellow. I'll see to you."

Shot, no doubt. Poor creature. But there was nothing she could do for it, and perhaps the man would be so keen to get his horse to help that he wouldn't search for the lady he'd rescued.

All she had to do was keep very quiet.

Then the man spoke louder. "Anne?"

Her breath caught. Surely she knew that light, crisp voice.

"Anne? Where are you? Are you all right?"

It was as if a mighty hand had shaken the world and turned it upside down. Or had *she* been shot and blasted out of her wits?

The avenging Horseman of the Apocalypse was Race de Vere?

"Anne?"

The clear anxiety in his voice cut through her daze. She tugged herself free again from the hedge and limped into the moonlit road, picking up her staff. The dark horse still had six legs, but one pair of legs moved. Race ducked under the horse's neck and into view.

Hatless, slender in comparison to the bulk of the horse, not far from a time of violence, he seemed completely at his ease. It infuriated her.

"What on earth are you doing here?"

"As usual, Lady Anne, getting you out of trouble."

"As usual!" She shook her staff at him. "I am never in trouble."

He laughed.

"I'm not! Or at least," she amended, being a stickler

for justice, "I have not been before tonight. And this is all your fault."

That was unfair, and she expected him to say so. Instead, he said, "You're doubtless right."

It reminded her of things. "You're a Rogue. Or at least, a servant of Rogues."

"True."

"You went to Benning Hall to . . . to do something for the Rogues."

"True after a fashion." He turned his attention back to the horse. "That pistol ball creased his back, poor fellow. I need to get him to shelter and help."

She stared. Was that it? He charges in here, rescues her from some unspecified but terrible fate—single-handedly against dozens—and now his main concern was shelter for his horse? She approved, but it struck her as extremely strange.

"How did you come to be here?" she demanded.

"Magic," he said.

For a moment, out here in the unreality of the night, she considered whether it might be true. Then she sighed. "Can you ever talk sense?"

He glanced back. "I do so frequently—as when I told you not to marry Ralstone."

"I didn't."

There was a silent question in the air between them—had she acted as if married? That was one she wasn't ready to answer.

"Come on," he said. "The horse can doubtless carry your light weight as far as Nun's Chase."

She put a hand to her dazed head. Finding her battered bonnet there, she tore it off and flung it on the road. She was very tempted to stamp on it. "You cannot simply appear out of nowhere and not explain yourself!"

Race looked at her, and an explanation occurred.

"Oh, heavens. Do my family know? Have they sent you after me?"

"Why me, not Uffham? I followed an instinct and checked on you in Greenwich. Unless anyone else does the same thing, you are safe."

"Safe?" She started to laugh.

Then she was in his arms, as it had been that first time

at Benning Hall, strong, solid, comforting. He thought she was distraught and she was not, but she let him think it because this was where she wanted to be.

Suddenly everything was clear. This man, this hero, this rock—for all his mischievous ways—was the only one she could share her life with. And he could not be indifferent to her.

Why else was he here if he did not want her, at least a little bit? She knew, however, that he was trying to protect her, just as people had all her life. He wanted to wrap her in flannel and tuck her safely away in aristocratic splendor.

How was she going to get what she truly wanted?

She drew back a little, looking up at him. "You saved me."

The moon was behind him making his expression a mystery. "I shouldn't have needed to."

Undeterred by his stern tone, she said, "Thank you." She slid her arm around his neck and kissed him.

He resisted for a moment, then his arms tightened and his mouth sealed hers. She heard her staff clatter to the ground, then her other arm was around him so she could kiss him back as she wanted to, as she never quite had before, with no limit, with no thought of limit.

For the first time she let her hands take possession of him, of his shoulders, his skull, his jaw. Twisting, she slid one arm lower, to his back, then to his strong buttocks. . . .

He pulled back, pushed her at arm's length. "Anne, stop it."

"Why?"

"Don't be stupid."

"I've been stupid. I'm not anymore. I want you."

That wasn't quite so gracious as she'd intended, yet she felt his hands tighten under the power of it. Before she could amend it, he put his hands at her waist and lifted her into the saddle. The horse shifted for a moment, and she clutched the mane, but at a word from him, it settled.

What a remarkable feat of strength to lift her like that. It melted her even more. She would not let him go. He was hers. She reached down to tangle her fingers gently in his silvery hair. She wanted freedom to do this all her days.

He looked up, seeming exasperated if anything. "It's fear, relief, and battle aftermath, Anne. You'll have your wits back soon."

She just smiled. A month ago, a week ago, yesterday, she would have shriveled at that and fled. She had, in fact. It was all different now. A deep instinct told her that he wanted her in the same way that she wanted him. She had only to break the barriers that he thought came of honor.

She didn't underestimate the challenge. Men, good men, took those things so seriously. On the other hand, she didn't underestimate her own abilities when it came to a challenge.

He was clearly determined on getting her to Nun's Chase. Then, she suspected, he would disappear. One way or another, she would not allow that. Would Tris lock him up for her until he saw reason?

He picked up her staff and took the reins to lead the horse down the road. She'd rather stay here, but what argument could she make? She was racking her brain when fate solved her problem.

"Pleeze," said a laconic, French-accented voice, "stand and deliver."

Anne stared at the stile, and at the man now sitting on top of it, a pistol pointed at them. The tone might be lazy, but the pistol was not.

The man was dressed in black, with black mask, mustache and beard, and the broad-brimmed hat with the sweeping white plume.

"Le Corbeau?" she said. "I don't believe this!"

Perhaps this was all a crazy dream.

Thirty

~

The man inclined his head. *"A vôtre service, mademoiselle."* Eyes and pistol remained steady.

Anne wondered how Race was taking this and prayed that he not do anything dangerous. "If you are thinking of a duel, sir," she said to the highwayman, "I assure you that I am not interested."

Le Corbeau grinned. "You refer to zat absurd play, *minou*. I would not give up my way of life for a mere woman."

Kitten. He was calling her kitten? She preferred Mouse.

Race spoke at last. "What do you want?" His tone was chilly, as if he addressed a thoughtless child.

Le Corbeau dropped down from his perch, pistol steady all the time. Fifteen feet or so lay between them, so Anne didn't think there was much they could do. If she weren't seated sideways she might be able to charge the horse at the highwayman. It was clearly cavalry trained, but she wasn't. She didn't know how to make it fight. And, of course, it was injured.

It was all intolerably frustrating, and she was sure it was worse for Race. She didn't want him to take risks, however. She had such high hopes for their future.

"Your money or your life," the man said, but again as if amused by the trite line.

"I have about ten guineas," Race responded. "The lady has nothing."

"I doubt it. Perhaps I should search her."

Anne heard Race sigh. "As we're trading clichés, *monsieur*—over my dead body."

Anne shivered with dread, but also, she had to admit, with a thrill at the absolute challenge of it.

Le Corbeau seemed to study Race for a moment. "She is your wife?"

"No."

"Your lover?"

"No."

"Your beloved?"

"No."

Was it her imagination that Race hesitated before saying that? It could simply be the mounting tension she sensed in him.

She plunged into speech, in French. "You, sir, are supposed to be in jail."

"My poor simulacrum," he replied in the same language. "I never thought to win so well by losing a few trinkets at dice."

That answered one question. He really was French. She had been taught by a Frenchwoman and could detect no falseness in his fluency.

"If you are known to be still working these roads," she pointed out, "they will have to let him go free."

"It seems only fair."

"Very well. Let us assist you. Permit us to go on, and we will immediately report your activities to the magistrates."

"How kind. However, to have full effect, it is necessary that I steal something from you. No necklace, my pretty cat? No rings? Or did those you drove off before take them? I heard a shot."

Her jewelry was in her pocket beneath her gown. "They were frame-breakers, not thieves, and I'm a poor cast-off maidservant with only the clothes I stand up in."

For some reason he seemed to find that amusing, but he turned his attention to Race. "And you, my silent sir?"

"Oh, I'm nobody."

Anne was touched to discover that while Race's French was tolerable, his accent was atrocious.

"Does Mr. Nobody fight with the sword?" Le Corbeau asked.

"It has been known. I fear that you, sir, have been

sneaking into Drury Lane to watch your own adventures. Why the devil should I fence with you?"

"For your lady's honor."

A silky menace in it made Anne come alert. This was all so strange, so dreamlike, that she'd been treating it like a play. But it was real, the villain was real, and he might well have foul designs on her body. If Race fought him, one or other might die. She hiked up her skirts and swung her right leg over so she was astride.

"This is nonsense," she protested. "I have money. Take it!"

"Oh, I will," the highwayman said, eyeing her exposed legs with interest. "You doubtless have it tucked away next to your skin. Beneath your garter, perhaps, or between your breasts. . . ."

Mouth dry, she realized that she might have made things much, much worse.

In a swirl of movement, Race tossed the reins to her, and slapped the horse to make it run. She missed the reins so clutched the horse's mane as it careered away.

She screamed, "No!" She was going to fall without balance or stirrups, and she wasn't going to leave Race to face an armed man alone.

Perhaps the horse obeyed, or perhaps it was its wound, but it halted, shifting nervously beneath her. Muttering about highwaymen, heroes, and men in general, she grabbed the reins, settled herself in the staddle, and turned the horse back. A fight was going on. And there seemed to be three men involved!

"Sorry," she said to the horse. "Go!" She kicked as hard as she could and, praise heaven, some warrior instinct sent it hurtling back to the fray.

Anne saw the three men stop fighting to stare at her—three white faces, two masked, and all ludicrously alarmed. She hauled on the reins to stop the beast, but she'd obviously found one of its battle cues. It reared up, slashing out with its hooves. She clung to the mane, praying not to fall.

The men all rolled for cover, but she heard one laugh. She knew who that must be.

She brought the horse down, soothing it, wondering exactly where her bravado had brought them. She'd split the men, but was Race alone, or with one of the villains? Should she now ride on to safety or try to rescue her hero?

This daring lady business was not so easy as it seemed.

She circled the horse, peering around. "Race?"

A movement. Before she could react, she was dragged off the saddle and over a broad shoulder. Struggling, screaming, she couldn't get free.

Then she was whirled to her feet, a gloved hand over her mouth. Race hurtled out of the shadows, but the man behind her said, "Don't."

Race stopped, but Anne saw a death-promise in his eyes, the sort made by a man who knew what it was to kill.

"Do not be rash, sir," Le Corbeau said from behind her, in English now, and wisely speaking very carefully, indeed. "As you know, I am not alone. My friend, he has two pistols and can stop you dead at any moment."

Anne tried to speak, to tell Race not to take any risks. All she could do was shake her head at him.

Race was focused on the man behind her. "You, sir, are a dead man."

"Perhaps. But at ze moment, you sir, are a man who must do exactly as I say, no? And what I say is, you walk. Over ze stile, down ze path a little way, to a cottage."

"Why?"

"You do not take ze orders very well, do you?"

"It has been said." It was as if Race relaxed, but Anne wasn't fooled, and neither, she suspected, was the highwayman. She didn't know where the third man was now, but she didn't doubt that he was nearby and with pistols. They had no choice but to do as Le Corbeau said.

"You want a reason?" the highwayman asked. "Very well. Ze swords are in ze cottage."

"And if we fight and I win?"

"Zen you both go free."

"If I lose?"

"Zen you are both entirely at my disposal, but I promise you your lives. You have been a soldier, I tink. You know it is good to live to fight another day."

Race nodded, but Anne was glad she wasn't the focus of his wide, steady eyes. Perhaps they gave the highwayman pause, for time passed before he spoke again, and then it was to her.

"Do not scream, *minou*. It will do no good." He then removed his hand from her mouth, though he still had an arm around her, pressing her to his body. He was a tall man, not heavy, but all muscle.

"Should I have ridden away?" she asked Race. "I'm sorry. I couldn't do it."

He smiled. "I don't suppose I could have either." He picked up her staff from the road and gave it to her. "Let's go to this cottage and see the end of this. Don't worry. I won't let anyone hurt you."

He couldn't be sure of that, and yet she felt as if safety had been wrapped around her. She wanted this security all her life.

Le Corbeau let her go, and she limped to the stile. "I wish I could make sure no one hurts you."

Race smiled at that, shaking his head, then went nimbly over the stile and turned to help her. Le Corbeau's henchman was on that side, pistols at the ready, but Race acted as if he didn't exist. A glance back showed Le Corbeau behind, a pistol pointing at them.

Anne faced the man, trying for the same nonchalance that came so easily to Race. "Someone has to take care of the poor horse, sir."

"But of course, my grand lady. As soon as you are at ze cottage. I see you limp. I am sorry for it. Would you wish me to carry you?"

She gave a deliberately theatrical shudder, turned, and made her way inelegantly over the stile. At the far side, Race swung her into his arms. "You don't find my touch repulsive, I hope."

What to say to that? She contented herself with a simple "No" and made sure her staff was not in his way. Despite their situation, the feeling of being in his arms was magical.

The henchman turned to lead the way down the rough, shadowy lane. He kept glancing back, however, and Le Corbeau was behind. Up ahead Anne saw a flickering light, and this time it really was the lit window of a cottage.

The highwayman's lair.

Where Race would fence with Le Corbeau if she didn't think of some way to avoid it. To add to her problems, at some point tonight she had to win Race de Vere. Her arm was looped around his neck, and she let her hand cherish his strong shoulder.

"I'm sorry for dragging us into this mess," she murmured.

"It would have been wiser to stay safely in Brighton."

Anne surprised herself by digging her nails into him and making a growl of irritation in her throat.

"Little cat," he said, and she heard amusement. "Is that an improvement on Mouse?"

"I wasn't *purring*. I fled Brighton because you threatened to turn my family against Ralstone."

"Ah, yes, Ralstone. Perhaps you wish to be returned to him."

"No!" A moment later she wished she'd softened it.

"What did he do?" That cold murderous edge was unmistakable.

"Nothing. Stop sounding as if you want to kill someone."

"If you're going to go adventuring, Anne, you are going to run into violence and bloodshed. Get accustomed to it."

"Ralstone did nothing particularly offensive. He was merely himself."

After a moment, she felt laughter shake him. "What a sad epitaph. You, however, deserve to be spanked for leading the poor man on."

Anne didn't have to find a response to that justified accusation and outrageous suggestion. They had arrived at the cottage.

The darkness hid many flaws, but even so *ramshackle* was the word that came to mind. It was so old that the small windows had no glass, only vertical wooden bars to keep out intruders. The whole place tilted, and the henchman had to heave the door up to get it to open. He went into the dimly lit interior, and they followed.

Race stood her on the earthen floor, and Anne straightened her clothes, glancing around. This must be the main room of the cottage because it had a large hearth in the center wall. A rough door to one side which would lead into another simple room. There would be a space above under the roof, perhaps once used for sleeping, but if there were stairs, they were in the other room.

The light came from a pierced tin lantern similar to the one the Luddites had carried, and the smell of tallow mixed with a general smell of damp and rot.

She turned to face Le Corbeau. "A suitable hole for a rat," she said in French.

"Does it not occur to you to be a little careful of what you say to me, *minou*?"

"I will be polite if you promise to let us go."

"Do I collect slaves? Of course I will let you go." He put on a look of horror. "My God! You think I will murder you? No, no. Too messy by far."

"The swords," Race said in that cold, forbearing voice.

"Ah, yes—the swords."

Le Corbeau looked between them, the light glimmering on his face. It wasn't the face, however, so much as the mischievous smile that made Anne's breath catch.

She knew that smile.

Tris! Le Corbeau was Tris.

What on earth was he up to, and why was he playing this game with them? To punish her for being in this mess? She almost spoke, but then remembered. Once this adventure was over Race would disappear. She wasn't sure even Tris could stop him short of tying him up, and where would that get her?

His eyes met hers. He knew she knew. He was telling her to say nothing. Heart beating hard, she obeyed for the moment.

"I am afraid, my dear sir," he said to Race, "that our fight will have to wait a little while. For one thing, I must go out and rob someone or my poor substitute might hang. For another, we can hardly fence in the moonlight, no matter how romantic that might seem. Morning is the time for duels."

"Then let us go, for God's sake."

Race's tone made Anne chill with guilt. He still thought this for real and was afraid for her. She should tell him the truth, but she had the feeling that Tris was on her side and had some purpose. He was not stupid in his mischief and adventures.

"I fear you might raise the alarm, sir," Tris said, the French disguising his voice so well, "and increase the risk of my capture. I wish to bring about the release of the innocent man, but not at risk of my own neck."

"What, then, do you intend?"

"Merely to keep you securely here until morning, at which time we can play our little game."

Race was cold as stone. "I, sir, am not playing games. The lady will be missed. A search will be made."

"For a cast-off serving maid?"

Now Anne knew why Le Corbeau had found that funny. Damn Tris and his wayward sense of mischief. At heart, he and Race were two of a kind.

And she loved them both.

It couldn't come to violence and blood, could it? Anne knew, without doubt, that Race was poised to take any chance to kill their captors and get her away to safety.

She moved closer to him.

Race glanced at her and put an arm around her. "Don't worry. I won't let him hurt you."

"I know." That was the problem. She'd moved close so as to be able to stop him doing murder.

"Take off your clothes," Tris said in his heavily accented English.

"What?"

She and Race said it together, and she was probably the more shocked.

"What on earth—?"

But again, the look in Tris's eyes stopped her. "Not all your clothes," he said, lips twitching. "Your outer clothes. Zen you will be locked in ze upper room. I don't think you will find a way out in the next few hours, but if you do, perhaps running across the countryside in your underwear will make you hesitate."

"We're not doing it, Anne," Race said. "He has neither time nor inclination to make a struggle over it. I don't know what makes the madman tick, but this is a game to him, nothing more."

An accurate assessment, but Anne would quite like to get Race out of some of his clothing. Wicked though it was, compromising them both was the only way to capture this man, and less clothing would be a step in the right direction.

A few months ago such outrageous ideas would never have occurred to her, but now she was a daring lady who knew exactly what she wanted—to make love to Race here, tonight, so that he'd have to marry her.

And Tris was on her side?

Perhaps this was a dream, but if so, she would enjoy it.

With a loud *click*, Tris cocked his pistol. "If you do not take off your cloak, dress, and shoes, *minou,* I am going to shoot your so gallant escort. I will try to do it in a nonfatal spot, but I cannot guarantee it."

"If you shoot me," Race said, "I can hardly fence with you in the morning."

"As you have guessed, I am quite mad. The best ting to do is to humor me. I am also a man of my word. If you win ze duel in ze morning, you both go free."

Race looked at Anne, exasperated and apologetic. "I'm sorry. He clearly is mad, and thus there's no point reasoning with him. I'd willingly be shot to save you, but it's unlikely to do any good."

"Of course it isn't. Don't even think of it. As it happens, I'm quite well covered underneath."

She leaned her staff against the wall, untied her black cloak, and let it fall to reveal the cream muslin dress she'd put on for dinner with Ralstone. Ignoring Tris and his man—doubtless some poor innocent groom forced into this mayhem—she turned her back to Race. "You'll have to unbutton it for me."

She stood there, eyes closed, sucking in every scrap of pleasure from his fingers working at the row of small buttons down the back. From just that, from the elusive brush of his fingers against her spine, something wild and fevered stirred deep inside her.

Plots and motives began to fade beneath a sharp, animal need. How easy it would be to turn, to move into one of their blistering kisses, to go on from there this time. . . .

He parted her dress and untied the laces that gathered the waist beneath her breasts, then she felt, surely she felt, his knuckles brush comfortingly against her skin for a moment. She had to catch her breath before she turned, dress loose, to face all three men.

Perhaps it was a lifetime of servants, or perhaps just that she knew that underneath she was almost as well covered as in the gown, but she felt no embarrassment. In fact, she quite enjoyed the discomfort on their faces.

Serve Tris right!

She pulled out of the sleeves, and let the dress fall to the ground. Beneath, she wore a petticoat of white cotton which was little different to the dress except that it was sleeveless. Beneath that—she knew at least—she had a light corset over her shift and drawers.

Chill hit her bare arms but she didn't rub them. Race would probably risk death to put her cloak back on her.

"Now you, sir," Tris said. "Ungallant to leave ze lady so far ahead of you."

"You're a lunatic." But Race shed his jacket, waistcoat, and shirt. "Will that do?"

"Oh yes." She saw that Tris was having trouble staying serious. For her part, she was having trouble concentrating on anything but Race and the feelings his strength and his beautiful body stirred in her.

"Is that all?" she demanded, desperate now to get Race alone. Surely that was part of Tris's plan.

"Alas, *minou,* your footwear. If you are willing to run around the countryside in your petticoat, perhaps you will hesitate to do so barefoot."

"The lady has a crippled foot," Race said. "She needs her boots."

"Even so. Perhaps, sir, you would help her."

Anne saw Race was close to breaking point, ready to fight. She sat on one of the rough benches that were the only furniture. After a tense moment, Race turned his back on their captors and came to kneel before her.

His eyes met hers and she winced at the angry tension there.

"Don't fight them," she murmured. "This is nothing terrible."

"You're very brave."

She winced with guilt. "Not really."

He shook his head and undid her left half-boot. She

could take off her boots herself, but she had no objection to Race doing it for her, especially wickedly naked from the waist up. She couldn't resist. Pretending to need the balance, she put a hand on his broad shoulder.

So warm, so firm, so strong.

He glanced up, perhaps puzzled, perhaps wary, perhaps warning her of something. He made short work of her boot then began to unlace her right one. The heavy boot she wore on her crippled foot.

He'd handled her right foot before, at the Swinamer ball, but worry tugged at her. What did he really think about it? Would it repulse him when it came to intimacy?

He eased the half-boot off, then looked at her again, and this time she saw nothing but assurance in his expression. He traced with his fingers the awkward turn of her ankle and the crease in her sole. Then slowly, he raised her foot and kissed the instep.

Her hand on his shoulder tightened of its own accord, and she felt him become still. Did something ripple through him as it did through her, dizzying her, shooting aches into private places?

It did. She saw it in his eyes, but he rose, took off his own boots, and faced their captors. "Now what?"

It was the same forbearing tone that said that their captors were simpletons. Harmless, and mindless. Anne prayed that Tris wouldn't fall out of his role and shoot Race for pure impertinence.

She could shoot him for excessive willpower, but it did not truly daunt her. He was hers, and soon would be in all senses of the word. He had to be. She could not bear for it to be any other way.

Apparently unmoved, Tris gestured toward the door beside the hearth, where his henchman waited with the lantern. "Now you follow my friend upstairs. We secure you up zere, and you peacefully await the dawn. See, it is perfectly simple."

"So is death," promised Race, extending an arm to Anne.

Shaken by nerves and desire, she needed it, but she did her best to walk with dignity. In many ways it was more comfortable for her to walk without the corrective shoes, but her limp was worse. Race moved to carry her, but she stopped him.

"I prefer to walk."

A bit of sanity remained, and she wanted him to see her like this before she bound him to her. If he couldn't bear it, she would have to let him go. With another man she could hide her blemish, but not with Race. With him, reality had to be all or nothing.

Had Tris known that, too? Was it why he'd insisted on her being in her stocking feet? As she made her way awkwardly up narrow stairs, she prayed that Race never learn who Le Corbeau was. God knows what he would do.

The stairs emerged into an empty space beneath the roof with a small window at one end. This was not much of a prison unless Tris intended to chain them to the rafters.

The henchman put down the lantern, went to what looked like an end wall, did something, and opened a rough plank door. Perhaps in daylight it would be clearer, but there would never be much daylight here. A secret room, doubtless where Le Corbeau kept his loot.

Where Tris kept his loot? She remembered to puzzle over his role in this. He couldn't really be a highwayman. A resolute traveler might put a pistol ball in him one of these nights. Could she be wrong about his identity?

She peered at him, and even in the dim light, she was sure. She'd known his voice, too, once she'd recognized him. Though he was pitching his voice a little higher, it was still his. What on earth could he be up to?

She had no time to fret about his role now. They were ordered into the shadowy space beyond the door.

The distant lantern light showed some locked chests and a rough bed. A place for Le Corbeau to live for a day or two if hunted? Other than that, the room was just another attic space, the ceiling being the timber roof frame and the thatch beyond.

She suppressed a shudder, imagining spiders and even bigger invaders dropping down from that thatch in the night. Race put an arm around her. That instantly made everything wonderful, but could she really attempt to seduce him in such a place?

Thought of pests raised other worries.

She turned to where Tris and his man stood in the doorway. "Are there mice here? Or rats?"

Race drew her closer. "There are bound to be, Anne. Don't worry—"

But Tris said, "Not as far as I know."

He was telling her that he knew nothing to Race's discredit. Of course. He wouldn't be throwing them together like this if he did.

And he was. He was clearly arranging things to make it as easy as possible for her to capture her elusive beloved. It was close to miraculous, but she'd take a miracle.

She blew Tris a kiss and saw him fight a smile.

They were both mad, and this was wicked, but she was sure of her course. She knew in her heart that Race loved her as much as she loved him. Rank and fortune no longer mattered. This was her chance for a true treasure, and she would not let it slip by.

"I no longer play for farthing points," she said, and saw Tris understand her, and Race fail to do so. In fact Race looked as if he feared she was scared out of her wits.

Tris smiled and put the lantern just over the threshold. "I wish you all pleasure of the night, my friends, and a glorious tomorrow."

And then he closed the door.

Thirty-one

Despite what she knew, the closing door sent a shudder through Anne and she moved into Race's arms. She might be terrified if not for him. Once their bodies touched, however, desire pulsed back into her, making her body and Race's body the only things that mattered.

The sounds at the door seemed distant to her, the sounds of Tris or his man locking them in here.

She rubbed against Race, waiting for a kiss, but he gently moved away from her and went to check both door and tiny window.

Willpower, damn his eyes.

She considered the bed. Unpromising though it was, it was her target. She limped over to sit on it. The wooden frame seemed solid, and the only smell was a faint one from the wool blanket. In fact, it was quite a respectable bed for its surroundings, and when she felt the sheets, they were fine cotton.

She suppressed a smile. Of course. Tris would not contemplate sleeping in a coarse and grubby bed. Worry pricked at her again.

Had he really left to hold up a coach in order to prove that the poor man in jail was not Le Corbeau?

She made herself put it aside. There was nothing she could do about it now, whereas there was something she could do about her future. As she watched Race move around the small room, never looking at her, doubts stirred. She fought them down. She remembered the way they'd kissed on the road. She remembered the look in his eyes downstairs.

He was hers. She only had to break him.

The sagging mattress made sitting on the edge of the bed awkward, so she hitched herself up onto it and leaned back against the low wall. The roof angled up just above her head. She tried hard not to think about spiders in her hair.

This would be a lot easier, she was sure, in a gracious bedroom. But perhaps not. Race was going to resist, and their circumstances were weapons she could use.

He'd picked up the lantern and turned from the door with it in his hand. "Unfortunately, I can't see any way of getting out. I could try battering the door down with one of the chests, but it's very solid and securely fixed in some way. This cottage may look run down, but it's well maintained where it matters." He moved back into the center of the space. "We could set fire to the bed and hope they rescue us."

"Don't!"

He turned to her. "I'm sorry. Damnable army instincts. Assess the possibilities and hazards."

"The roll of the dice?" she suggested.

He laughed and put the lantern on one of the chests. Then he came over to sit on the bed by her side, but a foot away. "You're very brave."

"I don't feel brave." It was true, but her fear was nothing to do with highwaymen, and all to do with failing here. She moved closer. "Hold me, please."

She counted his hesitation in heartbeats, but then he met her and took her into his arms. "You're cold," he said, and drew her closer.

"You're warm," she breathed with relief.

She pressed as much of herself as possible against him, exploring the wonder of her naked arms against his naked chest. He did feel delightfully hotter than she was, and the firmness of him, his strength, his self, warmed parts deeper than her skin.

She rested her head on his shoulder, breathing in his spicy smell.

She felt him tense.

That was doubtless good.

"Thank God you're here with me," she whispered against his skin. "He might have captured me when I was by myself."

"Or the frame-breakers might have slit your throat. What crazy impulse took you out into the night?" His tone was cool, but he began to stroke her, comforting her.

Such pleasure, such power in his clever, soothing hands, burning through the fine lawn and silk of her underclothes. She breathed in the scent of him. She longed to turn her head and kiss him, kiss his throat, his chest, his muscular torso. . . .

He'd said something. She should reply. . . .

"Out into the night," she echoed, most of her mind on other things. "I had to. I couldn't be there with Ralstone in the morning. If anyone found out, I might have had to marry him."

"Wasn't that the idea?"

Her arm rested across him. She dared to move her fingers, to explore a little. "Not by then. If I'd stayed and refused to go on with him, he might have revealed my identity to force me."

"He still might."

"Without my presence, it's just his story." If she raised her head, would he kiss her?

She felt him nuzzle in her hair. "Anne, you left your monogrammed luggage behind."

She winced. "Oh."

She looked up to see rueful amusement in his eyes. "And a note on your crested note paper. I tore off the crest, but I couldn't do much about your luggage. I added a postscript to your note, however, that should make Ralstone keep it all quiet."

"And I felt so competent, so brave!" All her confidence, all her courage, fled into the gloom. She moved away from him. "I'm useless, aren't I? A spoiled duke's daughter. I can't do anything right—"

He captured her shoulders and made her meet his eyes. "Your bravery humbles me. For you, for Lady Anne Peckworth, to set off into the night, to face down wandering troublemakers, to face down a highwayman, took more courage than I possess."

"Or a foolish miscalculation of the danger involved."

Lantern light showed his smile. "That's usually the

way it is. Few heroes really know what they're letting themselves in for. If they did, they'd run away."

"I don't think so. I'm sure you knew what you risked when you had a man flogged with ribbons."

His smile disappeared. "Who told you that story?"

"Ralstone."

"A gossip, too, is he? It was no act of heroism."

"You were almost flogged yourself."

"Almost. There was no real danger."

"You couldn't have been sure of that."

She realized that they were back to arguing and a foot apart. She had a strong suspicion that he'd arranged it that way. What did she do now? She'd assumed that they would fall into mad passion as they had before, but she saw now that he had himself under tight control.

Very well, it was a challenge, like a game of chess against a masterly player. She was good at chess. On the other hand, she didn't underestimate Race's intelligence and willpower. In a strange twist on Tantalus, she was sure he would deny himself water when dying of thirst if he thought it was the right thing to do.

She settled back into his arms. He could hardly refuse to comfort the poor maiden in distress. "Explain how you came to be on that road to rescue me, and how it was not the action of a hero."

He leaned against the rough wall, but she was aware now of how he kept himself a little apart, a little restrained. What if she stroked? Kissed? It seemed shamelessly bold but she would need to be bold to win. . . .

"It's hardly heroic to drive off a handful of frightened farm laborers when I had a cavalry-trained mount burning to attack."

"What was your weapon?"

"A stick."

"Whereas they had blades and a pistol. You were almost shot."

"A miscalculation of the dangers." She heard the smile in his voice and smiled herself.

"I see. If you'd realized one of them was armed, you would have left me to my fate."

She felt his chuckle. "No, love, I couldn't have done that."

She noted the *love* and gathered it to herself as a precious gift. His arm shifted to settle more neatly at her waist, and his head came to rest against hers. With deep satisfaction, she thought she felt another kiss in her hair. She inhaled slowly, struggling not to show her response. Yet.

Race inhaled the scent of Anne, struggling with his body and his conscience. He hadn't followed her to trap her, and he couldn't let that happen. Not even if she was maddeningly bent on her own destruction. Safer by far to keep his distance, but he couldn't refuse to comfort her when she was frightened.

Her delicate perfume alone could undo him, especially now, mixed with a tang of earthy sweat that said she'd left the safety of her elevated sphere to fall to earth. His task was to return her to her cloud, but for this brief time she was here, below, and intimately in his arms.

Perhaps she'd regain her wits when she realized how much of her situation was his fault.

"I couldn't have abandoned you," he said, "because your situation was my fault. I threatened to warn your family about Ralstone simply to scare you off him. And instead," he added, "I scared you into his arms."

"Not scared," she protested, but then said, "Oh, I suppose I was. Scared of failure. But how did you find me? I thought Ralstone's plan was quite clever."

"He stole it from an ingenious couple in Portugal, and I remembered it."

Then he described his visit to Ralstone's lodging and what had followed. All the time, however, he fought the enchantment of her slender body so close to his, her bare arm across him, the awareness of all of her, so close, so warm, so vulnerable, so desirable. . . .

He knew—God, how he knew—that she wanted to give herself to him now. She had some romantic idea in her head, perhaps because of her situation with Ralstone, perhaps because she saw him as a gallant hero. As he'd told her, it was battle madness. He couldn't take advantage of it.

She shifted. Pressed closer.

Damnation.

"But how did you know which way I'd gone from Buntingford?" she asked, looking up, so her lips were only inches away.

"Map. Looked at the map." Dear Lord, he was degenerating to incoherence. He forced himself to make sense. "I knew you were too sensible to set off into the night without a destination. When I saw that Nun's Chase was in the area, I gambled on that."

"Do you gamble a lot?"

"Rarely."

"Good."

Were her lips closer? Had she moved, or had he?

Resist, he commanded, while his body, on its own, strove not to.

"Thank you," she murmured, only an inch away now.

"For rescuing you?"

"For crediting me with sense after such a nonsensical adventure."

"Not nonsensical. Goaded you. Into it."

In her move, she'd shifted a leg over his. His right hand had somehow ended up above her neckline, on her naked back. Her knee pressed against the erection he was fighting. Did the minx know what she was doing? Lady Anne? She couldn't possibly.

Resist. Resist.

He moved slightly, but she moved with him.

"Goaded me into eloping?" she asked, sliding her cool hand up his chest to his shoulder, then across his shoulder to his arm. A ripple of fire.

"No." He grabbed her hand and moved it but then couldn't think what to do with it. "Not elopement. Bad idea." She moved his hand—or did he?—to his lips. "Hades, Anne, stop it!"

He surged off the bed and put the width of the small room between them. His body ached, burned, for what she so idiotically offered.

He waited for the innocent "Stop what?" but this was Anne, not some lesser woman.

"I want you, Race."

He turned at bay to see her sitting on the bed, apparently composed, an angel in white, pale skin, pale hair, pale hands narrow in her lap. How could he long to do such earthy things to an angel?

How could he not?

"I don't know anything about this," she said, "but I think there are natural forces, aren't there? I know what I want, and it is to become one with you here, now, tonight."

"No—"

"Because," she overrode, "if I don't, tomorrow you will leave my life forever."

He was shaking as if with a fever. "It's the only sensible thing to do." He was arguing with himself as much as with her.

"It doesn't make sense to me, and you said I was sensible."

"Sometimes."

"Only when it suits you, apparently."

He laughed, loving her more, desiring her more by the second. "Anne, sweetheart—"

"Am I?"

He didn't ask the stupid question, but he didn't answer, either.

She cocked her head. "When . . . when Le Corbeau asked if I was your beloved, you hesitated. Am I, Race?"

So easy to say no.

Impossible, though, here in this moment.

He found some cool spot in his mind and drew control from it. "Yes. But it wouldn't last, Anne. You'd be cut off from your natural sphere like a fish out of water. Haven't you read myths about marriages between humans and fish? They never turn out well. Especially for the fish."

She laughed, a lovely chuckle that wove through the room and into his aching heart. "We're not so different as that! I don't have a serpent's tail to hide like Melusine, nor do you." She drew her knees up and wrapped her arms around them, resting her chin on top. "Explain to me exactly why our union is so unnatural."

"Your world will not accept me."

"Yes, they will."

"A pleasant myth, but a myth. I suppose your family

might be polite out of love of you, but it would never be the same."

"The same as what? I've lived my life quietly and will be happy to return to that. As you say, my family will accept you, and I'm sure some of my friends will positively approve."

Some tone in that suggested a special meaning, but he had no energy to pursue it. "I don't believe that you want to live as privately as that. Where are your new friends to come from?"

"Perhaps from your circle. The Rogues?"

"They're not my friends, except Amleigh. And my relationship there is secretary."

She sat up straighter. "You're Lord Amleigh's secretary?" At last he had surprised her. Perhaps she'd see reason.

"Now and then."

She chuckled again. "As you please. I see. I have to warn you, Race, that when it comes to marriage it will not be as you please."

There were a number of things he could say to that, all of them dangerous. Verbal battles with Anne Peckworth, he was realizing far too late, had been dangerous from the start.

"As it is," she said, "I have a plan for the future that deals with your concerns. Of course, you may dislike it as much as Ralstone did."

"Is that why you left? Because he didn't like your plan?"

He hoped to distract her, but he also needed to know what Ralstone had done to her. Had he seduced her? Raped her? He'd kill him, but it might also be an excuse to take what was offered here, to marry her in order to save her.

"I left because we talked over dinner, and I realized we had nothing in common."

After a moment, he said, "That's it? Don't you think you should have realized that earlier?"

"Of course I do." She spread her hands. "I don't know why I didn't see it. He wants a life within society, and I want a private one. He wants a large circle of friends, and I want a small one. He does not want to live in my family's pocket—though I'm sure he was hoping to live out of it." She sighed. "I think he has a trick of telling people what they want to hear."

He hadn't seen that, but she was right. "It's not surprising that you were taken in by it."

"But mortifying. I hope no one ever knows."

"They won't."

"He might boast of it."

"He won't."

He saw her look become startled. "Did you threaten to kill him?"

He gave thanks for this conversation, which was giving back some control over his body and his wits. "Not in so many words—but yes."

"And would you?"

He wasn't sure what the right answer to that was. Women could be strange about these things. He gave her the only gift he could: honesty.

"If it came to it, of course, but a duel would hardly avoid scandal. I think he'll see sense."

Her gaze was thoughtful. "You are alien in so many ways, Race, but not because of your lineage. It's your wild spark and your army career."

"There are many men with an army career behind them."

"But how many who flogged a man with ribbons?"

Race shook his head. "I wish you'd forget that bit of foolishness."

"Why? You saved a man from unjust punishment."

"Not so unjust. Greely was a sloppy malingerer."

"Then why?"

"I simply grew tired of the bloody nonsense."

"Literally bloody. But I have to point out, sir, that your language is becoming a little strong for a lady's company."

She was teasing, and he'd never felt less like teasing in his life. "You, my lady, are trying to get me naked into that bed. A little swearing hardly counts."

He'd hoped the attack would shock her into sense, but the ethereal angel said, "True," and shrugged the straps of her petticoat off her shoulders. Then she undid the waist tie, and shimmied out of it, rising to get it under her bottom.

The only way to stop her was to physically restrain her, and getting any closer to her was the last thing he should do.

Smiling at him, she tossed the cotton-and-lace garment aside with all the ease of a naughty dancer. A delicate cloud of her perfume danced across to torment him. She was still well covered, but the sight of a corset could drive any man wild, and her shift reached only to her calves.

Then she raised it and untied her right garter. He watched frozen as she rolled down her pale stocking, uncovering her slender leg and long, aristocratic foot. He stood there, held up by the wall behind, able only to breathe as she slowly removed the other stocking to uncover the foot that was turned and misshapen.

He'd seen twisted feet that were worse—he'd seen a child with the ankle turned at ninety degrees—but the slight turn was enough to mean that she would never walk gracefully, never run, never dance except far from public eyes.

Resistance broke. He went, knelt, and took her foot to cherish. He stroked it gently, feeling the misplaced joints, the unnatural seam in her sole.

Her hand gripped his. "Don't."

He looked up. "It is nothing to be ashamed of."

"You're going to make me cry."

He let her draw his hands away. "That's the last thing that I want, Anne. Believe that."

Holding his hands she said, "Then make love to me." With a wicked smile, she added, "Once you're my lover, I'll let you fondle my foot whenever you want."

He hid his face in her hands, laughing, but close to crying. "Anne, for pity's sake. Where did you learn to be so ruthless?"

Her fingers moved to flex against the side of his face, to move into his hair, shattering him. "I'm a duke's daughter. I'm used to having what I want. I come from a long line of people used to having what they want. And I want you."

He captured her hands and looked up at her, forced her to look at him. "But who do you want to be? Think, Anne. Do you want to be a laughable de Vere?"

"I don't mind."

He had to tell her all of it. Quickly, before he lost courage, he explained that his father was in the process of annulling his first marriage so that the son of his second marriage could carry on his glories. Then he told her that he'd agreed to the plan, thus willfully destroying hope of marriage to any high-born lady.

"So you see, I'm worse than nothing. I am not even a de Vere."

"Then take your mother's name. I don't mind."

"Racecombe Racecombe?"

She chuckled. "Such names have been known, but Race"—she cradled his face and looked into his eyes—"it truly doesn't matter. I thought it did, but it doesn't. Most of the people I care about won't care, and we will make our name one to be proud of, whatever it is. If you don't want de Vere, or Racecombe, what of your father's original name? Despite the annulment, he's not denying that he's your father. Will that suit you better?"

He suspected by now that it wouldn't dissuade her, but he tossed it like a challenge anyway. "You want to be Lady Anne Ramsbottom?"

She stared, and then she broke into giggles. "Ramsbottom!" She leaned forward into him, gasping, "Ram! Derbyshire Ram!" He had to move onto the bed to stop her from falling off.

She struggled out of giggles to cry, "Bottom! Barnacles!" and then collapsed again. And he caught it like virulent fever, laughing with her, kissing with her, on the bed with her, on her . . .

His whole body burning for her.

"On your head be it," he muttered, and surrendered.

She'd won! That was all Anne could think as she responded to the most ravishing kiss of her life. It flowed like their other passionate kisses, but now, here, beneath him, with her hands feasting on his bare back, it consumed her.

He suddenly reared up, kneeling over her. "Say stop, now."

A spasm of something that was almost fear collided with agonizing need. She managed to choke out, "Continue. Now."

Perhaps he was hesitating, regaining control. She sat up and locked her arms around him. *"Now,"* she repeated.

"Bloody aristocracy," he groaned, but she laughed. She had him. He would not fight her anymore.

"I love you," she said. "That's all that matters."

"Damned nonsense, but I love you, too." He cherished her face. "I'll make it my life's work to ensure that it doesn't matter, Anne. You've won, you've won. Perhaps I could let you go, but I can't let you go into the sort of disasters you seem to court."

"Me?" she asked innocently, and laughed at his groan.

His hands were fumbling behind with her corset laces, but they stilled. She braced for another fight, but he simply said, "Let's try to do this with a little grace."

He slid off the bed and helped her off, turned her, and tugged at her laces. Staring through the tiny window at a tree and hedge touched with silver moonshine, she inhaled victory like a perfume.

Some fear lingered. She did not underestimate the drama of the choice she had made or the struggles yet to come, but she knew that her decision was right. She knew they could make it right simply because of who they were.

He was still tugging, and she heard a muttered curse.

"Hetty knotted them," she said, fighting the giggles again. "This morning—yesterday morning. She has a special way of doing it so they won't slacken during the day."

"A modern chastity belt? Someone should tell her that a corset doesn't secure the essentials."

Thirty-two

~

There was a series of sharp tugs, and the corset went slack. She instinctively held it on at the front. "What did you do?"

"Penknife. Our captors didn't think to search me. Not that a penknife would get us out of here."

"It's as well I'm not intending to put it on again soon," she said, letting the corset fall to the ground and turning to him in just her shift and drawers. "I have no interest in escaping."

"There is a little matter of a duel in the morning."

She froze. She really should tell him the truth now. But she didn't dare interfere with this magical process. It could evaporate in her hands.

"Perhaps Le Corbeau will be caught."

She wasn't sure he was listening. His attention seemed fixed on her breasts. She looked down and saw her nipples pressing out the fine silk. She'd always thought her small breasts lacking, but they didn't feel lacking at the moment. They felt swollen and tingly, and the cloth tormented them with every breath she took.

He wasn't doing anything, and she didn't know what to do. In the end she let her hands do what they wanted to and cradled her own breasts, comforting them, pushing them up slightly. An invitation, she realized, and utterly shameless, but watching him, she couldn't regret it.

His hands replaced hers, resting on her ribs, raising her breasts, and his thumbs brushed her prominent nipples. An astonishing ripple of pleasure shot through her, and she grasped his arms for balance.

Still brushing her sensitive flesh, he kissed her again,

hot and wet, so she sighed and shuddered into his mouth. Her legs trembled and ached. Perhaps he knew. He stopped his pleasuring, picked her up, and placed her on the simple bed.

Then he undressed.

She watched as lantern light picked out slim hips and strong legs. Definitely worthy thighs.

His male member jutted, ready for her. A tremor struck her, part nervousness, part longing in her most private places. He was utterly beautiful, lean and graceful. She thought again of faery, but a faery warrior, mighty and brave.

Suddenly aware that she was still covered she sat up and stripped off her drawers, and then her last shield, her shift. But nerves struck, and she sat there with it clutched to cover herself.

He took it from her, and his expression eased away every trace of doubt. She could weep for happiness to be the woman Race de Vere looked at like that. Her heart pounded with love, with desire, and with a raw burning need to be his.

He straddled her legs and took the silk shift from her powerless hands. He flipped it behind her, then drew her to him with it like a bond. "Last chance, Anne. After this I will not let you escape. You will be mine forever as if we'd spoken the most binding vows in a cathedral. Think well."

She slid her hands up to his shoulders. "Think? Now? I've thought, Race. I've done too much thinking, much of it wrongheadedly. I know now. I know. Don't you?"

His kiss was his answer, and they fell back together onto the bed. His sure hands stroked and fondled her, and she touched and tasted wherever she wished. As always with him she knew she had only to trust and the lights would shine.

She ran her hand down his long back and found his taut buttock to squeeze as he sucked on her nipple, sending hot waves of pleasure rolling through her.

Rolling. Legs tangled, they rolled so she was half over him, stroking his flank, his belly, his springy curls and the hot promise there. Hot, hard, satiny, moving beneath her tentative touch.

She looked at him and saw his hungry eyes, his need, his patience. She slid back under him, loving to be under his naked strength. She spread her legs, aching, burning, and knowing what she wanted. "Come into me, Race. Now."

He laughed. "Yes, your ladyship."

She braced for some mighty force, but he took his weight and moved slowly despite the need she heard in his unsteady breaths. The brush against her burning flesh made her want to scream with impatience, but she waited, stroking his tense arm, trusting him.

Then slowly, smoothly he slid inside her, making her inhale with the astonishing sensation of stretching and fullness. Of completion.

Then she understood.

"You are the first," she said.

"I know. Come." With that he began to move, and her whole mind locked on to a rhythm as natural as breathing. As her hips caught the pattern and met with his, she knew that at last she'd found a dance that she could do.

He was touching her breasts again, making her arch. He kissed her again, then when his mouth slipped off hers, she kissed his shoulder, filled her mouth with his flesh, pressing him closer, demanding, demanding. If she'd had voice, she would have ordered him to do something, she knew not what. . . .

Then her body arched itself with a pleasure she'd never known existed. Again and again it rocked her, making her choke out incoherent things. She assembled enough control to say his name. It seemed important then to say it.

"Race."

"Anne."

She felt him shudder and knew that he'd been in a similar place, swept up in a similar pleasure. Together. Forever.

As her body came together again, heart thundering, nerves singing, she thought it was no wonder men enjoy this so much, and women, too. That people sometimes made complete fools of themselves over it.

He shifted, sliding out of her, and held her close, kissing her again. She kissed him back, a new sort of kiss for them. Slow, lazy, sated, delicious. How perfect this was, this complete union of skin, sweat, breath, and self.

Marriage, indeed.

"Race?" she said at last.

"Yes, love?"

She smiled. "I like that."

"What we just did?" He sounded amused.

"Yes, but you calling me love."

He kissed her cheek. "You could call me love, too."

"Haven't I?" She rolled to face him, to kiss him between sentences. "You are my love. My dear heart. My precious. My sweeting—"

. He silenced her with a thorough kiss. "Enough." He climbed off the bed, pulled the blanket and sheet from under her, and covered her. Then he went to extinguish the guttering candle.

To be apart for a moment felt cold and empty, and when he slipped back into the bed she wrapped herself tightly around him. "You are mine now. Forever."

He nuzzled her. "And you are mine. Never doubt it. No changing your mind again tomorrow."

"Race!"

"You have been somewhat fickle, wench."

She bit her lip and told him about Alderton.

He shook with laughter. "Two engagements in two days! You never do things by half, do you love?"

"It's not the Peckworth way. But it was always you, Race. From Benning Hall."

"For me, too. That night in the corridor, I wanted to drag you into my bed."

"It might have saved a great deal of trouble if you had."

He slapped her bottom. "It would have caused disaster, and you know it." He rubbed the spot, that only stung a little. "We still have disaster on our hands, love. It's time for you to tell me your plan, the one that Ralstone didn't like."

She shifted to face him, though she could hardly see him in the shadows. "It doesn't matter. What life do you want?"

"I have no fixed point in the firmament, remember? It will be as you wish."

She growled. "You are not to be self-sacrificing about this. Tell me what your ideal life is."

His hand was still on her bottom, but now it flexed and played there, almost distracting her. "To replace Beau Brummell at the heart of society."

She heard the tease in it. "The Regent would doubtless be better for it. But?"

He shifted onto his back, drawing her half over his chest, hand still playing, sliding between her thighs, tickling a very sensitive spot.

"I became Amleigh's secretary for my own reasons but I enjoyed it. Or at least, I enjoyed the paperwork."

He slid his hand down to her knee and raised it, opening her against his hip. Her calf brushed hardness and her breath quickened. "You don't distract me so easily," she said.

"No?"

"No. Continue your explanation."

But her heart was pounding and a familiar ache built.

He sounded calm—and amused—as he went on. "I'd like to do more work with chaotic papers, but I'm not sure how to make a living at it. But even if there is such a way, it is hardly suitable for the husband of Lady Anne Whoever."

His other hand had found her private places, and moved in tiny, gentle, maddening circles.

"De Vere," she said, fighting not to gasp. "Lady Anne de Vere. People will become accustomed both to name and way of life. . . . *Race!*"

"Yes, love?"

Her breath came in gasps, her body clenched.

"You want something?" he whispered into her ear.

"You know what I want."

"To talk about our plans for our future . . ." His fingers slid into her, held her, as his thumb pressed.

"Wretch!"

He moved her onto her back and stroked between her thighs again. "I'm going to pleasure you, Anne. Let me."

His fingers slid inside her, his head lowered to her breasts. Anne clutched at him as hot waves built.

"What do I do? What should I do? Race?"

"Relax," he murmured. "Relax and fly."

So she surrendered and let her body move, let her mind dissolve, let her senses burn as she flew close to the sun. But survived. She buried her face in his chest as she came back to earth, not sure what to say after being played to a crescendo like a musical instrument.

"Do you not like that?" he asked.

She stirred to look where he was in the dark. "How could I not like it? It feels selfish, though."

"One of the curses of man is that we can't explode like that as often as a woman. A shame to deprive you of extra pleasure. But some time, if you want, you can do the same for me."

She smiled at the thought. "I want. I want a great many things." Her mind was back and clear. "I want our perfect happiness, and, Race, we are perfectly suited. You liked being a secretary, and my favorite way to spend time is among the chaotic papers at Lea Park!"

She expected the same delight, but he said, "I don't know about that. I hoped that you had just discovered an even better way—

She slapped his chest, shocked by the sting and the action. He laughed and retaliated with a kiss. "You're such a violent woman. Well, which is best? Paperwork or lovemaking?"

"One for night, one for day?"

"Sometimes I like to make love in daylight. Even outdoors . . ."

The idea sent a shiver of excitement through her. "There are always candles for night paperwork. Perhaps I can persuade my father to put in gas light in the library at Lea Park."

He ran his fingers through her hair and she felt his change of mood. "You're serious about this? You think you can be happy playing around in the Peckworth papers for the rest of your life?"

"I warn you, I don't play. I become lost in them."

"So do I." He moved so she was lightly in his arms. "So, what in particular are you engaged in?"

"Just women's papers."

Snuggled against him, skin to skin, she told him about the domestic papers and the picture they gave of the lives of the Peckworth women. Eventually she shared with him the last, most private part—her dream of writing a book based on them.

"Of course," she said, her hand circling his nipple, wondering if he found such things as pleasant as she did, "this won't interest you."

He caught her hand and sucked at her fingers. "Your teasing touch will always fascinate me. As for your papers, I'm enthralled already. I wonder how many other great houses have similarly neglected collections. . . ."

"You mean it."

"Oh, definitely. So, you want to live at Lea Park. If your father permits . . ."

She grasped her courage and told him the last bit. "Not actually at Lea Park. I was thinking of asking my father for a house as part of my dowry. Quoyne House. It's a simple manor house on the edge of Little Cawleigh, which lies just outside Lea Park. . . ."

He laughed. "I can imagine Ralstone balking at that, love, but it sounds like heaven to me. And if your family will accept me, I will be happy to be part of them. After all, I have no true family of my own."

"Your father can't be so unfeeling as that."

A silence made her think she'd intruded, but eventually he spoke. "He's not unfeeling, but I did abandon him, and for seven years I paid him little heed. What's more, I was never the son he wanted. He wanted one who would be a perfect gentleman, and also build the family both in grandeur and wealth."

"You are a perfect gentleman."

"With a strong undignified streak, you must admit."

"You have more dignity than Uffham!"

"Ah, and there you have a point that my father misses. He did too good a job of raising me to be one of the privileged set. I feel able to play fast and loose with the rules in the way he never could. But his main complaint is my lack of interest in achieving fame and fortune.

"Now my mother's dead, he's dabbling in trade again, making sure he can provide for his new wife and family, and making money to fund his title hunt. He dangled all kinds of opportunities in front of me, thinking they were bait. I only saw worms. He loves me, I'm sure, and in a way I love him, but we're mysteries to each other. I'm a Racecombe cuckoo in his Ramsbottom nest."

"Has he gone back to the Ramsbottom name?"

"Oh, no. He likes being a de Vere, but he made it legal before he married Sarah, so their children are completely legitimate. Little Tom will doubtless grow up to be just the sort of son he wants—the sort of aristocrat that England will need. One foot in tradition and the land, and the other in industry and new ideas."

"And you will truly be happy living quietly in the country spending large amounts of time among papers?"

He rolled over her. "Add in the frequent lovemaking and you have described my idea of heaven. . . . As you may have guessed, this poor male is ready for passion again."

She almost felt it was too much, that her nerve endings were too raw, but at first kiss resistance melted, and when he entered her it was the same, a natural fulfillment.

It was slow this time until the end, and she had more chance to know what was happening to her, to him. It was quieter for her, too, in the sweetest way, and she felt his wild explosion with delight. What a complex, fascinating mystery this all was.

She held him in her arms afterward, guarding him as he came back to earth.

"This is," she whispered, "perhaps almost as fascinating as a box of neglected household accounts. . . ."

"Almost?"

They settled together laughing, and tumbled into sleep.

Thirty-three

Anne woke when Race sat up. It was morning, and sunlight slanted in through the small window, gilding his lovely body. Warmth spiraled and tingled in her at the memory of what that body and her body had created in the night.

Birds sang, chirped, and complained, and a rustling in the thatch suggested other neighbors. She sat up, too, aware of aches in unusual places and of a deep, satisfied happiness.

She stroked the silken warmth of his back, full of wonderment that it was hers to do now as often as she wished. "What's the matter?"

He turned to her. "I think someone did something to the door."

Oh, Lord. Reality fell on her, and awareness that he still thought this morning would involve a duel with Le Corbeau. She had built heaven on a lie. She watched him get out of bed and walk splendidly naked to the partition wall to listen. She wanted him back in her arms, to touch him, stroke him, lick him, as she had in the night. She wanted reassurance that he would still be hers when he knew.

Perhaps he need never know.

He turned back, paused, and smiled at her. She could tell that he was thinking of her body exactly as she was thinking of his. Surely what they had created here could not easily change.

He came over and kissed her, one hand gentle on her face. "I love you, Anne."

She cradled his face in turn, delighted by the manly

mystery of stubble. "I love you, too. And we are, re-markable to say, perfectly matched."

"I think we are. But though I'd love to keep you naked in a bed for weeks, I think some covering wise before we venture out."

He found her crumpled shift and put it over her head. She wriggled into it, then scrambled off the bed to put on her petticoat and drawers. The corset was beyond hope, but she didn't really need it except to push her breasts up to fashionable heights.

By the time she was covered, he had his breeches on and was waiting by the door. There was a handle of sorts, and he pulled it. The door opened. They shared a wary look, then moved through it. The room beyond was empty.

She followed him down the narrow stairs to the de-serted ground floor, heart fluttering with nerves and hope. If Tris kept away, perhaps she could get away with this.

In the main room, their outer clothes awaited them, neatly folded. A plain breakfast sat on one of the benches—a covered jug of ale with two wooden beakers, and a loaf of bread and a hunk of cheese in a covered pot.

"*En garde* against rats," Anne said.

"A very strange crow we have. I'd like to think I frightened him away, but I don't believe it."

While she put on her gown, he thoroughly searched the ground floor, but then shrugged and came to fasten her buttons. Such a lovely domestic intimacy, especially when he brushed her hair out of his way.

"It must be a mess," she said.

He dug in his jacket pocket and produced a comb. She would have taken it, but he sat her sideways on a bench and sat behind her to work it gently through her hair.

"It's like silk," he said, discovering some pins and handing them to her. "Am I hurting you?"

"No, you're an excellent lady's maid, sir."

"I intend to enjoy this sort of service often."

She smiled with delight and sat in silence as he worked, savoring the pleasure of his caring touch. Oh, if only there wasn't one small dishonesty between them. But even now she would not change it. She was sure that if he'd known the truth he would never have surrendered and made love to her.

"There," he said at last, and she felt him quickly plait her hair, then coil it. "A pin."

She passed them back, one by one, and soon her hair felt in good order. She turned to him. "Thank you." She took the comb and tamed his hair, but alas, it did not need nearly so much work.

When she'd finished, he pulled on his shirt and tucked it into his breeches, but he didn't bother with his waistcoat or jacket. He produced his knife, and hacked up the bread, then passed her a piece along with some of the cheese.

She poured them both ale. He took his and went to stand by one of the small windows to eat.

She sipped hers. "It's good."

"Good enough for a duke?" he asked.

It took a moment for it to sink in, then a shiver passed through her. She put down the mug, unable to read his expression. She could pretend innocence, but she knew that was the last thing she should do. Fear tightened her throat.

"When did you guess?"

He was leaning against the wall, unreadable. "When did you?"

Perhaps it had been right to hold back the truth before, but not now. "Last night."

He drank some of his ale, looking at her in a silent command to continue.

With a *humph*, she picked up her mug and drank. "You were being too noble! I knew you'd ride away as soon as you thought I was safe."

"I didn't have a healthy horse."

"Then you'd walk away! You would have, wouldn't you?"

He rested his mug against his lip, considering her. "Yes."

"And it wouldn't have been for the best, would it?"

After a moment he shook his head and came over to

sit near her. "Right or wrong, it would not be what I want. You should be a general, love. Or an orator. You could tie Sophocles in knots."

Tears pricked at her eyes, tears of relief. "I was so afraid you'd hate me."

"I would be an ungrateful fool to do that."

"I was going to tell you. What made you realize?"

"The unlocked door and the considerate breakfast. I have no faith in chivalrous highwaymen. Then I remembered that we are within a mile of Nun's Chase, and everything fell into place. I'm disappointed, though. I rather liked the man."

"Disappointed that he seems to be Le Corbeau?"

"Disgusted that he forced you to undress before himself and a servant. He'll pay for that."

She grabbed his arm. "No, Race! He may be the only friend we have."

"Friend? He arranged for me to compromise you."

"No. He arranged for me to compromise you."

After a moment, he burst out laughing. "Talk about alien people! I do not understand you, Anne Peckworth, or your sort. No care for the proprieties at all?"

She felt her face heat. "I am assuming that we'll marry soon."

"And if not," said a voice from the doorway, "there is still the matter of a duel."

Anne blushed even more at the sight of Tris, completely the Duke of St. Raven, and here she was with what she'd done in the night surely obvious.

Race rose to his feet and walked over. His fist connected with Tris's chin, staggering him. The threshold tripped the noble Duke of St. Raven, sending him sprawling into the dirt path outside.

Anne stood but was frozen in shock. Before she could do anything, Tris scrambled to his feet and charged Race. The two crashed to the floor of the cottage, wrestling like village boys.

Race's shirt ripped.

"Stop it!" she screamed.

They paid no attention. Tris slammed a fist at Race. Race caught it on his shoulder with a grunt, then somehow rolled them so he was on top with Tris grunting, facedown. Then Tris was on top, his hands at Race's throat.

Anne looked desperately for something to stop them. Oh, for a bucket of icy water!

Race broke the hold and used his joined fists to deliver a horrible blow that sent Tris crashing into the wall. The whole cottage shuddered. Race leaped after, but Tris tripped him, and they were rolling together on the floor like madmen.

Anne grabbed her staff but then couldn't bring herself to swing it at either of them. The amber knob could do serious damage.

She hissed with annoyance and then let herself sink to the floor in an apparent faint. She heard another grunt. A thud. A curse.

Was it not going to work?

But then silence fell.

Tris said, "Anne?"

A scrabbling sound, then Race grabbed her hand—she knew his touch. "Anne? Love?"

They deserved some panic. She let them fuss over her for a few moments before opening her eyes. "You are both," she said, "quite mad."

Hunkered down on either side of her, they jerked back.

She sat up and grabbed a battered hand of each. "What was that *about*?"

"He hit me," Tris said, hand becoming a fist.

"You forced Anne to undress, and in front of your servant."

Their renewed urge to fight rippled up both of her arms. She tightened her grip. "You are my only two friends. You can't kill each other."

"Oh," said Tris, "I'm sure one of us would survive."

She growled. "And what good would that do me? I don't want to marry *you*, but we probably need you to help us sort this out."

Race jumped to his feet, then winced. He sent Tris a dirty look but held a hand down to Anne. When she took it, he pulled her to her feet.

She laughed, and it was with delight. No one had ever

treated poor Lady Anne so casually. She was sure Tris
would have tenderly lifted her, carried her to a bench,
then fussed over her for an age. In fact, he was on his
feet glowering at Race, presumably for the way he was
treating her.

The noble Duke of St. Raven had a split lip.

Race wasn't untouched. She suspected that he was
going to have a black eye, and from the wince she
guessed Tris had managed to do other damage. When
she thought of how much taller and heavier Tris was,
she was astonished that it had been such an even match.

And impressed. And yes, the way Race had knocked
Tris down thrilled a primitive part of herself, the part of
womankind that had screamed with excitement at
bloody jousts.

Race cocked his head at her. "You look like a cat
with a bowl full of cream, *minou*."

She blushed—but she grinned, too.

"Typical," Tris said, touching his lip. "Women always
enjoy blood."

She covered her smile with her hand. "I'm sorry. But
yes, it is rather thrilling."

Race picked her up and put her down on one of the
benches. "This isn't a game. Let's see what we can do
to get out of this mess without more bloodshed."

Tris sat with a wince of his own on the other bench.
"You're planning to continue with the elopement?"

"No."

"No."

Anne and Race had spoken together, and she sent
him a smile. He sat beside her, putting an arm around
her as if it were the most natural thing in the world. As
if they were country people in their cottage. As if they
were a china shepherd and shepherdess.

She leaned comfortably against his shoulder. "Perhaps
we could just live on here for the rest of our lives."

Race laughed. "Hardly."

She looked around and remembered that this little bit
of heaven was in fact a cottage that should be torn down
before it fell down.

"Hardly," she agreed. "So what are we going to do?
Perhaps Tris is right and we should carry on to Gretna."

"Anne wants marriage in her home parish," Race said to Tris, "and to live at a place called Quoyne House. How do we arrange that?"

Tris's eyes widened a little. "It won't be easy. I think the family would accept an elopement as a fait accompli, but getting the duchess's agreement to a proper wedding will take time."

"After last night, we may not have time."

Anne straightened to look between them. "I don't mind society counting the months after our wedding."

"I do," Race said, "especially if the count stops at six or seven. I won't have you subject to that sort of gossip." Race was still looking at Tris. "You'd better know the facts." He quickly outlined his family history.

Tris's expression grew more stunned as Race spoke. When Race arrived at the matter of the approaching bastardy, Tris looked at Anne. "The duchess will lock you in a dungeon and throw away the key."

"We don't have a dungeon."

"She'll have one built specially. Mouse, you are attempting to marry the bastard son of a tradesman. Gretna's your only chance."

She looked at Race and saw bitter regret, saw that for her sake he'd like to wipe out last night.

"I regret nothing," she said. "*Nothing.* If my family cast me off, so be it. But they won't. Yes, my mother will probably try to prevent our marriage, but I come of age in October. And my father, though generally ruled by my mother in these things, won't agree to cutting me off. I know he won't."

"He won't," Tris agreed. "He's softheartedly devoted to all his children. Too softhearted, in Uffham's case."

Race looked between them. "But he won't overrule the duchess in the matter of marriage?"

"No," Tris said. "Or not quickly or easily."

"What if we tell them that we have anticipated marriage?"

Anne gulped at that, but if it was called for . . .

"Lord," Tris said. "I don't know. I don't know. The duke's old-fashioned enough to have you horsewhipped. Fond fathers tend to be twitchy about *husbands* having their wicked way with their daughters, never mind upstart lovers."

Race pressed both hands to his face, then he ran his fingers through his hair.

Anne watched, heart breaking. "It would have been better for you, wouldn't it, if we'd never met? If I'd not pursued you. If I'd not seduced you last night."

"Seduced?" Tris echoed.

Race lowered his hands. "She did. Remarkably well, too." The look he sent her held regret, but memory and passion burned beneath it.

He pulled her to him and kissed her. "I regret nothing either, love, though I doubtless should. I can only hope that you won't regret either. It looks as if it has to be Gretna." He turned to Tris. "I'll have to ask a loan."

"I have money," Anne said.

"Very well." To Tris he said, "We should probably avoid Buntingford. Where's the next best place to hire a chaise?"

"The Swan at Stevenage."

In a few crisp moments the men had everything settled. Tris would have her trunk collected at the Black Bull and brought here. Then they would be taken to Stevenage, where they could hire a chaise.

Race's valise was apparently waiting for him at the White Horse in London. Tris would have it sent north. If it didn't catch up with them on the road, it would arrive at Gretna not far behind.

"Send it to the Angel in Chesterfield," Race said.

Anne asked, "Why?"

He gave her a rueful smile. "If we can't be at instant peace with one family, we might as well try for the other one."

"Are you perhaps thinking that if I meet your father, I'll change my mind?"

He laughed. "I doubt it. The Peckworths seem as changeable as a rock. It simply feels appropriate. I owe my father information about this important point in my life, especially as it's likely to cause trouble."

"Very well, love. I look forward to meeting your family." She smiled at Tris, but then a thought struck. "You're not Le Corbeau, are you?"

"Am I not?"

"No. I remember now that at Drury Lane, you didn't know who he was. That wasn't acting. Nor later when I pointed out that crow and raven are the same in French."

He looked rueful, but said nothing.

"You were out last night to protect the real crow, weren't you? Who is it?"

"Never you mind. You have enough tangles to deal with as it is."

She pulled a face but knew he wouldn't tell her. Or not yet. "Did you actually hold someone up?" she asked.

He grinned. "Oh yes. And it was a remarkable amount of fun."

"What folly!"

"That, from you?"

Race stepped between them. "Perhaps, Your Grace, we could set our plan in motion?"

Tris looked as if he'd like to pick another fight, but he said, "I am, of course, yours to command." With an ironic bow, he left to do his part.

Thirty-four

~

It took two days to reach Shapcott Hall, but despite everything Anne felt they were two of the best days of her life. Race was hers, and at last she could discover this man who had become so central to her life, and reveal to him more of herself.

They talked, sharing details from their pasts, but also spinning off into philosophical debates. They didn't always agree, but they always ended up in harmony.

They played cards and read books. He taught her brag, and she won a fortune off him. They bought a copy of *Headlong Hall* at St. Ives and read it aloud to each other, but soon abandoned it as cumbersome. She read parts of *Jeanne d'Arc* to him, but he refused to offend her with his French accent.

They spent a delightful night at a small inn on the outskirts of Stamford. Anne had abandoned her disguise—she was ready to face anyone—but they passed themselves off, suppressing laughter, as Mr. and Mrs. Ramsbottom. She had no ring, but kept her gloves on in public.

The next evening, however, when their chaise drew up before Shapcott Hall, she wasn't sure she was ready to face Race's father. He could not approve of this.

They paid the postilions to stay and take them on the next day—and also so that they would have transport if Mr. de Vere fell into a rage and would not let them in the house.

When the door opened and a sturdy man in country clothes stepped out looking puzzled Anne knew that would not happen. The instant he saw Race—out of the carriage and about to help her down—something moved across the father's face, part love, part loss, and part exasperated worry.

She could almost see the words, *What now?*

She let Race set the tone. He gave her his arm and led her toward the waiting man. As they crossed the few yards of driveway, other people emerged from the simple stone manor house. A sensible looking brown-haired woman, belly swelling beneath an apron, moved to stand beside her husband, a toddler in her arms. A bright-eyed blond boy ran out to clutch his father's hand.

Then the lad shouted, "Race!" and rushed forward.

Race freed himself from Anne and caught the boy, swinging him up. "Tom, my grand lad! But you know, you shouldn't rush at a gentleman who's escorting a lady." He put the boy down. "Make your bow to Lady Anne Peckworth."

The boy did a fine bow and then looked at her. "Lady? Are you very grand, then?"

What to say to that? "I suppose I am."

Race's father had come over by then, and he put a hand on his younger son's shoulder. "Tommy, we're going to have to teach you better manners." It was said kindly, however, though the look he gave Anne was wary at best.

"Father, this is Lady Anne Peckworth, who is to be my wife. I wished to make you known to each other before we tie the knot. In Gretna Green."

Race sounded smooth, but Anne heard a slight gulp before the last bit.

Wanting to laugh for tenderness and nervousness, she held out her hand to Mr. de Vere. "I'm very pleased to meet you, sir, and I assure you this is entirely my fault."

"I doubt that." He took her hand and pressed it. "You're welcome here, my lady, but I think we'll have to sort this wedding business out in better form."

Race had been right in his assessment. His father was a gentleman in the true sense, even if his speech carried a slight touch of his origins. Anne felt she could like him, but would he like her, who was bringing more trouble to his house?

She met Race's stepmother, who seemed flustered and worried. The toddler, little Amy, hid her face shyly against her mother's neck. Then they entered the oaken hall of Race's home, and all went into a cozy parlor, where tea was ordered.

She couldn't help thinking how different this was from her experience in Greenwich, and not just because Shapcott Hall was a solid, comfortable house. This was a home, and a happy one, and she immediately liked all Race's family.

Sarah de Vere had rid herself of her apron when she thought no one was looking and was presiding over tea, obviously thinking it a test. The little girl had been taken away by a nursemaid, but the boy was still here, fidgeting between his father and Race, who had clearly acquired another admirer.

They talked idly of the weather and the roads, and even a bit about fashionable gossip. It was all terribly artificial, but Anne didn't know what to do for the best.

Then Sarah stood, picking up the tea tray herself. "Come along, Tommy. It's time for your lessons. You can talk to your brother later if he's willing."

"Will you play soldiers with me, Race?"

"If I hear a good account of your lessons."

The boy pulled a face, but he went, and the door shut. Anne's nerves tightened. This was the moment of truth, and it mattered. She knew it mattered to Race.

"Well, my boy," Race's father said. "I don't like this Gretna thing, not at all."

Race flashed Anne a look. "Nor do I, Father, but Lady Anne's family won't approve of the marriage. And," he added, "we must marry."

Mr. de Vere's eyes flicked over Anne. "In the family way?"

She knew she was pink, but she tried to be composed. "We don't know yet."

He shook his head. "It's a bad situation, Race. Very bad. I'm disappointed in you."

"It was all my fault," Anne interjected. "All! You must believe me, Mr. de Vere. I pursued your son. I seduced your son."

He looked at her, bushy brows high. "Then you deserve a good whipping, miss."

"Probably. Especially as I started out yesterday eloping with a different man. And the day before that I was engaged to yet another."

"Anne!" Race protested, but when she looked at him, he was laughing.

"Oh, Lord, sir, I'm sorry. I should never have brought this mess here. It truly isn't as wicked as it seems, and a great deal of it is my fault. I never meant to upset you with it. I simply thought you should know."

Mr. de Vere sat there with a solid hand on each thigh. "I never have understood you, Race, but I'm wise enough to know that. I think I'm wise enough to know that you two are head over heels in love, aren't you?"

Race looked at Anne and said, "Yes."

"Yes," she said back to him, smiling.

"Well, I know a bit about that now. The truth is that I was never in love with your mother. I married her for her property and position, and she married me for my money. We rubbed along well enough, and I always did right by her, but it wasn't love. With Sarah, though, it's a different matter. So I reckon you should wed. Will money make any difference?"

Anne saw Race stiffen. "You owe me nothing, sir."

"Rubbish. You left before we could talk things over. You know I would never have gone ahead with the annulment without your say so, and I never intended to disinherit you."

"Father, you owe me nothing. I willfully left here—and hurt you in the process."

Mr. de Vere pushed himself to his feet. "Rubbish! You were always a high-spirited lad, and I drove you away with my follies. I won't make the same mistake with Tommy, even if he ends up the only lad we have. But whatever the case, you are my son. I want you to have your share of what I have."

Race had risen, too, and was looking rather exasperated. "Father, I will do well enough."

"Doing what? As far as I can see you know no trade but soldiering."

Race's jaw tensed, but he said, "I've been a secretary, and I intend to be a sort of librarian."

His father's blood rose into his face. "A *secretary*! A *librarian*! Is this what I raised you for?" Before Race could speak, he went on, "And how do you plan to support a lady born on those piddling sorts of wages?"

Race said nothing, and the older man turned narrow eyes on Anne. "I suppose you have plenty of money of your own, don't you?"

Anne had to say something. "Yes, but Race won't be a fortune hunter."

"You're right. He won't. He'll have a respectable income of his own!"

"Father, you don't want to take money away from Tom and your new family."

"There's enough."

"With the annulment to push through, and a title to buy?"

"Aye, and half a dozen more!" It came out as a bellow that made Anne flinch, but then Race's father rubbed a hand over his face looking, if anything, embarrassed. "Fact is, Race, that I'm more involved in trade than I let you know. I didn't think you'd like it."

"All the same—"

"Be quiet! I'm trying to tell you something. There were so many opportunities during the war," Race's father said, as if trying to excuse a sin. "And so many needs, too. And a mess of mismanagement that I just couldn't bear. Once your mother passed away, God bless her, there was no one to mind if I dabbled in trade. Things are harder now, of course, but I saw it coming so matters aren't too bad. I'm warm, now. Very warm."

"Father, I don't mind what you do. And a few hundred a year will not sway Anne's parents. They want her to marry a title. In fact her mother wants her to marry the Duke of St. Raven."

"An old fogy?" Mr. de Vere asked her.

"Not at all, but not the man I want to marry."

He turned back to Race. "Whether it sways her family or not, I want you to have your portion. It's only right. In fact, I'll feel very badly if you don't take it."

"That's blackmail."

"That's the truth!"

"I won't take it."

"Damn your eyes, boy, I'm your *father*. I have a right to give you money if I damn well want to!"

He'd turned red, but he looked at Anne and went redder still. "My lady, I'm sorry. But he drives me to extremes at times, indeed he does."

She went to take his hands. "He does the same to me, sir. And please call me Anne. I would be honored to be treated as your daughter."

He smiled at her. "And I'll be honored to see you so. I know this bastardy business isn't helping things, though he won't mention it. Too late to back down now, alas. The documents are in the hands of the church courts. You see how it is, though, don't you, Anne? It's my selfish plan that has you in a pickle, and I have to do something to try to set it right."

"Father," Race interrupted. "Your plan is pure common sense. With respect, there is nothing I want less than to live here and help manage this estate or your businesses."

Anne made her decision. She turned to Race. "Your father's right. He needs to give you some money, and you should take it. For his sake, and because it will sweeten the pill a little for my parents."

He met her eyes, and she worried that he was angry, but then he sighed. "Very well. How much did you have in mind, Father?"

Mr. de Vere seemed to be doing calculations, but Anne wondered if they were more to do with what he thought Race would take than with what he could afford. "I thought five thousand a year," he said at last.

Anne and Race both stared at him.

"Out of the question," Race said. "You'll beggar yourself."

"Do you think me such a fool? It's a fifth of my income now, but I've every expectation of making more once these hard times are over."

"I refuse to take that much."

"All or nothing," growled his father.

Anne stumbled over to grab Race's arm before he threw the offer in his father's face. "Race, stop and think." To his father she said, "You swear that your income is twenty-five thousand a year?" Given the simple state in which he lived, she had doubts, too.

"On the Bible, give or take. Plague take me, I'm fond

of the boy, but I have my Sarah and the children—and many more to come God willing—to think of. I'd not beggar them to satisfy some guilt of mine!"

"This is ridiculous," Race said as if he'd been offered a flogging rather than a fortune. He looked at Anne. "You want this money?"

She reined in her temper. "I neither want nor need any money. But your father needs to give it to you, and yes, it will help with my parents. In fact," she added, doing a rapid assessment, "with this money on our side we can roll the dice—turn back and see if we can marry properly."

"Five thousand a year will outweigh my origins?"

"It will help."

He sucked in a breath and turned to his father. "Very well, sir. Thank you."

"And that hurt to say," his father grumbled. "Believe it or not, I was just such a stiff-rumped fool as you when I was young. Wait here."

He marched out of the room, and Anne and Race looked at each other in puzzlement.

"Is he going to pour it out in front of us in cash?" she asked.

Race relaxed. "I doubt it. Am I being a fool over this?"

She took him into her arms. "No, love."

He kissed her. "All right, I know you're right about the money, and it means yours can go for our children's future. I'm not sure about your gamble, though. Wouldn't it be safer to seal things at Gretna before facing your family? We could marry again in an English church once the dust settles."

"Yes, but Race, I don't want a Gretna wedding. The closer we came, the more I disliked the idea."

He kissed her. "Then we won't do it."

Race's father returned with a few boxes, which he put on a table. "Your mother's jewelry. The stuff, such as it is, that she got from her family—they'd sold the best of it—and her engagement ring. I buried her in her wedding band."

They went over to the table. "Won't Sarah want these?" Race asked.

"She has those she likes of what I gave your mother, but she doesn't think the Racecombe jewels should come to her." Mr. de Vere looked at Anne. "These mostly won't seem much to you, daughter, but there's the ring." He opened a box to reveal a large diamond in a lovely setting.

"My goodness."

"I was so cock-a-hoop that a lady born would accept me that I bought her the finest stone I could find. Once we were wed, though, she never wore it. She said simplicity was the true sign of breeding."

Anne privately thought that Race's mother sounded unpleasant. How much of the trouble between father and son was her fault? And whose fault was it that there was only one child? If Race had had brothers and sisters, she was sure matters would have gone much better.

She looked at Race. "If you want me to have it, I would be honored."

He took the ring out of the box. "I never knew this existed. It is beautiful and deserves to be worn."

He slid it onto her finger. It was a little loose, but not so it would fall off.

"You're well and truly committed now, sir," she teased. "What next?"

Race looked at her, then at his father. "We rest. To-morrow we go south to hazard our future."

Anne enjoyed her evening at Shapcott Hall, and even helped Sarah bathe little Amy. Sarah was thirty-two and ill at ease at first, but soon they were like sisters. Like sisters, they laughed and complained about the men in their lives.

She watched Race play model soldiers with Tom. The lad sounded as if he'd be army-mad one day but his father didn't seem to be worried yet. He was probably right that it was a passing phase.

Later, the adults played whist, and she truly enjoyed their company.

After a nightcap, Race's father and Sarah went up to bed. Anne and Race had been assigned separate rooms, but tactfully no great attention was paid.

Anne wasn't sure what she wanted to do here. She was certainly surprised when Race took her up another flight of stairs to the attic.

"I have a surprise for you," he said, shining his lamp on a number of wooden boxes.

"What's in there?"

"The Racecombe records. No one's looked at them in at least two generations except to dump more boxes on top. Probably no one's looked at them at all after they were put up here."

Anne's mouth dried. "Oh, my. You are ruthless, aren't you, about binding me to you. I think I can bear to marry you, Mr. de Vere, if you promise me many trips back here to explore all this."

He chuckled and kissed her. "You understand me. I will use any weapon to hand."

When they went back downstairs, however, they went to their separate rooms by silent accord. This was his father's house, and it was how his father would want it to be.

Race's valise caught up with him the next morning before they left, which let him change his clothes.

"Where's the rest of your belongings?" his father asked.

"That's it, except for a horse still stabled at Somerford Court."

"That's it!" His father went off to his study and returned with a bundle of bank notes, thrusting them into his hand. "To tide you over. And get yourself some more clothes before you present yourself to the duke and duchess!"

Race pulled a face at the money, but then he put it in his pocket. "There's no time for that, Father, and you know it, and it wouldn't serve. I've been to Lea Park before. They know me as I am."

Mr. de Vere shook his head but waved them off with no further interference.

As they returned south they talked about sleeping arrangements on the road and decided to travel as Mr. and Miss Ramsbottom. There was a rightness to waiting till their wedding. Race wryly said it was like a knight fasting and praying on the night before a court battle.

He also said that the less risk of her being with child the better.

Anne had slept alone in a bed for years. Strange how unnatural it felt after two nights with Race.

As they passed through Hertfordshire, she sent a note to Tris at Nun's Chase alerting him to the new plan and asking him to go to Lea Park to be on hand in case of need. She prayed he was there to receive it. They might need all the help they could get.

Thirty-five

~

Anne arrived back in Brighton six days and a lifetime after leaving.

Caroline greeted them cheerfully, only expressing surprise that Anne had arrived in a hired chaise rather than sending for Welsford's coach. The situation was so strange that Anne didn't know quite how to open the truth.

She took off her glove to reveal the ring.

"Anne! It's lovely. Ralstone?" But then Caroline looked at Race, her eyes going wide. *"De Vere?"*

Welsford came downstairs smiling, but he caught the atmosphere and the situation quickly.

"The Duchess of Arran will be very displeased," he said. "A word with you, de Vere."

Anne watched Race go with Welsford into the back parlor, longing to go along to protect someone. She listened for blows or breaking furniture. . . .

Caroline linked arms and drew her into the front parlor. "Tell me everything!"

After a moment Anne surrendered and gave her the story she and Race had agreed on. She'd gone to Greenwich and discovered she and Ralstone didn't suit. Race had turned up to ask her to marry him, she'd realized he was her true love, and they had returned here before going to Lea Park.

It felt as if she was leaving out the most important part of her life, but it would be easier for Caroline and Welsford to support them if they didn't know about mayhem and wickedness.

She could hear nothing from the men. They couldn't have fallen into violence at least.

"I don't know how you could have been so confused about things," Caroline said. "With Welsford, I knew."

Anne pulled her mind back. "I knew, too, Caro. But I thought I couldn't marry Race, so I tried to marry other men. Mama is wrong. It isn't solely within our willpower. I know now I can't be happy with anyone else—nor can he. But there are problems."

"An understatement!"

"Other problems." Anne told Caroline about Mr. de Vere's origins and the plan to declare Race illegitimate.

Caroline slumped back in her chair in a pretend faint. "It's better than a play! *The Bastard Heir.*"

"And *The Daring Lady.* I know. But this is real, and I will have my way."

Race and Welsford returned then, not apparently bruised. Welsford was on their side, but not taking it lightly.

"The duchess acted as if *I* was aspiring slightly above my rights."

"That's because she wanted me to marry St. Raven," Caroline said. "It's an obsession of hers."

Anne nodded. "I've asked Tris to meet us at Lea Park. Perhaps he can persuade her that it's out of the question."

"Is there anything we can do to get the duke on our side?" Race asked.

Welsford thought about it. "Perhaps," he said. "Let's settle down and come up with a strategy."

Anne traveled in the chaise with Caroline. Welsford and Race rode alongside. Race had sent for his horse from Somerford Court, and Anne was touched to find that it was his favorite cavalry horse and getting on in years. Horse and man were clearly devoted.

"Joker?" she asked quizzically at a stop, stroking the bay gelding.

"He doesn't have a serious bone in his body. For more demanding moments, I asked St. Raven to get me that horse I rented from the Black Bull."

"Shouldn't you be riding it now, then?"

He smiled. "Probably, but the poor creature has already suffered in the cause. We're not in any hurry today as we head toward our fate." He led her back to the coach. "Onward to the last throw."

Anne's heart began to race as soon as they turned in through the gilded gates of Lea Park. She tried to concentrate on how lovely all the vistas were, on how much she'd always loved being here, but a strangling sort of panic was building.

Her parents couldn't completely prevent her marriage to Race. The days were surely past when daughters were locked up on bread and water and upstart intruders were whipped and thrown off a property.

She hoped.

She did remember one story of a young lady who had apparently been dragged off to Europe and kept in close confinement there to prevent an unsuitable marriage. Surely her parents wouldn't go so far.

They might if they felt they were saving her from disaster.

Welsford would be there.

Tris, she hoped, would be there.

Race would be there, but she wasn't sure how much he could do in this situation.

She looked to Caroline for encouragement, but she was looking rather pale, too.

They drew up under the porte cochere, and servants poured out to take care of luggage and horses. Anne climbed out, legs unsteady, hand clenched on her staff. She was glad of Race's arm as they walked into the west gallery and headed for the center of the house. He seemed completely steady, but he didn't have a joke for her. That was telling.

The first person they saw was Uffham.

He was crossing the hall, two hounds at his heels. "What-ho the sisters!" But then his tone turned frosty. "De Vere. What are you doing here?"

Race inclined his head. "Uffham. Good to see you again."

The duchess swept down the stairs. "Anne, Caroline,

Welsford. Not bad news, I hope?" As an afterthought she nodded at Race. "Mr. de Vere." Her expression cooled. "Come. Into the saloon."

Tris appeared at that moment. Anne sent a prayer of thanks, even if he did roll his eyes at her. As they all filed into the nearby room she resisted the urge to wring her gloved hands.

The duchess turned. "Now, what is going on?" Her gaze rested on Anne and Race, coldly.

Race said, "Your Grace. I have come to ask for Anne's hand in marriage."

Color flared in her mother's cheeks, but it was Uffham who stepped forward and said, "The devil you are!"

"Language, Uffham," snapped the duchess.

Tris moved to Uffham's side. "This is a matter for cool discussion, not dramatics."

"I'll give him dramatics," snarled Uffham, trying to shake off the hand Tris had clamped on his arm. His hounds started to bark.

"Uffham!" snapped the duchess. "Desist. And get rid of those dogs."

While the fuming Uffham obeyed, the duchess addressed Race.

"Mr. de Vere, what possible argument can you put forward in favor of your suit?"

"That I love him, Mama," Anne said, "and he loves me. I have tried to fall in love with a title, but I find I cannot. I certainly have no intention of marrying St. Raven."

"And I," said Tris, "have no intention of marrying Anne, fond though I am of her."

"Then you can marry Alderton," her mother said to her.

"It would be very unfair to him when I love another." Anne ruthlessly used her most powerful weapon. "I'm sorry, but my foot is paining me. I must sit."

Amid a flurry of concern, Race led her to a sofa. Her mother had little choice but to sit, too, and in moments everyone was settled. As she'd hoped, the tension did slacken, even when Uffham returned and sat glowering opposite her.

Anne realized that Welsford was no longer with them,

but that was part of their plan. He'd gone to talk to her father.

She sent up a prayer and peeled off her gloves.

Her mother stared. "You have accepted his ring, Anne?"

"Yes, Mama."

"Without consulting your father?"

"Yes, Mama."

"Is it paste?"

Anne kept her temper. "No, Mama." Time to try the most important throw. "Mr. de Vere is quite rich."

"Race!" said Uffham with a crack of laughter. "He's gammoned you well, Anne."

Anne could sense the tension pulsing out of Race beside her and knew he hated this kind of horse-trading as much as she did. But his voice was calm when he said, "My father is a wealthy man, Uffham, and he has settled five thousand pounds a year on me. The ring was my mother's, who is now dead."

Anne saw her mother's eyes narrow at the amount. It wasn't enormous, but it was respectable. But then she said, "You cannot *buy* a Peckworth, Mr. de Vere." Her cold eyes turned on Anne. "And didn't you travel to visit another gentleman's family? Captain Ralstone? A paltry match, but at least a family we know and a title in due course."

Anne swallowed. "I realized we did not suit, Mama. That was when I knew that Mr. de Vere was the man I *must* marry."

She saw her mother's eyes sharpen, but before she could speak the door opened and her father came in with Welsford.

They all rose.

"What's this, then? Strange goings-on." He frowned around the room, and Anne knew he was put out at being dragged into a messy situation. His decision could go either way, but they'd decided they had to try for his support.

He walked over to his wife. "Put me a chair here, someone."

Race moved another armed, upholstered chair beside her mother's. Her parents were going to look enthroned.

Her father nodded and sat. "Thank you, de Vere."

Was his acknowledgement a good sign? He wouldn't acknowledge a servant.

They all sat. It was like a court, either a royal one or a legal one.

"I assume Welsford has told you about this, Arran?" her mother said.

"Some of it. Whether it's all of it, I don't know. Anne, take off that ring until I give you permission to wear it."

Coloring, Anne obeyed. She passed it to Race, who smiled encouragement at her. He, she realized, had stayed standing. The prisoner in the dock.

"Good for you, Father," said Uffham. "We can't allow this."

"You were happy enough with de Vere's company, Uffham. You brought him here!"

"I bring my valet here. And my grooms."

"You don't bring them to the dinner table!" Anne exploded. "Don't be so insufferable. You *liked* Race."

"Behave with more respect," her father growled, perhaps to both of them. He looked at Race. "Mr. de Vere, I've seen you here apparently as purposeless as my son, and penniless to boot. You'd hardly expect me to give my precious daughter into the care of a man like that, would you?"

Anne wanted to leap to the defense, but she made herself leave it in Race's hands.

"Definitely not, Your Grace. However, may I argue that it was a furlough after seven years of war? Everyone, I think, is entitled to a holiday. And as I informed the duchess, I am no longer penniless. I can take care of Anne as well as you would like, and will do so."

"But what's your *purpose*, man?" her father demanded. "I detest idlers."

A silence settled that crept down Anne's spine like icy water.

"What purpose do any of the men in this room have, Your Grace?" Race asked at last. Anne wondered, hair rising, whether he'd glanced at Uffham. Her brother was turning red. "I could purchase an estate and take care of it. I will do so if it is a condition of your goodwill."

Anne watched her father's eyes narrow, and she

winced. Race was going to drive someone to violence again soon. It wasn't so much his words as his tone.

"You don't *want* to be a gentleman?" her father asked.

"I *am* a gentleman, sir. I have no particular interest in land management, however. My interests are scholarly."

"Scholarly!" guffawed Uffham. "You'll be telling us next you want to take holy orders!"

"Not at all. What I want to do is join Anne in the organization and study of documents here at Lea Park and in other places with a view to writing a book or books about history from the distaff angle."

Silence rang.

Uffham laughed again. "A fine ambition for a man!"

"Many men are scholars, Uffham. I have, I believe, done my manly duty."

Uffham shot to his feet. "I would have been in the army if my father had allowed it!"

"*I* went without my father's permission."

The duke raised his hand, which stopped Uffham from rushing across the room to throttle Race. After a blistering moment, he stalked out of the room, slamming the door behind him so the windows rattled.

Her father stared at de Vere, unreadable. "A general disregard for parental rights and authority, I see." But then he shook his head. "I sometimes wish I'd bought Uffham a pair of colors." He looked at Tris. "What are you doing here, St. Raven?"

Tris stood. "Witness for the defense, sir. Anne asked me to look into the men who were courting her. I'd have warned her off Ralstone if she'd given me the chance."

"Why?" Anne asked.

"He's careless with money and women, and he's been involved in duels."

"To defend a lady's honor."

"Is that what he said? He was defending himself against outraged husbands. Unfortunately he's a crack shot, so they suffered rather than him."

What a fool she'd been. "Thank heavens I changed my mind. You've checked up on Race, then?"

What had Tris discovered? She knew it couldn't be bad or he'd never have arranged that night together, but there could be something. They were going to have to tell her father about his father's origins and the bastardy, but they'd agreed to hold those things back until after they had his approval.

"De Vere's war record is excellent, sir," Tris said, "even if tinged with eccentricity. I think the field of war must be a reliable place to judge a man, and I found out nothing from his fellow officers to suggest that de Vere would not be a good husband."

With a slight smile he added, "My personal experience is that he is a man of courage and honor. I say, let them marry."

"This is not an election, St. Raven," said Anne's mother. "I have no doubt that Mr. de Vere is an admirable man. I have thought him so when he was here with Uffham. He was a good influence. None of that, however, makes him suitable as a husband for one of my daughters!"

"Then what does, Your Grace?" said Welsford, also rising. "Surely at the end it is the nature of the man not his rank that matters most to a mother's heart."

Anne gulped, watching her mother's frozen face.

"A girl who puts her mind to it can find a man who is both good and of similar rank, Welsford. Like should marry like!"

"But there are," said Race, "different qualities to consider. With respect, Duchess, Anne and I are like in all the ways that matter. I know you worry particularly about Anne because of her handicap. Perhaps you might consider that, with your blessing, we would choose to live close to Lea Park in order to pursue our work. You will be sure of her comfort and happiness."

Anne sucked in a breath. This was their last major throw.

"I have no estate," Race continued, "and no expectation of inheriting one. The income my father has settled on me is in lieu of my interest in his property. Anne has mentioned a place called Quoyne House."

"Quoyne House, eh?" said her father, looking at her. "Seems that you've thought about this quite a bit, Anne. I have to say that I'd like to have you close." Then he glared at Race. "You know what this means, sir. One moment of unhappiness, and I'll have your skin!"

"No, you wouldn't, sir." After a heart-stopping moment, he added, "I would have flayed myself first."

Anne saw her father's lips twitch and had trouble not whooping. They'd won. Surely they'd won!

"Arran!" her mother protested.

But her father cut her off. "You know our daughter, my dear. For all her sweetness and frailty, she has always had a mind of her own. Seems she's settled on this man, and he has a solid head on his shoulders. Better to let them wed and have her under our eye than have them running off somewhere."

"No daughter of mine would ever do such a thing," said the duchess with such fervor that Anne gave thanks that they'd changed their plans. Her parents would have accepted a clandestine marriage in the end, but they would have been terribly hurt.

She rose and went over to take her father's hand. "We have your blessing, Papa?"

He tried to glower, but it wasn't convincing. "Aye, you have your way as usual. I've not missed that fact over the years. De Vere!" he barked.

Race came over to stand beside her.

"You can give her the ring now."

Race slid the ring back on her finger and then raised her hand to kiss it—in the way of a man who knows how to please a woman.

Then he laughed. "Don't cry, Anne. Your father will skin me alive!"

She laughed with him, wiping away her tears. She kissed her father, and then her mother. The duchess was stiff for a moment, but then she hugged her back. "I only want the best for you all," she said.

"I know, Mama, and I love you for it. I will be happy with Race, though. And," she added, "in due course I will be here to wrap blankets around you and Papa and feed you gruel. You really cannot depend on Uffham marrying the right kind of wife for that."

The duchess laughed, but almost with despair. "Uffham, poor Uffham. I don't know what we are to do with him."

"As to that," said the duke, "Welsford pointed out that with de Vere in the family we might have a better chance of keeping him on sensible ground. Once he gets over his tiff, that is."

Anne saw Race cast Welsford a baleful look, but he didn't protest except to say, "I expect to spend most of my time quietly here with Anne, sir, but if I can help in any way, I will. Uffham is not unsound. He might benefit from employment. Perhaps a small estate of his own. . . ."

Anne made herself not react to that clever move. If Uffham had an estate of his own he'd be at Lea Park even less, and it might serve to make her brother grow up.

The room suddenly drifted into male and female. Anne said to her mother, "I would like to marry soon, Mama."

Her mother gave her a piercing look, so she hurried on, "So that Marianne can marry Percy. At the same time perhaps."

Her mother huffed out a breath. "Oh, I suppose so. He does seem to be coming along a little better. And there is always Eliza," she added, looking over at Tris.

Anne made a note to warn Tris. If he was wise, he would be married by the time Eliza left the schoolroom. And perhaps after all this the youngest Peckworth daughter would have an easier time of it.

Marianne was summoned and told, and promptly burst into torrents of tears. When she recovered, a wedding day two weeks away was settled on, and the duchess left to demand her secretary and start to make arrangements.

Race was taken away by her father for discussion of marriage settlements. This was the time they'd decided would be best for the final revelations, so Anne waited on tenterhooks, letting Caroline and Marianne chatter about wedding outfits and attendants.

It was still possible that her father would rescind his approval.

At last, however, Race appeared, smiling. She went to him. "It's all right?"

"Yes."

By silent accord, they escaped into the vastness of the great house, seeking privacy but propriety. They ended up on a window seat in the portrait gallery, chaperoned by ranks of Anne's haughty ancestors.

"Was he very angry?" she asked, drawn irresistibly against Race as she remembered being in a theater box at Drury Lane so very long ago.

This time they could kiss, but he eased away to say, "It was touch and go, but as you predicted, once committed, he didn't back down. I think he does truly like me, which helped."

Despite their decision to behave, his hands moved on her in the way that was already familiar, in the same way hers moved on him. Caring, marking, *mine*.

"And of course," he went on, eyes dark on hers, "part of the bargain is that I do my best to stop Uffham falling into serious folly while he grows up."

"He's the same age as you."

"And I might be as foolish as he is if I'd stayed at home. To keep my word, I'll have to spend more time away from here than I wish, love, but it will be as little as possible. Especially if you do that. . . ."

She had somehow ended up on his lap and was nibbling his ear, which she'd discovered had interesting effects on him.

He moved her back onto the window seat, capturing her hands, holding her away. "Pay attention. We're to have Quoyne for a wedding gift. Just the house. I said we had no interest in the tenant farms attached to it. I hope that's true."

"Perfectly true." She turned her hands and brought his scarred one to her lips, inhaling this precious new certainty. "We have heaven, don't we?"

"For all our days . . ."

She knew the same hunger rose in him as in her, but they had decided to wait. She stood and pulled him to his feet. "What now? We could go and look at Quoyne House. It's empty."

"Or you could show me your papers." His fingers wove with hers. "Papers or home? Home or papers?"

She couldn't stand it. "Or our other delight . . ."

"Wicked wench. No, we wait. Show me the library."

"Willpower!" she complained, but she guided him through her home to her special room. She found the key and opened the door. "With all my worldly papers, love, I thee endow."

Seen with objective eyes, it was a simple space, however, with one small window and lined with shelves and drawers. As with her naked body in the cottage attic, she had a moment's fear that this—her gossip and laundry lists—would be inadequate.

But he looked around with a grin. "I do so love an orderly woman."

She leaned back against some shelves, watching his delight with delight.

He trailed his fingers along a line of boxes, then took one down—an unlabeled one, one with papers yet to be read. It was exactly what she would have done.

He looked in it, and suddenly laughed with delight.

"I think my female ancestors are going to be competition," she said.

He glanced across at her, and the look in his eyes was all the contradiction she needed. "My laughter, love, was because of what's on top here. Come and see."

She limped over and took the faded, fly-spotted leaflet he handed her.

"A Warning to the Ladies and Gentlemen of this Fair Land of the Wicked Ruin that comes from the Game that Goes By The Name Hazard."

She laughed, too. "Wicked ruin, indeed."

"Speaking of Hazard . . ." He dug in his breeches' pocket, pulled something out, and put it in her hand—something small, thin, and hard.

Anne looked. It was an ivory gaming counter. "From Benning House? And I threw mine away! Along with the straw heart."

"The what?"

She realized that he couldn't know about that.

"That was before you came on stage." She blinked away tears, tears of happiness, tears of relief over what might have been.

"Let me tell you a tale," she said, taking his hand. "Once upon a time, long long ago, a princess was imprisoned behind walls of power, sadly weaving a heart out of straw. . . ."

Author's Note

I hope you have enjoyed the story of Race de Vere and Lady Anne. Most of Race's problem came from something that was a surprise to me. I gave him the name de Vere carelessly.

I knew the de Vere title had died out for lack of male heirs, but I hadn't realized that the situation was quite as sweeping as it was until enlightened by fellow author Margaret Evans Porter. (Thank you, Margaret.)

The de Vere name was ancient and important, and anyone bearing it legitimately would probably have a claim on the title of Earl of Oxford. In Regency England, anyone claiming to be a de Vere would be instantly suspect.

What a turn of the screw on my poor hero. I thought he was minor gentry, but when I probed into his name, I realized that it had to be worse than that. Once I realized that his father had won a lottery (I've always wanted to use a lottery in a book because they were very popular at the time), the legitimacy of Thomas de Vere's first marriage was in question.

All quite delicious, really!

Race first appeared in *The Dragon's Bride,* which is the story of Con Somerford and Susan Kerslake. The exciting events Race missed while in Devon occur in *The Devil's Heiress.* These books can all be read separately, but there are links. As you might have guessed, the next novel will be about the intriguing Duke of St. Raven. When he was off playing the highwayman that night, he had an interesting encounter.

As he says to a young lady in involuntary residence at Nun's Chase:

> *"It seems to be my night for knight errantry."*
> *"You've found another damsel in distress?"*
> *His lips twitched. "After a fashion."*
> *"This house must be becoming rather crowded."*
> *"Oh, I stashed her in one of my other residences. Now, your story, Miss Whoever-you-are."*

I don't have a title for this yet, but look for it in early 2003.

As for the dice game Hazard, it is the precursor of the modern game of craps. I hope I gave you enough to understand the action in Hazard. If you wish to know more, please visit my Web site below, where I have posted more information and also some links.

Dice have other uses, and have often been used for divination—for fortune-telling. If you want a little fun, try the following, which I have adapted from a Victorian fortune-telling book.

The Daily Oracle: using one die for daily wisdom.

Roll the die fairly and read the oracle's advice for the day.

1. Be open. You will meet someone of significance.
2. An act of kindness will bring an unexpected reward.
3. Be wary. There is a trap laid before you.
4. Someone in your family needs you.
5. Do not speak hastily. If you do, you will rue it.
6. Guard yourself around the one who smiles the most.

I have more forms of divination by dice on my Web page.

Here is a list of my other novels in print. You should be able to get any of these at your favorite bookstore. If they do not have a book, they can order it for you at no extra cost.

An Arranged Marriage (Regency. Company of Rogues.)
An Unwilling Bride (Regency. Company of Rogues.)
Christmas Angel (Regency. Company of Rogues.)
Devilish (Georgian. The Mallorens.)
Forbidden Magic (Regency.)
Lord of Midnight (Medieval.)
Secrets of the Night (Georgian. The Mallorens.)
Something Wicked (Georgian. The Mallorens.)
The Devil's Heiress (Regency. Company of Rogues. The Georges.)
The Dragon's Bride (Regency. Company of Rogues. The Georges.)

The excellent news is that the two other Malloren books will be reissued this year. *My Lady Notorious* will be out in July 2002, and *Tempting Fortune* in December. Soon the whole series will be in print.

I enjoy hearing from my readers. You can e-mail me at jobev@poboxes.com, or mail me c/o The Rotrosen Agency, 318 East 51st Street, New York, NY 10022. I appreciate a SASE if you would like a reply. My Web site is: www.poboxes.com/jobev

Dear Reader:

I hope you've enjoyed reading this adventure of the Company of Rogues.

I love these men, and I've had fun writing about them over the past thirty years. (Yes, really! My first Rogues novel was the first book I ever finished. It just took a while to get it right and sell it.)

The adventure started for them when they were schoolboys at Harrow. Boys' schools were rough places in those days and an enterprising lad called Nicholas Delaney gathered a group for mutual support—one for all and all for one—forging a bond that lasted into adulthood.

They're a mixed bunch because Nicholas chose the outsiders, the unusual, and the ones who needed protection most. For example, we have Miles Cavanagh, an Irish rebel, and Lucien de Vaux, Marquess of Arden, haughty heir to a dukedom. Leander Knollis was the suave son of a diplomat, who scarcely knew England at all, and quiet Francis Haile, Viscount Middlethrope, arrived at school grieving his recently dead father. Despite their variety, the Rogues are consistent in honor. Whatever their natures, they serve their country in Parliament, on the battlefield, or by tending the land, because that's what heroes do.

For me as an author, their differences have been a joy, because each Rogue has fallen into a different kind of adventure. Or perhaps I should say, they have run into a different kind of woman, seemingly designed to test their limits. A tempestuous ward. A Regency-era feminist. A woman trained in the erotic arts. A poet's widow who's fed up with being seen as the perfect "angel bride." (Want to guess which Rogue above gets which?)

All things come to an end, however, and they are nearly all settled in matrimony. *The Rogue's Return*, on sale in March 2006, will be followed by Lord Darius Debenham's story in 2007, completing the series.

However, there will be books about friends and relatives, all in the same "world." The Company of Rogues series (including some spin-offs*) is as follows: *An Arranged Marriage* (Nicholas), *An Unwilling Bride* (Lucien), *Christmas Angel* (Leander), *Forbidden* (Francis), *Dangerous Joy* (Miles), *The Dragon's Bride* (Con), *The Devil's Heiress*, Hazard*, St. Raven*, Skylark* (Stephen), *The Rogue's Return* (Simon).

I hope you enjoy them all.

All best wishes,
Jo

The Devil's Heiress

Clarissa Greystone is called the Devil's Heiress. Burdened with the wealth of a man she despised, she is a fortune hunter's dream. And no one needs that fortune more than Major George Hawkinville. But how will he ignore the hunger in his heart when Clarissa boldly steps into his trap?

"[A] deftly woven tale of romantic intrigue. . . . Head and shoulders above the usual Regency fare, this novel's sensitive prose, charismatic characters, and expert plotting will keep readers enthralled from first page to last."
—*Publishers Weekly*

"With her talent for writing powerful love stories and masterful plotting, Ms. Beverley cleverly brings together this dynamic duo. Her latest captivating romance . . . is easily a 'keeper'!"   —*Romantic Times* (Top Pick)

St. Raven

Cressida Mandeville agrees to Lord Crofton's vile proposal, but secretly she has other plans. She will trick the loathsome man, find her father's hidden wealth, and save the family from ruin. All goes well, until a daring highwayman, Tristan Tregallows, Duke of St. Raven, stops their carriage, whirls Cressida up onto his dark horse, and demands a kiss. When St. Raven discovers Cressida is on a quest, he knows he must become her partner and protector. But he doesn't expect the dangers to his heart.

"Beverley's delicious, well-crafted, and wickedly captivating romance is a surefire winner." —*Romantic Times*

"A well-crafted story and an ultimately very satisfying romance." —*The Romance Reader*

Skylark

Once she was Mrs. Hal Gardeyne, the darling Lady Skylark of London society, but now she's a terrified mother. Hal's death has made young Harry heir to her father-in-law's title and estates, and she fears Harry's uncle wants those prizes enough to commit murder. Then a mysterious letter that could change everything arrives. Is there a long-lost heir to the Caldford estate? Laura must uncover the answers even if it means turning to Sir Stephen Ball—a man whose heart she broke years before. Together, Stephen and Laura must discover the truth despite the dangerous obstacles in their path. Will they be able to overcome their enemies before the passion that has reignited between them sweeps them both away?

"Beverley is a master who sets the tone for a wickedly sensual romance."   —*Romantic Times*

"The story is told with charm and wit, with narrative limited to the pertinent, and plenty of lively and meaningful dialogue."   —Romance Reviews Today

"Wickedly, wonderfully sensual and gloriously romantic."
—Mary Balogh

"A delicious...sensual delight."
—Teresa Medeiros

"One of romance's brightest and most dazzling stars."
—*Affaire de Coeur*

New York Times Bestselling Author
Jo Beverley